Praise for *Fractured*

"Ossowki's smart, time-twisting novel is a gorgeous exploration of whom we love and why, and how the past sometimes—extraordinarily—can bleed into the present. A gorgeously written page turner."
—Caroline Leavitt, *New York Times* bestselling author of *Pictures of You* and *Cruel Beautiful World*

"Stellar. A complex and compulsive read. A beautifully written reflection on dreams vs. reality, self-determination and the people we're born to be."
—Christopher Meades, award-winning author of *Hanna Who Fell from the Sky*

"With the deftness of a magician, Tamar Ossowski masterfully whisks us into a world where the lines between dreaming and waking, between one life and another, dissolve. In this space of no-time, stories become palimpsests through which the truth blazes like a guide-star in a dark sky. Riveting and richly textured, *Fractured* bravely tackles themes of love, destiny, and freedom with a freshness and honesty that makes it impossible to put down."
—Rita Zoey Chin, critically acclaimed author of *Let the Tornado Come*

Praise for *Left*

"A haunting, sometimes harrowing portrait of the ways that love can go wrong—and how we can right it. . . . Trust me, you've never read anything like this—like a shadow, it will stick with you."
—Caroline Leavitt, author of the *New York Times* bestseller *Pictures of You*

"The vivid voices, deft plotting and, most of all, utterly original characters Tamar Ossowski has created in *Left* make it an unforgettable read. This is a book of unusual, even magical, compassion and heart."
—Holly LeCraw, author of *The Swimming Pool*

fractured

Also by Tamar Ossowski

Left

fractured

A NOVEL

TAMAR OSSOWSKI

AUTHOR OF *LEFT*

Skyhorse Publishing

This is a work of fiction. Names, characters, places, and incidents are either the products of the author's imagination or used fictitiously.

Skyhorse Publishing books may be purchased in bulk at special discounts for sales promotion, corporate gifts, fund-raising, or educational purposes. Special editions can also be created to specifications. For details, contact the Special Sales Department, Skyhorse Publishing, 307 West 36th Street, 11th Floor, New York, NY 10018 or info@skyhorsepublishing.com.

Skyhorse® and Skyhorse Publishing® are registered trademarks of Skyhorse Publishing, Inc.®, a Delaware corporation.

Visit our website at www.skyhorsepublishing.com.

10 9 8 7 6 5 4 3 2 1

Library of Congress Cataloging-in-Publication Data is available on file.

Cover design by Erin Seaward-Hiatt
Cover photo credit: ShutterStock

Print ISBN: 978-1-5107-4382-3
Ebook ISBN: 978-1-5107-4385-4

Printed in the United States of America

For Chloe.

Chapter 1

There aren't many people who know my real name.

But he does.

As I start to draw the big fancy loop of the *S* in my signature, I can see that he's staring at me. Lawyer looks up, maybe because I have suddenly stopped writing.

"Problem?" She asks, wiggling a pen between her fingers, back and forth like a synchronized seesaw.

He looks down, but I can still sense his impatience. I can feel it crawling across the table, poking me in the ribs, and I shift like I am trying to avoid being hit by a dodge ball. He never looks up, never checks on me, and it is at that moment I feel the first twinge. I hold the pen for a few more minutes and Lawyer busies herself with something as the sound of shuffling papers echoes throughout the room.

Windows that extend from the floor to the ceiling surround the office and I wonder whether anyone has ever sat in my chair and contemplated jumping. I imagine the initial crash through the glass and then the few minutes of freefall. Lawyer clears her throat, bringing me back to the room, and the man tapping his fingers on the table, waiting for me to sign the papers that will allow him a similar freedom.

Tap.

Everything is quiet except for that sound, suddenly magnified in my ear.

Tap. Tap.

I work on the lower case *a* and then the *l*. When my mother is angry with me, she stumbles across that letter, making it sound like *Solomon*. A king, known for his wisdom who later betrays his people. A solo man. Maybe that is what she should have named me instead. I stop, and this time Lawyer looks at me funny and I decide that I hate her, which maybe she knows, because just then she stands up and walks into the hallway. Now he looks smaller, shrinking as if, without her by his side, he cannot hold his shape.

I click the top of the pen repeatedly, and then because the ticking noise makes him shift in his seat, I click more. Lawyer returns with a bottle of water and places it down on the table. I lower my head, and when I look through it, everything appears distorted. He has gone back to tapping and I go back to working on my signature. Perfecting every curve of every letter making sure that my name is written with clarity and strength, maybe as if someone else has written it. I can tell they want me to finish and to stop stretching things out, but I finally have his attention.

And I like it.

I wish my name had more letters in it, I wish I could go on writing it forever, but I cannot, and before I am ready, before I want it to end, it does and we are finished.

Fractured.

As we stand to leave, he smiles perhaps in gratitude or relief, but I am not sure which because just then I push myself away from the table. I need to get out, to run from this room and get as far away as I can.

Part of me wishes he was following, but the rest of me knows that he isn't and that he never will again. Streets and faces and honking cars blur together until I stop running and realize that I am sitting on a park bench, the tears rolling down my cheeks like a toddler who has just dropped her lollipop on the ground. I cry harder, as if somehow that will make everything go back to the way it was but it is at that moment that I am suddenly overcome by the realization that nothing will ever be the same again.

Because I have allowed him to destroy me.

To break me.

As the shaking intensifies, I am overwhelmed by how damaged I have become. I try to take deeper breathes to calm myself. I probably look as though I am hyperventilating but there is no one around to witness my breakdown. The panic starts to recede but returns with a vengeance when I suddenly realize I can feel myself collapsing and literally crumbling away.

Because I am.

I look down at my hand. My fingertips have started to disintegrate, to slowly but undeniably disappear. I tell myself I must just be in shock and try to ignore the sensation of watching myself slip away. It's as though, instead of cells, I am made up of hundreds of little mosaic squares that begin to topple in onto themselves, and when I look down at my lap, I realize my hand has completely vanished. I know I should feel terror but all I can feel is relief. And then, because I can't make it stop, I don't. I softly tilt my head backward so that I can more comfortably fall into the act of disappearing, and then I take a deep breath and close my eyes because I know.

There is no turning back.

Chapter 2

When I opened my eyes, there was blackness.

Before I could determine if it was real, it vanished like a cube of sugar in a hot cup of tea and then I was surrounded.

By light.

As things cleared and I looked down, I saw that my knees were slightly bent like I had jumped from somewhere.

I was clutching a book to my chest.

I was standing beside the shore of a lake.

Next to a man who felt strangely familiar and yet completely unrecognizable. I tried to rewind my brain, to grasp the thread of memory that teased like a tickle, but it was too slippery, and when I reached out, it disappeared like a wisp of smoke and then I was left with nothing.

Nothing from before.

No matter how hard I tried, I couldn't remember back or then or since—all I could see was now.

The man beside me was poking with furious intent at something protruding from between the dried brown weeds. Morning light glistened across the water as he plunged the branch he was holding into the sludge, scraping away at the debris, trying to set free the thing that was trapped. A bit of mud gave way and when I looked down I could see what I thought was the neck of a swan, curved like the arc of a question mark.

Maybe it was the result of what I had just experienced, or maybe it was simply the idea of a bird forever trapped never to take flight again that shook me from within, but I suddenly lost my footing. He put out his hand to steady me and left it there even after I was no longer in danger of falling.

And we stayed that way, connected.

Attached.

Because all my memories had vanished, the only thing I could rely on was my intuition, which told me without a doubt that I had been here previously, beside this lake in this moment with this man. I looked at him again and realized that his face was so familiar, I could trace the curve of his profile with my eyes closed. Even though I knew we were strangers, there was no question in my mind that I knew him.

Intimately.

He gasped, this time as if he was in pain, and when I looked down I saw that he had managed to dislodge the thing further, and it was clear that it was not a bird. Even though it was still covered in leaves and dirt, there was no mistaking what it really was.

A bone.

When he spoke, his voice was soft, almost like he wasn't speaking at all. "I think it's human." Then he turned and vomited into the leaves at his feet.

When he finally looked at me, I felt a flood of heat that ended abruptly when I saw the woman.

She was walking down the path with a child strapped to her in one of those knapsacks. She was singing softly into the baby's ear, and the delicate way her hand cupped his little egg-shaped head filled my heart with the most excruciating ache. She smiled at me and instantly I knew.

I had to run.

I let go of his hand, surprised at how easily he let me slip from his grip. I raced past him, past the swan that wasn't, past the lake and the leaves and the birds. I ran out of the park as fast as I could until I was panting, each breath stinging more than the last, making my chest feel so tight I thought it might actually be my heart breaking into a thousand different pieces.

And then I ran faster.

Sometimes you end up where you should only because you have let go of where that is supposed to be. When I finally stopped running, I was standing in front of an apartment building, and I wondered if the amnesia was starting to lift because the building I was standing in front of felt compellingly familiar.

I'm not sure how it was that I knew this was where I lived.

The key in my pocket slipped effortlessly into the door.

"You okay?" She pointed to a hole in my pants. I must have fallen without even knowing, but I was too busy staring at the coffee table in front of her to answer. It was covered in red lipstick prints of her lips. "I was doing an art project with the kids. Folded butterflies and I thought lips would be cool too. A more interesting way of signing my name than just *Susan*."

Of course, her name was Susan, and she was an art teacher at an elementary school and she was my roommate. Maybe it was just a question of time? Maybe if I started to calm down, the effects of my blackout would pass and I would start to remember. Like my name? How could I not remember my name? I could have asked Susan, but something told me that she was not someone I could trust, and since all I had to go by was intuition, I decided to listen.

"You sure you're okay, Sam?"

"I'm fine."

Susan shrugged and went back to mashing her lips down onto the paper napkins. The light was on in the room nearest to where she was sitting so I guessed the other one belonged to me. The door stuck as I pushed against it, and when I nudged harder I heard something topple over. There were towers of magazines everywhere, some piled so high they were careening into walls and taking up every inch of free space in the room.

I pushed a pile off my bed and sat down to think. She had called me Sam. Was it short for Samantha? No, that wasn't my name. I closed my eyes and thought harder and then it came to me: it was the lie I told people when I didn't trust them with the truth. There are some things that even memory loss could not erase.

My name was Salmon, and my mother named me that because salmon always knew how to find their way home and she never wanted me to get lost.

How ironic.

I walked over to the desk, which was sloped like the kind an artist would have. There was a half-finished collage of *The Birth of Venus* made with what looked like magazine ads cut up into hundreds of tiny mosaic squares. I lifted it up to the light, which made it seem as though Venus's head was tilted to one side and, even though I knew it wasn't possible, it felt like she was disappointed in me. I put the collage back down next to an envelope that was stamped and sealed and addressed to a law school in New York, and because it looked important, I folded it in half and slipped it into my pocket.

"Forgot to tell you." Susan was standing at the door of my bedroom. "Your mother called. She said not to be late."

I nodded because I knew I couldn't ask more, and when she looked at me strangely I knew I made the right choice. I didn't know why, but she made me uncomfortable and I wanted her to get out of my room. She wasn't very good at reading my mind; instead of leaving, she took two steps forward. "Nice." She was pointing to Venus.

The line between where I had come from and where I was now started to blur, and I fell backward against the bed. I knew that I didn't want to share my Venus with her. I didn't want to share anything with her.

It took everything I had to smile because I thought it might get her to leave, which it finally did, and once she was gone, I propped Venus up on my desk and admired her. Had she actually come from somewhere inside me? Was this who I was? Someone who had the talent to make something so perfect? I couldn't stop looking at the way the shapes worked together to create movement and how angelic she appeared and how, if I squinted and turned my head just the right way, it almost seemed like she was smiling at me, like she was welcoming me back.

Like she was forgiving me.

I put on my jacket and walked out of my apartment building. I could feel the panic welling up inside me and I felt lost and alone. I forced myself to take in a few deep breaths, and then I closed my eyes. Once it was quiet, I could picture it.

My mother's house.

Maybe the first things to come back would be the important ones and the little things would come later. The house my mother lived in was pale blue with black shutters. Even though I couldn't remember the others we had lived in, I did remember that the one thing they all had in common was that every one of them had a white picket fence. If there was no fence, she would save up her money and have one installed. If it was not white, as soon as we got our things settled, she would go to the hardware store to buy paint.

White.

Always white.

This house was no different. The fence was so bright it hurt to look at, and as I ran my hand along the sharp points of the pickets, I was comforted by the fact that remembering this detail had to be a sign that I was getting back to normal. The front door was open, so I let myself in, and when she came out of the kitchen, she had a dishtowel in her hand.

"Finish up. I am going to take a shower." She sounded breathless, as though she was flustered. But I knew, just by looking at her, she never was.

The kitchen was painted yellow and filled with light. A drawing hanging on the wall triggered another memory: when I was little, my favorite things to draw were flowers, which my mother insisted on framing. She put them up and took them down every time we moved. Hanging on the wall now were daisies, drawn with thick black lines that gave no hint of texture or depth or perspective.

When I was in high school, other girls would talk about going to parties and I would listen to them whisper in the gym locker room the next day about how they had gotten so drunk they couldn't remember a thing from the night before. Which is exactly how I felt now. Whatever had happened to me, whatever was in control, was parsing out my memories as it pleased. Every time one would come, it was just enough to keep me from becoming completely unglued but nowhere near what I needed to answer my questions. I finished washing the bowls in the sink just as she walked back into the kitchen.

She came close and kissed my cheek and I got a whiff of her shampoo. "Trying out a new recipe." She opened the oven door and pulled out a pie with a perfectly peaked topping. "Have to let it cool."

We sat down and she placed a salad and a piece of grilled chicken in front of me, and I dipped cucumber into the dressing that had pooled at the bottom of the plate. She looked at me for a moment longer than was comfortable so I looked away.

She unfolded her napkin, positioning it gently onto her lap. "I had some interest in the Larson house. I knew it would go quickly."

My mother sold houses. I remembered now. She did it better than anyone else in her office. She did it better than anyone else period. And she was proud of it.

"How's work?" She poured herself a glass of wine. "It was really nice of Randy to give you that job and Anne Marie is such a doll."

I nodded. I would have to see if I could find a paystub in my room to figure out the address of where I apparently worked. "How was your day, Mom?"

She was looking at me funny again.

"I already told you about the Larson house. Is everything okay, Salmon?"

I flinched for a minute. It was my opening, my opportunity to tell my mother what was going on. Maybe she knew something that would help me understand.

"Where was I yesterday?"

"At work, silly. Where else would you be?"

The bottle of wine on the table was empty, and she walked over to the cabinet to find another.

I stumbled over my words like I was hitting large pieces of furniture in the dark. "Do you know if something happened to me?"

"Something happened? What happened?" Her intense stare made the breath catch in my chest, and I suddenly understood that even if I told her the truth, she wouldn't believe me. She would think I was crazy and somewhere deep inside I knew that was not something I could bear. I felt a familiar sense of defeat rise in my throat. "Nothing happened."

She looked at me a few seconds longer, her lip twitching like she was calculating a math problem in her head, but then went back to her salad seemingly convinced, and I went back to mine as well. I didn't want her to see the truth in my eyes.

"Did you send in the down payment for school?"

That must have been what was inside the envelope. I stopped eating and dug it out of my pocket and handed it to her like a kindergartner bringing her first report card home.

"Why didn't you mail it like I told you? Never mind, I'll just do it." She caught me eyeing the pie. "Sam, honey, one day you are going to pay for that sweet tooth." She smiled and brought it to the table. The topping had silky, sugary peaks that looked like caramel-colored hilltops. As she cut me a slice, all I could think of was losing myself inside the cloudy softness of that sweet puffy goodness.

"I'll mail it tonight. I promise." I greedily stuffed the pie into my mouth, more hungry for the comfort than the taste, and only slowed down when I looked up and realized she was watching me. I shoved the envelope back into my pocket and she nodded, pleased.

She picked up her plate and walked to the sink and I followed. She washed and I dried, and as the water hummed from the tap, we slipped into a routine that felt so natural I realized it was something we must have done often. Except that someone was missing.

My father.

I closed my eyes and waited until I could see him. He used to be here with us. It was the three of us until something happened.

Until she threw him out.

I tried to push down the salad that suddenly came up in my throat along with the feeling of uneasiness that I was somehow to blame. She ran the water so hot that steam floated up from the basin like clouds. I watched as she scrubbed, round and round, and then I waited until she handed me a dish.

"How is Dad?" There, I said it.

She turned and looked at me. "You mean Brian."

It sounded strange, but she was right, I always called my father by his first name.

"He's fine."

The strings of her apron were tied so perfectly they reminded me of a bow on a present. I could tell she didn't want to talk anymore because of the way her shoulders crept up toward the tips of her earlobes. She continued handing me dishes and we returned to our predictable rhythm. I was back within the cover of familiarity, back where I had stood after so many meals when nothing could ever harm me because I was with her.

Back to being safe.

It was at that moment that I decided that what I thought had happened to me earlier in the park simply couldn't have. I couldn't have been with a stranger who felt intimately familiar even though I had never laid eyes on him before or watched him unearth part of someone's decomposing body. My mother was always accusing me of having an overactive imagination and this was just another example.

Relief washed over me, and I was thankful that I had decided not to share this with her. I was more convinced than ever that it all must have been just a figment of my imagination. I still felt disoriented but maybe I was coming down with something. I had once seen a television program about people who got high fevers that led them to hallucinate. I was sure I would be back to normal after a good night's sleep. I forced myself to stop thinking about it and to trust that as time passed the details would fade and then everything would return to normal.

Because it had to.

It took a few minutes for me to realize that there was another voice in the room that belonged to neither of us. It was coming from the small black radio she had on the counter. A male newscaster with a deep booming voice and perfect articulation was speaking: "The police have uncovered what appears to be human remains along the banks of Daphne Lake and it could be weeks or even months before the coroner's office will be able to provide any more information. In the meantime, they are checking surrounding communities for missing person reports and asking anyone with information to call them."

My mother and I were no longer in sync, and I dropped a dish, which shattered into three sharp pieces and took my breath away.

"You're not yourself tonight, Salmon."

I was on my knees collecting the stray shards of china.

She stared at me for another minute, and I was grateful that my memories were so spotty, because at that moment I had the feeling that if she wanted, she could see right through me.

"Take the pie with you," she said and kissed my forehead.

I walked home.

The air was fresh and cool and I needed to fill my lungs with it to remind myself that I was real. The pie was heavy, and I shifted it from one hand to the other, which probably made me look even more unbalanced than I felt.

When I walked in, Susan was watching television. When she saw what I was carrying, she smiled. Before I could react, she jumped off the couch and removed the pie from my hand. I watched as she dipped the tip of her pinky finger into the topping and stuck it into her mouth. She made a loud sucking noise and then decided that she needed something more effective. As I left to go into my room, I could hear her rattling through a drawer looking for a spoon, and I didn't care because I just wanted to get away.

Venus was staring at me when I came in. I turned her so she faced the wall.

It was just all too much, too loud, for one day. I didn't even take my clothes off, just laid my head down on the cover of one of the magazines, which felt soothingly cool on my hot skin. When I finally closed my eyes, I dreamt of Venus standing upright in her clamshell, her leg curved and graceful like the majestic neck of a swan.

Chapter 3

If I had hoped I would wake in the morning to the discovery of my lost memories, I was disappointed. I felt as disoriented as I had been the night before about whom or where I was. I tried looking for clues by rummaging through my things and found a stack of photos held together with a rubber band in my nightstand.

Me and my mother, smiling.

The second one in the pile was of me and a man with a beard the same color as my hair with his arm draped over my shoulders.

It took a few minutes of staring at his face and even then, I was just making a guess.

My father.

I put the stack of photos under my pillow.

Maybe I needed to see a doctor.

But it was too much to think about now, and I decided if I just went about my routine, my memories would return by themselves. I continued digging through my things and found an old pay stub crumpled up and stuffed into a corner of my sock drawer. I would go to work today because it was very likely what I did the day before and the day before that and the only way to return to normalcy was to force myself back into my presumably quiet and ordinary life.

It turned out that I worked as a receptionist for a property management company in the basement of a large office building. Because there were no windows, the space was flooded with the unnatural blue glow of fluorescent light that made everything feel cold even though the air conditioning was broken.

My coworker, Anne Marie, seemed much more interested in talking to our boss, Randy, than talking to me. There were donuts in the break room, which were possibly meant to celebrate my last day at the office but no one said anything directly to me, and I couldn't help but notice that she kept rubbing up against him and coming in close to wipe the crumbs from his mouth. Even more glaringly obvious was the wedding band she wore around her finger.

That afternoon, I watched as she slipped into Randy's office and closed the door. They were so brazen that I could hear the desk thumping up against the wall, so I finally went to the bathroom to escape. When I came back, a man was standing in the reception area, shifting awkwardly from one foot to the other, but I recognized him from the framed picture Anne Marie had on her desk.

"Is Annie around? I thought I'd surprise her."

The way he said her name made her sound sweet, like she baked cookies and lived on a farm. I stared at him for too long. He cleared his throat to let me know he was waiting for me to go find his wife.

"Do you want something to drink?"

"I'm good."

My first instinct was to come up with a lie to cover for Anne Marie, but then something stopped me.

"Have a seat. I'll find her."

He ran his hands down his dungarees before he sat. They were covered in grease, and I guessed he was some kind of mechanic. He was too big for the couch and it sunk as he leaned into it.

I walked past my desk and then across to Randy's office. I knocked softly before I opened the door. Randy's pants were down around his knees and Anne Marie was bent over his desk with her skirt hiked up around her waist. Her hair had slipped from its bun and he held fistfuls in each hand like the reins of a horse. Her neck was arched from the strain of his pull and her breasts bounced up and down from the force of his thrusts. When he saw me standing in the doorway, he pushed her away and drew up his pants.

"Fuck, Salmon, can't you knock?" She sounded irritated, like I was the little sister barging in on her date. As she turned toward me, she picked up a file from the desk to cover herself.

"Your husband is here."

Her face paled and the file dropped from her hand, sending pink requisite slips to the floor. She stood motionless until Randy threw her a shirt.

"Tell him I went to lunch." She got a compact from her purse and began dabbing at her face. "Tell him I went to lunch." She repeated.

Randy was sitting at his desk staring at his computer screen as though there was something terribly urgent that needed his attention. He didn't look at either of us.

"You tell him," I said. "That's the least you owe him." I closed the door behind me and walked away.

I went back to my desk, and out of the corner of my eye, I saw Anne Marie come out with her hair still disheveled and her blouse half tucked in. I could feel what was about to happen like I was watching a movie in slow motion. I could imagine her husband's cries, broken and raw, and the way he would be holding his hands to his face unsure if the tears would ever stop or if the pain would ever end. He would be struggling to catch his breath, feeling his insides collapse onto themselves as he tried to comprehend how the person he loved most in the world could suddenly just stop loving him.

I don't know how it was that I could understand his pain so well, but I could.

She was walking down the hall, getting closer, but he still couldn't see her, and the next thing I knew I was standing in front of him, blocking him.

Shielding him.

"I can't seem to find her. She must have already left for lunch."

He hesitated for a moment, but I could see he wanted to believe me and then just like that he did.

"Could you tell her I stopped by?" He twisted his baseball cap in his hands, which for some reason made him seem even more vulnerable. "I'm Jimmy."

I nodded.

As soon as he left, she came out from the hallway, slipping on her shoe. "Thanks."

I didn't respond because she wouldn't have understood that I didn't do it for her. I knew somewhere deep inside that this was my way of making amends for something even if I didn't understand what. I knew that she would never understand that what I had done was not at all for her and maybe just a little for Jimmy.

But mostly for me.

I walked back to my apartment with the few things I decided probably belonged to me sliding around in a cardboard box. There was a book about New York City, a bunch of colored markers, and package of bright purple Post-its that I took just because I liked the color. Susan wasn't home, so I walked over to the fridge, but before I could get anything to eat, someone knocked on the door. When I opened it, I found the man with the beard the same color as my hair smiling back at me. "Fishhhh," he whispered and kissed me hello.

I didn't move.

"Hi, Brian. Thanks for coming over to help me pack," he said in an overly dramatic feminine voice and a sad attempt at mimicking mine.

I wondered why I called him Brian instead of Dad. Was it because that's what my mother called him, or was it just because that's what I had always called him and no one ever corrected me?

He walked into my room and I followed. "Guess we should get started." He found a box and went to work loading my things into it. I stood there for a few minutes until he nudged some things into my hand, and then I got to work too, losing myself in the physicality of the task, my mind finally quieting to the music of ripping duct tape. It was warm in the apartment, and soon two half-moons formed beneath the armpits of his shirt.

"We make a good team." When he laughed, his face lit up. He walked over to my dresser and picked up something. "Remember this?"

He was holding a book in the air. "Remember how we rode our bikes to the library every Saturday and took out the same art book every single time? You would stare at those mosaics for hours like they held some magical secrets. Remember I finally bought you a copy for your birthday?"

It was the first time I felt the loss of my memory so profoundly it took my breath away. How could I not remember something so important? How much more was there that I had forgotten?

"That's coming with me." I packed it in the bag I planned to bring in the car.

"And what about these?" He motioned toward my stacks of magazines and then shook his head. "I shouldn't have asked." He got out a cone of twine and went to work stacking and tying them into bundles.

It seemed to get warmer the harder we worked, so I turned on the fan and left my bedroom door open. When I looked up, Susan was standing in the doorway even though I hadn't heard her come home. She was staring at Brian and very slowly licking her bottom lip. She was wearing a jogging bra with the price tag still dangling from the corner. I watched as she came in and positioned herself in the seat closest to him. "Need any help?"

Brian must not have noticed her either, because when he saw her sitting there, he seemed surprised. "I think we're good."

More lip licking before she stretched out her perfectly bronzed legs and then pointed her toes. "You're sure?" She wiggled in the chair, and I could swear I saw her push her shorts just a bit further down her hips.

"I think we have this covered." Brian wasn't even looking at her.

She shrugged then stood, but before she left, she ran her finger along the edge of the art desk. "You can have this, Salmon. Consider it my going-away gift."

"I don't want it."

The determination in my voice startled us both. I didn't know why, but I knew more than anything that I didn't want that desk. "You keep it."

She rolled her eyes like she didn't understand and couldn't be bothered to try, and when neither of us paid her any more attention, she finally walked out. Even though it was warm, I closed the door behind her.

Brian was holding some twine in his mouth. "She's quite a number." He grabbed another handful of magazines. "Something going on between you two?"

Of all the people in my life somehow, I knew he was the one I could trust. He was different than my mother, and maybe I should have told him what was happening to me, but if I did, it would make it real, and part of me wanted it to believe if I didn't talk about it maybe it would just disappear as mysteriously as it arrived. I looked at him for a moment, still uncertain. Before I could find the courage to speak he did.

"Can I ask you something?"

"Sure." I put my hands in front of the fan, feeling the warm air blow between the V's of my fingers, grateful for the reprieve and vowing that I would answer whatever he asked as honestly as I could.

"Do you want to go to law school? I mean, really want it?"

He was looking at me with such sincerity that I had to look away.

He moved in front of the fan so that he was facing me. "Because it's import-ant, Sam, that you know who you are and what you want. It's really important. Do you understand?"

How was it that he knew me so well, but still not at all? There was so much I wanted to tell him, but when I looked more closely at him, I saw the pain and anguish in his eyes. And even though I had no idea why, somewhere deep inside I knew I was the cause. Something I had done before had hurt him, and I couldn't bring myself to do it again no matter how much relief it might provide. Maybe losing my memory was punishment. Maybe I'd gotten exactly what I deserved. So, I said nothing and just nodded, even though I had just promised myself I was going to be truthful. He looked like he wanted to say more, but then he picked up the twine and went back to stacking magazines and I went back to feeling hopeless and utterly alone.

That night after he left, I sat in my room.

I was restless, unsettled, and I couldn't find a sense of peace, so I picked up *Venus* and then I flipped through the art book my father had given me. He was right; the mosaics did feel magical. I found a magazine on my nightstand and began to rip out pages, cutting strips of rectangles and triangles, first stacking and then layering them on top of each other, and before I knew it, paper and glue danced between my fingers and shiny advertisements of cars and buildings effortlessly transformed into the mesmerizing blues and silvers of the ocean. I shifted the pieces downward and back up again, searching for position, and as my fingers flew across the page, I could feel myself slowly disappearing inside the movement of shape and form and color.

It happened in that moment of perfection, when every piece had fallen into place and all things were precisely where they were meant to be. It happened inside that tiny space between a breath and an exhale, so raw and genuine that I knew without a doubt that what I was about to witness would change me forever.

At first, the edges blended together softly like the blocks of color I had just held in my hands. But then as my vision sharpened and things came into view, it was as if I was watching myself in a movie. I was wearing black rain boots and could hear the branches crunching beneath my feet. I was making my way toward the lake, holding a sketchbook close to my chest, and I was there to look at the water for inspiration for the collage I was working on.

It all felt eerily familiar.

Had I been in this moment once before? I looked up and saw the same man I had seen before, poking at the same spot along the banks of the lake. I continued to watch, realizing that I knew exactly what he was going to find. I stared at him for a few minutes, wondering if maybe I knew him from somewhere and that would explain it. But no, even though I had come to Daphne Lake often, I had never seen him before. Not even among the groups of Frisbee players I had to dodge past when I walked along the grass.

He was tall with broad shoulders, and when he looked back, I saw that he was probably in his twenties like me. As he continued to dig, his intensity drew me in and I lost my footing and then just as he had the first time (or was it the last time?), or maybe we had never even met before, he reached out to steady me.

"You okay?"

I nodded, and he went back to prodding the thing that I knew was not a bird with his stick. How could it be that I knew what was going to happen before it did? How could I have gone from someone who remembered nothing to someone who could see what was going to happen next? I was like a rat in a maze that had been dropped back at the starting gate to redo the race. I closed my eyes, letting the images wash over me, lifting through me, and soon it felt like I was living it and it became real and stopped feeling like a movie.

He was still holding my hand, maybe because he forgot to let me go or because he was too focused on what he was doing. From my vantage point, I had a good view of his profile and I liked the dramatic way his brow framed his face. He dug for a few more minutes, and when he realized what he had unearthed, he gasped. He turned and vomited in the reeds behind us.

As if on cue, the woman with the baby strapped to her chest came down the path, but this time when I saw her I felt nothing like I did before, so instead of letting go of his hand, instead of running away, I stayed where I was. It was then that I sensed it, real and profound and raw—a feeling of despair so thick and biting it was almost like I couldn't breathe, and something inside told me I had to stay, so I buried my face into his jacket and closed my eyes.

I didn't understand the significance of the choice I made to remain by his side instead of running away. At least, not at the time. All I knew was that he was in anguish and he needed me and that felt more important than anything else.

He didn't push me away, so I held on even tighter. I don't know how long we stayed that way, braided together in that strangely intimate bond, but after a while I could hear talking around me. As it got louder and more heated, I realized someone must have called the police because now they were there, and when I opened my eyes and looked down, I saw that we were still holding hands. It wasn't until the officer began asking questions that we broke apart, but we were still so close that our shoulders touched.

"Which one of you was here first? Did you move anything? How often do you come here?" The officer had his hand on his gun belt, shifting sideways every few seconds as though to balance himself.

The man did most of the talking while I clutched my sketchbook to my chest. After a few more questions back and forth, the officer gave us information on how to contact him and the man started to walk away and I followed.

We still hadn't spoken, but I followed him into a bakery at the end of the block, and when he sat down at a table, he motioned for me to sit. He ordered his coffee black and wrapped his fingers around the cup, blowing tiny bubbles across the surface. I got a Coke and we stared at each other, drinking in silence until finally he extended his hand.

"Sol." The way he said it made it sound like Soul.

His hand felt unnaturally warm from the coffee mug he had been holding. "Sam."

He took another sip. "Short for?"

His jawline was so chiseled it was almost like he was carved from marble. It occurred to me that he was handsome, maybe even striking, and even more so when he smiled because it made the black stubble around his chin soften. I was supposed to meet my mother for dinner soon. I dug my phone out of my pocket and texted something along the lines of how I couldn't come because I wasn't feeling myself, which I decided was partially true. He waited for me to finish before pointing to the sketchbook I had placed on the table.

"What's that book you've got?"

"It's nothing." I pulled it in closer. "Just some ideas."

"Can I see?"

"I should get going."

He seemed to hesitate for a moment, like he wanted to ask more, but then he threw a few crumpled bills onto the table. "Give me your contact information, you know, in case the police need us for something."

I scribbled my name and phone number and email address onto a napkin and handed it to him.

"Ever going to tell me what it's short for?"

"My dad wanted a boy." I had told the lie so many times it almost sounded true and my answer seemed to satisfy him. We stood and walked out of the shop, but then he stopped.

"I don't want to go home yet."

There was something about him, maybe the way he looked at me like he wasn't ready for me to leave either, that made me want to stay. As we walked, I tried matching my step to his, but his legs were longer than mine and it took some work before we were moving in the same rhythm.

"At the lake, you seemed to be looking for something," I said, breaking the silence that almost felt like a pact.

He shrugged but then he quickened his pace and I missed a step, throwing off the dance I was sure he had no idea we were performing.

"I'm always looking for something." He was smiling as he said it, which didn't match the sadness in his voice.

We didn't talk much after that. Just kept walking until we reached a row of shops. I watched our reflection in the storefront windows and thought about the way we fit. He was tall, maybe even too tall for me, and every time I spoke, he had to stoop down to hear me. Which he did every single time.

"What do you do for work?" he asked.

"I'm a receptionist in a property management office. You?"

"My father owns the Ice Cream Man shop. I work there."

I had been inside the store before. It was bright and decorated with pink and brown polka dots and I couldn't picture him working there. "Do you like it?"

He didn't answer so we just kept walking. He seemed distracted, and I wanted his attention, which is probably why it flew out of my mouth. "I'm going to be starting law school."

Again, he didn't answer, so I wasn't sure he'd even heard me.

"In New York."

Something about the way he moved changed, and suddenly I found it difficult to match his steps.

We said our goodbyes, and that night when I got home, I felt like I was walking on air. The next morning, the first thing I thought about was how his jacket smelled when I buried my face into it and I imagined how his stubble would be feel against my skin.

I didn't hear the knock on the door and jumped when Susan walked in.

"Forgot to tell you. Someone called. Sal?"

"Sol."

"He said to meet him at ten. Said you'd know where."

She closed the door behind her.

He didn't need to tell me where to meet him because of course I already knew. The area by the lake where we first met was cordoned off by yellow tape, so I sat on a bench on the other side and waited. Dew had formed along the seat, and I could feel it seeping in through my pants, but I didn't care because I liked the shocking feeling of the cold. Birds were chirping, but other than that, the air was still. I heard a crackling sound behind me and then he was there.

"Cold?"

I shook my head, but he untied the sweatshirt from around his waist and handed it to me anyway. There was a camera hanging from his neck and he unscrewed the cap from the lens.

"Is that why you came here the other day? To take pictures?"

He got that sad expression I had seen before but didn't answer, and when he began to walk away, I followed. Whenever he saw something that interested him, he would stand high above it and zoom in to shoot.

"That's kind of a weird way to take pictures."

He shrugged. "I like to see what things look like from high above."

"Like you are flying?"

He didn't answer.

"Let's see what's up there." I motioned toward a dirt path through the trees that veered off the paved walkway. Sunlight filtered through the branches like a million shiny tightropes. I moved my hands back and forth, slicing through the golden lines. Then I heard the *click click click* of his camera, and when I turned I saw that he was pointing it at me.

"What are you doing?" I turned away and tried to hide behind one of the trees.

"Your hair. It's beautiful."

My hair. Was not. Beautiful. It was thick and orange and suited my name perfectly because it was the exact color of the flesh of the fish.

"Do you ever take it out of that ponytail?"

"No."

"That's a shame because it really is beautiful."

Click. Click. Click.

A butterfly landed on a tree stump and caught his attention. He hovered over it and then turned the camera sideways as it flew away, and as I watched him, I couldn't help but remember what he had told me.

About always looking for something.

"Do you like working at the shop?"

He smiled the smile I had come to realize didn't necessarily mean he was happy. "I've always known that's what I would end up doing. It's what was expected of me."

"Why?"

"For the same reason you are going to become a lawyer."

Maybe it was the moment, or the way the sunlight hit the top of his head making him look like a fallen angel, but I felt like I could trust him, and for the first time, I said the words out loud.

"I don't want to be a lawyer."

He nodded like it was obvious, then ran his fingers along the length of the camera strap. "What is it you want then?"

Such a simple question and one I had no idea how to answer. I bit my lip because of how raw I suddenly felt. I wanted to be truthful and tell him about Rome and my dream to see the mosaics from the art books in real life, but somehow it felt silly, and he was special. I knew if he laughed it would break something inside of me, so I said nothing.

"What is it that *you* want?" I asked, buying myself some more time. The insects flying through the air sparkled like glitter, and as we walked further down the path, my heart quickened because I could hear people talking past the trees and I knew that whatever was happening between us was about to end.

"You first," he said.

I took a breath, trying to find the courage to speak, to find the words that might capture what was inside of me, but it was too misshapen and unwieldy and I didn't know how to explain. Then too much time passed, and we were already back on the paved walkway where joggers and elderly couples weaved in and out of each other. We had left the magic of the trees behind and were now back to being just like everyone else, and I don't think he even realized that I hadn't answered him.

Chapter 4

When I opened my eyes, I looked down at my hands, speckled in dried webs of glue. It was morning, and even though my heart said what I had just experienced was real, my mind told me it must have been a dream.

The collage of Venus sat in my lap.

I jumped when all of a sudden someone began pounding on my bedroom door. "Have you been up all night?" My mother barged in and began gathering the few things I had forgotten to pack. "I told you I would be here bright and early. It's time to go, otherwise we will never beat the traffic."

I felt dizzy, like I had just gotten off a merry-go-round, and took in a deep breath to help remind me of who I was and why I was here. Slowly, I remembered I was going to New York and I was going to become a lawyer and she was there to take me.

Sol was just a dream. I whispered it under my breath like a chant. Even if I'd wanted it to be, none of it was real.

None of it.

"Sam, are you okay?" Her eyebrows were knit in frustration.

I knew that I couldn't tell her the truth, maybe because I barely understood it myself. So, I nodded and let her push me out the door and into the car.

Brian sat in the back seat while I sat in the front with her. But as we started to drive, I could feel myself beginning to shake, and all I wanted was for the thoughts and the doubts and the worry to stop crashing around inside my head. Maybe she read my mind, because instead of making conversation, she began to sing and I let myself slip into the magic of her music, the silkiness of her notes sweet and billowy like cotton candy. When she sang, there was a softness about her that I didn't recognize.

"You have a beautiful voice, Mom."

She stopped singing.

We drove in silence before she spoke. "You've never told me that before."

I stared out of the window as cars drove past and Brian snored quietly in the back. I drew in deep breaths to calm myself. She started singing again after a few minutes, like she couldn't keep it in, like she had no choice but to let it out, and I wondered what had happened between us to make it so I had never told her how lovely her voice was. But then I forced myself to stop thinking, and I leaned back and closed my eyes. Between the steady controlled motion of the car and the clean, pure strength of her music, I fell asleep. I dreamt I was eating donuts dipped in white icing. The mechanical hum of a bus engine finally woke me.

Brian had already unlocked the trunk and was busy filling a cart with stacks of my magazines. I came up behind him to help. I'm not sure what it was he saw in my face, but after the third box went in, he whispered, "It'll be okay, Fish," and I wondered how many times before he had said those very same words.

We rode the elevator to the eleventh floor while my mother searched for a parking spot. Brian had to fiddle with the key and push hard against the door, and just as we were about to give up, it flew open as though it was just testing our commitment.

The furniture was standard dorm fare—a desk, a chair, a single bed, and a dining table. There was a hot plate and a sink and a tiny private bathroom beside it. Because the room was so small, the cart didn't fit inside, so we had to leave it in the hallway and carry things into the room. It wasn't long before the space felt cluttered.

My mother finally came in, and if she was disappointed, it didn't show. "Cute," she said, pulling out a handkerchief from her bag to mop the film of sweat that had formed across her forehead. "At least there's air conditioning."

She pressed a button and the room filled with the unnatural smell of electric air. She got to work unpacking my clothes into the small dresser next to the desk. I hadn't noticed the shopping bag she was carrying until she reached inside. "A little bit of home." Out came a drawing of a rose I must have made when I was little, but because I had added too many petals, it looked flat and misshapen. She hung it above the dining table. "Perfect."

We had dinner at a pizzeria a few blocks away where the two guys behind the counter spoke the fastest Spanish I had ever heard while simultaneously tossing pies into the air. We sat at a fake marble table in plastic outdoor garden chairs and drank our sodas out of cans.

Afterward, we bought Italian ices that the girl behind the counter scooped into paper cups. Brian and I licked ours, but my mother insisted on eating hers with a spoon. We ate them outside, walking on the street, listening in on other people's conversations and feeling the rhythm of music streaming from someone's open window. From the graffiti on the fronts of the buildings to the gum-cemented sidewalks, I felt completely immersed in color and sound and texture. It was the first time I felt at home, and when I looked up, I saw Brian smiling and I knew that he felt it too. It was like walking through a living painting.

My mother took out the handkerchief that seemed to appear freshly pressed even though she had been using it to wipe the perspiration from her face for most of the day. "Make sure that you take care of yourself, Salmon."

"She'll be fine, Jay." Brian smiled at me.

I'd forgotten that was what he called her when he used to live with us. My mother's name was Jayne, and I liked that he called her Jay because it gave the Y in her name a purpose. It reminded me of a time when all we cared about was who got the best spot on the couch for TV and how many books I could trick them into reading me at bedtime. Memories of my childhood swirled together, spinning so quickly in my head that I stumbled from the dizziness. My mother reached out her arms to catch me. "Remember what you are here to do and who you are going to become and know that I love you, Salmon." She kissed my forehead with her cherry-stained lips.

I didn't anticipate how sad I would feel to see them leave.

Brian hugged me while my mother stood beside him smoothing out the wrinkles in her pencil skirt. Her pocketbook was open, and I could see some of her business cards poking out. They had been late meeting me, and I knew it was most likely because Brian had needed to stop and buy peanuts from the street vendor on the corner while my mother handed out cards to the concierge when she checked out of the hotel. She believed there was opportunity everywhere and acted as though it belonged to her. I breathed in her perfume, crisp like a pear and so different than the buttery sweetness of Brian's beard. I breathed them in even more deeply one last time so I could more fully take in the comfort of their predictability.

After they drove off, leaving me behind, I decided to walk.

Life in the city was busy and loud, and it was easy to get lost, which is what I wanted—to feel invisible. I stopped inside a bakery with its breads lined up against the back walls like decorations. Cookies and pastries filled the insides of glass cases, but there were so many that even by the time the clerk made her way over to me, my mind wasn't made up. I smiled at her but she didn't smile back, and when she went on to the next customer, I just gave up.

Back on the street, I walked some more and after a few blocks, I found myself standing outside of an office supply store. I went inside where parents and students milled about, filling plastic green baskets with school supplies. We moved like a herd, and I ran my hand along the tops of boxed pencils and markers and brightly colored folders. It was the paper aisle that caught my attention and the one I lingered at the longest. There were several sketchbooks displayed in multiple sizes. My dorm room was too small to work at the scale I was used to, and I didn't even have an art desk any more. I wandered down a few more aisles and that's when I spotted the perfect compromise: a roll of cash register paper perfectly sized for mosaic making in a tiny dorm room.

For dinner that night, I ate half a bag of white powdered donuts and a can of soda that I bought from the vending machine in the basement of the dorm. It was sweet and tasty, but more importantly, I could eat it while sitting on the edge of my bed, which was necessary since I had already arranged the roll of cashier's tape along the width of my dining table and set the magazines up above it, leaving no room for eating.

I wanted to create something to represent the energy and life of the city streets, and as I began to cut out the different values of grays and blues and sort them into piles . . .

It happened.

Chapter 5

I was in my apartment building waiting for Sol in the lobby.

My hair was loose, falling to my shoulders. It had taken me a full thirty minutes to brush out the bend that had formed from the rubber band that usually held it together. He smiled when he saw me, which made my cheeks turn red and then I wished I had left it in a ponytail.

"Where should we go?" he asked.

"You decide."

As we walked, he held my hand so gently that only our fingertips touched and all I could think was how little it would take to break our connection.

The restaurant he took me to was called the Early Bird and was filled with older couples eating dinner and an irritated looking waitress named Dorothy. She smiled when she saw Sol and he addressed her by name.

She looked me up and down. "Who's this?"

"My friend, Sam," he said.

She frowned and stared at me a little longer before turning back to Sol. "The usual?"

He nodded and winked.

"You?" She focused hard on the pad of paper in her hand.

"Grilled cheese. White bread. American."

She scribbled something down.

"White bread?" he asked.

"I like it."

"How about rye or whole wheat or pumpernickel?"

"I only eat white bread."

Dorothy waited as if there might be a chance I was going to change my mind, which there wasn't, and finally turned and walked away.

"One day you will tell me what Sam stands for and you will eat something other than white bread."

I focused on stacking some packets of jelly into a tower. "How do you know her?" I asked, looking at Dorothy a few tables away taking someone else's order.

"I come here a lot."

A group of giggling teenagers came in and sat near us. Two girls crammed themselves into one side of the booth while the boys sat across from them, their skinny overgrown legs jutting out from underneath the table. I watched them until Dorothy came back and slammed my dinner down so hard it made my fork jump.

"Hot plate." She smiled at Sol.

His "usual" turned out to be two slices of meatloaf covered in a reddish-brown gravy surrounded by a mound of mashed potatoes and a pool of green peas. He pierced a piece of meat onto a fork and reached across the table. "Want some?"

I smiled and shook my head, realizing this was going to be our little joke.

"Can't fault a guy for trying."

I had always been a picky eater and not even adulthood changed my compulsions. I stared at his plate, at the way the peas were pressed up against the potatoes, and I didn't know how to explain how much I hated when one kind of food touched another. I watched him eat and then I picked up my sandwich. The teenagers next to us were talking loudly and laughing.

"Remember those days?" Sol asked when he saw me staring.

I nodded because I didn't want to tell him that I didn't. That most of my growing up was spent in my room surrounded by cut up magazine strips and art books. We finished eating and Dorothy came to clear our plates. "We have your favorite. Banana cream."

Sol smiled and nodded his head.

"I'll have the same," I said, even though she had already turned and walked away.

She brought over two plates and sprayed a white pyramid of whipped cream over each slice. I was almost finished with mine when I looked up and realized he had barely started.

"Looks like we found something you like." He reached over with his napkin and very gently wiped the cream from my chin. Then he ate a few forkfuls before pushing the plate toward the middle of the table.

"Aren't you going to finish?"

He was quiet for a few minutes as if he was trying to decide whether to tell me something. "I don't really like it," he admitted.

"Then why did you order it?"

"Because Dorothy thinks I do, and I don't want to hurt her feelings."

"You don't like banana cream pie and you only order it to please the waitress?" I reached over and scooped some of the custard onto my spoon.

"No. I love banana cream pie. I just don't like this one."

"Why?"

His cheeks turned the slightest shade of pink that I would not have noticed had I not stopped eating to look up.

"My mother makes the best pie. It's like nothing you have ever had. Ever."

"Then why don't you just eat hers?"

There was that quiet again, and he looked across at the teenagers who had finished their meals and were now all simultaneously texting on their cell phones. He turned back to me. "Because she's not here anymore."

His words hit the table with a heavy thud. He sat a bit more upright, as if a boulder had just been released from his shoulders, and the air between us felt thick.

"I'm so sorry, Sol."

He suddenly looked angry. "There's nothing for you to be sorry about. I didn't say she was dead. I just said she was gone. And I will never stop searching until I find her."

I couldn't help but think of how he was that first time at the lake and the desperate way he was looking for something. I needed to say something to fix it, to make it right, but I didn't know what.

It took me a few seconds, but then I said the first thing that came to my mind:

"What was it like?"

"What?" I could tell he was still mad. Maybe he thought he misheard me or that I misspoke and that I wanted to know about her. Maybe I did, but not in the way that he thought.

"Her banana cream pie. What was it like?"

He hesitated for a minute, perhaps trying to determine if I was sincere, and he must have decided I was because soon he began to speak. "The crust was made of graham cracker but it had a nutty flavor, the custard was light and yellow with little black specks, and the topping was sweet and tangy all at the same time. I have never tasted anything like it." He closed his eyes and took in a long deep breath, and suddenly more than anything I wanted to be in his mother's kitchen and feel what it was like to know that everything in your world was perfect because the person you adored the most in the world, who also happened to be perfect, was feeding you a piece of pie that was better than anything else you had ever tasted. I reached across to touch his hand and he let me. All I could think was that I wanted to ease his pain and that I had never felt that way about anyone else before.

He walked me home that night, but we didn't say much. When we got to the front steps of my apartment, I reached toward him, but he turned his head so that my kiss landed on his cheek and I felt foolish.

"Thanks for dinner."

He nodded.

"And thanks for telling me about your mother."

He looked at me for a few minutes more and then he came in very close and cradled my head in his hands. "Promise me you'll show me what's in that sketchbook of yours." Then he kissed me, and every last bit of my sensibility disappeared and I knew I would have done anything he asked, given him anything that he wanted.

I had two boyfriends when I was in college: one who was very interested in me until I slept with him and the second even more shy than I was. He was kind and sweet, but we had very little to say to one another, and most of the time I would fall asleep when we were together and when I woke he would be gone. When it finally ended, I felt indifferent, and then after that there was no one and I resigned myself to the fact that there probably wouldn't be.

I had never been with a man who made me feel the way that Sol did, someone who electrified me and whom I knew could get me to do whatever it was he wanted. I had never felt so weak. He kissed me again, and when he pulled away, I was desperate for a sign that he felt the same. But all I saw was a profound sadness, so infinite and bottomless that I knew if I stepped the wrong way, I would fall inside of it and lose myself forever and that I would never find my way out.

I knew it with every part of my being.

Being with Sol was dangerous.

Chapter 6

I opened my eyes in my dorm room in New York, the strip of cashier's tape dangling off the edge of the table with bits of gray and black squares glued along the sides. I was confused and undone, and when I looked down at the half-finished collage, I couldn't help but wonder if there was a connection between my art and the dreams or if they just happened to come at the same time because of coincidence.

Or maybe it was all just because I was going mad.

All I knew was that I felt unbalanced, like I could topple over the edge at any minute. I hated feeling that way. My hands were shaking so I took a few deep breaths and tried to regain my composure. I couldn't stop thinking of the last few seconds with Sol and how they had terrified me, and I was grateful that I woke up when I had. He was risky and unpredictable, which was also how he made me feel. I hated that even in a dream, the man I was in love with had so much power over me that I didn't even recognize myself.

Like I'd forgotten who I was.

I was here to go to law school. I got the sense that my mother and I had argued about it for a while and finally, she'd won. She always seemed to know what was best for me, whispering her words of reassurance like the embroidery letters on a needlepoint sampler over and over so I wouldn't forget. Even though I had clearly resisted at first, maybe she was right. If I focused on school instead of the art, it might stop these dreams and even help me regain more of my memory.

Maybe it would prevent me from going crazy.

Yes, my mother was right—what I needed was to focus on why I was here. It was the only way to move forward. I needed to commit to the life I was living and forget the one I was dreaming.

I quickly learned about the importance of study groups. Mine was formed by pure chance. During Civil Procedure, the girl sitting in front of me, but slightly to the right, had been eyeing the two guys sitting in front of her for most of the class, and then because she needed a fourth person, turned around and asked me. It was without question an example of being in the right place at the right time. Or at least that's what I thought. Later, she told me that I was her first choice from the very start.

Margaret was focused and determined and had decided she was going to become a lawyer when she was ten. She wore her hair in a nautical knot low in the back of her head and each day chose a different colored pencil to secure it into place. John was married and always brought a packed lunch from home. Lucas was serious and intense and hated when anyone shortened his name to Luke. We worked well together, like one of those pinwheels that becomes a single ring of color when you blow on it.

Everything was moving along smoothly until one day in Contracts when the professor walked into the classroom late. He cleared his throat and slammed his briefcase hard onto the desk. An uncomfortable hush filled the room as one of the girls in the front row bent over to collect the papers that slipped onto the floor. She was probably just trying to get in his good graces since he was notorious for asking dauntingly grueling questions. At the start of every class, there were several moments of collective breath holding while he selected his victim.

When he called out "Salmon Baird," I wasn't sure if the rustle I heard coming from the middle of the classroom was the sound of relief or the stifling of laughter. I slowly rose to my feet, which made me feel even more awkward. All I could think was how much I hated my name and that I wished I had remembered to tell him to call me Sam. I opened my laptop and tried to position my textbook strategically so that I could make sense of the notes I had written. Even though I wasn't looking at him, I could sense that the professor was pacing at the front of the room like a lion waiting to pounce. It didn't help that all eyes were now on me and that every fact that had been in my head from the night before had suddenly disappeared. I tried to will it back, to picture the text, but all I could make out were jumbled words, completely unintelligible like they were written in a foreign language.

Margaret kicked me, and I realized he had just asked me something.

"Yes, sir." *You will not make me cry*, I mumbled to myself, and maybe he thought I was speaking to him because he stopped what he was doing, walked up the aisle, and the next thing I knew, we were a nose length apart.

"*Hawkins v. McGee*. You are prepared. Yes?" He spoke like a drill sergeant, his words crisp and clear and perfectly enunciated. He had his hands tucked behind his back as he slowly swayed back and forth.

"Yes."

"Speak up, Ms. Baird. Or should I call you Salmon?" He smirked.

"Ms. Baird is fine." I hated that I was whispering.

"Facts!" he barked and a few people in the back row gasped.

"The case is about breach of contract."

"Facts!" he hollered again, this time louder. Now there was complete silence.

I didn't know what he wanted, and fear began to creep up my legs and across my chest, and then the shaking began in my core, slowly vibrating through my neck and into my head. I bit down on my lip to make it stop. "No."

"Did you say something, Ms. Baird?" He had a stress ball in his hand, which he squeezed so tightly it looked like the number eight.

I couldn't find my place on the page or the words in my head. But then I looked over at Lucas, who was smiling at me. I don't know why on that day he had forgotten to shave, but he had, and the little bits of stubble that formed along his chin gave me courage.

"The defendant operated on the plaintiff's hand and guaranteed to make it 100 percent perfect. After the operation, the plaintiff was left with a hand that was in worse condition than prior to surgery. The plaintiff claimed that the damage was the fault of the defendant."

He was still standing close to me. He waited for another very long minute before he spoke. "You can have a seat now, Ms. Salmon Baird."

Fear had a numbing effect, which seemed to make my hearing fail and it took a few minutes for me to understand what he was saying. It wasn't until Margaret squeezed my hand that I realized he was done with me and had already moved on to someone else.

The next few days, we studied even harder, breaking only to eat. After what happened to me, everyone else wanted to make sure they were doubly prepared.

"You did fine, Salmon," Lucas said as he bit into an apple.

"Thanks." I smiled because I knew he was just being kind.

"You really did." John said as he unwrapped the tinfoil from around his sandwich. His wife packed his lunch every day, alternating between cream cheese and strawberry jam and tuna fish. I hadn't yet figured out if that was all he liked or if it was simply all she knew how to make. In any case, he always seemed pleased and licked the tips of his fingers when he finished.

"Back to work." Margaret instructed. She had already thrown out her trash and was standing with her books in her arms.

Good thing, too, because the next day it was her turn.

I watched as she rose and positioned her feet like she was at home plate and about to hit a ball, clutching the edge of the desk to steady herself.

The professor began like he always did by pacing at the foot of the classroom. But there was something different about Margaret, something so dynamically capable that it seemed to energize him and make him pace even faster. His questions became more complex, more difficult, and after she answered them she took another breath and answered the ones he hadn't even asked. She was so strong, so powerful, that I couldn't take my eyes off her. The eloquent way in which she expressed her thoughts and how she connected her arguments was breathtaking. When he finished drilling her, he walked up the aisle so that he could get closer to where she was standing. She was someone who knew exactly who she was and precisely what she was supposed to be doing with her life.

It was as though she was sparkling, and maybe he also felt the heat coming from her, because he pulled a handkerchief from his suit pocket and dabbed it at his temple. He stared at her for several seconds longer and then he motioned for her to take her seat, but the way his hand was outstretched almost looked as though he was asking her to dance. She smiled and stood for a few seconds longer just as I had except that she was not doing it because she was frozen in fear. She was standing from the high of battle and the rapture of victory.

When she finally sat down, I could feel the relief and the glory wash over her. It made the tops of her cheeks blush and her eyes shine. It was that feeling you get when it all falls into perfect place, slipping effortlessly into the very spot it was intended to fit. I pushed away how intimately recognizable the feeling was because I couldn't let myself think about my art.

We went out that night for a celebratory dinner at a Japanese restaurant. Even John decided to join us, but not before calling his wife and inviting her to come, as well. Margaret did most of the ordering. Somehow, she knew me well enough to know that there was no way I could force myself to eat the endless array of raw fish sitting on balls of rice. I saw her whisper to the waitress, and a few minutes later a tray with fried chicken breasts came out. I was so touched that when Lucas poured sake into my glass, I took a sip. I could feel it burn its way down my esophagus and then warm my belly. He poured a second glass and then a third and I lost track after that. I liked how springy my legs suddenly felt, as though I could leap across the room, which was quite misleading because when I did finally stand, instead of taking flight I stumbled into the chair next to mine.

Lucas took my elbow, promising Margaret that he would get me home safely. He tried to steer me along the sidewalk, but I didn't want to be led. Each time I convinced him to let me go, I would wobble and then lose my balance like I was walking some invisible tightrope.

"Why don't you just hold on to me and let me take care of you?"

We weaved along the street with all the others who'd had too much to drink. Someone was throwing up in a trash can and Lucas pulled me in tighter. We made it back to the dorm and he stopped at the vending machine to buy water. He walked me to my room and we stood at the door for a few minutes.

"Do you want me to come in?"

I touched his face, rubbing my hand along the side where there was still a line of stubble. I fished around in my bag looking for my key but then gave up and just handed it to him. It took a few minutes for him to find and then he shoved his shoulder into the door until it finally gave way.

It was dark inside, and I could see him trying to find the light switch, but I wanted it to stay dark, I didn't want to see. "Stop."

I tripped over a stack of magazines and he turned to make sure I was okay. As I fell toward him, he reached out his arms and then he kissed me. His lips tasted like the Vaseline he was always rubbing on them. I closed my eyes, moving my fingers along the stubble on his face, and I couldn't help but think of Sol.

"I promise I'll shave tomorrow."

"Don't."

He shrugged and kissed me again and I tried to pretend I saw fireworks.

That's how it began for us. During the day, we acted like everyone else, but at night we were lovers. He was easy to please because he didn't ask for very much. He never questioned why I didn't want to turn on the lights; he simply let me have my way. I could barely admit it to myself let alone tell him that sometimes when he was on top of me, I pretended he was someone else.

Aside from his occasional stubble, he looked nothing like Sol. His hair color was as ginger orange as mine and I often wondered if people thought we were more like brother and sister than a couple. It looked less orange in the dark, which was another reason I preferred turning off the lights.

When Lucas got called to present in Contracts, he was confident and self-assured. He wasn't a natural like Margaret, but you could tell that he was smart and determined. He seemed pleased with his performance and afterward he turned to me and smiled.

That evening when he got into my bed, the smell of menthol covered me like a blanket. He had a habit of brushing his teeth several times a day, which made him smell medicinal, which was even worse than the Vaseline. I couldn't get the image that we were about to have intercourse in a hospital ward out of my head. When he got on top of me, he closed his eyes and buried his face into my hair so that whatever sound he made got muffled inside my pillow. When he finished, he lay back down and kissed my hand like he was thanking me.

"You did well today."

He smirked.

"I meant in class."

He kissed my forehead. "I guess you'll have to practice keeping up."

Then he fell asleep, snoring softly in my ear, his words leaving behind a cold sheet of sweat that made the sides of my hair stick to my face.

After that night, I worked harder.

I brought cardboard boxes from the supermarket to store my magazines, and when our study group ended for the evening, I stayed up later reading and highlighting and crafting the most magnificently detailed outlines. Lucas pretended to be supportive, but I knew that he missed me. He would knock on my door every few nights, casting down his head when I sent him off. Even on weekends I locked myself away and when exam time finally came, I felt ready. I went to bed early, ate a healthy breakfast, and approached the test confidently. I was having lunch with Lucas when the results came in. I probably looked like I was smiling as I was reading them, but that was because the muscles in my face had frozen into place.

Nothing had changed.

I made the same grades I had before. I pretended to be pleased, pretended that everything was wonderful. He patted me on the back and kissed me on the cheek like he knew the truth anyway, which made it even worse. Everyone else in the group did well and decided to go out to celebrate.

We ended up at a loud bar where there was nowhere to sit so we stood. John and his wife were there, and he had probably had a little too much to drink because he had a funny smile on his face and looked glassy-eyed. "Hi, Sammy." He burst into giggles as his wife swatted his shoulder.

Margaret was out on the dance floor. Her hair was out of its knot and flew down the length of her back like a river. Her hands sat on the tops of her knees as her hips swayed back and forth. She chose the guy closest to her and wound his arms around her waist from behind. He quickly matched his movements to hers and then it was like they were one person.

Lucas asked me if there was something I wanted to drink. There wasn't. What I wanted was to get out of there. There was an energy that made me uncomfortable, a letting go that felt well deserved for all the rest of them but not for me. I felt bad for leaving after I had promised to come, and he tried to leave with me but I insisted that he stay. He had worked hard and deserved to celebrate.

I didn't turn him away when he showed up at my door that night smelling like disinfectant. Maybe I cried a little while we were having sex, maybe I let my body go limp as he silently climbed on top of me. As much as I wanted it to be dark, I was betrayed by the moonlight slipping in from behind the window shade. When he kissed me, I was overcome with spearmint and Vaseline and beer. Maybe he sensed my reluctance, because the next time he kissed me, he did it more adamantly, like I imagined a vampire would. He stole my tears and my breath and whatever remaining images I had left of Sol.

And I let him.

Chapter 7

Lucas liked to go to the movies.

He liked to go in the middle of the day when there weren't many people around. His favorite theaters were the ones that let you squirt as much of the fake gold butter onto your popcorn as you wanted. My favorites were the old-fashioned kind where the projection screens were flanked by dark maroon velvet curtains tied back with thick, gold cords.

I let him choose the movies we went to see. His tastes varied from action thrillers to crime dramas to comedies. He laughed so hard that even if there weren't many people around, they still always turned to stare. He especially liked movies from his childhood, and one day he took me to see *Back to the Future*. It was playing at one of my favorite cinemas with arches over the front windows and red carpets lining the floors. We stopped at the concession stand to get popcorn and candy and then made our way inside the main theater.

Lucas was very particular about where we sat, and I waited impatiently, balancing the candy and soda in my hands, while he made his choice. We almost always ended up in the middle, and sometimes I wondered if it took so long because he was calculating dead center in his head. Once we settled into our seats I opened a box of Sugar Daddies while he glared at anyone who even remotely thought of sitting within his line of vision.

I offered him some candy, but he was too busy eyeing a woman and her preschooler who had just walked in. He must have succeeded in scaring her off because she quickly moved to the other side of the theater. In addition to her, there was a man with a baseball cap slumped down into his seat, three teenagers with neon-colored hair, and an older looking Asian woman with knitting needles and a ball of yarn in her lap. I started thinking about what would happen if life as we knew it came to an end and the only people left were the ones sitting in this theater. Would we form a little society or simply continue eating copious amounts of popcorn while watching movies as the universe crumbled to bits outside? I wanted to talk it over with Lucas, but the previews had just begun and he waved his hand to shush me, so I sat back in my seat and chewed my candy instead.

After the movie, we stopped at a diner where he ordered a hamburger for himself and lemon chiffon pie and coffee for me.

"Didn't you love that movie?" He wiped something from the corner of his mouth and cut me off before I could respond. "I mean that scene where she thinks his name is Calvin because it says Calvin Klein in his underwear, totally priceless." He continued to snicker to himself as he sipped his soda.

Silky yellow lemon coated my lips. "What do you think would have happened if Marty hadn't tried to go back to 1985? If he had just decided to stay where he was and accept the life that he was living?"

Lucas looked up with his mouth slightly open. "Sometimes you confuse me, Salmon. That's the whole point of the movie. Marty is in the wrong time. He has to go back to where he came from so that he can make everything right again."

I didn't know why I was pushing it. Well, maybe I did. "But why? Why couldn't he have just stayed where he was? Just make the best of it?"

Lucas smiled. "You're such a silly thing. Because that's the way these plots work. Whenever a character is thrown back in time, they spend the rest of the story trying to get back to where they started."

He was right, of course, this was the way that all these stories went. The protagonist always spent the rest of the book trying to return to where she started in order to fix the future. Lucas was humming the lyrics to a song about two worlds colliding and I suddenly wondered if he could read my mind.

"I told you. That we could fly. Cause we all have wings. But some of us don't know why."

He took another bite of his hamburger, and I waited, thinking maybe it was possible that he understood me. Maybe I had really found someone who could see inside of me, whom I could trust with my secrets without hesitation, without judgment. But he said nothing more, and when he motioned for the waitress to bring over the check, I knew he didn't know and I told myself it didn't matter. I scraped the last few bits of pie into my mouth because when you chew it makes it harder to cry.

My parents came to help me find a new place to live at the end of the school year.

It never occurred to me that it might seem strange that we were still a family even though they were no longer together. One night, after I finally remembered the password to my Facebook page, I discovered that even though I rarely posted, my mother did, proudly and often. From her photos, I saw that I spent a lot of time with my parents—both of them, together. Through the memories I was able to retrieve, I knew without question that they were always there for me and that we were a team.

They had two hotel rooms, and I first went to see my mother, who was busy circling listings in the newspaper. She was wearing a fancy black suit and spritzed extra perfume behind her ears before leaving to search for my new summer apartment. Once she was gone, I went to see Brian, and we rummaged through the nightstand until we found a room service menu. We ordered cereal and ate it on the fancy little cart that arrived with a flower in a vase and then afterward, I read a book while he worked on a crossword puzzle from the newspaper. I liked sitting in the room with him and listening to the sound his pencil eraser made as it rubbed across the surface of the page. Suddenly, an image of us drawing together when I was little came to mind. I closed my eyes for a minute, losing myself in the tranquility, breathing in the peacefulness. I know that my mother never understood quiet the way that Brian and I did.

My mother was the loud, powerful force in my life. Maybe that's why the memories that were slowly returning seemed to predominantly center around her.

She found me a sublease in a two-bedroom apartment with a girl who was earning her degree in engineering. The girl's hair sloped like a tent in front of her face so that I could barely see her eyes, and when she spoke, her voice was so soft I could only hear every third word. She was so nondescript that if she hadn't been there that afternoon, I wasn't sure I could have picked her out in a crowd.

Everyone in my study group had landed impressive internships. The one I found was at a small two-person firm a few subway stops away from campus. I wasn't put off when the lead attorney explained that much of the work would be answering phones and filing documents mostly because that was the kind of thing I was used to doing. Except for the stale smell of cigarettes that seemed to always linger in the air, the office suited me just fine.

Lucas moved in with three other people from our class. The night after we settled in, my parents took us out to an Italian restaurant to celebrate. The nice thing about New York was the way that one thing could so easily transform into something else. What had once been an old hardware store now had quaint wooden flower boxes beneath the windows and a red-and-white striped awning over the doorway.

Lucas arrived exactly on time. He shook Brian's hand and then commented on the scarf my mother was wearing. When she batted her eyes, I know he thought he had her right where he wanted and that she might have even been flirting with him.

But I knew better.

She hated him from the start. Even though he was ambitious, came from a good family, and had landed a prestigious internship, she hated him. She tapped her fingers on the table like she was drumming the beat to an executioner's song.

Lucas beamed when he thought she approved of his wine selection and again when, in nearly flawless Italian, he ordered a fancy veal dish from the menu. When the food arrived, he laid his napkin in a perfect square across his lap.

My mother picked up her wineglass. "Lucas, what are your plans for the summer?"

"Working at the firm, probably lots of late hours. And spending time with Salmon, of course." He put his hand over of mine.

My mother's lip twitched. "Am sure Sam will be happy to have the company."

The sip of water I took sat trapped in my mouth before passing over the lump that had started to form at the base of my throat. I told myself it was just the beginnings of a cold.

"Lucas is interested in real estate, Mom."

Even though she hadn't eaten much, she pushed away her plate. "Really." She tipped the wineglass into her mouth and when it was empty, filled it up again. Brian was looking down at his meatballs and spaghetti. His hands were in his lap and I could hear the sound of his knuckles cracking.

"My father is in real estate development. It's an area I'm interested in pursuing after graduation." Lucas spoke perfectly, like he had rehearsed it a hundred times, like he was sitting at a job interview.

"That's terrific, Luke." A little of that southern drawl I remembered from long ago made its way into how the *u* blended into the *k* of his name.

When Lucas turned red, it made his already orange hair look even more carrot-like. For a moment he hesitated, not sure if he should let it go or take the bait, and I could tell that he was not used to being thrown off that way. He wanted to stand up for himself and correct her but in the end, he said nothing, so I spoke for him. "It's Lucas, Mom."

She laughed, pleased. "Of course, it is, forgive me, Lucas." She stared at him, still red-faced, and then she smiled some more, maybe because she thought she had won or perhaps because she actually had.

During dessert, she was more at ease, lingering over her coffee and then scraping up every last bit of her panna cotta. When we left, she slipped her arm through mine and pulled me in close enough so all I could smell was her perfume. We walked Lucas to his apartment where we said our goodbyes.

"It was nice meeting you, Mrs. Baird."

She waved like she was in a beauty pageant. "The pleasure was mine."

I waited until we were at least a block away before I spoke. "You hate him."

She shook her head. "I don't."

"You do."

She adjusted her purse so that it fit more snugly inside the crook of her arm. It was patent leather and shaped like a trapezoid. Math was always my most difficult subject and Brian had spent hours teaching me geometric shapes. "Why?"

"I don't hate him, Sam."

We passed a music store and Brian went inside. I lost sight of him because the windows were plastered over with concert posters.

"You have so much to learn, Sam."

Before she could say anything else, I walked into the store. It was filled with vinyl records held in plastic crates that you had to bend down to sort through. I started in the A's and made my way from Aerosmith to Blondie to the Doors. They were frayed and held together by strips of duct tape, and as I carefully lifted one of them to my chest, I realized that I had known what she was going to say before she said it. I'd heard those words before, spoken a long time ago in a different place in a different world and about a different man.

But the words, they were the same.

It was easier once they left.

Easier to go back to living the life I had been living before they came. If Lucas's interactions with my mother impacted him in any way, he didn't let on. It was as though we were reading from a script, and once we made it back onstage, everything picked up just where it had left off.

Lucas worked long hours. Sometimes he would come straight to my place and other times he would just bring a change of clothes to the firm and sleep on a couch in one of the empty offices. My experience was nowhere near as intense. It didn't take me long to figure out that the two attorneys I was working for were father and daughter. He was elderly and stuck in his ways and insisted on doing research using books he stored in a backroom that smelled like mothballs. His daughter spent most of her time rolling her eyes behind his back and trying to talk him into updating their computer system. They handled a wide variety of cases so I never knew whom it was I would find in the waiting area when I arrived in the morning.

One day when I was a few minutes late, a woman was already waiting outside the office. Her hair was shiny and black with a sharp part running down the middle. There was a boy with her whom she seemed to be pushing in my direction.

"Señora Whitting's office?" His eyebrows were two thick caterpillars and his voice shook when he spoke.

They were looking for the daughter. Most of the women who came to the office were looking for the daughter. I unlocked the door and they came inside and watched as I fanned some magazines out onto the coffee table.

"Do you want something to drink?" I pointed to the water dispenser and the box of tea bags sitting on the table beside it.

It wasn't until that moment that I noticed the half-ring beneath her eye. It had already started to turn a yellowish gold and blended into her skin seamlessly like it had been there before and somehow belonged. She was sitting in the chair, her arms folded neatly in her lap. It was the boy who told me again that they were there to speak with the lawyer.

Fredrick Whitting always arrived half an hour before his daughter. He walked into the office with a newspaper tucked under his arm and a cigar hanging from his mouth. His daughter hated the smell as much as I did so he begrudgingly agreed to only smoke it inside his office. The rest of the time, he carried it unlit in his mouth. He grunted something that sounded like a hello but was muffled by both his lack of effort and the cigar wedged between his lips. He glanced at the clients in the waiting room and then stomped into his office, making it clear he knew they were not there to meet with him.

The woman's hands remained folded in her lap and she sat with her back straight. When I spoke to her, I tried not to stare at the ring beneath her eye.

"She will be here soon."

The boy translated and she nodded her head.

Abigail Whitting had three gray suits between which she alternated. She always came to work wearing sneakers and then changed into a pair of sensible black shoes she kept stored behind her desk. Even though she was much closer in age to me than her father, she intimidated me more.

I handed her the few messages I had retrieved from the answering machine. She looked over at the woman and the boy sitting on the couch, and as the woman started to rise, she motioned for her to sit back down. She went into her office and came back out after a few minutes wearing her ugly black shoes. She kept them in such perfect condition that I couldn't envision a time when they would ever need to be replaced. After she slipped a tea bag into her mug and filled it with hot water, she motioned for the woman to follow. The little boy stood as well and then all three walked into her office.

The walls were thin enough that even though I couldn't decipher what they were saying, I could make out the tone of their voices. I had sat in on enough of Abigail's meetings to know that what sounded random and haphazard was actually a perfectly choreographed piece of music. I also knew how long it would take to go over the details of custody and child support and the resources available to battered women, so I was surprised when after only fifteen minutes, the office door flew open and the woman with the dark hair came rushing out with her bag clutched to her chest. She was holding a tissue in her hand and I could tell she had been crying. The boy stood between his mother and Abigail. The woman looked down at the carpet, the boy still standing silently between them. Abigail approached her slowly like she was trying to lure a stray cat from underneath a porch. "Su tiempo."

The woman continued to look down at the floor, and I wondered if she was staring at the large brown stain that had been there longer than I had or if, for a moment, she was actually considering changing her mind.

But she wasn't.

She took the boy's hand and walked out of the office without ever once looking back.

Abigail stood quietly staring into the hallway as if she could somehow will her to return. We heard the chime of the elevator and both looked up at the door as it swung open, but it was only the UPS man with a package and some paperwork for me to sign.

"She may still come back." It sounded naive even to my ears.

Abigail shook her head. "She was here asking me to represent her husband. She wanted me to convince the DA to drop the charges against him so that he could come home."

I had seen enough in this little law practice so that not much should have surprised me, so I was taken aback by the fact that it did.

"I don't understand." I immediately regretted saying it.

Abigail stared at me like she had never really noticed me before. She tilted her head just a tiny degree to the left, reminding me of an owl. "There isn't much to understand. It takes some people longer to learn to fly," she rubbed the stain on the ground with the toe of her very sensible black shoe, "and sometimes they never do."

The woman never came back.

Every now and then, I wondered about her and about her boy and whether she was all right, but Abigail and I never spoke of her again. There were so many more women who came into the office that I wasn't sure if Abigail even remembered, but I could not forget, and sometimes when my dreams turned into nightmares I saw her face with the golden ring around her eye.

I ached for my art boxes but was too frightened of the dreams they might provoke so I tucked them away neatly beneath my bed and distracted myself with Lucas, who was over more often now that summer was nearing its end. Maybe he noticed that I was feeling sad, because one day, he invited me to an ice-skating show with his mother and sister and nieces. It was a production of *Swan Lake*, and I agreed to go mostly because I thought that watching the figure skaters flying across the ice would remind me of the acrobats at the circus I had always loved.

Lucas's mother was perfect. She wore her sparkling silver hair swept into a bun and, even at the ice arena, she was dressed as though she was hosting a luncheon at the country club. She never left home without a strand of pearls and always referred to Lucas as *darling*. We had met a few times when she and Lucas's father came in from Connecticut to take us out for dinner. Her makeup was flawless, and I smelled the faintest hint of Chanel No. 5 when she leaned in to kiss me hello. We made our way inside the arena where Lucas's sister Elizabeth was waiting for us. Her girls, both under the age of six, were chasing each other up and down the stairs while she was feverishly texting someone on her cell phone.

She looked up when she saw us. "Hello, Mother."

The girls were dressed in matching pink tulle dresses and one had pulled the bow out of the other's hair. Elizabeth quickly tossed the phone into her bag and gritted her teeth as she spoke, "Come here and let Mommy fix your hair, Madeline." She tugged hard and the child began to squirm. When she finally gave up, the little girl ran off.

"I guess we should have bought a ticket for the nanny, too." Lucas smirked. Elizabeth rolled her eyes while Lucas gave the girls a hug and then walked them over to the snack bar. They returned with two oversized cones of fluorescent pink cotton candy.

"You get to clean them up afterward." Elizabeth pointed her perfectly manicured finger at him, but he just shrugged and laughed. We handed our tickets to the usher but then just as her mother's back was turned, Elizabeth pushed Lucas so hard that he had to grab onto the railing to steady himself. "Sorry." She was smiling but her voice trembled with rage.

Rows of folding chairs surrounded the ice rink, and once the usher pointed them out, his mother and the girls settled into their seats. Out of the corner of my eye, I saw Elizabeth move toward Lucas again, but this time the heel of her shoe got stuck between the seam of the rubber mats that lined the floor. She flew backward, and as the breath rushed out of her, it made a funny whistling noise like the air escaping from a balloon. She landed on her bottom still clutching her expensive bag to her chest. She remained motionless and, for a minute, I wasn't sure that she was ever going to get up.

It was Lucas who came to her rescue.

"Don't move," he said.

"I can do it myself," she growled.

"No. Elizabeth. You. Can't." The words slipped off his tongue with such ease that I knew he had said them a thousand times before. He gave her his hand, and when she pushed it away, he pulled her up anyway. She could not seem to stand on her own, so she leaned up against him and I could see that she was used to having him save her.

And that he was used to it too.

He went back and collected her phone and a pack of tissues and the lipstick that had fallen from her bag, and then he asked me to get her some ice and a Diet Coke. When I returned, I saw that whatever spirit she had shown earlier was gone. She was sniffling into a tissue and pointing to where it hurt, and he was twisting her foot back and forth.

I had watched enough medical dramas on television to know what he was doing was wrong, and I started to speak but he interrupted me with a wave of his hand. He must have felt bad for cutting me off though because then he winked and smiled awkwardly. "I've got this, thanks."

He made her breathe in deeply, and when she finished, he handed back her shoes but one of the heels had come loose and was dangling from the outer sole like a broken finger. He left with an usher, and when he returned, the heel was refastened with a strip of shiny silver duct tape.

She held it in her hand. "Bruce is going to kill me."

"I'll deal with him, Lizzy."

I had never heard anyone in his family use a nickname to refer to anyone else except for his father's beloved Airedale Terrier, Reggie.

She was looking down whispering something, thanking him again and nodding her head slowly, and I was shocked at how small she suddenly seemed. Lucas made his way back to his seat and his mother reached over and squeezed his hand, and I realized that she too was probably accustomed to having him take care of things.

He leaned in close to speak to me, his words leaving damp spots where they hit my neck. "She's always needing me to bail her out of one mess or another. It's been that way all our lives." It was the pride with which he said it that made the goose bumps rise beneath the freckles on my arms. He waited for me to respond but my heart was beating so loudly I couldn't speak.

Elizabeth was spoiled and incompetent and helpless and maybe she got what she deserved. What was I getting so worked up about really? She shouldn't have pushed him or worn those silly high-heeled shoes in the first place. Even though she had behaved poorly, he was still the first one to rush to her side, making sure she was all right. He was the one who took care of things so that she didn't have to worry. I tried to stop the trembling that had begun in the tips of my fingers and then I looked over at Elizabeth, who was sitting solemnly with one of her daughters in her lap, and I wondered how much it must have cost for her to give herself away and whether the price was worth it.

I swallowed the spit that filled my mouth, as if somehow, I could push down the realization that was trying to make its way up. Then I stopped thinking because it was too much too soon and too hard. I turned my attention toward the rink, and even though it was beautiful, breathtaking even, to watch the figure skaters dressed in white feathers floating gracefully across the surface of the ice . . .

It also made it so much worse.

A few days passed before we saw each other again, and then we only did because I ran out of excuses. I didn't really know how to explain something I didn't fully understand myself. He came by on a Friday night after having a few too many beers with the other interns from work. He wrapped his arms around me, holding me tighter than he had in the past.

"You missed me, didn't you?" he whispered into my ear.

"Yes," I said too quickly, maybe because I was trying to convince myself as well. I weaved my fingers through his orange hair the color of autumn leaves. I had worked hard to forget what had happened with his sister, turning it into a bruise you could still see but couldn't remember how you got.

"Good." He kissed me hard, as though we were sealing the deal, and then pushed his hand up my skirt.

He stripped off my clothes and we got into bed. I tried to pretend that I wasn't counting the minutes until it was over. When we finished, he got up to use the bathroom, taking his bag of toiletries, and returned smelling like mint.

"I think I ran into Mouse, but she scurried off into her hole, so I didn't get a good look."

He was talking about my roommate whom he had gotten into the habit of making fun of. Even though he was laughing, there was something mean in the way his lip curled when he spoke about her.

"Her name is Mickey."

"Don't be so serious."

"Her name isn't Mouse." I'm not sure why it bothered me, but it did.

"You're the boss." He shrugged.

He fell asleep before me, snoring quietly on my pillow, and I noticed that he was quite handsome when his eyes were closed. His lashes were long and there was a softness about him that wasn't there when he was awake. I ran my hand along the curve of his cheek, but it must have bothered him because he swatted at me and then jerked away.

The street lamp outside my bedroom window was flickering and I stared at the pulsating light, waiting to see which one of us would outlast the other. It had a hypnotizing effect; after a few minutes, I was asleep. I dreamt that I was standing up, presenting the woman with the golden eye's case in Contracts class and the professor was grilling me and I knew that I was doing a terrible job. Every time I got an answer wrong, her husband got to punch her, sometimes in her face and other times in her belly. She was crying, begging me to help her, yet no matter how I tried, I could not get the answers right. I woke at the point when she was crouched over on the floor and he was kicking her with his work boot. I sat up in the bed and screamed and then Lucas woke, too.

"What happened?"

"I'm going to be a terrible lawyer."

He pulled me back down. "You'll be fine."

"Tell me the truth. I want to know." For whatever reason, hearing him say it felt urgent, perhaps even critical.

"You are perfect just the way you are."

I know he didn't mean for them to, but the words sent chills down my spine. "I don't want to be a lawyer. I don't want to be perfect." It was the most honest thing I'd ever said to him, but I spoke it too softly for him to hear.

"Come here. You're cold. Let me warm you."

I let him wrap his arms around me and said nothing more.

"It doesn't matter anyway. One day we'll be married, and you'll stay home and take care of our kids and I'll take care of everything else and you'll never have to worry about anything ever again."

My heart was beating so hard, it made it difficult to breathe, and the only thing I wanted was to find my art boxes, to cut up my magazines and feel the tranquility that always happened once the pieces fell perfectly into place, but when he fell asleep, he held onto me so tight, it hurt.

I couldn't move. And I was too scared that if I fell asleep, I might dream about Sol. So, I lay in bed awake most of the night thinking about Elizabeth wearing that taped up shoe on her foot, broken and defeated.

And perfect.

I broke up with Lucas on a Wednesday one week later because that's how long it took for me to find the courage. As tempted as I was to do it via text, I felt I owed him more than that. The problem was that in addition to hating confrontation, I also didn't know how I would explain things so that he would understand.

We met at a diner with domed desserts on the counters and I ordered tea and he ordered cheesecake. When I began to speak, it was too sudden, too fast, and I stuttered over my words. I tried not to look at his face, which became paler the longer I spoke.

"Why are you doing this?" he demanded.

The table we were sitting at was unsteady and rocked back and forth between us like a seesaw. "It's just not working out."

"You've met someone else?"

Would that have made it easier for him to bear? "No, of course not."

"Then what?" He was getting angry, and his skin went from the white of shock to the bright red of rage. "Tell me why?"

"This just isn't what I want." It was the first honest thing I'd said since we sat down and something inside of me unclenched.

"You're fucking that Mouse bitch now, aren't you? Is that it?"

I laughed, which probably infuriated him even more. "You know that's ridiculous."

"What I know is that the girl with the stupidest name I've ever heard is breaking up with me even though I am and will always be the best thing that ever happened to her, and there is absolutely no comprehensible or logical reason for why."

He was breathing heavily, and for a moment I thought he was going to choke.

"Since we are being brutally honest with one another, there's something else you should know." He paused for dramatic effect. "You will be a terrible lawyer and I have no idea why or what it is you are doing here besides wasting everyone's time, Salmon."

The way he curled his tongue over the silent *L* in my name reminded me of the way my mother said it when she was angry, and the similarity startled me. He sat there a few minutes longer as if he was waiting for something. He wasn't used to not getting what he wanted, so maybe he thought I would change my mind. I had no idea what to do or say and then my head began to spin and everything sounded like the squeaks Brian's old tape recorder made when I pushed the buttons too quickly forward and back.

Finally, Lucas gave up waiting for me. I didn't realize he had been keeping the table steady with his hand, so when he stood, the whole thing shifted downward and the tea in my cup shimmered and splashed across the surface. I watched his face soften like it did when he collected the contents of Elizabeth's purse, like it did when he wanted to take care of things. I felt my resolve start to shift so I looked away until I was certain the feeling had passed. When I turned back again he was gone, leaving a few crumpled dollar bills and a stack of napkins behind to sop up the mess.

I watched as they turned from white to the color of February snow and then something unfamiliar and unexpected came over me. I pushed the napkins aside, and when the bus boy came over, I asked for a rag. I slid it across the Formica, feeling the table rock from the strength of my force. I didn't stop; I was scared that if I did whatever it was that I was feeling would disappear. So, I scrubbed until the girls sitting at the booth beside me paid their bill and stood to leave, until the skin on my knuckles began to chafe and the entire surface of the table was so shiny I could see my own reflection. And then I scrubbed a few minutes longer because even though what I was experiencing was microscopic, I had never really felt before what it might be like to take care of things for myself.

I went back to that coffee shop three days in a row, trying to conjure up the feeling like a witch hovering over her cauldron, but nothing came. I sat at the same wobbling table until my tea turned cold but all I felt was a confusion so encompassing I couldn't breathe. The only thing I could think to do was walk.

I wound my way through streets and neighborhoods that changed every time I remembered to check. I passed street vendors who handed out hot dogs engulfed in steamy clouds of vapor. Some neighborhoods smelled like yeast and oregano, and on one block I counted four different pizzerias. When I got tired of smelling food, I watched people, some alone like me and others huddled together sharing a soda, a cigarette, their hands wrapped around Styrofoam cups of coffee. I stopped inside a bakery where I picked out unusual sounding flavored donuts like blackberry lemonade and maple bacon and red velvet licorice. I slipped my fingers through the brown twine the clerk used to tie the box, letting it cut into my skin because the pain reminded me I was alive. I walked until I couldn't walk anymore, and when I came home I was tired but never tired enough. Lucas's words haunted me, and I could not shake the possibility that he was correct, and that even though I thought I was doing the right thing by being here, it was all very wrong.

As big as the city was, eventually the walking became routine, the routes too familiar, and I felt like a hamster trapped inside a wheel. The streets were loud and filled with life when what I wanted was quiet so that I could just disappear.

It was inevitable really.

Digging through one of the boxes buried underneath my bed, I found my sketchbook. Yearning swept through me, like binging on an entire cake, the temptation too strong. I opened it and found a half-finished sketch of a mermaid. Even though I knew it was going to happen and that I shouldn't let it, I just couldn't stop myself.

Maybe it was simply my destiny.

Chapter 8

Sol and I had become inseparable, drinking from the same glass and eating from the same plate, and when we weren't together, we were making plans to see each other. It had become so consuming that I couldn't remember life before him or imagine it moving forward without him. I knew if it ever ended something would break inside of me, which made it even more intoxicating and exciting.

And terrifying.

He was all I could think about.

He pressed his fingertips against mine when he kissed my upper lip and made me dizzy with fever. The connection between us felt so powerful that it joined me to him in a jolting way whether I wanted it to or not.

But I wanted it.

We were standing on the stoop of my apartment building.

"I don't want you to move to New York." His arms were wrapped around my waist and he pulled me in close.

"Then I won't," I whispered into his ear, and maybe he didn't hear because he didn't answer. Instead he held me so close it was like we were taking the same breath. I had never felt such love combined with madness for anyone before.

Later in the week, I went to my mother's house for dinner. I was pushing a piece of pie around on my plate, hoping to find courage in the crumbs for what I was about to say.

"Did you send in the down payment for school?" she asked.

I didn't answer, just scraped up the last little bits.

"Never mind, just give it me." Her hand was outstretched but I still didn't respond.

"Give it to me and I'll mail it for you," she repeated.

I shook my head. "I don't have it."

She came closer and put her hand on my shoulder. "You're scared. Things that are important will always make you feel that way."

"I am not going."

She smiled. "Sam, just give me the check."

"I am not going to law school and I'm not going to become a lawyer." I waited for her to say something more, but when she didn't, I decided to act like nothing had changed between us even though it felt like we were already a million miles apart, staring at each other from different hemispheres of the world. I tried to take my place next to her by the sink, but she pushed me away and then turned her back as she washed one dish after the next, stacking them up carefully and making sure that I understood that I was not needed.

Or wanted.

The music on the radio stopped as the announcer read out the news headlines that detectives were still investigating the events that happened at Daphne Lake.

My mother said something under her breath that I couldn't hear.

"What did you say?"

Finally, she turned to me. "Take the pie home. I don't want it."

And that was it. I waited a few more minutes, unsure of what to do next, and when she didn't say anything more, I picked up the pie and walked out of the house. On the way out, I slammed the door of the fence so hard it bounced three or four times before it finally shut for good.

At work the next day, I thought about my mother as I sorted through the mail. The truth was that I had never defied her. The reason I did what I was told was because there was never anything important enough for me to fight for. Law school had always been her idea. She was a go-getter, a successful career woman who was determined that I would never be dependent on a man for anything. Law school, she had assured me, was my ticket out. My way of ensuring that I would be financially independent and never need to rely on anyone, ever. There was rarely very much I fought her on. I had been an obedient child who had now grown into an obedient young adult who did as I was told.

Until now.

Until Sol.

I tried to get my mind off things by opening the mail, but a copy of a newspaper mixed in with some outdoor furniture catalogs caught my eye. In the upper left-hand corner where my thumb left a smudge was a picture of a young woman named Sarah Jacobs. I remembered when she disappeared several years ago seemingly without a trace. I looked closer and saw that the story contained an interview with her mother, who expressed her thanks to the police department and her hope that someday soon they would be able to bring her daughter home.

I folded the paper in half. Sarah was young and beautiful and at the beginning of her life. Was the reason her name was back in the headlines because of the bone Sol and I had discovered at Daphne Lake? I couldn't think about her lungs filling with water and her body coming apart like that, her soul trapped inside the underbrush forever and her mother never knowing what really happened.

I must have looked strange because, as she passed, Anne Marie stopped at my desk. "Everything okay?"

I nodded, which seemed to be enough for her. She appeared to be in a hurry.

At first when things between her and Randy began, she would disappear into his office during lunch breaks, but after a while she gave up on keeping appearances. She would close the door behind her in the mornings, reemerging an hour later with a file pressed up against her chest. Sometimes her husband would call and I would lie and say she was in the bathroom. She never asked me to, but I did it anyway.

Randy wore pin-striped suits every day and a bracelet made of thick gold links around his wrist. His aftershave smelled like cheap soap, and every time he walked by, I had a sudden desire to wash my hands. He was darkly tanned, and when he smiled, his teeth looked like Chiclets pressed up against his skin. Anne Marie wore tight gray pencil skirts with three-inch-high black heels and Randy would stick his fingers into his mouth and whistle softly whenever she passed.

I'd never met her husband, but she had a picture of him on her desk. He was big and round and stuffed into a suit that was a few sizes too small. His name was Jimmy and they met in high school and had been together ever since.

Today things were busier than usual, and when she came out of his office, he came out right behind her with his shirtsleeves rolled up to his elbows.

"Leaky boiler in Building Three." He barked as he rushed past us and out the door. Anne Marie leaned against the desk with that file pressed up against her chest like a shield. She stood quietly for a few minutes until the telephone rang, startling her out of her daze.

"Remington Development," I answered. "Let me see if she's available."

She waved her hand in the air as if to say she could not be bothered, but then quickly changed her mind, grabbing the receiver and pushing the blinking red button down hard. "Hey, Jimmy." She twisted her finger around a loose strand of hair. "Can you pick up dinner?" She made a loud kissing noise and then hung up the phone.

I watched as she walked back to her desk and kicked off her high heels and I was struck by how small she suddenly seemed. She came out from behind her desk with a white box in her hand. She lifted it open to reveal a cake that read GOOD LUCK IN NEW YORK! in neon green frosting.

I pushed the newspaper away. "I meant to talk to you about that. Change of plans. I don't think I'll be going back to school anytime soon."

She put the cake box down and turned toward me. "Salmon." She knew my real name because of the tax forms I had to fill out when I started working there. Seems that we were both privy to each other's darkest secrets.

"Sam." She continued, but this time her voice was softer. "Don't do something you are going to regret later."

I snickered because the irony was just too much.

She must have heard because her hands came down to her sides and balled into fists. "You think that you can judge me?" She was speaking so fast that spit was spraying from her lips. "You don't deserve any of the things your mother does for you. You're an ungrateful bitch."

Her anger caught me off guard and I dropped the letter opener I had been holding, which made a sharp tinny sound as it hit the floor. I was relieved when the telephone rang, breaking up whatever it was that was happening between us, and I thought I was safe until she picked up the receiver and plunked it back down, hanging up on whomever had just called.

I started to stand. "I'm meeting someone for lunch."

She grabbed my wrists. "Don't screw this up."

I tried to wriggle out of her grip, but she was determined. Without her shoes, she only reached my chin. She held me with such force that it was beginning to hurt, and I must have winced, but she kept holding on. Because I couldn't stand the way she was looking at me, I finally turned away, which gave me a perfect view of her desk and that photo.

Of sweet, stupid Jimmy.

I made my way down the line, listening as people put in their orders.

"Chicken fingers and fries and a roast beef sandwich with mayo."

"Lettucetomatonion?" the man asked, speaking so quickly the words blended together.

I shook my head. "Just mayo."

He scribbled something onto his pad then looked back up at me as if he was waiting for me to realize the mistake I had made. When I didn't say anything, he shrugged and went about preparing the food and then handed me a brown paper bag already stained and glistening with grease. I walked out of the shop and onto the street filled with people and walked until I reached a row of apartment buildings. His was the fourth building on the left. I walked up the stairs, letting myself in through the lobby door with the busted lock. I walked up the staircase until I reached the third floor and used my key to let myself in. He was standing in the middle of the room with his back to me and his head tilted to one side.

"Fisshhh," he whispered softly when he looked up and saw me standing there. The goatee at the tip of his chin was the same color as my hair. "Is it lunchtime already?"

"Yes, Brian."

He ran his hands down the front of his shirt and pushed a second folding chair up to the table. I sat beside him, pulling out chicken strips while he retrieved packets of ketchup from the bottom of the bag.

"How are things?"

I looked down at my lap.

He took a bite of his roast beef sandwich and waited.

"I told mom that I'm not going to law school."

He took another big bite and chewed so loudly I almost wondered if he was choking. He wiped his mouth with the back of his hand. He looked at me for what seemed like a second too long. "Do you want me to speak with her?"

I didn't even need to think. Didn't need time to reflect or contemplate. "No."

He was about to say something else, but I interrupted. "No, Brian. Thank you. I can handle this." We continued eating in silence, but my mind was racing.

To the last time he intervened for me.

I was in high school and had been accepted to a summer art residency program in Rhode Island because my art teacher had encouraged and coaxed me to apply. It was the only other time I had ever fought for anything that I really wanted. But my mother had gotten me a job answering phones at a law firm because she thought it would give me good exposure to the lawyers and was an opportunity she decided I couldn't pass up.

I spent weeks begging her to let me go to Rhode Island and Brian took my side. I could hear them arguing about it late at night. One afternoon, I went back to school because I had forgotten a textbook I needed to finish a home-work assignment. I passed by my art teacher's classroom, and even though her door was closed, I could see through the glass pane that she was speaking to someone. She was young and pretty with blond hair so shiny it sparkled. Her voice was soft and wispy, and the way she was speaking made me feel like I couldn't walk in and interrupt.

I pressed up against the wall trying to gather the courage to take a better look. Maybe it wasn't a surprise, maybe somewhere inside I knew it would be him.

My father.

I watched for a few minutes longer, and even though nothing overt happened and even though I was looking at them through the glass pane of the door, I could sense their familiarity.

Their intimacy.

It's funny the way things happen by chance. I ran home as fast as I could and found my mother home early from work, which almost never happened. She could immediately tell that there was something wrong and all I wanted was to find relief, to unload it all onto someone else. It was as if I wasn't in control as the words tumbled out of me and into the air.

The next day he was gone, and I knew she had thrown him out, and even though we never discussed it, I knew that it was my fault. My father rarely fought my mother. The only reason he and my art teacher's paths even crossed was because he was standing up for me, for my dreams of becoming an artist. His punishment was the loss of his family. It took a long time for me to work on my art after that because I knew I was to blame.

It was because of me my father no longer lived with us.

Remembering made my stomach queasy and I pushed away my lunch. I needed to think about something else—anything else. "What's that you're working on?" I pointed to a canvas leaning against the window covered in different hues of purple strips of paint.

He shrugged. "Not sure yet. Just how I was feeling today."

"Purple?"

He smiled. "Sometimes you just have to go where it takes you."

He was so committed to his craft that he took small jobs here and there to support himself because the only thing that mattered was his art. His paintings were abstract and chaotic and unnerving, and I wished that I liked them more than I did. He never asked my opinion and I hoped it was because he really didn't care what other people thought.

"Are you sure you don't want me to speak with her?"

I shook my head. "I'm sure."

He walked back to the kitchen and came back with a big round chocolate chip cookie. He smiled as I took a bite, and I hated myself even more for how easily he thought I could be bought.

When I got back to the office, Anne Marie's hair was combed and pulled back and her lips were shiny and red. She smiled at me as I walked through the door.

"Nice lunch?"

I shrugged because I was tired and because it wasn't.

She walked over to my desk and handed me the file she was always holding up to her chest when she disappeared inside Randy's office. "Do you think you can take care of this?"

I nodded without looking at it or her.

"Sorry about before. You're a smart girl. I know you'll end up doing what's best and of course you can stay as long as you need."

She reached over and touched my hand and I shook away the image of her holding me. Begging me. I smiled and she smiled back and then walked away. I put my pocketbook in a drawer and got to work on the file she had given me, which was filled with overdue bills for paper towels and toilet paper and garbage bags. And then when she slipped away inside Randy's office, I crumpled one into the shape of a ball and threw it as hard as I could at her desk where it hit poor Jimmy squarely in the face.

That night all I wanted was Sol, but he was working late so I fell asleep rereading the old texts that he sent on my phone. I slept peacefully, but when I woke, it was to the sound of determination in the form of a knock.

I pulled the covers over my head, which made the knocker knock harder.

"Coming." I stumbled over a stack of magazines, hitting the right corner of my toe. The pain coursed through me until it reached the back of my throat, turning into a soft guttural groan. When I finally reached the door and opened it, she was standing there, smiling.

"Rise and shine. Brought you muffins," my mother said, swinging a crinkly white bag in her hand.

"Thanks," I said, rubbing my eyes because I was still half asleep.

"How are you?" she asked, sliding herself onto the chair in front of my desk.

Besides a few quick telephone conversations, we had not spoken since I told her I wasn't going to law school. She came into my room and sat on the chair, smiling and batting her eyelashes, and instead of trying to figure out what she was up to, I decided to eat a muffin. They were still warm. I chose one filled with chocolate chips. I knew she was watching so I turned around to take a bite so she couldn't see.

"Delicious?"

Agreeing with her would be paramount to giving in, so I took a second bite and said nothing.

"What's this?" she asked, pointing to the corner of my mirror.

It was a photograph Sol had taken of me that day in the park. I don't know why it bothered me to have her look at it but it did. "Just a photo."

She picked it up and tilted it in different directions in her hand. "Why don't you get dressed and we'll go for a drive."

I grabbed some clothes out of a drawer and went into the bathroom to change. Something about the way she was looking at my things made me uncomfortable and I wanted to get her out of my apartment. I splashed water on my face and then hurried to get dressed, stumbling over a button that left my shirt hanging unevenly over my pants. She was standing when I returned, and I could see her eyeing the outfit I had chosen but she said nothing. Instead, she smiled funnily and clutched the bag of muffins to her chest. "Might as well take these with us."

She was parked behind the building. Even though I did not own a car, she insisted that whatever apartment I rented come with a spot so that she would have a place to park whenever she visited. My mother loved to drive. When I lived at home, she would wake me in the morning and we would take drives together. We never talked because her second other favorite thing to do was sing. Sometimes with the radio on and other times without. Her voice would fill the car with a pure and steady sound that was sweet and light as confectioner's sugar. When I was little, I was sure the birds could hear her too, because when I looked out the window, they always seemed to be flying to her rhythm. I remember thinking she was magic.

I got into the car and crossed my arms across my chest. She turned on the radio, first spinning the dial forward and then back, and when she couldn't find what she was looking for, she turned it off. For a few minutes, we drove in silence, and I could feel something churning and building inside of me and I wondered what would happen if I let it come out. I opened my mouth to speak but just then she began to sing. She started slow and soft, the sound of her voice so pure it made me catch my breath. Her music swirled through me, strong and clear, and when we stopped at a red light, she closed her eyes and tipped back her head. A car honking startled us both. She gripped the wheel and started to drive again.

I felt unnerved and dizzy, like someone had spun me around and then left me to drop. I rolled down the window so I could breathe some outside air.

"You're fine." She smiled, patting my knee.

I hated myself for wishing she would start to sing again, for wishing that I could disappear inside the sound and not have to think. I stuck my hand out of the window, weaving my fingers through the passing air as if there was something there to grab. After a few minutes, I closed the window, leaning my head against the glass.

"There's something I want to show you." She pulled the car over and parked it on the sidewalk. "Are you coming?" She smiled in a way that let me know I had no other choice. In my haste, I had thrown on a pair of sandals, and when I got out of the car, I stepped directly onto a soggy patch of grass. Wetness seeped in under my soles, making my feet feel slippery and unsteady. She walked toward me, linking her arm through mine like we were old friends who had not seen each other in years.

"This just came on the market and I wanted you to see it."

It was not unusual for my mother to take me to a listing. Growing up, many of my weekends were spent being dragged to one real estate open house after another. But something about this one was different. Something about her was different. Two large trees blocked the house from view, but as we walked up the path and I saw it, I knew. I knew without her needing to say a word or squeeze my arm the way that she was.

From the time I could remember, my mother told me stories about the house in which she was raised. It was white with pale blue shutters. Every year, her mother planted white impatiens in the window boxes because she could never find flowers the right shade of blue to match.

It was the impatiens I noticed first. White and crisp and just beginning to cascade over the sides of the planters. "What is this place?"

She smiled and squeezed my hand even harder. "Isn't it amazing? I couldn't believe it when I saw it."

"I don't understand."

"It's like it just fell out of a fairy tale. Come inside."

She pressed some buttons on the lockbox and then pushed open the door. The rooms were small and bare and the bathroom needed work. The kitchen was clean and white with room for a table.

"It's lovely, isn't it?" She sounded like she already knew the answer.

Even though it was empty, it had a charm that I sensed the moment I walked inside. It was sweet to see how enchanted she was, and I wondered if this is what she had been like as a child. "It's nice."

She shook her head. "It's perfect."

I took another look around. "I bet if its priced right it will go fast."

"It already did."

"What do you mean?"

"The moment I saw it, I knew it was right. I bought it for us. I bought it for you."

I stumbled back both from shock and the fact that she was walking toward me dangling the key from the lockbox in front of my face. "What are you talking about?"

"It's yours," she said, spreading her arms out like a gymnast who had just stuck her landing. "We'll rent it out while you are in law school, which will give you some income. Then when you graduate, you can come back here to live."

All the things I wanted to say collided inside my head so that, ultimately, I said nothing.

"It's perfect," she said again, twirling around the living room.

"Mom."

She stopped dancing. Stopped smiling. And for a split-second, I felt bad that I was the reason.

"Is there a problem?"

"I already told you."

"What is it that you told me? That you are willing to walk away from the opportunity of a lifetime? Everything that we have worked for?"

"You don't understand."

"For whom?" Her voice got louder and became hard and mean. "For him?" She pulled out the photo that Sol had taken of me.

"You had no right to take that." I reached toward her, but she moved away too quickly.

"It's a lovely photograph of you. The angle is unusual and he captured something special in your expression. He's very good at what he does." She waited for me to react, and when I didn't she sighed. "Sam, *this* is what he loves." She lifted the picture up again as if what she was saying should have been obvious. "I promise it has little to do with you."

I wished that what I was feeling was pure anger but instead it was sprinkled with tiny shards of doubt that stuck into my heart like glass splinters. Words strung together inside my head in the most eloquent and thoughtful way but none of them came out.

"You're wrong. You don't know anything about him."

She lifted the photo up again, but this time she dropped it so that it fell to the floor.

"You have so much to learn. He's already talked you out of going to school."

"You don't know him. You don't know anything."

"Sam, why can't you see? He can't do what he wants with his own life so he is going to try and control yours." She began to turn. "And instead of standing up for yourself, you are just letting it happen."

Her words whipped through me like a brisk wind, knocking out my breath, and we stared at each other for a few minutes before she picked up her purse and walked out of the house. After a few minutes, I heard her car start and then she was gone.

Leaving me behind.

It was a longer walk than I had anticipated, and my feet squeaked inside my sandals, the straps rubbing unpleasantly against my heels. But I didn't care. As much as she liked to drive, I liked to walk. And that's what I did. I passed houses and then apartment buildings. I saw people buying coffee and newspapers. I breathed in trees and air and car exhaust. And most of all, I tried not to think about her words.

I had walked past his shop a few times but mostly at night when it was closed. Now I found myself standing there watching young families stream past, not sure about what it was I wanted to do or why I was even there. Maybe I just wanted to see his face, or maybe I wanted to prove her wrong. Anyway, each time the door opened, a blast of cold, sweet air swept past, and finally I decided to go in.

There was a line by the counter where a young girl was taking orders. A little boy was running his fingers along the outside of the glass case, and his mother was trying to help him make a choice.

"Chocolate?"

He shook his head.

"But you love chocolate."

He shook his head again, and this time licked his finger and drew a circle in the glass.

"Tommy!" she yelled and pulled at his arm. "Sorry," she said to the girl behind the counter, who looked back at her with utter disgust.

"We'll take a cup of the chocolate."

"Sprinkles!" Tommy yelled.

His mother smiled and rubbed the top of his head. "Of course."

The girl pointed toward two canisters and mumbled something.

"What kind do you want, baby? Chocolate or rainbow?"

But Tommy had moved on to pulling napkins out of the canister and throwing them up into the air.

"Sorry," his mother said again, but the girl just shrugged her shoulders. "Let's have rainbow."

Tommy crouched down on the floor and dragged his car through a mound of napkins. Once she had paid and had the ice cream in her hand, she called out to him. "C'mon, Tommy." He flicked the car so hard that it went careening across the floor and smashed into her foot. I watched as her face turned red and kept watching as she tossed the cup of ice cream into the trash and hoisted Tommy over her shoulder. They walked outside and down the street, and it took several seconds for the sound of his wail to stop echoing throughout the shop.

Unfazed, the girl turned to me. "Can I help you?" She was chewing gum, blew a bubble. I jumped when it popped.

"Is Sol here?"

He smiled when he came out from behind the counter. He looked different than when I saw him with his camera strapped around his neck. Maybe the crisp, white apron made him look more subdued, less intense. He kissed me as if I came in every day, as if I belonged. We sat at a table in the far corner of the store. The girl finally stopped watching us when a man and three kids came in and ordered shakes.

"This is a nice surprise," he said, and I hated myself for wondering if he really thought it was.

I wanted him to tell me that I was making the right decision and that my mother was wrong about everything. I tried to speak, but my insides felt so twisted I had no idea where to begin until finally the words came out. "I told my mother, Sol. I told her that I'm not going and that I want to stay here with you."

He didn't say anything at first, but then he got up and told me he'd be right back. I sat at the table watching the girl blend ice cream inside a tall silver cup, the sound of the whirr both soothing and irritating at the same time. He was gone long enough for me to start to wonder if he really was coming back. It was quiet at the counter now, and she was eyeing me up and down, and for a second, I wished I had at least buttoned up my shirt properly.

He swept past, lowering a plastic bowl on the table in front of me. "Try this." He pushed it forward and handed me a spoon. I looked back at him, trying to figure out what it was he wanted. He pushed the bowl closer. "To celebrate."

I scooped some into my mouth. Banana ice cream covered in graham cracker crumbles with a sweet white topping that was a combination of marshmallow and whipped cream. "You inspired me." He smiled, looking so hopeful, and then all it took was another spoonful to push my mother's words out of my head.

"Everything is going to be perfect, Sam. You'll see." He laid his hand on top of mine.

I waited as the sweetness filled me, and as he watched me enjoying myself, I couldn't help but think how familiar it all felt.

Chapter 9

When I opened my eyes, it was to the sound of sirens streaming down my New York City block. I looked down at my lap to find the image of the mermaid complete but the surrounding water still untouched.

Just like the time before, I felt unbalanced and shaky. I stood slowly, putting one foot in front of the other, and by the time I made my way into the kitchen, I finally had my bearings. I often had recurring dreams but never ones that seemed to pick up exactly where they left off every time I dreamt them. My feelings for Sol were so intense, I could barely breathe. Even now. Even here.

Even though I was awake and back in my real life.

My hands were trembling, and I needed to think things through. In the kitchen, I found a box of donuts I had bought earlier sitting on the counter, and when I looked up I saw that Mickey had walked in too. She started to back away, as though she had somehow broken our silent roommate code of never being in the same place at the same time.

"Stay," I said, and she hesitated, which was better than turning around and leaving. I suddenly realized how incredibly lonely I was. "Please."

I found a small paring knife in one of the drawers and used it to cut the string. The box sprang open like a jack-in-the-box. I put the donuts on a plate and cut them into quarters. I went to get glasses for milk, remembering what it was like sharing desserts with Susan, and then even though I didn't know Mickey at all somehow, I knew that she was nothing like Susan.

But when I turned back around, she was gone. I sat at the kitchen table, staring at the sad little plate of donuts I had set out on the table. I wondered if I looked as pathetic as I imagined when she came back a few minutes later holding a white box of her own.

"Wagashi," she said as she opened it.

Inside were perfectly sculpted cakes so beautiful they looked like delicate pieces of art. Each was lovelier than the next, which made it difficult to choose, but I finally picked one shaped like a fish. As I lifted it up to my mouth, she laughed, which also took me by surprise because it was something I had never seen her do. "Salmon," she said, pointing at both the fish cake and me.

I smiled.

She put a teakettle onto the stovetop and brought out two mugs that looked like bowls. I watched as she poured hot water over scoops of green powder and then whipped it all together with a whisk made of bamboo. Her movements were quick and meticulous, and when she finished, she handed me the greenest tea I had ever seen. I held the bowl in my hands, taking small sips of the froth, and even though it was bitter, it blended perfectly with the cake I had just eaten.

"Your boyfriend's an asshole." She said it without judgment, like it was a simple fact. When she pushed her hair out of her face, I saw that her eyes were black and shaped like almonds, and I realized that even though we had lived together for an entire summer, I hadn't ever bothered to look at her. We sat at the table and ate donuts and Wagashi and when I finished the first cup of tea, she went to make another. As she turned on the water to refill the pot, I thought about what she had said about Lucas.

"I'm not dating him anymore."

She looked at me and nodded. I didn't tell her that I had kept one of those tea-stained napkins from the coffee shop in my bag and had rolled and kneaded it so often that it had turned to shreds in my hands. I wrapped my fingers around the next cup she handed me and inhaled the steam that felt like the first fresh breath I had taken in a very long time.

Mickey's mother and grandmother lived in Queens, and sometimes she would take me home with her for meals. Her grandmother made soups with dumplings, and if she knew I was coming, there was always a plate of Wagashi for dessert and extra for us to take back with us. On our bus rides home, Mickey told me stories about her family, particularly her great-aunt who had been enslaved as a comfort woman for the Japanese military. She was so brutally raped she finally died from her injuries.

"That's why I'm going to school," Mickey said, and as the bus we were riding hit a pothole, it felt like her words jumped out at me. "I will be so educated that no one will be able to take what I have because it will all be inside my head." She tapped her finger to her temple.

When we reached our stop, Mickey pulled the cord and moved with such intense conviction that she almost tripped the person next to her. She was always so determined, and when I was with her, it gave me hope that I could be that way too. As I matched my pace to hers, I imagined her strength coursing through me and then it suddenly occurred to me why Lucas hated her:

She was brave.

The truth was that for the past few weeks, I had been considering packing my bags and going home. I couldn't help but think that Lucas was right and that I was going to be a terrible lawyer and that staying here was just one colossal mistake. His words were like monsters that grabbed at my ankles and tormented me from beneath the bed. The only other thing I could imagine doing was becoming an artist, but because it was twisted up in my betrayal of my father and had become a portal into some dream life that made me feel like I was going mad, it was something I just couldn't consider.

Even though we lived several states apart, I could still hear my mother's voice, reminding me to focus on my task because she knew what was best— because she always knew what was best for me. Maybe there was a time earlier on I might have put up a fight but that was then. Now, I couldn't even imagine having the strength to defy her.

So, I forced myself to keep going.

When things got so bad that I couldn't stand it anymore, I would sneak into the kitchen and brew the green tea I had learned to make by watching Mickey. I never realized how terribly I was shaking until I wrapped my hands around the mug and felt the heat spread past my palms and into my fingertips. It was the only way I knew to get the trembling to stop.

There were more electives to choose from during the second year of law school, so I was able to avoid Lucas as much as possible. The times I did run into him, he looked right past me as though I wasn't there. He told everyone that he had been the one to end things, and when I saw Margaret, I didn't tell her the truth but I could tell she knew anyhow. About six months into the year, Lucas started dating a girl from the first-year class. I heard she came from a wealthy family and I could see that she hung on to every word he said. After that, he began acknowledging me in the hallways again, sometimes even saying hello. She was always with him, her arm slung through his, casting me dirty looks. I wanted to tell her there was nothing for her to worry about, but I didn't.

Now that Lucas was no longer part of my life, I needed to find different ways to distract myself, and since the possibility that my dreams of Sol were triggered by my collages, I had to do whatever it took to avoid the temptation.

But it was hard, and I was weak.

So, I did the next best thing: I wandered through art museums, going through rooms that were so eerily quiet the acoustics made my voice sound funny. Sometimes Mickey would come, too, but she was so tired from her course load that she would fall asleep on the subway ride home leaning against my shoulder. When I was sure she was fast asleep and that no one was looking, I would take deep breaths, trying to inhale her strength like it was a perfume she dabbed behind her ears.

But no matter what I did, it didn't work.

I felt broken and empty and lost inside, and because I didn't know what else to do I visited the museums even more. I skipped classes so that I could go twice a day, convinced there was respite hidden in the art in those buildings and it was only a matter of time before I would find the calm for which I was searching.

During one of my subway rides home, I became frantic. My despair was so thick it formed a wall around my chest, making each swallow of air sting more than the next. Tears I hadn't realized I was crying poured down my face and into my mouth. I wiped them away just as the conductor announced the train had become express. It lurched forward, and then amid the groans and complaints of the other passengers, flew into the dark tunnel at maximum speed.

We passed one stop after the next at such an exhilarating pace that the stations meshed together into one long colorless blur. I closed my eyes so I could drown inside the vibration of sound and movement and color. It filled my head with such a fierce and glorious rumbling that it almost hurt. The rocking motion soothed me, and for a few moments, I lost my troubles inside the roar. The hum continued and began to resemble something amazingly close to silence, and as I stared out of the dirty window, I marveled at the fact that inside this fast-moving graffiti covered subway car, I was finally able to find peace.

After that, I was like a junkie searching for a fix.

Every time I rode the trains, I searched for the fastest one I could find so that I could once again disappear inside the deafening sound of reckless speed. I was like a baby rocking within the gurgling safety of her mother's womb. The faster the train went, the more silenced the voices of my demons became.

I was adept at reading the NYC subway map and soon had it memorized. I searched for stations circled in white because I knew that was were where the express train stopped. Sometimes I woke up hours before class to catch the ones running during rush hour. I liked holding onto the bar above my head as my body swayed to the rhythm of momentum. If I was feeling exceptionally brave, I would let go and carefully bend my knees like a surfer on the crest of a wave.

Early mornings meant businesspeople closely packed together with newspapers clutched in their hands. Later, it was students and restaurant and retail workers plugged into their iPhones. One day, the doors flew open and the car filled with a large group of tourists speaking a language I didn't recognize. Their guide had a purple flag with a yellow smiley face that she lifted into the air every few minutes when she wanted to get their attention. I tried to lose myself in the movement of the train, but they were snapping pictures and some of the men were pointing to a map and arguing so loudly I couldn't focus. When the train stopped, they moved off like a herd, and the next thing I knew I was swept up along with them. It wasn't until they marched off toward an exit that I regained my bearings and found myself standing inside the Lincoln Center Station. As I started to make my way back to the train, something caught my eye.

I moved in closer, ignoring the neon green spray paint surrounding the edges. There was a pool of unidentifiable goo on the floor, but I didn't care because all I could focus on was what was staring back at me, calling me as if it had simply been waiting to be found.

Mosaics.

I ran my hands along the tiles of the one with two beautiful dancing girls each with flowing hair as orange as mine. I pressed my body up against them, the tiles cool against my face. Even though I wasn't a religious person, I closed my eyes and sent a prayer of gratitude to the tourists who had picked me up like a lost child in a department store and delivered me safely back into the arms of my ever-waiting and welcoming mother.

My salvation.

The subways became my roller coasters, my therapy, my art museums. I made sure to always have my cell phone handy so that I could take snapshots of all the mosaics I found. I discovered animals on Eight-First street and a flying pig on Eighty-Sixth. I became obsessed with the intricate detail that went into creating the lettering on the Canal Street, Grand Central, and Lexington Avenue signs.

My second and third years of law school passed in a blur of green tea and subway rides, and the next thing I knew my parents were in town to celebrate my graduation. I came home to find Brian and my mother standing in the living room I shared with Mickey. The bouquet of peonies my mother held in her hand cast a pink glow across her face, and I had never seen her look happier. She wrapped her arms around me and kissed the space between my eyebrows.

"I'm so proud of what you have accomplished, Sam." She held me too tightly, like she wasn't sure she could let me go.

On our last night together, Mickey and I sat in the kitchen drinking tea. I had never come so close to telling anyone my secrets. But the longer we sat, the more the words twisted up inside of me, and I knew I could never make them sound right. Even though I wanted to blurt it out, to share it all, I said nothing.

The next morning, it was harder to say goodbye than I had expected.

"It will be okay, girls. You can write to one another," my mother said, like we were twelve-year-olds heading home after summer camp.

My mother must have sensed my hesitation. "We should get going now, Sam." She walked toward Mickey. "Thanks for taking care of my girl."

Brian came up behind me and took my elbow. He had one of my bags in his other hand. "Looks like that's the last of it."

We stood at the threshold, and as I turned to say goodbye, Mickey handed me the bamboo whisk she used to whip my tea. "For you." She was composed, elegant even, as she pushed her black hair from her face. As I hugged her, I breathed in her strength one last time, and it was only when my mother cleared her throat that I finally let go.

On the ride home, my mother sang while I stared out of the window, pressing the bristles of the whisk into my hand until it made the inside of my palm feel red and raw and alive.

Reminding me to be brave.

Chapter 10

My mother pulled up to a little white house.

She got out of the car and opened my door, and I could feel my legs give out from under me. Suddenly, I felt as though I was sinking.

"C'mon, silly."

As she slipped the key into the lock, my heart filled with panic.

"Aren't you going to come inside?" she asked.

This was the house.

The one I had dreamed about when I dreamed about my life with Sol.

It was the house my mother had tried to bribe me with to leave Sol and go to law school, and it was the first time that something from my dream life had crossed over into my real life and maybe that was why I was suddenly filled with such uneasiness. Or maybe there was another reason that it upset me so much and made it so that I wanted to do only one thing.

Run.

Bolt as fast as I could from that moment and everything it came with. But I couldn't since I could barely even walk let alone understand why I was having these feelings. I took a few tentative steps.

"I've been keeping it for you as a surprise. Isn't it spectacular?" My mother spun around, and the skirt she wore lifted like it was propelled by clouds.

I closed my eyes, trying to retrieve the memory that was sitting like a forgotten word at the tip of my tongue, but then it was gone and there was nothing.

Nothing but dread.

Brian put his hand on my back. "Give her a minute, Jayne."

"It's for you baby girl. All of it." She spread out her arms.

I couldn't keep it down. I tried to swallow it back, but it didn't work. I ran into the bathroom where I knelt over the toilet and heaved green frothy bile, and then I thought about the girl whose leg bone looked like a swan entrapped in the mud.

Never to take flight again.

The rest of the day passed in a daze. I heard Brian tell her that I just needed time to adjust and that soon everything would be fine. My mother gave me cups of flat ginger ale to help settle my stomach and then insisted on showing me around the rest of the house, which she had also furnished. One bedroom was painted lavender with a brass four-poster bed with white and purple hydrangeas decorating the bedding. The other bedroom was turned into a home office with a dark mahogany desk and a matching bookcase lining the wall.

That night, we ordered Chinese takeout and ate around the wooden table she had bought for the kitchen. I pushed the fried rice and chicken around on my plate. I didn't understand what it was I was feeling, but I knew I didn't like it, so I drank from my water glass and didn't stop until I felt bloated and uncomfortable. It helped distract me from the inexplicable feeling of uneasiness that tickled my nose like a sneeze about to come.

My intuition screamed that something terrible had happened to me in this house, and as much as I hated not knowing, I was also terrified of finding out what it might be. It was like stumbling blindly through a dark room knowing there was a monster behind every shadow.

"I'm sure you're tired." Brian said more to my mother than to me. They locked eyes like they did when they were talking to each other without words. It was usually in those moments that I felt like an outsider, but tonight I didn't care.

My mother insisted on washing the dishes, and she and Brian worked together until everything was done to her liking. Then they got ready to leave, and I swallowed down the urge to beg them to stay. Maybe they noticed because they hesitated, but then Brian whispered something to my mother and they promised to come back first thing in the morning. I told myself I was just being silly and waved as they drove away.

Once they were gone, I walked into my new office and sat in the chair. My mother had placed a large leather blotter on the desktop and a pen stand with SALMON BAIRD ATTORNEY AT LAW engraved onto the brass plate. As I ran my fingers across the letters, I couldn't help but feel like an imposter.

I didn't want to think about the fact that parts of my dreams were seeping into this life or what that might mean about my sanity. I didn't want to acknowledge that this house gave me the creeps and that every time I swallowed, a lump of pure and unadulterated fear planted itself squarely in my throat. If my intuition was correct, and something bad had happened to me here, I didn't want to know what it was. That's when I made my decision.

To just give in.

She had always been confident that she knew what was best for me and maybe it was because she did. I would put my trust in her and live the life my mother had planned for me—as a lawyer who was self-sufficient and financially independent.

I would do my best to move forward and stop jumping backward.

For the first time in a long time, I felt a sense of relief as though I had a purpose, a goal. I felt like I finally had a road map to follow. Maybe she had been right about things all along, and it was better than waiting to see the next thing my dreams might reveal if I allowed them to return. It was safer to commit to this life and not look back.

It was safer not to remember.

His name was Stu Russell. He was another friend of my mother's, and when he introduced himself, he said his name so quickly that it sounded like streusel. After that, whenever I saw him, I thought of coffee cake with a crumbled cinnamon topping, which is probably why I liked him.

Stu ran a law practice handed down to him from his father, whose oversized and looming portrait hung in the reception area. He was posed in a leather chair from which he stared disapprovingly at everyone who passed.

I made sure to keep my attention squarely on the receptionist whenever I walked by because it always felt that he was looking at me with disdain.

Stu was in his late forties with a wife and children. He was self-consciously tall and always stooped over as though he was worried about hitting the ceiling. Sometimes his wife brought the children into the office to visit, his daughter tall and lanky like him and his son thick and stocky like his wife. They made a strange looking couple because she was so round and short, but after a while I forgot about how they looked because of the way his face would light up when he saw her. It was sweet how she kissed the lower part of his chin when she greeted him, probably because that was as far up as she could reach.

Stu's practice focused primarily on real estate, and my mother had talked him into taking me under his wing. I worked part time throughout the summer months because Stu wanted to make sure I had enough time to prepare for the bar exam. I signed up for a study course, but I hated the other students and the anxiety-laden buzz that surrounded them. The girl next to me was so consumed with nerves that the vibrations from her leg shaking passed from her seat into mine and sometimes I left before the end of class.

I missed Mickey and the apartment and the sound the subway made as it rushed across the rails. I missed the feeling of being beneath the ground with nothing but roar in my ears. In my heart, I knew that what I really missed and what I hungered for the most was my art.

But I also knew the consequences of succumbing to my temptation.

I didn't want to know, didn't want to remember, the secrets it might reveal, so I worked harder at distracting myself. I knew that I had to succeed because the consequences of failure were too grave. I tried to ignore the sense of listlessness that was working its way steadily back into my life by immersing myself in deeds and real estate closings and contracts. I showed up on time for work every day, smiled at clients, and waited for a sign that I was on the right track. It finally came exactly two years, four months, and fifteen days from the day that I started, but it wasn't what I expected.

Stu called me into his office and I watched as he took out a pack of Tic Tacs from his pant pocket. He tossed several of the white candies into his mouth like they were Vicodin. I shook my head when he offered me one.

"I don't know how to say this."

The smell of peppermint on his breath reminded me of Lucas and I suddenly felt sick. I looked at the man whose name sounded like pastry and noticed the dark circles under his eyes. He muttered something that I couldn't hear because he was staring down at his lap. I cleared my throat to get his attention, and when I did he seemed startled, like he had almost forgotten I was sitting there.

"Things have not been going well."

I didn't want to hear what he was going to say next. I had done everything that was expected of me. Day after day, I sat through monotonous closings chitchatting with nervous clients while plowing through thick stacks of complicated contracts. As tempting as it had been, I hadn't worked on one collage, not even one drawing or sketch. I had done my part, kept my word. My head began to throb. I wanted him to stop talking so that I could turn around and leave and we could go back to being who we were ten minutes before I walked into his office.

"It's the economy, Sam. Things are bad. Those damn mortgages."

The throbbing shifted into my ears so that it now sounded like there was a thunderstorm in the room.

"And I have to let you go."

He had the decency to look me in the eye when he said the last part, but it didn't make me feel any better.

My first instinct was to plead but something stopped me.

"I've barely been able to keep things afloat this long. I am not my father. I have never been." This was said more to himself than to me, and he looked back down at his lap and fiddled with the Tic Tac box. I had a sudden urge to walk into the reception area and scratch out his father's eyes with my ballpoint pen.

"What am I going to do?" I could hear the despair in my voice, and I was ashamed of how it sounded. I don't think he understood how much I had invested and how close I was to slipping backward.

Literally.

When he looked up, I could see his sadness. "I can give you some severance. I have a little put aside, and of course references if you need."

I nodded.

"Salmon. Can I speak truthfully?" He leaned in closer so that the rings beneath his eyes were even more prominent. "I don't think that you want to be a lawyer. This job isn't for you. You only live one life. Go do what you love."

Even though he was kind, the impact of his words was no different than Lucas's had been, and the insecurity I thought I had managed to bury torched through me like a flame.

"Stay as long as you need. I'm not throwing you out."

My mouth felt dry and searching for something to say felt unimaginably difficult.

"This isn't your fault, Sam. It's mine."

But he was wrong. It was my entirely my fault.

It turned out that all I needed was a few hours to gather my things and find a box to put them in. As I walked out, I took out a wad of the pink gum I had been chewing, and when no one was looking, pushed it onto the tip of Stu's father's nose.

Like I did when I always needed to disappear, I walked.

First through streets and then around Daphne Lake, which was surrounded by orange- and red-leafed trees. But walking led me to thinking, which was the last thing I wanted, so I began to pick up speed until I was running down the path. I ran so hard that each breath I took hurt. I ran until I was panting, and then I leaned over, holding onto my kneecaps because I no longer had the strength to stand upright or outrun my demons. I had given everything I had to give and still it wasn't enough.

I spent the next week in bed, watching *Jerry Springer* reruns and eating ramen noodles out of Styrofoam cups. But seeing other people's misery on television didn't make me feel any better, and soon my self-pity became so ravenous it felt impossible to feed. That afternoon, I put on a clean T-shirt and walked to the liquor store where I bought a bottle of wine. For the first time in a long time, I came home with a sense of determination and resolve. Millions before me had drowned their sorrows this way, and if it worked for them, I expected it would work for me.

Because I had stopped washing dishes, I couldn't find a clean glass. After searching for a few minutes, I found a mug with a picture of Donald Duck hidden deep in the back of the cabinet probably left behind by the previous owner. I turned Donald the other way, so it wouldn't feel like he was judging me, and filled the mug.

I sat in front of the television and watched the Spanish channel even though I didn't understand very much. A good-looking dark-haired man was speaking very quickly to an equally attractive woman. I took a sip and it burned as it went down, reminding me of how much I hated the taste. Now the man had his hands on the woman's shoulders, shaking her. I pinched my nostrils closed and swallowed down half of what remained in the mug like it was cough medicine. The couple was now locked in a passionate kiss and dramatic sounding music played in the background. I took another sip and this time didn't need to hold my nose, and before I knew it, I was back in the kitchen for a refill.

I was looking for relief, something to untie the knot that now seemed to permanently reside in my stomach. What I got was a hazy stumbling stupor that made me feel unbalanced and bloated. I tasted the acidic flavor of fermentation every time I burped. I went to lie down in my bedroom but ended up thrashing and getting twisted between the sheets like I was drowning. I spent the rest of the afternoon and evening with the television on mostly because it was better than sitting in silence.

The next day, I decided that I needed something stronger, liquor perhaps. I headed back to the store without brushing my hair, which hung around my head in frizzy red clumps. I wore the same shirt I had worn the day before, but if he even noticed, the pimple-faced teenaged clerk said nothing. I rinsed out Donald, got some ice, and filled the mug with straight vodka, but each sip tasted like I was drinking Sea Breeze acne astringent and that was all it took to push me over the edge. And then I just gave in, gave up. Even though I told myself I would only do it for a minute, I knew better.

I knew it was a lie.

But at that point, it didn't really matter anymore.

Nothing mattered anymore.

I couldn't help myself; it was like a magnetic pull over which I had no control. I found the mermaid I had been working on in New York. My problem had always been in trying to recreate water. On one of my last weekends before moving back home, I had taken the train to the ocean because even though I had lived for three years on an island, most of it was spent underground.

And I had forgotten about the water.

It was a gray and cool day, and each time I tucked my hair behind my ear, it slipped out and whipped past my face. It was early spring and not yet warm enough for the beach, but I took my shoes off anyway. There weren't very many people, and still lots of areas under construction from the effects of the last hurricane. I followed a flock of screaming seagulls that picked at the bivalves left behind by the tide. The sand was smooth except for the rocks and shells that popped up every few feet.

Halfway up the shore, a line of water formed a crest that came crashing down and then exploded like a can of soda. I gave up trying to keep my hair back because by then the wind had built enough strength to lift my jacket up like a parachute. I remembered the same feeling from that day in the coffee shop with Lucas. Like I was being untied, released, and even though I knew it was silly, I lifted my arms as though I could fly. The ocean roared what sounded like words, and I stood and listened for as long as I could, but then I lost my courage and turned away when a man passed by with his dog. As desirable as they were, I hated those moments of freedom because all they did was remind me that I wasn't. I drew a line in the sand, trying to ignore the sadness that now felt stronger than the waves, and that's when I saw it: a piece of undiscovered treasure peeking out from the froth.

I turned it over in my hand and realized it was just the other half of a mussel shell. The outside was weathered and drab, but when I turned it back over again, I saw that the inside was the color of shimmering silver. I rocked it slowly back and forth, and as it caught little bits of light, I knew that it was what I had been searching for. I moved carefully across the beach collecting as many as I could.

I stored them in a plastic bag that I had packed away with me when I moved home and forgotten about. But there they were here at the bottom of my sock drawer. I went to the kitchen and got the wine bottle out of the trash. I used it to roll over the bag and crush the shells and then went to work sorting the broken pieces into piles. I found a pair of tweezers and practiced arranging them into the collage, changing them back and forth, the whole while telling myself that this was all I needed to feel better and that I could stop at any moment. An hour passed, maybe more, before it happened, before I lost myself inside the curl of the wave, its silvery crest twisting into itself as if it was protecting the faintest whisper of a secret.

Chapter 11

Sol invited me to his house for dinner.

He said his father would be out playing cards and so it would just be the two of us. I wore a soft green sweater and a skirt, but as I left I couldn't help but wonder if it just made me look even more like a carrot.

Susan promised to help me pick out a bottle of wine, but then texted me at the last minute to tell me she had her own date that night and wouldn't be coming back home beforehand. Left to my own devices, I ended up at my favorite bakery. It had bright fluorescent lights and a black-and-white checkered floor sprinkled with sawdust. The staff all had thick waists and even thicker accents and always slipped an extra cookie or two into my bag. I tried hard to think about what Sol might like and ended up choosing two large chocolate cupcakes. The clerk put them into a white box that she tied with red and white string.

I decided to take the bus to his house, but as it lurched forward, I was suddenly overcome by the thought that Sol had probably already made plans for dessert and that bringing something was silly. When we reached my stop, I got off and handed the box to a homeless man sitting beside a grocery cart who God Blessed me and tried to kiss my hand before I managed to slip away, knowing I didn't really deserve any of his blessings.

Sol and his father lived a few blocks from the bus stop, and as I walked I poked my head into different shops, hoping an idea would come. The sky was starting to darken and streetlights lit the sidewalk. I walked past a liquor store and contemplated just grabbing the first bottle I saw but then changed my mind. As I got closer to his house, I began to panic and contemplated running back to the homeless man and explaining why it was I needed my box of cupcakes back. I even started to turn around and would have kept walking if he had not come out on the stoop at that very moment.

"I was wondering where you were."

I waved, hoping he didn't notice that I had come empty handed. My mother always told me it was proper to bring the host or hostess a small gift. She would have been furious with my lack of social grace and for whatever reason the thought of that made me smile. Sol must have thought I was smiling at him because he smiled back and gave me a kiss on the cheek.

"Come in." He pushed open the screen door.

The house was small and very tidy. The furniture was old but looked as though it had been taken care of so well it would last a lifetime. There were framed photographs on the wall and a vase with flowers on the table.

"I thought you might like these," he said, pointing to the yellow daisies.

I nodded, thinking that he had, in fact, thought of everything.

He took my coat and hung it in the closet and then I followed him into the kitchen. There was a small butcher-block island in the middle of the room where he motioned for me to sit. He turned toward the cutting board, and as his arm moved up and down, I was suddenly struck by how intimate it all felt. Watching this man prepare food.

For me.

Unlike my mother's kitchen, which never felt completely lived in, this one seemed old and solid and comfortable. I wondered if this was the very same spot that his mother had fed him that famous banana cream pie. He must have read my mind because at that moment he turned and said, "I've lived here all of my life." Then he shrugged. "I guess that doesn't make me sound very adventurous."

"It sounds perfect," I said but not loud enough for him to hear.

He pushed a bowl of potato chips toward me. I must have told him that my favorite kind was the one with the ridges because that is what was in the bowl, and I wondered how much else he knew about me that I didn't even realize. He returned to the cutting board, and the sound of his knife strokes against the wood soothed me.

"What are you making?"

"Something I know you will like."

"How do you know?"

He shrugged. "Because I do."

He reached up and pulled two glasses out of the cabinet and then took a large bottle of Coke out of the refrigerator. As he poured, I watched the frosty brown foam sizzle alarmingly close to the top and then slowly deflate. I stood up to look for plates thinking I could help. "Is it okay to eat here?" I pointed to the kitchen table.

He shook his head. "Dining room."

The table was already set with silverware and crisp white linen napkins folded into perfectly shaped triangles. He followed me into the room and then lit the two white candles that sat in the middle of the table.

"I'll be right back."

I could hear him moving around in the kitchen, the clink of pots and pans like music in the background. The room was a pale blue that turned even softer from the glow of candlelight. I gently blew across the table, watching the flame shimmer delicately back and forth. I sat down and felt my cell phone buzz in my pocket—a text from Susan apologizing for disappearing followed by three bright red kisses. I scrolled to a news site and saw a story about Daphne Lake. There was a photo of a rusted car and beside it an interview with the sheriff explaining that after they had drained the water, divers had uncovered a vehicle at the bottom of the lake. They were asking for the public's help in identifying it by make and license plate number.

Had the bone Sol and I found come from inside that car? Were the two connected somehow? The very next story had a photo of Sarah Jacobs's mother clutching a framed picture of her daughter close to her chest. I started to read it, but I couldn't stop looking at her, the pain in her eyes so raw. I jumped when Sol came in and placed a plate of food in front of me.

It was a relief to be able to put away my phone. I didn't want to think about the possibility that Sarah had drowned in that lake or about who put her there or how her mother must have felt both wanting to know the truth but terrified that she might. Sol smiled at me and I reminded myself how lucky I was to be sitting across from a man who had just painstakingly prepared a meal for me. He watched as I cut into a breaded chicken breast that was golden brown and perfectly crisp. Beside the chicken there were french fries, meticulously cut so that they were all the same size.

"Homemade," he said.

I bit into the crunchy outside, which then gave way to the white fluffy interior.

"Told you you'd like it."

He watched me for a few more seconds then went about eating his own.

"It's delicious," I said.

Even though he was in the middle of chewing, he got up and walked into the kitchen. He came back with a notebook filled with recipes cut from magazines.

"It was my mother's." He was quiet for a few minutes, pushing a french fry around on his plate. "Sometimes when I miss her, I make her food. Mostly because of the way it makes the house smell. Like when she was in it."

The image of this little clean house filled with the smells of her cooking made my insides clench, so I shoved a piece of chicken into my mouth. He didn't say anything, and when he finished eating, I helped him clear the table but that was all he would allow me to do. "You are my guest." He moved quickly through the small space, opening cabinet doors and running steaming water into the sink. Before I knew it, the kitchen was clean, and he handed me a large mug filled with silky brown hot chocolate. I followed him into the living room and sat beside him on the couch. I took long slow sips, letting the warmth and the sweetness fill me.

"Things will be different with me," he said.

"Like what?"

"You will be different with me."

He put his mug down on the coffee table and picked up a camera. He flipped the lens cap off and began turning dials and then he lifted the camera high up above both of our heads and started clicking.

"What are you doing?"

"Capturing this moment and the color of the room and the feel of the air." He closed his eyes and moved the camera around, quickly snapping pictures without looking. Then when I wasn't expecting it, he reached across my back and pulled me toward him, adjusting the camera so that we were facing it.

"We belong together," he whispered as he kissed the lower part of my earlobe and at that moment, in the solid and sturdy couch his mother had most certainly picked out, I knew without hesitation that Sol Green was in love with me.

My body felt warm, and when he slipped his hand into mine, I realized I had never wanted anyone or anything more. I probably would have held on for most of the rest of the night if not for the jingling of keys. Sol disentangled himself from me and the camera fell to the floor just as the door flew open.

"Dad."

The man grunted something that sounded like *Sol* or maybe it was *son*; it was simply too hard to tell. His hair was gray and combed to the side and glistened as if it had been oiled. He was tall and leaned over onto a cane that made a muted thud each time it hit the wooden floor.

"You're home early. What happened to the game?"

He grumbled something that I didn't understand, but Sol must have because he nodded his head.

"This is Sam," Sol said, and I realized I was still sitting on the couch watching the scene unfold as if it were happening on a television screen. I stood and walked toward him, pulling down my skirt, which suddenly felt too short. I reached my hand out to shake his.

"Henry Green," he said in a voice I was certain had frightened quite a few people in the past.

I had no idea if I was supposed to address him by his first or last name, so I nodded my head and went with what I thought was right. "It's nice to meet you, Mr. Green." His half smile told me I made the correct choice.

"How was dinner?" he asked as Sol took his coat and hung it in the closet.

I waited for Sol to speak and when he didn't I did. "Delicious."

"You can always count on your mother's recipes." He winked at Sol and for the first time his face softened. "She knew how to make everything perfect."

"I have some hot chocolate on the stove. Would you like some?"

Henry nodded then sat on the couch. "What kind of name is Sam?"

Older people usually liked me because I was quiet and serious, and I was not used to having to work particularly hard to gain their approval. However, with Henry Green it felt as though every question was a test that I was desperately close to failing made worse by the fact that Sol disappeared into the kitchen leaving me to fend for myself.

"My father wanted a boy," I mumbled.

Henry stared at me, and I could tell by the way his upper lip curled that he was displeased. "Sol works hard. He needs someone to take care of him."

Not wanting to get anything else wrong, I nodded my head.

"He needs looking after," Henry said. He had a habit of tapping his cane against the floor even while he was sitting. I couldn't help but become distracted by it, wondering if he was trying to send me a secret message. Neither of us said anything more until the kitchen door swung open and Sol came back with a mug of hot chocolate for his father.

"Dad, I'm going to walk Sam to the bus stop."

Henry's fingers wrapped around the cup, and I watched the curls of steam rising to his face. "Yes." He nodded his approval and then moved his hand through the air as if to tell us we were dismissed. "You walk her to the bus."

Sol helped me with my coat.

"Goodbye, Mr. Green. It was a pleasure meeting you."

Mr. Green nodded slightly, but it was apparent that he was much more interested in his hot chocolate and, to be honest, I was grateful. He took long deep breaths that made his chest expand each time, like he couldn't get enough.

Like he was breathing her in.

I hadn't realized how warm it was in the house until we got outside. The cold air felt good, and Sol took my hand as we walked. We didn't talk much except for when I complimented him again on the meal. There were things I wanted to ask about Henry, but something about the way Sol was walking made me know that now wasn't the time. So instead I practiced matching my gait to his, and when we got to the bus stop, he waited with me until the bus pulled up. As the engine rumbled in the background, Sol lifted my hand to his mouth and kissed the tips of each of my fingers.

"Text me when you get home so I know you got there safely," he whispered.

My hand tingled for the entire bus ride and for most of the walk to my apartment building.

Chapter 12

It had been such a lovely night, and I fell asleep dreaming of Sol only waking to the buzz of my cell phone.

My father was calling me.

Which was unusual since we almost never talked on the phone. But he called, and because he seemed uncomfortable, I immediately realized that my mother had put him up to it.

"I was wondering if you wanted to come for dinner."

"Tonight?"

"That would be great."

"Where?"

There was a moment of hesitation, and then a crackling noise as if he was far away hovering in a spacecraft somewhere above the Earth.

"How about at the house?"

The "house" did not mean his house. It meant hers. And that is what she had put him up to.

I contemplated my choices. Maybe I contemplated too long, because after a few minutes, he repeated my name to make sure I was still there.

"How about seven? Can we see you at seven?"

A million excuses ran clumsily through my head. I wanted to just grab one and throw it in his face for taking her side.

For setting me up.

But there was something in his voice, in his distance, that made it impossible to say no. So, I didn't, even though I spent the rest of the day regretting that I did not make it harder for her.

I arrived at 7:30, because the one thing she insisted upon was punctuality. As I walked in through the gate, I could see inside the house. She was in the kitchen, opening and closing the oven door, probably making sure things were not getting too hot or too cold. I knocked and she turned and smiled.

"Just in time."

Even though I had made sure that I wasn't.

Her hair was pulled back, and she was wearing a white apron with ruffles. My father was leaning against the doorframe smiling at me and cracking his knuckles, which he did when he was nervous. She took my arm and guided me inside.

"Fishhh," he whispered and kissed my cheek.

I nodded in response. I never understood why even after she had kicked him out of our lives, he still did whatever she asked.

She motioned for us all to sit so we did. She set out china rimmed in vines of pale pink roses paired with her favorite crystal water glasses. She had made a roasted turkey breast with stuffing and mashed potatoes, and I couldn't help thinking that it all felt very Thanksgiving-like, but I wasn't sure which one of us was supposed to be the one giving thanks. She smiled a lot during the meal, talked about a house she had recently sold while I pushed the turkey around on my plate.

I noticed that she and Brian would look at each other in a funny way, and I couldn't help but sense their connection. It was something I had experienced throughout my entire childhood and sometimes it made me feel hurt and left out. I think Brian must have noticed because he smiled and rolled his eyes a few times when she wasn't looking, but it was hard to take his offer of solidarity seriously when he was the reason I was sitting there.

Dessert was a mixed berry crumble topped with scoop of vanilla ice cream. I was halfway through my second helping when I made the mistake of letting down my guard. She reached across the table and touched my hand and then cleared her throat. "Salmon."

I knew I was in trouble. I focused harder on my dessert.

"We want to talk about your future."

Cracking knuckles popped throughout the room.

"I know that we have our differences, but I am hoping we can find a way to work them out." She stirred sugar into her teacup.

"That would be nice," I said.

She looked seemingly encouraged.

"Your mom just wants what's best," Brian said.

Traitor, I thought but I said nothing. Just tapped my fork against the bottom of the plate like Mr. Green liked to do with his cane.

"I know that you think you love this boy." She took a breath that made me realize she was gearing up for the rest of her monologue.

"But I really do have your best interests at heart. We have talked it over, and law school is just what makes the most sense." She smiled like she had just closed a million-dollar deal on a house. "So, it's settled."

I suddenly realized that if I didn't speak up, she would have me packed and moved to New York before the dishes were washed.

"Can we agree that we will follow through with our plan? And then after law school, if you still want him, you can have him."

She said it as if she was buying me a present for doing a good job on my homework. I was quiet for a few minutes, and I guess she assumed it was because I was relenting. She used to tell me what a good baby I was, never fussing and sleeping soundly when she put me down to nap. Since the moment I came into the world and she held me in her arms, I had given in to her. Neither one of us had entertained the possibility that a time would one day come when I would not. I wasn't sure what it might look or sound like, so when it came out of my mouth, it surprised me almost as much as it did her.

"No."

Because she had prematurely anticipated her victory she was still smiling. It took her several minutes to understand what it was I had just said.

"Excuse me?" The shrill in her voice sent it an octave higher than usual.

"I said, no."

She pushed her chair back and her face went from pink to red. "What is it that gives you the right to throw away everything we have worked for?" Now she was growling, or maybe it was more like a low groan.

"Jayne," my father said.

I always wondered why she insisted on the *y* in the middle of her name when the only people who even knew it was there were the ones who mis-spelled it whom she then had to correct. When my father said it, he drew out the *y* so that it drowned out all the other letters.

She glared at him. "Stay out of this."

He cracked a few knuckles in response.

"You are going to school like we planned and that is the end of it."

I must admit that part of me enjoyed watching her get more and more red. "No."

She stood up from the table and turned away from me. It was quiet for a few minutes until finally my father spoke.

"Sam, why don't you invite the boy over so at least we can meet him. Maybe we can all sit down together and figure this out."

My mother's lips pursed around the beginning words of her protests.

"You promised you were going to be civilized about this, Jayne."

She walked out of the kitchen and he followed.

I could hear the soft muted tones of his voice in contrast to her yelling. I took my spoon and stuck it into the berry crisp like some flag of victory and then I slipped out of the house, leaving my father, my mother, and a sink full of dirty dishes behind.

When I got home, the living room was dark except for the flicker of the tele-vision screen. Susan was sitting on the couch wrapped in a pink satin robe. Every few minutes, the color of the screen would cast an eerie blue shadow across her face, but the sound had been turned off. It was Sarah Jacobs's face plastered on the television, the media again becoming obsessed with her story. Susan's hand sat on top of what looked to be a half-empty box of donuts.

I took off my coat and draped it over the arm of a chair, and she reached into the box, taking out a donut dusted in powdered sugar. She took a bite, which left a circle of white around her mouth, and I watched as she wiped it with her sleeve. I picked up the remote and switched the channel, because even in silence I didn't want to see Sarah's face. I settled on a talk show instead. Susan didn't seem to notice as she pushed the box of donuts closer to me. All that was left was cinnamon. Not my favorite but it would do in a pinch.

"He broke up with me."

I had been so involved with Sol lately that I wasn't completely sure whom she was even talking about.

"I'm sorry."

She slouched down, and her robe began to open but she did nothing to conceal herself, nothing to cover up. She sat with her feet propped up on the table, semi-exposed. "It always goes to shit." She dropped the half-eaten donut back into the box.

"You'll meet someone else."

She turned toward me, the smell of alcohol heavy on her breath. "What do you know?"

Maybe I was just tired from the evening with my parents or maybe I just said the first thing that came to my mind. "I don't know a lot, Susan, but one thing I know is that you and I really aren't that different."

She made a noise that sounded like a snort but must have been a laugh because she was smiling. "The truth," she said, as flexed her toes forward and back like a cat, "is that we are exactly alike."

She grabbed the bottle of wine from the table and took big ugly gulps like she was trying to wash away the taste of those words from her lips.

Chapter 13

Sol bought a new car.

It wasn't exactly new, but for him it was the most exciting purchase he had ever made. It meant he didn't have to borrow his father's car.

It meant freedom.

The first time he came to pick me up, he honked from the street. He pulled into a spot and when I came downstairs, he held the door open as if it was a chariot.

It was not.

It was green, and the fabric in the driver's seat had worn into the exact shape of the previous owner's behind. It also carried an unpleasant smell of smoke, but Sol didn't care. He hung an air freshener in the shape of a pine tree from the mirror, and when I got in, a shot of mint hit me in the face.

Like my mother, Sol loved to drive. He didn't, however, like to sing in the car; in fact, he didn't even turn on the radio. Instead, he talked. As he spoke, he would stare straight out onto the road and because he never broke his focus, I wondered if he was even speaking to me or if it really mattered that I was there. He announced his thoughts and ideas to the windshield without ever once turning his head.

It became a habit, and because of that, I stopped taking my morning walks. He would come early when the sun was just beginning to rise and we would drive. He talked while I stared out the window. He told me about the latest ice cream recipe he was thinking of testing, how he suspected one of the workers at the shop might be stealing from him, and about a photo he had recently taken that reminded him of summer. He spoke in a monologue that rarely stopped and reminded me of flowing water. His hands fit firmly around the steering wheel as he stared out onto the road never once looking across at me.

It was during one of these moments of feeling invisible that it came out. I wasn't sure he heard what I had said so I was taken aback by his reaction.

"My parents want to meet you."

I watched as his fingers tightened around the wheel.

"Forget it. It really doesn't matter."

Silence sat in the space that was usually filled by the sound of his voice.

He slowed down the car to let someone cross. "Yes."

"What?"

"I think we should meet."

"Really?"

He nodded and kept driving. He was quiet for what seemed like a very long time. Then he reached over and took my hand, and without ever taking his eyes off the road said, "I'll take care of everything."

She offered to have us over to the house, but I insisted that we meet at a restaurant because it seemed like a more neutral place from which to storm out. I spent the days preceding our meeting conjuring up the various dramatic scenes that might take place while Sol reassured me that everything would be fine.

He arrived cleanly shaven and dressed in a suit, looking as though he was heading off to a graduation. I noticed a nick in his skin, and for some reason my eyes filled with tears. As we got in the car, I contemplated the odds of talking him into heading to his favorite diner instead, but he seemed so determined that I knew there was no turning back. A shiver ran through me and he reached over and turned up the heat.

"You know I don't really care what they think," I said as I adjusted the seat belt that was slowly making its way up toward my chin.

"It will be fine." He was staring at the red light, waiting for it to turn, but when it did, he lunged forward too quickly and the seat belt cut into my neck. "Sorry," he said as he moved his arm across my chest to protect me from falling forward. I felt the tears again, but I turned toward the window so he wouldn't see.

It was drizzling outside, and everything sparkled from the dampness. The rain wasn't heavy enough to run the window wipers, but he turned them on anyway, and they made a sharp squeaking noise that lulled me with the sound of their continuity. I could feel myself beginning to relax, my breath matching the sound of the squeak, when suddenly Sol hit a bump and the next thing I knew, we were airborne.

It was probably only seconds that we flew through the air, but it didn't matter because I still felt it, the indescribable sensation of flight, of soaring.

Of freedom.

I wanted to freeze the moment and not allow anything to come after because I knew that nothing could ever compare to the feeling of being lifted. I wanted to make everything around me stop so that Sol and I and his old tired car could break up into a million pieces and disappear into the black night air with the feeling of lightness still in our lungs. I felt giddy and dizzy like when you reach the very top of a roller coaster and anticipate the thrill that is about to come. I tried to grab his hand, because I wanted him to feel what I was feeling and because I didn't want it to end.

We landed with a thud, and he swung the steering wheel to the right, getting us safely back onto the road. When I turned to look at him, I could see the color had drained from his face. The second of flight that had given me an exhilarating taste of freedom had given him something else.

Terror.

And because of that, I could not admit that I had loved it.

"Are you okay?" I couldn't put into words what it was I had experienced, so I just said what it was he expected me to say. What he wanted me to say.

He nodded, but as his hands shook, I started to feel shame for enjoying something that was clearly so traumatic for him. "We're okay."

He nodded a second time.

"Sol?"

He turned to look at me, and I saw that his eyes were damp, and he used the back of his sleeve to wipe them. "I said I was fine."

I knew that I probably should have made more certain that he was all right, but I didn't. Instead I sat in the passenger seat, closing my eyes, desperately trying to re-create the sensation of flight. By the time we arrived at the restaurant, the drizzle had stopped, leaving behind dark patched puddles that were deceptively deep. I held on to the crook of his arm, trying to avoid them, and looked like I was playing some crazy game of hopscotch.

The hostess greeted us with a smile and I saw my mother in the background stand and wave. Mildly aware that the possibility for escape still existed, I shifted, but Sol slipped his hand inside the curve of my back and propelled me forward.

"Sa—" my mother said, but before she could get anything else out, I shot her a look. My name was my secret to reveal.

"Sam," my father said and kissed me on the cheek.

"This is Sol," I said and watched as my mother extended her hand. I immediately recognized the suit she was wearing. It was smartly tailored and so dark that it made the white blouse she wore underneath seem even crisper. She bought it after closing on one of her largest deals, and it usually sat in her closet in a dry-cleaning bag like the spoils of war.

"It's a pleasure to meet you," Sol said.

The waiter handed out menus, and as he chatted with my parents, it became clear that they knew each other, and I couldn't help but sense an advantage. I looked across the table at my mother, who looked up at the same moment and smiled.

"Would anyone like something to drink?" my mother asked while the waiter stood at attention, pen and paper in hand.

"Whatever you have on tap," my father said.

"Me too," Sol said.

Spin the wheel. Move three spaces.

"Me three," I said as my mother's menu slipped from her hands.

Move three more spaces.

"Sam," she laughed, "you don't drink beer."

I shrugged. "I do now."

She looked at me for a few minutes then finally back at the waiter. "A glass of chardonnay, please."

It was quiet for a few minutes while everyone looked over their menus.

"The steak is delicious here," my mother said.

"The chicken is great, too," my father added.

My mother shook her head. "I could order for both you and Sam with my eyes closed." She went back to looking at her menu.

It probably should not have infuriated me to the extent that it did, but I hated how easily she could make me feel like a child. How stuck and predictable and dull she painted me out to be. The waiter came and set down our drinks and then asked if we were ready to order. My mother began to speak, and when she finished, pointed to my father and I and said, "They'll have the chicken."

Now that the ordering portion of the meal was decided, she folded up her menu and handed it back to the waiter whom she referred to as "Jim."

"Actually, Jim, I will have the New York sirloin," I said casually as if it was something I ordered every day.

"Sam?" she said it like it was a question. Like an alien had invaded my body and she needed to make sure I was really in there.

"Yes, Mom."

She shrugged her shoulders like it meant nothing to her.

"How would you like that cooked?" the waiter asked.

When I looked up, I could see she was looking at me.

Grinning.

"We'll both have ours medium," Sol said as he took a sip of beer and the color finally returned to his face. I took a sip, too, hoping that either the taste had changed since the last time I had tried it or that I had matured enough to develop a liking.

I hadn't.

Lose a turn.

It was bitter and overly carbonated, and I stifled a cough. And then because I could see her still watching out of the corner of my eye, I took another sip.

My mother's fingers were pressed around the stem of her glass, slowly twisting it forward and back. "Sol, I understand you run your family's business."

Sol had just taken a bite of a roll and nodded his head as he passed the basket to me.

"It's an ice cream shop that my father started."

I tore open one of the rolls and watched the steam rise from it.

"My grandfather had a dairy farm and this sort of came from that."

I wondered why I didn't know that. It was such a simple question with a simple answer and one that it had never occurred to me to ask. I spread a pat of butter, watching it melt and turn the surface of the bread the color of sun.

"His ice cream is delicious," I said, and Sol smiled.

"Sam has shown me some of your photographs. They are lovely."

I had not shown her. She had seen because she pushed herself into my house and my room and my life.

"Is it something you are thinking of pursuing professionally?"

My breath quickened because I knew when she was setting someone up, but Sol just smiled politely.

"Sol takes pictures for fun," I said, taking another swig of beer and resisting the urge to spit it back out.

At her.

Appetizers arrived, and the waiter busied himself with remembering who had gotten what. I had chosen French onion soup and slurped it just loudly enough for her to hear. Unfortunately, in the process, I also burned the roof of my mouth.

"Sam has always been a very good student. It was my hope that after law school, she and I could start a business together. Like you and your father."

Move back two more spaces.

Sol busied himself with cutting up a piece of lettuce on his plate.

"When did you become interested in photography?" my father asked.

"My mother gave me my first camera when I was ten."

"My dad's an artist," I said.

"I paint," he said, as if I had made a mistake that he felt compelled to correct.

The bus boy came and all it took was the blink of my mother's eye for him to understand it was time to clear the plates. As he set them on top of one another, they made a loud clinking noise that made me jump. Sol rubbed the spot between my shoulder blades.

When the entrées arrived, I could feel regret pushing out through the insides of my stomach. My steak sat on a stark white plate with dark brown juice pooled around it.

"Is everything to your liking?" the waiter asked.

We all nodded.

I couldn't help but stare longingly at the chicken on my father's plate. He looked up at me, and for a second, I thought he was about to offer me some but he didn't.

Sol handed me some steak sauce and I poured as much on as I could, managing to get down the first bite.

"Enjoying your meal, sweetheart?" my mother asked.

I nodded, struggling to swallow a piece that was especially chewy, and then took a sip of beer. I don't think I could have chosen a more revolting flavor combination had I tried. She smiled in a way that made it obvious she was enjoying every moment of her triumph.

"Excuse me." I pushed my chair away from the table. "I need to use the restroom."

She didn't follow, which I found both a surprise and a comfort.

The bathroom had dark paneled walls and marble sinks. A woman was putting on lipstick in front of a mirror, so I went into one of the stalls. I rocked slowly back and forth as the steak and beer churned inside of me and willed it not to come out, but suddenly the stall felt like it was closing in on me. The lock on the door seemed to be stuck, and as I tried to slide it back and forth, I could feel the panic rising in my chest.

"Lift up and turn," the woman instructed.

I did as I was told, and when I finally felt it open, I burst through like someone was chasing me. She looked up for a second and then went back to blotting her lips with a napkin. She ran a comb through her hair and then twirled in front of the mirror like she was filming a Maybelline commercial. I turned the water on, hoping the warmth would thaw my fingers, which felt so cold they were numb, and when I looked back up she was gone.

I stared at myself in the mirror and tried to smooth down the hairs sticking up around my forehead. I looked paler than usual and my eyes seemed sunken in. I splashed water on my face, but some of it got onto my blouse, leaving big dark stained circles. I thought about flying and wondered if twirling would feel the same. I stood the same way the woman had, but just as I was about to try, someone walked in.

Things were quiet when I returned to the table. All the plates had been cleared except for mine, and everyone was looking at the dessert menu.

"I wasn't sure if you were finished." My mother pointed to the steak.

"I am finished."

She motioned for the waiter to take away the plate.

The dessert menu soothed me. The descriptions of ice cream and cake and pies slowed my breathing and brought warmth back to my cheeks. I chose a banana and raisin bread pudding.

When it arrived, I shoveled spoons of it into my mouth, letting the warmth heat me from the inside out. I wrapped my still cold fingertips around the ramekin. I breathed in the cinnamon and nutmeg, and when I closed my eyes, I was sitting on a brown velvet couch in front of a roaring fire. The clearing of her throat startled me out of my daydream. Harsh and scratchy like a chair scraping against the floor.

"More to your liking?" she asked.

I didn't answer. I went back to finishing my dessert, and it was only as I was taking my last bite that I realized Sol hadn't ordered one. Instead, he seemed to be mindlessly stirring his spoon inside a cup of coffee.

"I would have shared with you." I reached under the table and squeezed his knee and he stopped stirring.

Dinner was over, and I was pleased that we had managed to get through without any serious explosions. As we said our goodbyes, my mother hugged Sol and whispered something in his ear that I couldn't hear because at that same moment my father hugged me too. "He's very nice," he said, which meant a lot even though I didn't want it to.

Sol was quiet the entire ride home. He pulled up beside my apartment and told me that he was tired and wanted to go home. He smiled one of those smiles that was supposed to make me feel like everything was fine even though I immediately knew that it wasn't.

"Tell me."

He fiddled with the miniature compass hanging from his keychain. "She offered to fund my photography career."

Maybe I had my mother all wrong. "Really?"

He looked down. "She said she will give me whatever it is that I want."

I could feel my heart beating through my eardrums.

"And there is only one thing I have to give her in return."

He turned toward me so that I could see the gold flecks in the brown of his eyes. "You."

There was quiet between us as the words sunk in.

He reached over and took my hand. "That will never happen, Sam. You will always be mine."

He said it to reassure me, to comfort me, and even though some part of me knew I shouldn't, I let him because I wanted him to.

Because when he was there protecting me, watching over me, I could close my eyes and I could disappear.

Chapter 14

Sol didn't say much when he called the next morning, but I knew he wanted to drive and that he wanted me to come with him. I called in sick to work and then turned on the television while I got ready, and it was only as I was brushing my hair that I saw her image reflecting back at me from the television screen.

Sarah.

Smiling and hugging a friend whose image had been blurred. She was so naturally beautiful it was like staring at pure sunshine. After a few minutes, the image panned to Sarah's boyfriend, the son of a police officer who had initially been interviewed when she first disappeared but was then released. His name was Stephen Markworth, and he was as handsome as she was pretty, with perfectly white teeth and a squint that made him look rugged. I imagined that when they walked through the halls of their high school together, they appeared to be the perfect couple. He and his lawyer pushed past a horde of microphones and got into a black SUV. A few minutes later, Sarah's father was shown at the podium with her mother standing quietly in the background looking disheveled and undone.

It was clear that the media had decided the boy had something to do with her death and it disturbed me more than I wanted to admit. Somewhere inside of me, I wanted to believe that the perpetrator had been a stranger and that what happened was the result of some random inexplicable act of violence because that would have been easier to bear than the possibility that not only had she known him . . .

But that she had loved him.

And as a result, he had broken her.

I turned off the television when I heard Sol honking outside. He was pulled up near the sidewalk and didn't say anything to me when I got inside his little green car. It was so quiet that every noise became amplified and I covered my ears to drown out the silence. I turned the radio on, hoping to find distraction, but it was the top of the hour and every station I hit was doing a news segment and all I could hear was her name, *Sarah*, over and over. I spun the dial faster until the words broke apart and smashed back into each other like rough surf.

I opened the window and the space between us filled with cool air and car honks. Sol began to rub the curve of the steering wheel like a person would stroke the neck of a horse. I sat with my hands clasped in my lap feeling the air hit my face harder the faster we drove. Soon we were on the highway and I wanted him to stop being so cautious, always so safe. I wanted him to go faster so that I could remember how it felt to fly, so that it wouldn't feel like we were drowning as other cars swept past. One mile looked the same as the next, and after a while it became difficult to gauge time. After what seemed like hours, or maybe it was just minutes, he exited onto a winding road where the houses grew further apart. He continued to drive along the lines of a creek, and as he slowed, I stuck my face out of the open window so I could hear the water dancing over the rocks.

Some people blurt their sadness out loud. Others do it so softly you can barely hear, and still others do it with no words at all. We followed the creek to a mill town where it wound itself loosely around an old building with shattered windows. As we passed, I tried to look inside but all I could see was darkness, like a child had scribbled across them in black crayon.

Sol drove into the town and then up a street that was lined with parking meters. It was not difficult to find a spot because there weren't many people about. He pulled up beside an old-fashioned diner.

"Hungry?" he asked with a smile that seemed so broken it made me catch my breath.

He got out of the car before I could respond.

He was holding open the door, and when I emerged, he put out his arm and I slipped mine inside the *V* shape that it formed. He looked down at the ground and then back up, and I had the overwhelming feeling that he was looking for something. He dug around in his pocket and found a quarter to put in the meter.

The waitress smiled when Sol and I walked in. He led me to a table in the corner. Once I got settled, I opened my menu but found it hard to focus because Sol was tapping his foot so loudly on the linoleum floor.

"You okay?"

He nodded and went back to tapping.

"What should I get?" I asked, hoping the game would change his mood. It was something we liked to play even though we both knew full well that I already knew what I was going to get.

He shrugged.

The waitress came to take our order. She wore her hair in two braids, the ends of which were dyed bright pink like two tips of a paintbrush.

Sol folded his menu. "I'll have coffee and an apple pie. She will have a Coke and a grilled cheese. American and white."

She nodded and took our menus. The diner was small with a curved ceiling. There was a jukebox in the corner, and lining the space between the ceiling and the tops of the windows were license plates—hundreds of them stuck side by side like railroad cars from every corner of the country. A woman came in with a little boy who pointed up to them and laughed. The waitress sat them at a booth across from an older couple.

"Food should be up in a minute," she shouted in our general direction. I looked over at Sol and was surprised to find him staring at me. He blinked. It may have been more than a blink, actually, because his eyes remained closed for a few seconds too long.

"My mother liked to come here."

The little boy began singing. "Five little monkeys jumpin' on da bed." His voice was sweet and light. "One fell off and bumped his head."

The waitress set our food down on the table. "Anything else I can get you?"

She was waiting for me to respond but I didn't say anything. Instead, I looked down at the old-fashioned style Coke bottle she had placed in front of me. I remember someone had once told me that drinking it helped take away headaches.

"We're all set," Sol said, and I think he may have even smiled before he ripped open a packet of sugar and poured it into his coffee and then the pink-haired waitress walked away.

"I need to tell you about that day. The day that she disappeared."

Sol's face turned red, as if the pain was pulsing up through his veins. He put his elbows on the table and rubbed his fingers across his temple, and I wondered if all the news stories about Sarah were as upsetting for him as they were for me and if it was why he suddenly needed to talk.

About his mother.

He took a deep breath and then expelled it like he was emptying his insides of something. "I was working at the store with my dad. I remember I was tired because it was the day after my twenty-first birthday and I had been out celebrating. She was up waiting for me when I got home with a cup of tea." He stopped speaking, maybe to swallow down the ball of pain that seemed to be working its way up. "I went to work the next morning. When I handed my father a pitcher of milk, it slipped and shattered onto the ground. There were slivers of icy white glass everywhere."

He looked down at his pie and pushed a piece around the plate with his fork. "I was on my knees cleaning it up when I got this terrible pain, like I couldn't breathe." His fork made a tinny sound as it scraped across the plate. "She was supposed to come to the shop that day, but she was late." He took in a shallow breath and whispered, "When I looked at my father, he made a noise like I have never heard a person make and then his legs gave out from under him."

I hadn't realized he was crying until he pulled out a napkin from the metal dispenser and wiped his eyes. "I don't know how it is that we both knew something was wrong."

The little boy began to whine, and his mother handed him a small plastic airplane. I watched him fly it through the air. The waitress came to clear our plates, but this time she didn't ask how we were doing. In fact, no one in the diner seemed to be talking. I ran my fingers around the ridges of my Coke bottle. The glass still felt cold and I thought about how sturdy it felt. Old and reliable like it had fallen from somewhere out of the past.

"The doctors say my father is fine, but he's convinced he can't walk without that stupid cane."

The little boy dragged his mother to the jukebox. He put some change into the slot and she pressed the buttons. When the song began to play, he clapped his hands and she rubbed the top of his head. It was a happy song, with a loud fast beat, and he skipped back to the table.

When I looked at Sol, I realized he had been watching me watch the boy.

"I didn't know it then, but that day I lost them both. We called the police when she didn't come home, but they never found anything, so I started digging through her things, searching for any clues, and I found this matchbox and on the cover was the name of this place so I decided to drive up."

The song finished playing and the little boy went back to zooming his airplane.

"She recognized my mother's picture." He nodded in the direction of the waitress. "She told me she came here a lot." He looked down at the table. "Sometimes my mother was so sad and I could hear her crying in her bedroom." He swallowed hard, as though he knew the words he was about to say next were going to cause him physical pain. "I asked the waitress if there was someone she was meeting here, but she said all she could remember was that she came in a lot and that she always asked to sit at this table, in the seat that you are in."

A man with a shaggy gray beard dressed in overalls walked in. He sat at the counter, shifting his weight so that his seat swiveled slowly back and forth. Someone from inside the kitchen called him Corky, and when he heard his name, he smiled and waved. I realized that from the moment Sol began to speak, I had said nothing. I reached across the table and touched his hand, startled by how cold his fingers felt.

He took a final sip of his coffee. "Have to use the restroom."

Corky swiveled harder and his seat squeaked like a seagull. The pink-haired waitress came out of the kitchen and when she handed him a bagged lunch, I saw him wink at her. When he left, bells I hadn't even noticed jingled as the door shut behind him, and I knew this was a scene that had been replayed many times over and one that Sol's mother probably watched repeatedly. I thought about Sol's suspicions, and even though I knew little about her, I knew she wasn't coming here to meet someone.

I stared out the window and wondered why it was that she had been so sad.

I stretched out a little further so I could see the cars driving past. A small blue car came along, but because the dip was so steep when it went down, it seemed to disappear as if it had had plummeted off the edge of a cliff. I felt my breath catch in my chest for the few seconds it was completely out of sight like it had never even existed.

Like it was inconsequential.

Like it was never coming back.

I don't know why I worried about that car, but it suddenly felt like knowing it was safe was the most important thing in the world. Then, just was I was about to give up, it reappeared as if by magic in a puff of white exhaust and I felt something.

Relief.

Which I suddenly realized was what Sol's mother probably felt when she watched it happen. It gave her a sense of reassurance, proof that she too would not fade away. It was from this seat in this old-fashioned diner that she was reminded she would also rise back up. I watched a second and then a third car disappear and then reappear and I understood why this place was so important to her.

It gave her hope.

I felt Sol standing beside me. He threw some crumpled bills onto the table. "C'mon."

Even though it was cool outside, I didn't wear my coat because I wanted to feel the air against my skin. We drove back the way we came, through the narrow streets and then past the abandoned mill that had at one point been the heart and soul of the town but now stood empty and ragged like a monument. Water still rushed around it, blind to the fact that its purpose had disappeared.

I thought about the diner and the pink-haired waitress and how much it meant to Sol's mother to find Corky waiting for his bagged lunch at the same time each day, hear his stool squeak and spend her afternoon watching those cars disappear and then reliably spring back up every time. There was comfort in being in a place where you could rely on the fact that everyone was doing the things they were meant to be doing, day in and day out. What appeared routine and mundane to everyone else was special to her, and she came back to the diner in the town with the old forgotten mill because it reminded her to have faith. Which is exactly what I was about to tell Sol except he had pulled over onto the side of the road with such purpose that it made me jerk back into the headrest.

"Sorry." He turned off the ignition and we sat in silence.

He got out and I followed. We walked to the edge where the land started to slope toward the water. Leaves had already begun to fall and there was a smell of decay in the air. The water from the creek moved swiftly, making a humming noise that surrounded us like a swarm of bees.

"There had to have been someone else, someone who hurt her. She would have never just left me." The sky was a vibrant blue and he suddenly looked gray against it. "Sam." He started to speak and then looked down, nudging a branch with his foot. "What if that bone we found?"

"No."

"But Sam. What if?" His color went from gray to porcelain white, and a blue vein I had never noticed before appeared across his brow.

I took his hands in mine. "That bone belongs to Sarah Jacobs. Why else would her case be back in the news?"

His eyes darted back and forth across my face like he wasn't sure he could trust me, but then after a few seconds he nodded and then he seemed different, like he knew that I understood.

How important it was to him that I believed.

"She is out there, Sol, and we will find her." As soon as I spoke, I knew it was a promise I probably couldn't keep. But it meant so much to him, so I told myself they were just words and that after I spoke them they would drift up into the air where they would innocently disappear into the cold churning rush of the water and no one would be the wiser.

Chapter 15

I opened my eyes to the sound of a drip.

The glass of vodka I had been drinking from was tipped over, leaving a large wet circle in the middle of the carpet. The mermaid collage sat in my lap and the crushed shells surrounding her tail sparkled and came alive with light. When I stood, it slipped down and fell to the ground next to the wet vodka spot.

And I didn't care.

I felt like I was suffocating, like I couldn't breathe, and I realized it was because of the dreams I was having about Sol.

No.

It was because of the person I had become when I was with Sol.

A desperate liar who was willing to say (or maybe do) whatever it was he wanted. I detested the girl in those dreams.

Maybe even more than I hated who I was in real life.

Where I was alone, unemployed, and miserable.

I needed another drink.

I searched through my fridge for something to mix into the vodka, but all I found was a carton of spoiled orange juice. I poured it into the sink, where it left clumps of coagulated pulp clinging to the drain. I left my house in search of a convenience store, passing mothers with strollers and the elderly who didn't have jobs to go to and could be out enjoying the crisp fall air. I felt uneasy and conspicuous and tried to stay focused on my mission: juice for the vodka.

I finally found a store, but the lights were off and there was a for lease sign plastered across the door. Right next door was a paint-it-yourself pottery studio called The Creative Outlet, and I'm not sure why I walked inside, but I did. The floors and walls were decorated with children's handprints and a woman was busy covering a long rectangular table with a vinyl-coated tablecloth.

She nodded a greeting in my direction.

I wasn't sure what it was I was doing there or why I had felt compelled to come inside. I reminded myself about the juice, but suddenly it didn't seem so important. I walked from one display of unpainted plastered figures to the next feeling a surge of excitement like the first time you open a box of crayons and see that they are all freshly sharpened and still fit inside the box perfectly because they are brand new.

There were kittens and superheroes and cartoon characters. There were shelves of paint and buckets of paintbrushes and, hidden in the far back of the store, on a small table against the back door, was a display of gargoyles and dragons and griffins. I picked one up.

"Good choice." She pointed to the one I was holding. "Griffins mate for life, and after their partners die, they spend the rest of their lives alone. They're used to guard treasures."

She went back to setting up tables while I decided on paint colors, and then once I sat down, I lost myself in the task. This was different than creating collages, and I liked the way the paintbrush moved inside the feathers of the griffin's wings, along the surface of the beak. It had the face of an eagle, majestic and proud but also sad. I could not figure out how it could possibly fly with the body of a lion, and I couldn't imagine a fate worse than having wings that were unusable. It was lunchtime before I looked up again, and when I went to the register to pay, the woman promised to fire it so that it would be ready to be picked up in a few days.

That night I couldn't sleep.

I went back to the store the next day and painted a gargoyle, then again two days later to paint a dragon. I loved the smell of the place, the peace that came over me when I was painting that felt different than when I was working on a collage. The next week, the woman asked me to watch the store while she ran out to get coffee. When she returned, it was with two cups and a bag of donuts. We sat at one of the vinyl-covered tables and ate.

"What's your name?" she asked.

I had chosen a fat, overstuffed jelly donut, and red stickiness dripped over the side of my lip. She handed me a napkin and I wiped my mouth. "Salmon."

She smiled but not in the confused, uncomfortable way that many people did when they first heard my name.

"Your name comes from the Latin *salmo*, which comes from *salire*, which means 'to leap.'"

I pictured myself flying through the air, and at that moment I understood that she was special.

"Can I ask you something?" she said.

I suddenly had the horrible feeling that she was only being nice so that she could tell me in a kind way to stop coming as often. Of course, it was strange, my connection to this place. I was a grown woman with an expensive legal degree. What on earth was I doing spending my days painting medieval plaster figurines? Maybe she was worried I was making her customers uncomfortable. Obviously, the donuts and the information about the origin of my name was her way of making the blow she was about to deliver more tolerable. I choked down the bite I had just swallowed and prepared for the worst.

"I was thinking, if you are interested, maybe you could help me out a few mornings a week?"

I held my breath so that the excitement wouldn't blow out of me like an explosion.

"I mean, that is, if you are interested. If you have nothing else going on."

Which is how it came to be that I went from practicing real estate law to becoming a part-time employee at the paint-your-own pottery studio, The Creative Outlet.

Alice always arrived at the store before me, and on my way, I picked up breakfast for us to share. She was fascinated with Greek mythology and was also a captivating storyteller, and while we sipped our coffee, she would tell me her favorite myths. She especially liked the story of Orpheus, who fell madly in love with Eurydice, who died after being bitten by a snake. Brokenhearted

Orpheus followed her down to the Underworld where he was miraculously able to negotiate her release on the condition that as he guided her to the world of the living, he would not look back. He agreed, but then seconds before they were free, he turned around. Eurydice was swept away into the Underworld and Orpheus was left alone, broken and grief-stricken.

When she finished telling this myth, I got quiet. Alice patted my knee and smiled. "Moral is don't ever look back. Always look ahead." I thought of her words at night and about how so many of the stories sounded as though they were handpicked just for me. I liked that she didn't ask me a lot of questions, like if I had a boyfriend or what I had been doing before I came to her. She told me that life brought you what you needed and that when I walked into her store, it was for a reason and that it was not her place to judge. I was grateful for her blind optimism.

I was working three mornings a week and leaving before lunchtime. The truth was that during the rest of the week, when I wasn't there, I was counting down the hours until I could return. Even though it didn't make sense, for some reason, while I was filling up pots of paint and washing out brushes, I felt calm. Alice and her store and her plastic-covered tables were the best medicine I could have asked for.

In December, things started to pick up and Alice asked if I could work all five mornings. I enthusiastically agreed. It was on a Tuesday that I noticed a little girl sitting at one of the tables coloring. I looked around, but it didn't seem like she was with anyone.

"Who's that?"

Alice looked toward where I was pointing. "That's Birdie, daughter of a friend. She comes on Tuesdays and Thursdays and stays until lunchtime when her dad comes and gets her. I'll introduce you."

As we walked closer to the little girl, I saw that her name suited her perfectly. Her hair was a medium shade of brown and it was wispy and feathered. Everything about her was dainty and delicate, from the tiny upturn of her nose to the way she held the crayons in her hand.

"This is my friend, Salmon."

Birdie looked up for only a second before she went back to what she was doing. Even though she was tiny, I could tell she was probably between four and five years old. Alice put a second stack of paper on the table and smiled at her. Birdie nodded but didn't smile back.

As we walked away, Alice explained, "Birdie doesn't talk."

"I was quiet at her age, too."

Alice shook her head. Even though she was only in her forties, her hair had already begun to turn gray, but because she always wore it in two braids on either side of her head, she still looked youthful. "I mean she doesn't talk. At all."

My knowledge of kids was limited, but even I knew that probably wasn't normal. "Is something wrong?"

Alice shrugged, which I understood to mean that she extended the same nonjudgmental philosophy toward Birdie as she did to me. "She's a beautiful little girl who doesn't use words to communicate, which is okay because she will find her voice in her own time."

Sometimes when the sun shined through the window, it made Alice's hair turn from gray to shimmering silver. Sometimes she reminded me of the goddesses from the myths she loved so much.

Sometimes I wished she had been my mother.

One of my jobs was to paint figurines so customers could have a sample to copy when they worked. Once Alice finished her paperwork and I had taken care of washing down the tables and brushes, I picked out a figurine to work on. That day it was a kitten curled up in a basket.

"Mind if I sit here?" I asked.

Birdie looked up from what she was doing. She didn't respond so I decided just to take my chances. I sat beside her, and over the odor of turpentine and hand soap, I breathed in her little girl smell. She was serious, too serious, hunched over the drawing she was working on. That first day I didn't say anything at all to her. We just sat side by side, lost in our thoughts and our colors and our art.

I couldn't explain why I was so drawn to her except for the fact that things between us felt remarkably simple. I started looking forward to Tuesdays and Thursdays because I knew I would get to see her. After the first few times of just being quiet, I started talking to her. Having a one-sided conversation was hard in the beginning, but once I realized she was listening, that she heard me, it became more natural.

I told her about my mosaics and how much I wanted to travel to Italy. I told her that I understood about funny names like Birdie because I had a funny name, too. If no one else was there, I would sing her songs. I sang to her about a fish and a bird that loved each other but couldn't be together because the bird couldn't live in the ocean and the fish couldn't live in the sky but that even that couldn't stop them from loving each other. Birdie was smart, and even though she didn't speak, she would tear off scraps of paper and write new words she had learned. She gave them to me as though they were presents, scrawled crayoned insights into her soul—*BIRD, FISH, SAMMMONE*. I kept them at home in a box and set the griffin on top to keep watch. I took a picture with my phone to show her, and she nodded so I knew she was pleased.

Even though it should have been enough, and I wanted it to be enough, the truth was that it wasn't and that I missed him.

Terribly.

It happened late one night during a futile attempt at sleep. I told myself I would only do it for a few minutes, just to relax. I started on a simple sketch of Birdie. When I closed my eyes, I could see her face, the way that her eyebrows scrunched up below her forehead when she was concentrating on something. I promised myself I would stop, but there was a travel magazine on my night-stand and before I knew it, I was ripping pages out from the seams, cutting up images of sandy beaches to replicate the sweet, soft delicateness of her skin.

Chapter 16

Susan always asked quietly so that if I said no she could pretend like she had never asked at all, but most of the times on the Sundays when Sol had to work, I said yes.

Our first stop was to the grocery store where I would push the cart while Susan threw things in. She chose packages of tea biscuits and cans of soup and sometimes the occasional piece of fruit. She stood in the aisle, holding the cans close to her face so she could read the list of ingredients. Sometimes she would shake her head and put the can back, and other times she would toss it into the cart. I never understood what it was exactly she was looking for, mainly because I never asked. I just kept moving whenever she nodded her head.

On this particular Sunday, she was determined to find lamb chops. "My mom used to make these for me when I was little. I loved them," she said as we walked toward the meat aisle. I watched as she scanned shelves of chicken and pork and beef. Sometimes I forgot how pretty she was, but when she smiled, I remembered.

This time, at the checkout, she counted her money and realized she was short ten dollars. She promised to pay me back once she got her paycheck and I wondered if it was the lamb chops that put her over.

We loaded the bags into the trunk and drove for about twenty minutes until we reached a street filled with one-story homes. We walked up the path to a door with paint peeling off in long, flappy strips. Susan rang the doorbell and then jostled the doorknob. The weight of the bags cut lines into my hand so I set one on the ground. Susan rang the bell again, this time jiggling the door with more force.

"I'm coming!" a woman yelled.

We heard a loud bang as if someone had fallen. We waited a few more minutes before she finally came to the door.

"Hi, Ma," Susan said.

Ma motioned with her hand and then stumbled backward.

Sometimes when we came, Susan's mother would be dressed in a blouse and skirt, greeting us with a polite smile when we walked through the door. Other times it was like this.

"Happy birthday, Ma," Susan mumbled so that mostly only I heard. It didn't matter anyway, because her mother was now sitting cross-legged on the foyer floor, motioning for Susan to join her.

"I need to put the food away," Susan walked into the kitchen, leaving me alone with Ma.

"Come here, Sally."

On the Sundays that she was like this, she called me Sally.

"Know what?"

I shook my head.

"It's my birthday." She lifted the glass I hadn't even noticed she was holding. "Time to toast." She scrambled to her feet, spilling the dark liquid onto the floor. "Oops." She giggled, covering her mouth with her hand.

I walked into the kitchen to get a paper towel. Susan was putting away cans of soup. She didn't look at me. I went back to clean up the spill, but Susan's mother was gone, and when I went to the living room, I found her lying down with her legs dangling over the arm of the couch. Her skirt was hiked up to her thighs and I could see she had forgotten to put on her underwear. I turned away, but she didn't seem to notice or to care.

"I'm going to make you some lunch, Ma," Susan called out from the kitchen.

Her mother's hand flew up, twisting back and forth as if she were trying to shoo her away.

She swung her legs back down so that she was sitting upright and patted her hand on the empty cushion beside her. "Come sit, Sally," she demanded.

I did as I was told, and she moved in closer and put her head on my shoulder. Then she slipped her hand inside mine and I was surprised at how small and frail it felt. Her breathing slowed, and after a few minutes I could tell she was asleep. Every so often, she would snort and cough as though she was choking.

The television was on, but the volume was turned all the way down. Beside it sat a radio, which was playing at full blast. The man and woman on the screen swayed gently back and forth, as though they could hear the music, and for a moment I wondered if they actually could. The radiator along the wall began to hiss, and I realized how warm it was inside the house. I stood and Susan's mother toppled over, mumbling something before falling back asleep.

Although the living room was small, there was a piano pushed up into the corner with photographs sitting on it. Susan Waving. Susan Drawing. Susan Swimming. Susan Pouting.

"She wasn't always like this." Susan was standing behind me, wiping her hands on a towel embroidered with strawberries. "She used to play the piano, and when she did she was beautiful."

It was more than she had ever told me. When she finished speaking, she turned around and went back into the kitchen. I stared at the photo of Susan Graduating High School, wondering what it was I would tell her if I could pull her through the frame. The smell of cooking meat wafted into the living room and I choked down a wave of nausea.

"Wake up, Ma." Susan leaned over her mother. When she didn't respond, she shook her, first softly and then with more force. Saliva sputtered from her lips and I could hear her moan.

"Why do you do this to me, Suzie. Why can't you just let me sleep?"

"It's your birthday, Ma. Come eat."

Her mother grumbled something but then swung her legs onto the floor, and I watched Susan help her along, broken and stumbling, to the dining table.

The place setting she had made for her mother was beautiful. Everything was laid out on a white linen placemat and the food was arranged on a plate trimmed in gold. There was even a vase with a single yellow rose.

"Happy birthday, Ma."

Her mother nodded. She cut into one of the lamb chops, and after she took a bite, she closed her eyes and for just one second I could see whom she must have been.

Before.

"You used to love these with those petite green peas that came in a can. They were your favorite." Her mother smiled and then took another bite. "I need a drink."

Susan stood. "Lemonade or water?"

"Suzie, I need a drink."

"I heard you, Ma. What would you like?"

Her mother stood and went into the kitchen where she pulled a blue plastic cup out of the dishwasher.

"Ma, those dishes are dirty."

She stood on her tiptoes, reaching up behind the cereal on top of the fridge and pulled out a bottle.

Susan grabbed her arm. "Not today. Please." She sounded small.

Just for a moment, I thought that maybe she had won. There was softness in her mother's face that I didn't remember ever seeing. She looked over at the plate of half-eaten lamb chops and she hesitated. For a second, she hesitated. And then she grabbed the bottle and poured whatever was inside into the plastic blue cup. "It's my birthday."

If Susan was heartbroken, I couldn't tell. Maybe her heart was so broken that another crack simply disappeared inside all the others. Her mother came back to the table with her drink and Susan cleared the dishes. I waited as she prepared the cake we had bought. It was white with perfectly formed pink roses and a purple HAPPY BIRTHDAY scrawled across the top. She stuck one candle in the middle and we sang loudly, as though we were at a six-year-old's party. Susan's mother sipped her drink and giggled and then blew out the candle.

Afterward, I sat on the couch with her while Susan cleaned up. I turned the television on to a game show that seemed to hold her attention until it didn't and then she leaned back and fell asleep with the cup still in her hand. When I went into the kitchen, I found Susan smoking a cigarette. She pushed the pack and lighter across the counter toward me.

I took one out of its box. I had smoked occasionally but mostly because I wanted to infuriate my mother. I lit the tip of the cigarette, and as I inhaled, I could hear the crackle of the tobacco igniting. I watched Susan blow the smoke out in a lovely white stream.

"You are good to her," I said.

"No, I'm not."

"You are a good person, Susan." And at that moment, I truly meant it.

She stared at me for a minute. "Ever think about the fact that they are both alone?"

She waited for me to say something, and when I didn't she kept going.

"Both of our mothers are completely alone." She was looking out the window into the dark alley. "That will never happen to me." She dropped the cigarette into one of her mother's cups, and it sizzled as it hit the liquid inside.

Back in the living room, her mother had woken and was now frantically pacing across the carpet.

"The world is coming to an end."

"It's not."

"It is and I can't find my fucking clocks."

"Why do you need your clocks if the world is coming to an end?"

She looked at Susan as if she had suddenly grown a second head. "Because, sweetheart, I need to know the exact time that it happens."

"Why?"

"Because."

"Because why?"

I shot Susan a look I'm sure conveyed "because she's crazy drunk, that's why."

"Mom, you have millions of clocks. Don't worry. When the world ends, you will know."

"Promise you will get me another one."

"This is insane."

She grabbed Susan's hand and brought it to her lips. "Promise me."

"Let's get you ready for bed."

Her mother allowed herself to be led out of the room like a child. She slung her body onto Susan, who couldn't seem to manage the weight.

"Can you help?"

I nodded, moving to the other side and grabbing her arm.

In all the times I had come, I had never been inside her bedroom. At first glance it looked like any older woman's bedroom with flowered wallpaper and a dusty pink carpet but what made it different was the clocks on every free surface in the room. There were alarm clocks, cuckoo clocks, digital clocks, and even an old wooden grandfather clock that stood beside her dresser. We managed to get her onto the bed, and Susan began to look for a nightgown. I stood in the middle of the room, overwhelmed by the sound of ticking, which made it feel as if a bomb was about to go off. Seconds passed, each recorded by a resounding tick. I wondered how she could sleep there with the passage of time being so assuredly announced. Susan helped her get into bed and then turned out the light, and we walked out of the room.

We spoke nothing of the clocks. As if they were normal. As if everyone had a room filled with them.

"We can go."

I nodded.

We gathered our things, and Susan went to turn off the radio, but then she turned it back on. Music filled the room and I wondered if maybe she was trying to drown out the ticking that now seemed to vibrate through the walls.

She didn't say much in the car, and she didn't need to, because there were only two places we went after visiting her mother. On a day when she dressed in a skirt and blouse, we went to the bakery and picked out cupcakes. On a day like this, we drove to the art supply store.

Once inside, we separated and I headed straight to the scrapbooking section, which had shelves filled with different-colored papers. I was working on a collage of a girl flying and was excited when I found translucent paper the color of silver.

We got in line and when it was our turn to pay, I unloaded the cart. Because it was buried beneath some brushes and a few tubes of paint and a stack of blank canvasses, it took a few minutes for me to uncover. But there it was, a clock face set inside a plain unpainted pine frame. Susan was lost in thought or pain or indifference, and as she turned away, she tapped her fingers against the handle of the cart and I wondered if she knew.

That she was drumming in perfect rhythm to each and every spiteful tick.

Chapter 17

A woman with a child straddled to her hip on the escalator distracted me.

I was going up and Brian was coming down, and just as we intersected, his hand reached out and touched mine. I heard a soft swooshing noise, like what it might sound like if you could hear time pass, and then he was at the bottom waving at me. When I finally reached him, he kissed me on the forehead and smiled. We talked for a few minutes about how funny it was to run into each other, but my father knew me well enough to know exactly why I was at the mall and where it was that I was headed.

Candy.

I wanted gumballs, and licorice and gummy bears and anything else that would force me to chew hard enough to make my jaw ache and make it so that I didn't need to think about how I had chosen Sol.

Over my mother.

We pushed our way through a crowd of ten-year-old girls until we reached the front of the store where canisters filled with candies sparkled like jewels. I chose purple and green and then little hard ones with multicolored swirls. I picked red ones shaped like raspberries, the outside of which crunched when you bit into them. The clerk at the counter asked if I wanted a bag, as if I was buying something illicit that I needed to hide. I shrugged, which she must have understood as yes because she slid them into a brown crinkly sack.

My father and I walked around the mall and I stuffed Swedish Fish into my mouth two at a time. Even though it made it hard to breathe, I liked the feeling of fullness, so I crammed in even more. I offered him some and he stuck two pieces of licorice into the corners of his mouth. They hung down like two red strands of spaghetti, which made me smile.

"That always gets a laugh out of you."

We walked toward the food court, which was almost empty because it was too late for breakfast and too early for lunch. Brian went to get something to eat while I waited. He came back with two Cokes and an enormous cinnamon bun and handed me a fork. Together we went about unraveling and pulling off the sweet, chewy pastry, and I closed my eyes as the sugar slowly seeped through me.

"You okay?"

I nodded.

"What are you going to do?"

We both knew what it was he was talking about.

I didn't answer, because I knew he understood that I had already made my choice.

He took a sip of soda, sucking so hard that it made a broken slurping sound as it came up through the straw.

"What is it you want? I mean, for yourself?"

Suddenly, I felt tired. Like all I wanted was to crawl up into a ball and sleep on his lap like a kitten. Like I used to when I was little. I didn't know what to say so I said nothing. I breathed in deeply and thought about Rome and my mother and law school and Sol. I needed to find a way to explain to him about Sol, but I couldn't find the words, so I looked away. When I looked back, I realized he must have given up on me because he was already clearing the mess from the table.

"Do you need a ride?"

I shook my head.

He pulled me close and whispered as if he were telling me a secret I had to promise to keep. "I will help you. No matter what you decide, I will help you."

I knew he meant it, too, which made my heart ache even more. He turned away, making sure to take along the things he had just purchased. I recognized the bag because of its gold and white lettering and the fact that it came from my mother's favorite makeup counter at Macy's. As I watched him walk away, his errand complete, I thought about strands of red licorice and mascara and wondered how much longer he could bear the cost of his freedom.

I recognized the laugh immediately.

It was high and shrill and usually happened in the hours and days my mother spent wooing her clients, convincing them they were incapable of making decisions without her. It was disarming because of its innocence. It was fresh and genuine, except when you listened more closely and realized that it wasn't.

I had taken the bus home from the mall and gotten off a stop or two early, hoping the walk would clear my mind, but it hadn't. I stood in front of my apartment door, listening to that laugh and wondering if I should just turn around and leave. Instead, I walked inside, and to my surprise, instead of my mother, I found Susan with her head tilted back and laughing so heartily that her breasts bounced up and down underneath her T-shirt. Sitting in the seat across from her was Sol, and he was laughing too.

I wiped away the leftover sugar from the candy smudged across my face. They stared at me as if I had just walked in on a joke that had become too private to join. My hands were sticky, and I felt like a five-year-old.

"I should get going," Susan said.

I had forgotten that it was Sunday. I had promised to help with her mother, but I couldn't imagine anything worse than sitting in the house of ticking clocks.

"You don't have to come, Sam," she said, even though I could tell she didn't really mean it.

The shirt she was wearing was so thin I could make out the outline of her nipples. I couldn't tell if Sol had noticed too since he was looking down at the floor.

Maybe it was the candy or maybe it was something else, but suddenly I felt sick. "Thanks."

She looked a little surprised, but then she picked up her jacket and moved her fingers in a delicate wave, which was a move I could have sworn I'd seen her practice in front of the mirror once. I waved back, which she didn't seem to notice since she was looking at Sol, who didn't seem to notice because he was looking at me.

After the door closed behind her, he walked over and kissed me. "You're sticky."

I pulled away.

"I like it."

"I didn't know you were coming."

"I thought I'd surprise you."

"You did."

I walked into my bedroom and Sol followed, but I could feel him hesitate before coming in. I watched as he bent over the scattered piles of magazines and gathered them into a pile before finally sitting down on my bed. "Come here."

He opened his legs and I stood between them. He looked up at me and smiled, and then he ran his fingers underneath my shirt. The two boys I had been with before were clumsy and eager to finish quickly, afraid that I might suddenly change my mind. Mostly they were lost in themselves, which didn't really bother me because it meant that I didn't have to work very hard at pretending I was enjoying myself.

But Sol was different.

He liked to pull down all the shades in my bedroom and light candles, and sometimes he would use his camera to take close-up shots of the flickering flames. Other times he would take pictures of me. He made me stand so close that the yellow glow almost touched my skin. He told me that afterward, when he looked through the images he had taken, it always seemed as if I were made of gold.

When we were together, he never took his eyes off me, and if I closed mine and opened them again, he would still be watching. Afterward he would roll over and lie beside me and we would play a game he had made up. He always let me go first.

"Ice cream for dinner."

"Done," he said.

"Really?" I asked.

"Yup."

"Your turn."

"Nikon AF-S lens."

"Snore."

"Rule is you get to wish for whatever you want, and the other person can't judge."

I nodded. "A slice of the perfect banana cream pie."

He squeezed my hand and then he took a long time to think. So long that I fell asleep and dreamt that he was still whispering wishes into my ear. "Promise you will never leave me. Promise," he said with such sadness that I woke with a gasp. The room was now dark, the candles having burned out long ago, and he was asleep beside me with his arm tightly wound around my waist.

Chapter 18

Sol and I picked the perfect weekend to go away.

Things at work between Anne Marie and Randy were becoming strained, and I spent most of my time trying to avoid getting caught in the middle. I wasn't sure if she was demanding more from him or if he was simply growing tired of her, but whatever it was, I was left feeling like the child asked to choose between which parent she preferred.

The ice cream shop was chaotic, too, because summer was nearing its end and most of Sol's employees were going back to school. He was constantly covering shifts, so when he was finally able to take the weekend off, we were both excited.

He showed up at my apartment early on a Saturday morning, telling me to pack lightly but to bring a bathing suit. He was more quiet than usual, keeping his eyes on the road, only saying how happy he was to be getting away.

We checked into a small hotel that had a bell at the desk, which we had to ring to get the owner's attention. When she finally came, I saw that her skin was tanned leathery brown and her hair was dyed blond and that her name tag said Sunny. She used the palm of her hand to slap the bell hard, and after a few minutes a teenaged boy came out of nowhere.

"Show them to Room 225." The boy picked up our bags and motioned for us to follow.

"It's pretty here," I said but he wasn't interested in making small talk. Maybe he had seen too many young couples just like us. "Having a good summer?" I didn't know why I was trying so hard to be different than the ones who had come before. Sol gave me a funny look.

"Call downstairs if you need anything," the boy said as Sol stuffed a few dollar bills into his hand.

He left and then Sol opened our bags and began putting our things away. I pulled the drapes open and lifted the window so I could breathe in the air.

"I think the air conditioner is on," he said.

I closed the window and went over to lie down on the bed.

"Stop!" Sol shouted. "Don't you know how filthy those things are?" I stood as he pulled the bedspread off the bed.

"Why don't we change and walk down to the beach?" he suggested.

Sol filled a canvas bag with sunscreen and towels while I went into the bathroom to change. I had brought a black one-piece swimsuit, but after putting it on, I decided it made me look like a twelve-year-old girl so I threw a T-shirt on over it, which probably made it look worse.

Sol was rubbing sunscreen on his face when I came out. He looked me up and down and then smiled. "Ready?"

It was only a short walk to the beach, but he was walking too quickly, always a few paces ahead and I couldn't catch up. I grabbed his arm to slow him down.

"Just excited I guess," he said.

The tide was beginning to come in, and there were groups of people sprawled out everywhere. We found a spot between a family with two little boys and an elderly couple sitting in chairs and reading. The boys were digging a hole that they were then surrounding with sand castles. Their father was orchestrating the project and directing each step.

"Over there, Ethan," he shouted, pointing to part of the hole that seemed to be caving in. He sent the younger boy to collect water while Ethan tried to repair the damage. Their mother was lying on a towel, occasionally lifting her sunglasses and squinting in their direction. When the boy came back, he poured what he had into the hole, which made it collapse even further, and made Ethan burst into tears and the mother jump from her spot and the older couple look up from their books. After several minutes, all was resolved with a juice box from their cooler.

"How many do you want?" Sol asked.

I was so engrossed in watching that I had forgotten he was there. "Not sure that I want."

He turned to look at me. "C'mon, Sam. There's no such thing as not wanting kids."

I just shrugged.

"They are what completes your life. They make it perfect."

I stood up. "Let's go for a walk." I reached out my hand to help him up.

I didn't want to talk about babies or why I didn't want to have them. The ocean air blew across my face and made me think of my mother. As complicated as my relationship with her was, there were moments in which the realization of how well she knew me made me want to cry. Like how she knew about my silly name and how well it would suit me.

I loved everything about water. I loved rivers and ponds and lakes. At the ocean, I loved the smell of the salt, the rushing sound it made as it teased the children playing at its edge and the crash of waves that sometimes sparkled so intensely it looked like shattered shards of glass. Sol and I held hands as we picked our way along broken shells and the strands of seaweed that lined the shore. Seagulls squawked like angry rats and then took off into the sky, floating majestically above us. Breathing felt easy and clean, and I turned to look at Sol to see if he was feeling the same. He was staring at a sailboat far out in the distance, so I could not catch his eye. We walked back to our spot, not speaking, and I hoped it was because he was equally in awe of the surroundings. By the time we returned, the family had packed up their things and only the older couple was still there. The woman was reading, holding her book in one hand and the man's hand in the other. Her husband smiled when he saw us coming.

Everything was turning that orange color that warms the air as the afternoon comes to an end. Sol dug through the canvas bag and pulled out his camera. He took his usual stance of standing up high and pointing it low and shot images of an abandoned sand castle that was slowly being demolished by the tide. The water swirled over the turrets, melting it into a soft flat lump, and Sol moved his camera quickly, capturing every second of its demise. Even though a breeze was coming off the water, when he came back to me his face was damp with sweat.

"We should get going," he said, throwing the camera back into the bag.

"Why don't we take a picture of ourselves first?"

The old man must have overheard us. "Happy to help."

After a few minutes of instruction, Sol stood beside me and, through a clenched smile, told the man when to click.

"Perfect," the man said.

We had dinner reservations at a restaurant in the center of town, and Sol showered first while I lay on the bed feeling bits of sand crumbling into the sheets. I walked in on him just as he was finishing up. I leaned against the sink and drew little faces onto the foggy mirror.

"Hurry up and get ready," he said then kissed me on the lips.

Even though I had used sunscreen, my cheeks felt pink, so the cool water was soothing. I came out, wiped off what remained of my smiley faces, and tied my hair in a loose braid.

"You ready?" Sol called.

"Just a minute."

When I came out, he smiled. "Beautiful." He kissed the tip of my nose. "But you need to be more careful about your skin."

On our way out of the lobby, Sunny waved to us and told us to have a good time. Sol thanked her for the restaurant recommendation, and I thought she said something else, but he pushed me along so I wasn't sure. There was not much opportunity to talk once we got outside since this was a resort town and the street was bustling with tourists. Fathers were dragging red plastic wagons with sleeping children inside and teenage girls in teeny shorts and glittery flip-flops were licking ice cream cones. There was desperation in the air, a palpable need to cling to the last fleeting moments of summer. We passed a clam shack with screens on the windows, and I could see the patrons inside wearing bibs and cracking lobsters and kids eating hot dogs. Sol noticed me looking and asked if I wanted to go there instead but I shook my head.

The restaurant he had chosen had a shimmering candle and a couple staring lovingly at each other at every table. As the host handed us our menus, Sol smiled at me. "Don't worry, we will find something you like."

Sol ordered duck a l'orange for himself and a half a roasted chicken with purple potatoes for me. After a glass of wine, he seemed to relax, and as he reached his hand across the table to touch mine, we became the same as every other couple sitting in the restaurant. I don't know why that troubled me, but something about it did and I felt myself pull back a little.

"You okay?"

I nodded, picking out the most familiar looking roll I could find from the breadbasket.

"What's this thing about not wanting kids?" he asked, kicking my foot softly under the table as if we had some kind of inside joke.

I took a bite of the bread. It was brown with pieces of oatmeal stuck to the sides but there was a sweetness about it that I liked. "It's not something I want."

He shook his head. "Serious?"

I nodded, still chewing. "Yes."

He smiled. "It's what makes you a family. It's what makes everything," he hesitated before finishing, "perfect."

Our meals arrived with a flourish, looking more like artwork than food. He smiled at me as he cut into the duck. "I promise, Sam, you will love being a mother."

And then he winked.

I pushed the chicken around on my plate. It was too fancy for my taste. I'm not sure if he noticed, because I had become good at repositioning my food to make it look like I had eaten more than I had. Besides, I was just killing time until the dessert menu arrived, which is what I focused on so that I could forget the conversation we had just had. I didn't want to have a child, had never wanted to have a child, and to be honest, the idea of it terrified me. I told myself it was not something I needed to worry about since we hadn't even talked about marriage or even living together. Anyway, it was much easier to think about the dessert menu, but when it came, I must have spent too much time looking because finally Sol cleared his throat. "You aren't happy."

"No, it's fine."

There was brie and blueberries, quince berry jam and pumpernickel cake, and lemon-filled raviolis with currants. The rest of the choices I couldn't even pronounce. Finally, I found something called peaches and cream that at least sounded familiar. I pointed to it when the waiter came and hated that I suddenly felt like a tourist in a foreign country.

What arrived were stewed peaches sitting atop thick, whipped, unsweetened yogurt sprinkled with basil. I forced myself to eat every single bite. Sol sipped his coffee, smiling at me.

"I love you," he said.

On the way back to the hotel, Sol kept his hands in his pockets and I linked my arm through his. He hesitated as we neared the hotel, as if there was something he wanted to say or something for which he was searching, or maybe it was just my imagination because as we got closer, he said nothing. The teenage boy who had helped us with our luggage saw us coming and quickly stamped out the cigarette he was smoking. The fumes lifted through the air and seeped inside the hotel lobby and I couldn't help but cough, and then all I wanted to do was get inside the room and lie down.

I must have fallen asleep, and when I woke Sol was asleep, too, with his arm around me. I woke a second time, but this time Sol was gone, and I called out his name, once—twice, maybe even a third time—in that frightened way a child calls out in the night when she wakes up disorientated and alone. That's when I saw him, sitting at the foot of the bed, head in his hands, crying.

I crawled through the sheets to reach him. "What is it? What's wrong?"

He shook his head and wiped the tears with the back of his hand. "I'm sorry, Sam. I meant for this to be perfect. I really did."

"What are you talking about?"

"I went to see your father last week."

"Why?"

"I went to ask for your hand in marriage. Because that is what you're supposed to do, right? That is the right thing to do."

The words sifted through me and were then replaced by pictures. Mostly of Brian, probably covered in smears of paint, listening to Sol bare his soul. I wondered if my mother was there, too, but I couldn't bring myself to ask.

"What happened?"

Sol shrugged. "I promised him that I would be good to you. I told him that I love you and I want to be with you. Forever."

He walked over and stuck his hand into the pocket of the shorts he had been wearing most of the day. "I've been trying to find the perfect time to give you this." He knelt and opened a velvet box, and inside was an emerald-shaped diamond that looked like it belonged on the hand of a queen. "Samidontknowwhatyourrealnameis, will you marry me?"

I felt the breath suck out of me. My heart may have stopped; and, suddenly, it felt as though things were happening without my having any say. He took it out of the box. "This belonged to my mother. It is very special to me. And I know she would have wanted you to have it."

The ring was elegant and stylish and looked like something a woman of high nobility would wear. It was also clearly two sizes too big and slid up and down my finger like a yo-yo.

"I promise our lives will be perfect," he said.

Had I even said yes? I wasn't sure. But he was holding my hand to his face, kissing it, and all I could think about was whether these were the very same words the last Mrs. Green who wore this ring had heard.

Chapter 19

A few days after we returned from our weekend away, my cell phone rang.

"Sam, it's Lucille," my mother's coworker said, like she called me every day, which she didn't.

"Is everything okay?" The pitch in her voice had lifted to a place where I knew that it probably wasn't.

"I was wondering if you'd heard from Mom? She hasn't been to work in a few days."

The slow cadence of her speech made it sound like she was talking to an eight-year-old.

"I'm sure she's fine. Just probably needed some time off."

"I thought I'd let you know just in case."

I hung up after reassuring her a second time that all was okay and promising to check in on my mother, even though we both knew the possibility of her taking time off was very unlikely.

My mother never took vacations because she believed there was always someone looking for a house and a truly committed realtor couldn't waste her time lounging on a beach chair or sitting around a golf course when there was work to be done. I wondered if Sol's conversation with Brian was what was behind her disappearance from work.

That Saturday morning, I went for a walk mostly to clear my head. I started off on the streets of my neighborhood hoping to find quiet. It was still early, and all the shops were closed and there weren't many people around except for some dogwalkers and a few middle-aged women jogging in tight Lycra tops and shorts. I tried not to think and instead just focus on my steps. I took one and then another, hoping to fall into the rhythm that happens when the only thing left for your body to do is move, but the pavement was buckled, and after tripping twice I decided to head to Daphne Lake.

It had been a long time since I had walked there, mostly because Sol liked to drive in the mornings so that is what we did. I dodged a few more joggers but finally arrived at a part of the path that seemed peaceful. I took deep breaths in through my nose, but that only made me feel dizzy. I tried to appreciate the leaves above me that looked as though their tips had been dipped into pots of yellow and red paints, but lost interest when a woman with short cropped gray hair and muscular legs ran past. I could hear the huff of her breath each time her sneakers hit the ground and could see the film of sweat that glistened across her shoulder blades. Her determination distracted me from my attempt at getting lost inside myself, so I just gave up and went to where I knew I would end all along.

On my way, I stopped at my favorite bakery to pick up muffins. The old women who worked there were from some eastern European country and always seemed angry. They grunted at the customers, but I didn't mind that at all. In fact, I liked turning to the person behind me and rolling my eyes, as if somehow, we all belonged to the same club. On this morning, there weren't many people in the shop, so she barked at me and me alone. I think she said something about being too skinny as she threw an extra cookie into my bag.

I picked at a raspberry muffin that had pockets of sweet fruit dotted throughout and tried not to think about where I was going. I wasn't sure why it was exactly I was bringing them to her. Maybe as a peace offering or maybe as something to talk about in case we ran out of things to say. "Aren't they delicious?" I pictured myself asking just the way my mother often would when she was watching me try some new dessert she had made. It was the perfect thing to talk about when you didn't really want to talk at all.

As it turned out, I didn't need to worry very much about making conversation. When I arrived and peeked through the window, I saw that she was asleep on the couch. The door was locked, but I knew that she hid a key under a flowerpot on the porch and used it to let myself in.

She was making loud, guttural snorts sprinkled with short snaps of silence. Her arm was stretched out in an unnatural-looking way, but she was still holding the remote control. There was a bottle of Jack Daniel's whiskey on the table, and its pretty amber color reminded me of maple syrup. I cleared my throat and she stirred for a minute, the remote slipping from her hand and landing softly onto the carpet.

I had only seen her this way once before, when I was sixteen and she and Brian had gotten into the fight that resulted in her throwing him out. She drank for three days straight afterward, but I never saw her drink anything stronger than wine after that.

Until now.

I touched her shoulder but she didn't wake. Her hair was matted and wild, and when I looked closely, I could see that her roots needed to be retouched. Her mouth was open. She was drooling. I touched her shoulder again. "Mom."

She opened her eyes first slowly and then big, as though she couldn't believe I was sitting beside her.

"Salmon. Why are you here? Are you hungry?" She tried to sit up, but then she winced and rubbed her forehead with her thumb and forefinger slowly back and forth.

I pushed the bag of muffins toward her, which she clumsily pushed back.

"Lucille called me because she was worried."

My mother swung her legs down onto the floor and laid her head back. "She's a drama queen."

"You're okay?" I sat on the arm of the couch, curling the top of the muffin bag opened and closed.

"I'm great." She poured more whiskey into her glass.

When Susan's mother drank, I could sense her sadness, but all I felt with my mother was anger, like with any misstep I would ignite a firestorm.

"This is what it has come to." She took three large gulps of her drink.

"I don't know what you mean."

She put the glass down on the table and some of what was inside splashed out.

"Yes, you do, Sam. You're selling out. Giving up. Giving in." She slurred her words so that they bounced in a funny way off her tongue and made her sound like she was from the south.

"That isn't what I'm doing." Why was I whispering?

"Yes, it is. You are smart. You can have a profession. You can live without ever needing a man."

I shook my head. "I don't need him, Mom."

"Then why?" As she stood, she shifted right and then left, trying to find her balance. She came toward me, bringing her face so close I could smell the Jack Daniel's on her breath. "Are you pregnant? Did he knock you up?"

The way she said it, like we were teenagers fooling around in the back seat of his car, made me smile.

"Is that it, Sam? Because you know these days it doesn't matter. We can get rid of it or you can have it on your own. You can still go to law school. I will help you. Whatever you decide, I will help you. I will raise it myself for chrissakes. But it doesn't mean you must get married and give up everything. Everything we have worked for."

"I'm not pregnant, Mom."

I'm not sure that she believed me, because she stared at me a few minutes longer, as if by doing so she could see inside me.

"Then what is it?"

I shrugged. "I love him."

"Love him all you want. But you don't have to marry him. You don't have to give up everything for him." More of the southern twang I had never heard before.

She used the arm of the couch to steady herself. "First that art shit and now this silly boy. I thought you were smarter than this. I thought I'd raised you better than this."

I didn't know how to explain about feeling so invisible and overlooked that part of me believed that if I disappeared into thin air no one would ever notice. I had gone through my life as a passenger in a train, irrelevant and unnecessary. I didn't know how to tell her that when I was with Sol, he made me feel special and accounted for. He made me feel like I was important.

All because I was with him.

I hated that even though no one before in my life made me feel the way that he did, she could still make me doubt myself, so I didn't even try to stop what came next. "At least I won't be alone for the rest of my life. Like you."

She hesitated for a minute, maybe because she was hurt or maybe just surprised. She stared at me so long and so intensely that finally I had to turn away. "You have nothing to worry about, Salmon. You will never be anything like me."

Suddenly I was the one who had become unsure of my footing, as if a wave was about to come crashing through the window and sweep me away.

She walked to the door and held it open. "Get out."

I left the bag of muffins on the coffee table.

She turned her head so that she was looking away, looking straight at the drawing I had made of daisies when I was eight that had been hanging on every kitchen wall we had ever had since the very first day I made it.

Even though she had stopped speaking, I could feel her pulling me toward her like a nail to a magnet. I hated that I was wavering, that I was always so weak. I hated that she could make me question myself. For a minute, I wondered if all it would have taken was a few more words and she would have won, and I would have been standing by her side like I always did.

Like a trophy.

But she said nothing.

"I am going to marry him." It came out like a surprise, like a balloon that pops without warning. I felt a burst of energy that started in my chest and rushed past my lips, which suddenly made marrying Sol the most important thing I could ever do, because when I was with him I was memorable and significant and valid.

As long as I had Sol, I mattered.

The door made a rusty creaking sound as she pushed it open even more.

I walked past her, inhaling a mixture of sweat and booze. I had never done anything without her approval, and it took a few minutes to get my bearings. Even though I told myself not to, I turned to look back, but she had already closed the door and gone back inside.

I didn't tell Sol about my confrontation with my mother.

Instead, I let myself get swept away in his excitement, mostly because it was like a whirlwind that distracted me from the hurt sitting just beneath. Sol had immediately taken the ring to be sized, and the first day I wore it to work, Anne Marie fawned over me. It was still a little too big, so I slipped it off and put it in my desk drawer after lunch, but she immediately noticed and made me put it back on. She thought I should be proud and show it off to the entire world.

She started bringing bridal magazines to work, ripping pages of dresses and headpieces and collecting them in a binder that she labeled Sam and Sol and decorated with little red hearts. She and Jimmy had gotten married at the Holiday Inn down the street and she was excited to show me pictures. Her bridesmaids wore dresses the color of pink frosting, and Jimmy was dressed in a white tuxedo with a cummerbund that matched. She proudly pointed to a photo of the sign in front of the hotel that had both their names up in lights wishing them luck in their new life. I wondered if she saw the irony in showing off her wedding pictures while the man that she let pull up her skirt in the copy room darted between us, grunting orders like an angry dog. Things between the two of them had cooled, but he did not like it that her attention was now diverted, and he certainly did not like the glaze that came over her when she reminisced about her wedding day.

"Get back to work!" he shouted as he snapped his fingers in her face. She would slap them away and then he would smile. Whatever it was that was going on between them confused me and I preferred to stay out of it.

"Have you thought about the ceremony?" she asked as she flipped through a magazine while Randy sat in his office, sulking with the door open so that we could see.

The truth was that Sol and I had not discussed the ceremony. In fact, we had not discussed very much of anything. We just went about our everyday lives understanding that a decision had been made and smiled at each other a lot. During the day, I was good at being brave about my mother's anger, but the truth was that at night it became more difficult. I found myself walking the rooms of my apartment long after Susan was asleep. I could feel the anxiety pulsing through me, and I got into the habit of washing my hands until my skin cracked.

Sol must have noticed because he bought me a tub of hand cream. "I'm sure it's just from the dry weather," he said.

I nodded, rubbing a scoop of lotion into my hands and then another and a third when he wasn't looking.

Brian called once or twice but only during the day when he knew I was at work. His voice sounded broken as if he was reading from a crumpled piece of paper. I never called him back mostly because I knew he didn't want me to. I knew that no matter what he said, he still belonged to her.

One morning, when we were driving, Sol asked me where I wanted to live. I don't know why the question took me by surprise.

"I was thinking you can move in with me after we get married and then we can save money and start looking for a place of our own."

The idea of living where his mother had flawlessly arranged the furniture and created the perfect slice of banana cream pie terrified me. I said nothing, but I could feel myself wringing my hands even though there was no soap and water.

Days and then weeks passed, and Anne Marie became even more excited. I had never seen so many variations of pink, and every time I thought there couldn't be, another would appear. She cut pictures of flowers, tablecloths, boutonnieres, champagne glasses, and balloons and pasted them inside the binder. Her taste in dresses leaned toward those so outlandishly poufy they looked like antebellum ball gowns, and after a while I stopped giving my opinion and just nodded my head, which seemed to satisfy her. She insisted that I needed to decide where to register. Blenders, sheets, punch bowls, and silverware began making their appearances and I watched as the binder grew even thicker.

One afternoon I needed to take a break from it all, so I decided to take a walk. Anne Marie had her head buried in a magazine and waved me off without even looking up. It felt good to be outside, and instead of getting lost in the crowd like I usually did, I took a different direction and ended up in front of a store I hadn't been inside before—a thrift shop with its name, Pandora's Box, written in stylized gold script above the door.

The woman who worked there smiled when I walked in, and I noticed she was wearing two different-colored shoes. Clothing was displayed on glamorous looking mannequins, one of whom had her eye covered with the kind of eye patch a pirate would wear. Her head was turned over her shoulder, which made her look even more mysterious. I started at the rack closest to her and began flipping through dresses. I found it stuffed between a black sequined cocktail dress and a purple floor-length prom gown.

The dress I would wear to become Sol Green's wife.

It was sleeveless and short with a creamy white bodice and vanilla-colored beads sewn around the neckline. It was so perfect that I didn't even try it on because I could not bear the possibility that it might not fit. The clerk with the different-colored shoes wrapped it in tissue paper, but when she started telling me about the woman who brought it in for resale, I quickly changed the subject. This was my dress and I didn't want to know anything about the person who wore it before.

I don't know why, but I didn't want Anne Marie to know, so I slipped the bag inside the janitor's closet when I got back to work.

"Have a good walk?"

I nodded.

"Look what I found. It's perfect!" She held up a picture of a dress that looked like an enormous cotton ball. I nodded again.

"I knew you'd love it."

It took three days before I could get back to the closet because Anne Marie kept leaving for the day when I did. On the fourth day, she stayed late, and when she and Randy snuck into his office, I was able to retrieve the bag without either of them noticing. When I got home, I carefully unfolded it and tried it on. It fit awkwardly across my chest, and my bra straps slid down over my shoulders like the handles of a pocketbook.

There was a soft knock at the door, and Susan came in, looking me up and down.

"Take off your bra."

"What?"

She unzipped the back and tugged at the hooks while I slipped my arms through. She left the room, and when she came back she had something in her hand.

"What's this?"

"A bustier."

She must have seen the look on my face.

"Trust me."

I adjusted myself into it and she helped me close it up in the back.

"Let me see."

I turned to her.

"Better."

I looked at myself in the mirror. My breasts were lifted and perfectly shaped and my waist was pinched. She took my hair out of the ponytail and braided it onto one side so that only a few strands fell onto the other.

"Perfect."

And it was.

My hair swept over to one side of my face made it look soft and light.

I turned to thank her, but she was gone. That night I didn't walk through the apartment and I didn't wash my hands. I hung the dress in the closet and stared at it for hours, rubbing my fingers through the folds of milk-colored silk. At 4 a.m., I took it off its hanger and slipped it back on. I stood in front of the mirror, turning my head over my shoulder like the mannequin in the shop. I loved its creaminess and the way the small-embroidered beads sparkled so delicately. I arched my neck and slowly lifted my arms, feeling graceful enough to soar, and then I closed my eyes, imagining what it must be like to be a beautiful white bird.

Chapter 20

We got married at Daphne Lake beneath the weeping willow tree.

Its leaves had begun to turn yellow, which matched the color of the late afternoon sun. I wore the dress I had found in the thrift shop with a silk shawl draped around my shoulders and a simple veil that Susan made for me. She was my maid of honor and stood solemnly beside me, adjusting it anytime a breeze pushed it into my eyes.

I invited both Randy and Anne Marie, but only Anne Marie and Jimmy came. He seemed uncomfortable in his suit, which fit him as snugly as the pictures I had seen of him in his white tuxedo. He kept handing her tissues, which she used to dab at her eyes.

There were several other guests, mostly Sol's family and friends, all standing behind us. His father stood next to him, leaning so heavily onto his cane that I thought he might tip over. I hated myself for doing it, but I turned back a few times to see if, at the last minute, she would give in. If my mother would show up beautifully dressed with her hair pulled back and smiling like nothing between us had happened. Birds chirped as if in preparation for her entrance.

But she never came.

After a few minutes, I stopped looking, and instead turned my attention to the man I was about to marry. When he smiled, I realized he had been speaking to me. I nodded even though I wasn't completely certain what it was I was being asked. I took his hand, which felt warm and clammy. I noticed the sun had gone behind a cloud and that it had stopped being warm and now there was a cool breeze. I tried to focus on what the Justice of the Peace was saying, but his words just swam through my head, and all I could think about was the way in which the branches of the weeping willow moved and that my face felt damp because it had begun to drizzle.

"I do," Sol said.

More words, more drizzle, and then I said it too.

Everyone clapped, and Sol turned to kiss me. He put his arms around my waist, pulling me in close, and I thought he whispered something in my ear but I couldn't hear if it was "I love you" or maybe it was "Don't leave me."

We turned toward the small, clapping crowd, and that's when I saw him standing in the back, smiling.

I made my way over and he hugged me. "Fisshhhh," he said, kissing me on the forehead.

"I'm glad you came."

I wondered what it must have cost him. His goatee was trimmed, and he wore a white shirt underneath a chocolate-colored wool jacket and I noticed some of the women eyeing him.

"You look beautiful," he smiled.

I could feel Sol come up behind me.

"Congratulations," Brian said. Sol nodded.

"We're having a thing at Sol's dad's. If you want to come." I felt Sol stiffen.

Brian shook his head. "That's okay. I just came to see you."

Sol wandered away.

"I wanted to give you this. It's from her." He handed me an envelope. I didn't need to open it to know what was inside. I could feel the outline with my fingertips. A key.

"Even though she doesn't approve. She wants you to have it."

Someone with more self-respect would have handed it right back, but I slipped it carefully into the little white purse I was carrying.

And then I thanked him.

"Enjoy your new life, Fish. I'm so happy that you know who you are and what you want." He kissed my hand and then blew on it as if making a wish.

I wanted to talk more, to convince him to stay a little bit longer, but Sol grabbed my arm and took me to meet more of his family. When I turned around again, Brian was gone.

Sol smiled the whole ride back to his father's house.

"We are going to be so happy," he promised.

Cars were parked up and down the street, and people were sitting on the front steps when we arrived.

"Congratulations!" they shouted. Sol beamed and lifted my arm up as if we had won a boxing match.

Inside, Sol's father was positioned on the couch and overweight middle-aged women were bringing him food from catering trays that lined both the dining room table and the kitchen counters. He motioned for me to sit beside him and I did.

"Sol's mother was the most beautiful woman I have ever seen."

Someone handed him a plate with half a corned beef sandwich and a pile of coleslaw. He took a bite and bright yellow mustard dripped down his chin.

"My parents were teachers. But then that no good McCarthy happened and anyone with a brain lost their job. That's when they bought the dairy farm."

A woman brought him a napkin, which he used to wipe it away.

"Rachel's family owned a jewelry store in the city and Rachel worked at the counter. One day I came in to get my watch fixed and I couldn't take my eyes off her."

He stopped speaking to take a few gulps from his mug. I waited to hear what happened next, as if he was telling me a fairy tale.

"I married her three months later. I bought the ring from her father. He told me it was a perfect ring and the woman that wears it will be perfect, too."

Henry Green turned to me. "And he was right."

I nodded and nervously slid the ring over the bump of my knuckle.

"Take good care of Sol just like his mother took care of me and you will have a good life."

I looked around the room; at the pictures placed at just the right eye level and the furniture so well cared for that even though it was outdated, it looked like it could withstand another ten years. It all seemed incredibly right, yet I felt a sadness so profound I had to turn away from Mr. Henry Green so that he wouldn't see the tears dripping down my face and landing in the lap of my secondhand thrift shop wedding dress.

We stayed for a few more hours, waiting for the last few guests to leave. Susan helped with some of the dishes and then got a ride home with one of Sol's cousins, who winked at Sol before he left. The middle-aged ladies covered what they could in tinfoil and stowed the leftovers away in the refrigerator. I had long ago taken off my shoes and was sitting on the couch with my legs tucked under me when Sol walked in.

"Ready?"

"For what?"

"Did you think we were going to spend our first night as a married couple in my childhood bed?"

To be honest, I wasn't sure what the plans were, but I had packed an overnight bag just in case. Sol got our things and the ladies sent us off with bags of cookies, whispering and giggling as if they knew a secret we didn't. Suddenly, I missed my mother so much it caught my breath.

"I know what you're thinking," he said as he threw our bags into the back seat of the car.

"You do?"

"You are thinking that you couldn't imagine being any happier than you are at this very moment."

I smiled.

"See how well I know you?"

We drove for about half an hour and then he pulled into the driveway of a hotel that was nicer than any other he had ever taken me to. He told the woman at the front desk that we were Mr. and Mrs. Sol Green and then he squeezed my hand.

We took the elevator to the fourth floor. The room had a large four-poster canopy bed and there was a bottle of champagne sitting on the table. I went into the bathroom to change. I had bought a pretty pink nightgown, but when

I put it on and turned a certain way in the light, I realized it was see-through. There was not much else I could do so I came out anyway. I crossed my arms over my chest while Sol poured us both a glass of champagne.

"To us," he said, swallowing it all down in one gulp.

He led me to one of the posts of the bed and had me lean against it, and when I went to cover myself with my hands, he pulled them down. He took out his camera and began snapping pictures, the sound of the click buzzing in my ear. He unbraided my hair and shook it out and I closed my eyes and let him have his way. I felt him zoom in and out, the sound of the closing shutter changing depending on how close he stood. I could feel him breathing within inches of me. He slipped one of the straps of my nightgown over my shoulder and gently kissed my neck. He touched me so softly that when he went to slip off the other strap, I didn't stop him. Every time I tried to cover myself, he pushed my hand away until finally I just gave up and let the nightgown slip down around my ankles. I kept my eyes closed while he took pictures and kept them that way until he was finished.

"Why is it, Mrs. Green, that you always seem so sad?"

He kissed me and then he pushed me onto the bed, his face on my skin, smelling me, licking me, sucking me. He ran his fingers slowly across my naked body, as though now that I was his, he could explore every part of me. I lay down with my hair splayed across the pillowcase and stared up at the canopy of the bed like a medieval princess. I didn't move or speak; I just kept looking up the entire time that he consumed me.

After he was done, he fell asleep with his head on my chest. He was snoring quietly, but I didn't sleep much that night. Even though it was hard to breathe with his head on me, I lay perfectly still with the weight of him pushing me down.

When he woke in the morning, he cradled my face like I was a doll.

"I love you so much," he said.

I got up to use the bathroom, and when I came back in, he was on the telephone. "Room service," he mouthed. I listened as he ordered for us both.

After we ate, we sat on the edge of the bed.

"I have something for you."

When we got married, I asked the Justice of the Peace to call me Sam so Sol still didn't know my real name. I stayed up very late the night before the wedding so that I could finish the collage. It took me a long time to figure out a way to re-create the sensation of flight and I was excited when it finally made sense. I used the Coke bottle I saved from the diner Sol had taken me to. I smashed it into shards with a hammer and then glued on the sprinkled pieces. It was not until I was almost finished that I realized I had cut myself and drops of my blood mixed in between the pieces of glass. I hoped that once they dried, they would become unnoticeable and that only I would know they were there. I wrapped the whole thing in newspaper and tied it with ribbon.

I watched as he tore through the paper and then looked at it. "Thanks, Sam." I had been so consumed with being with him, I rarely had time to work on my art, but he knew that I made collages and this was the first one I had made for him.

"It's really pretty."

I waited, but he didn't say anything more, and I knew the reason was because he didn't understand about the way the glass sparkled or about how you could see through it or that if you squinted just the right way, you could imagine yourself flying through the air.

He didn't understand about freedom.

I told myself it didn't matter.

"There's more." I pointed to the lower left-hand corner where I had carefully printed my new name. "Salmon Green."

He smiled.

"Salmon."

I nodded.

He said it again, stretching the parts out slowly like he was pulling on a piece of saltwater taffy.

An awkward layer of silence settled around us, and all I could think to do was start talking so I launched into my script. "My mother told me she named me Salmon so that I would always know my way home. Brian told me that he liked it because it reminded him of mermaids." He was looking at me in that funny way that some people do when they hear my name for the first time and I tried to push away my doubts.

My disappointment.

Sol leaned the collage against the side of the bed. "It's cute. We can be Sol and Sal."

I didn't respond.

"C'mon, Sam, I'm just kidding."

I shrugged and then turned away; I couldn't help the tears that began to fall. Suddenly, he leapt across the bed, sat on top of me, and tickled my armpits. Deep intense squeezing that produced cries of joy that mixed with pain until I could not distinguish between the two. He tickled me so long and hard that I was panting and begging him to stop. I had crossed over to the place where it just simply hurt.

"Please don't be sad, Sam."

He hugged me tight, running his fingers through my hair, kissing me. He put his face to mine and it felt wet, but I couldn't tell which one of us was crying. He said it again and this time I could hear in his voice.

That he was pleading with me.

Chapter 21

We moved into the little white house a few days after the wedding.

It was easier convincing Sol than I thought. He was making breakfast because I still wasn't comfortable doing anything in his mother's kitchen. I waited until he was sipping his coffee before I showed him the key, which I had placed in tissue paper like a delicate piece of jewelry. He unwrapped it, turned it over in his hands a few times, and then slipped it onto his key ring. I thought his pride might stand in the way, but it didn't. He told me that she owed us. Afterward, we went to tell his father and Henry handed him an old, beat-up tool chest and told him to get on with his life.

And that was the last time we talked about it.

I didn't have very many things so the move wasn't difficult. Susan helped me pack and then sat on the edge of my bed smoking a cigarette. "I can't believe you're married."

"I'm sure you will be next." I was rolling some shirts so I could fit them into a duffel bag.

"What's it like?" She took a long, exaggerated drag.

I shrugged and bent down to look under the bed and she grew quiet.

"I can still help out with your mom sometimes if you need."

She stubbed out her cigarette and the last wisps of smoke curled up into the air. "That's okay. You have better things to do now."

"I don't mind."

She shrugged. "You can keep this," she said as she ran her fingertips along the wooden top of the art desk she had loaned me. "Consider it my wedding present."

"That's so sweet of you, Susan."

She smiled and then she was gone, and I wondered if maybe she wasn't that bad after all.

Sol promised that with hard work, he could make the house perfect. I wandered through the rooms, imagining who had lived there before and whether they moved out for happy or sad reasons. I looked outside at the empty window boxes filled with dried brown leaves and cobwebs and thought about my mother. I couldn't help but think about what she had been like as a little girl or imagine her running through the rooms of a house like this one. I couldn't help that I missed her terribly.

Sol and I went to the hardware store and I let him pick out paint colors only disagreeing with him once when he tried to convince me to paint the bathroom mustard yellow. We settled on a lighter shade instead, and afterward I just let him make the rest of the decisions because it seemed so important to him.

He worked at the ice cream shop during the day and on the house at night. He came home, changed his clothes, and spent hours chiseling old paint and stripping wallpaper and then he would crawl into bed too exhausted to shower. He put his arms around me, pulling me into him, and I could feel his sweat seep through my nightgown.

Weeknights and weekends passed, and he was more determined than ever to make good on his promise, which is why I didn't have the heart to tell him that despite all his hard work, there was one thing he would never be able to fix. I tried to pretend that it didn't bother me but no matter what I did, I could not ignore the fact that everything from the tip of the roof to the grade of the cellar floor was unequivocally and undeniably crooked.

The toilet seat was always askew, and there was a swoop along the kitchen floor that was so uneven you could slide across it in your socks. The carpet we laid down on the living room floor never lined up with the baseboards and the cupboard doors in the kitchen hung so unevenly they looked like crooked teeth. It was like living on a boat that shifted from one side to the other, never finding its equilibrium. Sol didn't seem to notice or care and just went along happily changing into his paint clothes, slipping a pale blue surgical mask over his mouth, and humming to the songs coming out an old radio he found in the garage. But I couldn't help feeling the shakiness, the instability that surrounded me.

I thought it might help if I could work on my collages. The house had two bedrooms, but when I suggested that I use one of them as an art room, Sol just smiled. He put his arms around my waist so that his hands rested on my belly and whispered in my ear. "Sammy, that's going to be our baby's room." Something small and angry began to grow inside of me, but I pushed it away because I had given up so much, and more than anything I needed it to work between Sol and me. I told myself that the right time would come to one day tell him about Rome and the mosaics and I didn't say anything more when he moved my magazines and my art desk into the garage, which was unheated and filled with unopened boxes. I didn't say anything because there was just too much to lose.

Every night, we had sandwiches for dinner because they were quick and simple and Sol could get to work right afterward. White bread for me, brown for him, and mostly just peanut butter and jelly in between. He was so focused on the house that he didn't seem to even taste what I put down in front of him. One evening, when I was sitting on the couch watching television, Sol came out of the bathroom covered in white powder from scraping through plaster. He went outside to shake himself off and returned with two cardboard boxes from inside the garage. The tops were weaved closed and then sealed with packing tape so he got a box cutter and sliced them open. Inside were magazine and newspaper clippings.

"My mother's." He pushed the boxes toward me. "She collected them. Sometimes she'd try them out. Sometimes she didn't. Many of them ended up in these books."

At the bottom of the boxes were photo albums with plastic sheeting covering each page. Rachel had spent hours cutting out her favorite recipes and then organizing them into books. The corners of the pages were yellowed with age, and even though I could see she must have spent years putting them together, there were still recipes that she hadn't yet sorted through.

"I thought maybe you could go through these. Maybe even try making some."

I hadn't noticed the sound of crickets before, but now it was as if their chirping was coming from inside the house, marking each second as it passed. How could I say that I wasn't interested in going through his estranged mother's things? How could I even hint at it? He acted as though it didn't really matter, but I saw that he watched as I carried the boxes to the dining table and began leafing through his mother's prized possessions. He didn't say anything, just stood quietly in the middle of the room, and when I glanced back up, he was gone.

The recipes were cut with perfect precision.

Some she chose from magazines, others from newspapers, and there were even some from actual books. I knew so little about her, and now I had a box filled with the things that she loved most. I tried to find a pattern to her taste, to see if she preferred appetizers or main courses or desserts, but because she had enough recipes to fill up every single category, I learned nothing. Her choices were random and generic; it almost seemed that she was more interested in arranging them on the page than she was in the food. The recipes all came with photos, some directly from magazines and others taken with a camera.

I immediately recognized Sol's photographic style of hovering high above what he was shooting. The images came out looking like they were taken through a kaleidoscope. There was one of a pecan pie with nuts around the edge, which looked like a flower in bloom, like it was made from mosaic tiles. Rachel had written the year on the back of the photo so I knew that Sol was only ten when he took it. I needed to find him, to talk to him. I needed to know how, at such a young age, he already knew how to make something so simple appear so beautiful.

I went to see if he was in the bathroom, but it was empty and the lights were off. I found him in the bedroom sprawled out on the bed and realized how late it was. He had fallen asleep with his arm stretched out. I took off my clothes, and instead of putting on my nightgown, I stood at the foot of the bed, naked. When I slipped in beside him, he woke and wrapped his arms around me. He buried his face into my hair and then pulled me into him so that I could feel the rising of his chest. I matched my breathing to his and we moved up and down that way, slowly and rhythmically, until we disappeared inside the safety of each other's dreams.

After a few days of begging, I finally convinced Sol to take a day off and we bought tickets to the circus. When I was little and the circus came to town, it was always Brian who took me because my mother said that it was dirty and that the animals smelled. For lunch, Brian bought me candy and popcorn and made me promise not to tell my mother. I still remember licking salt and chocolate off my fingertips. Afterward, he would buy me a spinning toy that lit up, and when the lights went down, I would lift it up into the air and when I looked around, it was as if a thousand fireworks were going off at the same time.

Brian liked the tightrope walkers best. He told me it was because they were both delicate and powerful all at the same time, and I remember thinking that I really didn't understand what he meant. After a visit to the circus, his paintings would fill with the red and white and yellow strokes of the carnival tent.

I loved the animals most, but as I got older, I hated myself for loving them. I clapped my hands when the tigers leaped into the air or when the elephants stood on each other's backs but then I cringed each time the ringmaster cracked his whip because I knew it was his way of reminding them that they belonged to him.

That he controlled them.

So, I turned my attention to the acrobats. I became mesmerized by the way they twisted and turned and by how effortlessly they danced in the air. Some would hook their braids onto ropes and spin through the darkness like a modern-day Rapunzel. I pretended that they could really fly and imagined that one would suddenly break free from her trapeze and glide effortlessly past the lights and the noise and grab me from my seat and together we would soar above the audience, like two beautiful birds.

Sol came back from the concession stand with two hot dogs and a bag of chips for us to share. I stared at the little boy in front of me who was spilling kernels of yellow popcorn onto the floor but got distracted when Sol handed me a bottle of hand sanitizer.

The lights came down and energy surged around us like it was alive. The people seated next to us began stomping their feet as the ringmaster lifted the megaphone to his mouth and welcomed children of all ages. Music played and a small car came out onto the stage, and when the door opened, clowns began to spill out. They jumped through hoops and blew terrible sounding music from trumpets and pulled rainbow colored scarves from the tips of their shoes. The children around us clapped and laughed and pointed as the clowns piled back into the car and drove off, honking their horns in short, ear-piercing intervals.

Then, an enormous silver cage came out with eight beautiful tigers inside. The trainer used his whip to get their attention, and I jumped each time his switch hit the floor. His assistant brought out a steel ring, which she lit on fire, and again I heard the whip as he made each one jump through. Someone in the audience cheered, but I must have turned away because the next thing I knew, I was staring down at the floor, at the straw wrappers and M&M's and peanut shells scattered at my feet. There were a few more tricks, one of which elicited even more applause. When he finished, the tigers got back up on their stools and he threw chunks of meat at all except for the last one. He swung it in front of her, taunting her with it, but she sat frozen, stifling her instinct because that was what she had been trained to do. Finally, he tossed it to her and only when he gave her the sign that it was okay did she devour it. Afterward, he turned to the audience and bowed to thunderous applause. Sol clapped, too, but I didn't because I knew what it must have cost to get her to behave that way. I knew that the only way he could contain her power was by stealing her will.

The lights lowered, and I could feel the tears slipping down my cheeks. Motorcycle daredevils came out next and the zoom of racing motors vibrated throughout the stadium. I told Sol I had to use the bathroom, pushing past everyone in our row so I could pass. I found the ladies room, and when the woman in front of me let me cut her in line, I knew I must have looked awful. I sat in the stall and sobbed, the kind of crying that is so loud it makes you swallow your own snot. I rocked back and forth on the toilet seat thinking about that beautiful tiger and the humiliation she must have suffered and then I cried some more. When I came out, a female security officer asked if I was okay and I lied and told her I had gotten my period and gotten sick in the bathroom. She brought me a cup of ice and I wrapped a few cubes inside of a napkin and used it as an ice pack, like you do when something is broken. It was so cold it made me catch my breath, and suddenly there were people everywhere because intermission had started and then Sol was there asking if I was okay.

"Do you want to go home?" I could see the panic in his eyes.

I shook my head.

"Really, Sam, I think we should call it a day." He put his arm around my shoulders.

"I want to see the acrobats."

Ten minutes later, I was back in my seat, the napkin soggy from the ice that had since melted still pressed up against my face.

"You okay?"

I nodded. "Must have been something I ate."

He handed me a cup of ginger ale, which I hadn't even seen him buy. I took a sip and the lights went down and he held my hand as the acrobats came out to perform.

They were dressed in shiny white leotards, and when they moved, it looked like liquid ice. They danced on the ground before being lifted into the air. I shifted to the edge of my seat like I did when I was a little girl and believed that they could really fly. The next thing I knew, they were swinging back and forth, holding onto each other's arms, white dashes of light flying through the blackness. I held my breath because I was hoping, because I had never really stopped hoping that one of them would break free and come and sweep me away.

But in the end, they returned to the platform, like they always did, lifting their arms up into the air as everyone applauded.

That night, I went to bed before Sol because I didn't want to think anymore. I curled up and pulled the blanket over my head. I must have been exhausted; I didn't even remember falling asleep. When I woke, it was with a gasp that was sudden and off-putting and disorienting. Sol was kissing me in a way that he never had and it was still dark and I couldn't make out the time on the clock.

"What are you doing?"

"Shh," he whispered as he licked the patch of skin right above the crease of my elbow. The stubble on his face mixed with the softness of his lips both tickled and hurt. He held my arms above my head, and as I tried to wriggle out of his grasp, he held on tighter, using his tongue to move down my arm and then around the curve of my nipple. He kneaded it between his thumb and forefinger until it was hard and red and then he cupped the back of my head, kissing me so deeply I almost forgot to breathe. His hands moved quickly and with purpose, and before I realized it, he was on top of me easing open my legs.

Tonight, there was no camera and no candlelight. His breath in my ear was heavy and damp and he whispered things that I could not hear. He pushed himself inside of me, and the headboard made a soft thudding sound every time it hit the wall. When he stopped to bite the skin between my neck and shoulder, I could see that his face was glistening with sweat. If he experienced any pleasure at all, it was hard to tell since he didn't make a sound.

When he finished, he collapsed on top of me. "Sam." He was still inside of me, lying on my chest and running his finger through a tangled clump of my hair. "I think we just made a baby."

We hadn't.

And we didn't the next month or the month after that. What was worse was that we hadn't even had a conversation about having a baby. Sol simply stopped using condoms and the decision was made. I knew I should have spoken up, but I didn't know how to explain and I didn't think he would understand even if I could find the words.

When I was little, I never played with dolls or baby carriages. The only thing I ever wanted was a pet, which is what I wished for at every birthday, but my mother hated animals, hated the smell of them, and wouldn't even entertain the possibility of a dog or a cat. But still I begged, and somehow Brian convinced her to at least let me have a hamster. At the pet store, I chose the one huddled in a corner and separated from the others. I named him Fluffy, but my mother insisted that we keep his cage in the garage. Sometimes, I would put him inside a clear plastic ball and let him roam around, but he would always bang into the walls. I felt bad for him, so I set him free in the garage, and since my parents usually parked their cars in the driveway, he had the whole space to himself. He loved exploring and sniffing at the cobwebs and I loved watching him.

Until one day when everything changed.

I wasn't careful, vigilant enough, and the worst happened. I didn't realize there was a small opening at the side of the door where the wood frame had splintered, and before I knew it, before I could even understand what had happened, the neighbor's white cat was inside, and within seconds Fluffy was dangling from between his teeth.

I was frozen in fear, paralyzed. I must have found it in me to scream, because the next thing I knew my mother was there and without a second thought, she ripped that hamster right out of the cat's mouth. I don't remember much after that except that we rushed Fluffy to the vet, where he was stitched back together. Hamster fur eventually covered the incision, but in my mind, it was always there.

Reminding me of my recklessness.

Even months later, all I could think about was that he almost died and that I had done nothing to stop it. We never talked about it afterward, but I didn't let him go free again.

After that day, I knew two things:

One was that I would never let myself grow that attached to anyone or anything, and two, what happened was my fault and had it not been for my mother, Fluffy would be dead. In the face of fear, I was the one who froze, who hesitated, but she never faltered. Even though she hated animals, found them repulsive, she was the one who swooped in and rescued him from danger. In that moment, when he was about to be eaten alive, she was the one who saved him. As grateful as I was, it made it clear that I was not like her and that I could never be someone's mother.

Because I didn't have the instinct.

It was my truth, and even though it was something I discovered about myself at an early age, I knew it was indisputable because I felt it in every cell of my being. What I didn't know was how I would ever explain it to Sol. He would just dismiss it as the misguided musings of a six-year-old, or worse, see me as some terrible hamster-killing monster. So instead, I decided to take matters into my own hands and resolve the matter in secret. After some research online, I discovered you could use vitamin C to prevent pregnancy. I bought a bottle of pills at the health food store and filled the bowl on the kitchen table with oranges. Whenever I ate one, I tried not to touch the skin because I hated how the smell would permeate my hands afterward, the odor clinging to me no matter how often I washed, acting as a constant reminder of my betrayal.

The house was starting to shape up. The bathroom had sparkling white tile and a brand-new sink. Sol painted and rehung every single cabinet door in the kitchen, and even though they weren't perfectly straight, they looked better than they had originally. He kept his word about making it a nice home, a good home, and now it seemed he was ready to move on with even more enthusiasm to the next project on his list. One night, I found him sitting on the couch in the living room reading a book titled *The Perfect Pregnancy* with a half-peeled orange in his lap.

"When did your period start this month?"

I took the fruit away from him. "Excuse me?"

"I'm trying to figure out when you are ovulating."

I shrugged. "Don't remember."

"C'mon, Sam. Can you be a grown up for once?"

The segment of orange I had just bitten into had a seed and I walked over to the kitchen sink to spit it out. When I turned around, he was standing behind me. I hoped he hadn't seen the tears welling up in my eyes. I leaned against the kitchen counter. I hadn't realized he was still holding the book in his hand. He put it down on the table and slipped his hands around my waist and kissed me. I breathed in the taste of citrus on his lips.

"We've been going about this all wrong. I promise, Sam. I will fix it."

He was so earnest and sincere that I didn't say anything and he kissed me again, and I closed my eyes so that he wouldn't see my shame.

A calendar suddenly appeared on the bulletin board in our kitchen. Sol printed it off the computer and designated the best days for conception with yellow smiley-faced stickers, like the kind that teachers give out for doing well on a spelling test. He read somewhere that it was better to have intercourse in the middle of the day, so he got someone to cover his shift at the ice cream shop and made me rush home from work to meet him. There would be a sandwich waiting for me, but before I could even take a bite, he would push me into the bedroom and pull down my pants. What had once been slow and thoughtful was now rushed and frantic. He would lie on top of me, straining as if he was focusing on getting it right, like it was his fault that it wasn't working.

Which just made me feel worse.

Most of the time, I stared up at the ceiling waiting for him to finish. He told me it was important to stay tilted afterward so he stuffed pillows underneath my bottom to prop me up. Since I hadn't had a chance to eat my lunch, he offered to bring me tea, or cookies, or the rest of my sandwich, but I always asked for the same thing.

An orange.

Because I felt guilty, I made it up to him by letting him talk about the baby he dreamed we would one day have. Maybe that was cruel, but somehow it made me feel better. He told me he didn't care if we had a boy or a girl first. I coughed at the word *first*, but he didn't seem to notice. He talked about it during our meals or when we would take drives. He talked about it when he brushed his teeth at night, his wishes dripping with toothpaste and saliva. More than anything, I wanted to tell him the truth but I couldn't.

Because I knew I would lose him.

I needed a place to escape, but there was nowhere to go. My art desk sat in the cold garage, because even though Sol had promised, he had not gotten around to unpacking the boxes that surrounded it. Instead, I spent more time sorting through his mother's recipes. I sat in the kitchen, underneath the fluorescent lights, organizing them in the way I imagined she would. First in alphabetical order, then in the order of course, like how they would have been presented at a dinner party. I stared at them for hours, as if they held some secret message I wasn't smart enough to see.

One night while he was cooking dinner, following one of the recipes from the boxes, I decided to ask.

"Tell me about them."

He lifted a wooden spoon to his lips and blew on it. "Tell you about what?"

"Why she kept them, what they meant to her, and why they are cut so straight it looks as though the lines were made with a ruler."

He put the spoon back inside the pot and continued stirring. "I remember when I was little there were scraps of paper everywhere. Ripped from notebooks with jagged edges at the tops. They were spread all over the kitchen, in her purse, even in the silverware drawer."

"Recipes?"

He shook his head. "Poems. Scribbles mostly."

Something in the air changed, like when you find the missing piece of a puzzle underneath the box cover. He stopped what he was doing and turned to me. "Remember the moment we first met? You were standing beside me with that sketchbook clutched to your chest and you were so secretive about what was inside. You made me think of her."

So that was what drew him to me. That I reminded him of his mother.

"It was kind of dumb, actually. All her silly little scraps made such a mess, and I don't think my father liked it very much." He turned back toward the stove as one of the pots began to boil, making loud gulping noises that sounded as though someone was gasping for air.

"Then one day they were gone. Just like that. Disappeared like magic and I never saw them again."

He threw a box of pasta into the boiling water and I waited for him to finish talking.

"Then what happened?"

"I don't know, Sam. They were gone, and the next thing I knew, these recipes were in their place." He set a timer. "Doesn't your mother cook from recipes?"

I was taken aback. We hadn't discussed my mother since I had given him the key to our new house. "My mother takes things that someone else has made and then doctors them up and pretends they're hers."

Sol had bought the kitchen timer to match the walls, and it was simple and white and made a loud ticking noise that pierced the air.

"My mom followed these recipes meticulously. She never changed a step or a measurement or an ingredient and she never made a mistake. Her food tasted the same every time. It was always perfect."

"Like her," I whispered, but he didn't hear because he was draining the pasta into a colander. I stood beside him, breathing in the steam rising from the sink until it made me feel like I was suffocating.

The next morning, Sol woke up earlier than usual and talked me into going for a drive. As I slid into the passenger seat, he handed me a blanket. "Haven't had a chance to get the heating fixed. Sorry."

I wrapped the blanket around myself, but the coldness nipped at my toes and made them hurt.

"I'm out of ideas, Sam." There was frost on the glass, and I closed my eyes and pretended we were gliding on a crystal sheet of ice.

"Did you hear me?"

I pulled the blanket in closer.

"Nothing we are doing is working."

I turned the dial on the temperature control back and forth.

"I told you, Sam, it isn't working."

"Is it okay if I see for myself?"

"I don't mean about the heat. I mean, about the baby."

We drove in silence, and as the morning sun rose, it cast a white light across the sky.

"I think we should see a doctor." He turned away from the road and looked at me as he spoke.

I spun the control again slowly back and forth as if, somehow, I could coax it back to life. I knew he saw, but this time he didn't say anything. I laid the back of my hand against the air vent, hoping for the slightest puff of warmth.

He turned to me and smiled and then reached over and squeezed my knee. "Please, Sam. I promise you won't regret it."

The next thing I knew, we were pulling into the parking lot of the medical offices of Dr. Judith M. Goldman and Associates, and before I even had a chance to react, he jumped out of his seat and ran to the other side of the car to open the door. He held out his hand, as if he was escorting me to a royal ball, and I knew there was no way out and that I had to go.

Because it was a family practice, there was an old man and his wife sitting across from us, and a crying baby with his mother to our left. Sol knew the receptionist, who smiled when she saw him. I think she may have even asked about his father, but I was too busy working on the stack of paperwork she had given me to be sure. I couldn't remember what vaccines I'd had, if I'd ever had the measles or very much else about my medical history and, honestly, I was too angry to care. When I finished, I picked at the stuffing poking through a crack in the leather chair.

"Everything okay?" Sol asked.

"No, not really."

He smiled as if he hadn't heard what I said.

"Mr. and Mrs. Green?" Sol made small talk with the technician as she led us to the doctor's office. "The doctor will be right with you."

On her desk, there were four framed photos of a little boy and his dog. In the first two, he was playing in the snow, and in the others, he was at a lake, but in all he had his arms wrapped around the yellow-haired dog.

"Sol," she said as she opened the door to her office.

He stood and they shook hands. "This is my wife, Sam."

She looked down at the file she was carrying in her hand and then back at me. "Hello, Sam."

As she settled into her chair, I stared at the boy in the frame, who seemed to be smiling back at me.

"What brings you here?"

Sol looked at me as though he was silently asking if he could go first, and when I didn't respond, he reached over and held my hand. "I want to have a baby. I mean, me and Sam, we want to have a baby."

Dr. Goldman looked up from her notepad. "That's wonderful, Sol."

He smiled, encouraged. "We love each other very much and this would make everything between us perfect. But the thing is, Dr. Goldman, we've been trying so hard, and for so long, and nothing seems to be working, so I thought maybe you could help." He shifted in his chair, and I could sense his relief, as if he was finally able to unload his burden onto someone.

She clasped her hands in her lap. "How long have you been trying?"

"Six months."

She smiled. "Not long enough. You are both young and presumably healthy. If nothing happens in one year, then come back to see me."

Sol's shoulders sunk, and he looked like the wind had been knocked out of him.

"You don't understand. We need some help. This is really important." Even I could see he looked desperate, frantic.

She stared at him for a few minutes longer. "Why don't you let me talk to Sam for a few minutes. Privately."

He looked excited again, as if the school vacation he thought was canceled was back on. As he stood, he squeezed my shoulder and kissed me on the cheek and then closed the door behind him.

She pushed her chair away from the desk. "It's a pretty name. Why don't you use it?"

I shrugged. "It's easier to just be Sam."

She nodded, and I wondered if she really understood what it felt like to have to hide who you were from the rest of the world. I focused on the little boy captured in that perfect moment of love for his dog.

"I have treated Sol and his family for years. They are a good family."

She stood and walked toward me, sitting on the corner of the desk and blocking my view of the photos. "Is there something you want to talk with me about?"

I don't know why it happened, maybe it was the boy or the dog or the way she tilted her head when she asked me. But the next thing I knew, I was crying and talking about oranges and Fluffy while she emptied out her box of Kleenex, handing me one white square after the next.

"Salmon," I liked that it didn't sound silly when she said it. "You have to be honest with him. Tell him the truth."

"I can't. He wants this so much and I love him and I couldn't live if I lost him."

She was sitting beside me now, in the seat that Sol had been in earlier. If she thought I was being pathetic, she didn't let on. "I will speak with him."

Relief.

I knew it was something I should have done myself, but she was so comforting, and it was so easy to do nothing but take her up on her offer. I wanted to give her something in return, so as I stood to leave, I pointed to the frames on her desk. "He's very sweet."

She nodded. "Want to know a secret?"

I dabbed my eyes with the wadded-up tissue that had turned to shreds in my hand and nodded.

"He was in the frames when I bought them."

There was no one left in the waiting room so I read an article about healthy snacks while Sol went back in. When he came out of Dr. Goldman's office, he looked pale. As we made our way to the parking lot, I tried to match my stride to his but I couldn't. We got into the car and he turned the ignition.

"I'm sorry, Sol."

He didn't look at me.

Chapter 22

It was my idea to go bowling; I thought maybe it would ease the tension that had permanently settled between us. Bowling was something my family did when we wanted to forget our troubles. Even though at first my mother found the idea of wearing shoes that someone else had worn to be repugnant, Brian bought her a pair of her own, and after that she had no more excuses. We went on Sunday afternoons once her open houses were over. We typed our names into the scoreboard and Brian and I would compete to see whose was the most outrageous. Sometimes I was Slim, Slam, Sham and he was Brain, Ban, or Bam. My mother just rolled her eyes. She was always Jayne.

I decided to invite Susan to join us. She was dating someone new, and I thought it would be fun. As uncomfortable as things had become, we hadn't spoken a word about what happened in Dr. Goldman's office, and I hoped that going out with another couple would distract us from each other.

I picked a bowling alley called Lucky Lanes that was built in the early 1970s. The seats were made of gray plastic and the counters were covered in orange Formica. Susan waved to us when we got there and pointed out John, who was standing in line waiting to get their shoes. She giggled and put her arm through mine. "He's cute, right?"

I hadn't seen her this way in a long time.

John came over and handed Susan her shoes and then leaned over to give her a kiss. Then he reached out to shake Sol's hand and smiled at me.

"Our stuff is over there." John pointed toward a lane beside a group of high school kids.

By the time we got settled, John and Susan had already typed our names into the machine, and she winked at me when she saw me looking up at the board, which read Sam.

"Let's get started." John rubbed his hands together like he was about to roll the dice in a game of craps.

Susan beamed.

He lifted the ball up to his chest, and as he let it go, his arms flew out like the wings of a mangled bird. At first, I thought that maybe he was kidding but not when his stance for the second frame was exactly the same.

"You did great, baby," she said without even looking to see how many pins he had knocked down.

It was Sol's turn next, and I watched as he stood quietly, eyeing the pins for a few minutes. The next thing I knew, the ball flew down the lane with such precision and strength that it knocked down everything in its path. I couldn't help but feel proud seeing that he was that good. I tried to make eye contact with him, but he was staring down at his feet, retying one of his shoes. John congratulated him and then ordered a round of beer. Susan was next, and I watched as she wiggled her hips and sent the ball veering off to the left, landing it straight into the gutter. She didn't seem to mind just put her hands up into the air and shrugged as she walked past John, who patted her rear end.

It was finally my turn, and like I did when I was a kid, I ran my hand across the smooth coolness of the balls, hoping if I chose the right one, it would do all the work for me. I picked a black one, shiny with only a few scratch marks across it surface. I held it in my hand, feeling the heaviness of its weight, and I thought about straight lines and perfection and then pulled my arm back and let the ball go. It stayed in the center until the very last second when it shifted to the right, missing every single last pin.

Things did not get much better after that. It seemed no matter how hard I tried the ball had a mind of its own. After a while, I stopped paying attention, but Sol's focus was the exact opposite of mine. He continued to launch every ball flawlessly as if his life depended on it.

The high school girls next to us were taking silly pictures of each other with their cell phones. The boys they were with were arguing about sports, and every few minutes the two conversations would merge. At one point, one of the boys posed with a ball between his legs, which made everyone laugh. I stopped watching them when Susan waved her hand in my face, reminding me that it was my turn. But my heart wasn't in it anymore, and the moment my turn was over, I went back to staring at the people next to us, which is why I didn't realize that our game was finished and that Sol had won.

I smiled at him, and even though he should have been happy, he didn't smile back. I couldn't stand another night knowing I was the reason, so I invited Susan and John to go out for a drink.

I could tell Sol wasn't pleased, but after we turned in our shoes, John and Susan led the way out and we followed. There was a bar a few blocks away, and we managed to get the last table near the back. I ordered a frozen daiquiri because it reminded me of a slushy. The waitress returned, balancing the drinks on her tray, and then set them down, mine first, and then beers and shots for everyone else.

"Ready?" John yelled above the music blasting over our heads.

Sol and Susan nodded, and I watched as they sprinkled salt on the back of their hands, swallowed the tequila in one gulp, and then sucked on the lime. The table shook as they slammed their glasses back down, and then John smiled and lifted his arm into the air, motioning for the waitress to bring another round. I had never seen Sol drink very much, and I thought for sure he would bow out but he didn't. As quickly as the waitress brought them, Sol drank them.

John moved in closer to Susan and laid his arm across her shoulders. I looked at Sol, but he was busy rubbing his finger along the side of his beer bottle where the label had started to tear.

"One more round," John said.

Sol nodded and took another sip of his beer.

The music got louder and I started to feel hot.

"So how do you two know each other?"

Susan's chair was now so close to John's that she was almost sitting in his lap.

"My brother-in-law teaches at Susan's school."

John dropped something on the ground, and when he leaned over to get it I saw that he was balding.

"How about you guys? Where did you meet?"

Sol had been quiet up until this point. "We met at a grave. It was love at first sight, and I knew I couldn't live without her." He finished scraping the label off his beer and the shavings sat in a pile next to the shot glasses that had accumulated. There was something cruel and ugly in his face.

It was so loud around us that I'm not sure if they heard him, and if they did neither of them said anything. After the next shot was done, I knew I wanted to get out of there as fast as I could. Luckily, at that point so did Susan and John. My old apartment was only a few blocks away, and I watched Susan cling to John's arm as they made their way across the street after we said our goodbyes.

Not only could Sol not drive, but he could barely walk. He leaned hard against my shoulder and slowly and ungracefully we made our way to the nearest taxi stand I could find. He didn't say a word during the ride home, just propped his head up against the window. When we reached the house, the driver helped me get him to the front door.

"You okay, lady?" He was in his sixties and had an accent and grease stains that ran down the front of his shirt.

I nodded and thanked him. He waited until I put my key in the lock, and as he walked away, I hoped all he remembered was the smell of the Douglas fir wreath I had hung over the door and not the sight of my husband retching green-tinged tequila all over our brand-new welcome mat.

I managed to get him inside and onto the sofa. I handed him a small trash can, which he held onto clumsily either because he was too drunk to do any better or he was too drunk to care. I had been around Susan's mother enough times to know how to handle things. I filled a glass with ice-cold water and got him aspirin from the medicine cabinet. At first, he shook his head no, but after I insisted he swallowed.

I put a wet dishcloth across his forehead and once he seemed settled, I left him to go clean the mess he had made outside. After gagging a few times, I finally gave up and tossed the entire mat into a trash bag. When I came back in to check on him, he was still awake.

"You could have just cleaned it up. You didn't have to throw it away."

I took the compress off his head and sat beside him on the couch.

He closed his eyes. "He just wants to fuck her. I know she thinks he's going to marry her but he's not. He just wants to fuck her."

"What are you talking about?"

He rolled over and grabbed the trash can and coughed. "Susan."

He spit out stretchy balls of saliva and then he spoke again. "She's so obvious. So desperate. So needy."

"You're drunk." I left him and walked into the kitchen, but then I heard him start to vomit again. He was calling out to me, calling me Salmon, which he never did.

He closed his eyes as I leaned over to clean his face with the dishtowel. I wiped away the beads of sweat that had formed along his hairline then dipped my finger into the ice water and ran it over his lips, which had become white and chalky. He leaned his head back into the pillow.

"I heard them arguing and I came downstairs to see what was going on."

He looked at me to see if I understood what he was talking about and didn't continue until he was satisfied that I did.

"The night before all her scraps of paper disappeared."

He took my hand and laid it on his chest. "She had a suitcase." As he spoke, his breath skimmed the tops of my fingers. "And even though I was little I knew what was happening."

I could feel his heart beating through his skin, drumming to the beat of his fear. "She was always so sad."

His eyes brimmed with tears and I let them fall without wiping them away.

"My father pushed me so that I was standing in her way. Blocking her." He covered his face so that his words were muted. "She stood at the door, and I knew that she was going to leave and that I was never going to see her again. She turned away from me and I remember feeling like you do when you are in the middle of a dream except this was real because I could feel my father's fingers digging into my shoulders."

His breath caught in his throat and he swallowed hard before he continued. "He said her name like she was far away, like he was calling her from the edge of the ocean. He pushed me toward her and I could feel his despair, his need to show her that because of me she would always be tied to him. He said,

'Rachel, don't leave the boy.' His hands felt so heavy, and after what seemed like a very long time, she picked up her suitcase and went back upstairs and I could hear her heels clicking across the floor."

Sol began to cry tears for the little boy who had come so close to losing his mother. "My father and I stood in silence like you do when you wait for the last crack of lightning to hit in a thunderstorm. We waited, and when nothing else happened I told him I was hungry. He got out a box of cereal and let me fish around to the bottom looking for the prize, and when I was finished eating, he let me drink the milk out of the bowl. We left the dishes in the sink and when we woke the next day, they were washed and her poems were gone and we never talked about it again." His breathing slowed and then it was like he was empty and there was nothing left except for one tiny little bit. "I knew I was the reason she stayed."

I could tell he was fighting it, his eyelids heavy with sleep, but before he allowed himself to let go, he searched my face to make sure I understood, that I could see what it was he was asking me for. I stayed up with him until he fell asleep. I watched over him, making sure the blanket I had found at the bottom of the linen closet didn't fall off. I turned the light on above the kitchen sink so he wouldn't wake up to blackness. His eyebrows were arched in pain, and as I kissed his forehead, I felt a sense of relief. He loved me so much and he needed to know that no matter what happened, that I would always be there and I would never leave him—he needed proof.

Which was the reason he needed me to have his child.

There is a sense of comfort when you are suddenly able to see things clearly; like you've been suffocating for so long but then suddenly are given the gift of a deep breath. There was only one way to show him how much he meant to me, and once my decision was made, it was all very easy and I immediately stopped having doubts or feeling scared. Sometimes, love is all you need to power through your insecurities.

I threw out the bottle of vitamin C stashed in my nightstand drawer along with every single orange I could find, and as I laid in our bed, I could hear him in the living room and I counted the seconds between his snores. This was finally my opportunity to take care of him instead of it always being the other way around. This was my chance to prove to him how much I loved him. I must have fallen asleep, because I dreamed I was bowling outside during a rainstorm and every time I hit a pin, lightning would strike. When I opened my eyes, I saw the flash of Sol's camera. He had stripped down naked and was standing above me taking pictures.

"What are you doing?" I covered my face as he took another.

"You." He lowered himself down and kissed me, and I could still smell the alcohol on his breath. "Are beautiful."

He flipped through the screen on the camera, showing me images of my orange hair spread across the pillow like waves. "See." He pointed as he jumped into the bed and slid under the covers, and it was almost like he knew that now I understood. He wrapped his arms around me and laid his face beside mine so that I could feel his breath on the back of my neck. "You are absolutely perfect."

Chapter 23

Anne Marie and I were in the break room. I was drinking a Coke and she was holding an "I love my secretary" mug with a red heart where the word *love* was supposed to be.

"Do you think you'll have a kid one day?"

Anne Marie shrugged. "Jimmy can't."

"How do you know?"

She stood up to get more coffee. "Some doctor told him once." She had her back to me. "We keep trying anyway."

"You want one?"

"Jimmy does."

"But you don't?"

She turned the water on to rinse out the carafe. "It's mostly Jimmy's mother. She never liked me. She told him a baby would tame me." Anne Marie rolled her eyes. "Spends every waking moment praying to Saint Jude."

"Who is Saint Jude?"

She laughed. "The patron saint of all things hopeless."

I had some free time on my hands because Anne Marie and Randy had redis-covered the desk behind his locked office door. I answered the phone when it rang and spent the rest of the afternoon reading up on Saint Jude. I wasn't raised with religion and had never stepped foot inside a church so I knew very little about saints but this seemed pretty simple. All you had to do was say the prayer nine times per day for nine days. Almost like wishing on a falling star.

I didn't say anything to Sol because I didn't want to get his hopes up. It seemed strange to suddenly be praying so fervently for something I had just recently been trying to prevent. I said the prayer in the shower in the morning and before bed. I said it while I was standing on line waiting to pay for grocer-ies. If Sol asked me what I was doing, I just smiled, kissed him on the lips, and told him not to worry. I kept remembering how vulnerable and scared he had been that night, and I needed him to know that I would take care of things.

If it was a baby he needed to prove it, then that is what I was going to give him. I pushed the memory of Fluffy out my head, convincing myself I had just been a silly child and that things would be different as an adult. Now when we had sex, I was the one who was frantic. Afterward, I closed my eyes and whis-pered my prayers, imagining that Saint Jude could hear me directly. I prayed and wished and waited. I found the "how to get pregnant" books that were bur-ied under the magazines on Sol's nightstand and I read them until I had them memorized. I researched diets and vitamin supplements and taught myself to meditate. Finally, when I could not take it anymore and I was convinced there was no possible way that I was being heard, something happened.

But it was not at all what I expected.

I walked into the bathroom muttering to St. Jude, and that's when I found her. She was crying and wiping her tears away with a paper towel. Her eyes were red and her makeup blotchy and streaked.

"Are you okay?"

She nodded and snorted and then ran to the toilet where I heard her retching.

It seemed that Saint Jude had heard my prayer, but rather than bringing a baby to me, he had sent one to Anne Marie instead.

To pretend that I wasn't devastated would be a lie. What complicated matters more was that it was clear she resented every moment of her pregnancy—a pregnancy which somehow in my head I believed she had taken from me. It was difficult to be excited for her when all I wanted to do was cry.

In her defense, she didn't gloat about it, mostly because I think she was too worried about what was going to happen. I could hear her talking to Jimmy on the telephone, convincing him that the baby was nothing short of a miracle. As for Randy, as soon as she started to show, he stopped paying her any attention. The larger her belly grew, the more invisible she became. She stopped wearing makeup and much of the time looked so tired I offered to cover her phone so she could rest in the break room. Most days she took me up on my offer. Jimmy's mother was right: having a baby was going to tame her.

I felt sorry for her but mostly I felt sorry for myself, which is why I pretended to be sick on the day of her baby shower. I just couldn't bear to witness the callousness with which she treated the thing that Sol and I wanted so badly. Instead, I made Sol take me bowling, and I comforted myself by watching my strong, handsome husband bowl a 170. His movements were smooth and swift and his focus intense. I relished in his victory as if it was really something worth celebrating. I tried with all my might to distract myself from the thing that I could not stop thinking about.

Even though I had worked hard at keeping my sadness at bay, one night it was too hard. I didn't cry, but I moved around the house without purpose, and once I found a warm corner of the couch, I had a hard time leaving it.

After flipping through his mother's recipes, Sol made a creamy tomato soup with grilled cheese sandwiches. We ate with our feet propped up on the coffee table, and after cleaning the dishes, he held my hand while we watched television. He even kissed the tips of my fingers like he had when we first started dating, which made me feel even worse for not being able to give him the one thing that he wanted most.

I had been taking pregnancy tests at work because I didn't want Sol to see, didn't want him to get his hopes up. I kept them inside my desk drawer like symbols of my fading hope. I researched home pregnancy tests online and read the backs of the boxes in the aisles of drug stores. I found ones that detected pregnancy at the earliest point possible, and when Anne Marie went on her lunch break, I would slip them into my pocketbook, head for the ladies' room, and rip through the packaging. Unwilling to accept the first result, I would go back to my desk, gulp down a soda, and come back to try again twenty minutes later.

We used to chatter back and forth, but now Anne Marie and I sat in silence, interrupted only when the telephone rang or when she ate. She had gotten into the habit of snacking throughout the day and would lay Kleenex tissues across her belly to keep her dress from getting dirty. Her diet consisted of things that were crunchy and salty and orange and she indulged her every whim by buying bags of Cheetos and Doodles and Puffs in bulk. She used the Kleenex to dab at the fluorescent dust that settled around her lips.

Randy barely talked to her anymore, directing all his requests to me. A few times I noticed her trying to smile at him, but he just stood at my desk flipping through the mail, ignoring her until she just gave up. Sometimes she would bring him folders, and because these days the door was always left wide open, I could see him point to the file cabinet in the corner without saying a word. Now when he closed his door, it was because he was on the telephone, the sound of his voice echoing through the emptiness in the front office like he was speaking through a megaphone. I was too busy reading up on the most accurate pregnancy tests available on the market and Anne Marie was too busy eating chemically tainted orange things to care.

And then one day everything changed.

I was in the ladies' room about to pee on a stick, even though it was much too early to test, when I heard Anne Marie walk in. I slipped the unused test back inside my bag and came out of the stall.

She was turned to the mirror, leaning in close and applying a shade of red lipstick I had not seen her wear in months. She rubbed some onto her finger-tip and then onto her cheeks.

"Sam."

She was looking at her reflection in the mirror as she spoke. "My water broke."

I wanted to scream or dial 911, but instead I watched as she twisted her lip-stick back down, recapped it, and slipped it inside her purse. We walked into the main office and ran into Randy, who was putting on his jacket and heading out to lunch.

"I am leaving for the day and I am taking Sam with me."

"Who do you think is going to watch the phones?" He was fiddling with his zipper and wasn't looking at her as he spoke.

"That's your problem."

She turned on her heels and pulled me along with her. Outside the air was cold and it hurt as it hit my face. More than anything I wanted to run, but instead I watched as she hailed a cab. "Northeast Medical Center."

"Do you want to call Jimmy?" I asked.

She nodded, but she didn't make any attempt to reach for her phone. Each time the taxi hit a pothole, she jumped a little in her seat.

"It's going to be okay," I said.

She was staring out the window so I couldn't see her face. Once we got to the hospital, I helped her out of the car but she refused to use a wheelchair, insisting that she was fine to walk.

She sat on a bench while I checked her in.

"Did you call Jimmy?" She had found her way to the vending machine and was crunching through a bag of bright orange crackers and didn't answer.

"Maybe you shouldn't be eating now."

She shrugged.

"It's all going to work out," I said more to myself than to her.

She nodded as she brushed crumbs from her lap. A nurse came out with a chart and pointed in Anne Marie's direction. If only Jimmy were here, I could make my escape, but Anne Marie looked back at me as she stood and I knew I was supposed to follow. We were led to a room in the middle of the floor and Anne Marie changed into a dressing gown. A nurse in blue scrubs asked me to wait outside as they pulled the curtain around her bed.

I scanned the halls watching for Jimmy's hulking frame to come flying through the doors and relieve me of my duty, but so far only two nurses dressed in the same blue and a doctor with a scrub cap on his head came out.

"You can come back in now."

Anne Marie was staring out the window.

"Your friend is pretty far along."

"I don't understand. Isn't labor supposed to take hours?"

"She's been in labor for hours." I must have looked confused because the nurse went on. "Everyone handles pain differently."

I realized that Anne Marie had never told me when her water broke. Most likely, she had been sitting at her desk in silence, suffering one contraction after the next, as she listened to Randy laughing on the telephone.

"You should probably get a hold of the dad and have him come if he doesn't want to miss this."

Anne Marie grabbed onto the railing of the bed and clenched, and I could see the ache radiate through her. Instead of letting the pain come out in one long scream, she made short little grunts. Someone knocked on the door, and we both looked up, but it was just an orderly wheeling in a cart and then she went back to panting.

The pain was coming faster and sharper. I could tell by the way she was wincing and by the tears that had formed in the outside corners of her eyes. She wiped them away with the back of her hand.

"It's going to be okay." I hated that was all I could think of to say.

The tears were now streaming down her face, and I didn't know if they were from the pain of giving life or the pain of being left. She grunted through a contraction because she refused to dignify it with a scream. There was something breathtaking about her courage, her strength. I had never seen her so powerful.

The nurses set her legs into stirrups and then the doctor came in to examine her.

"Any time now, sweetie." One of the nurses smiled and patted her head.

She clenched her jaw and made a sound that came from so far within, I think it startled even her. The nurse held her hand, and as she strained against the pain and the hurt and pushed past the possibility that she wasn't strong enough to handle it on her own, Jimmy came flying through the door with a bouquet of red carnations from the gift shop in his hand.

"I'm sorry, baby. I'm here now." He tossed the flowers onto a chair and I got out of the way so that he could take his wife's side.

"Just in time, Daddy."

Things were moving at a fevered pitch, but then everything froze and there was a moment of indecision, a split second when what you are about to choose will change everything that comes after. Anne Marie stopped panting, she stopped fighting, and instead of holding onto the railing, she let go, reaching for Jimmy's hand, and suddenly I realized how small she looked in that big bed next to her big husband. I started to back away, which was easy since everyone was focused on her. I stood outside for a few minutes, and I listened to the screams coming from her room. The ones she had managed to curb for so long when she believed she was brave, when she believed she was strong. Now she was wailing, crying Jimmy's name over and over again, like a child.

The baby was a girl and she let Jimmy choose her name. He named her Miranda after some Victoria's Secret model. Anne Marie didn't tell him that it reminded her of the list of rights a suspect gets when he is about to be hauled off to jail or the name of the man she had been sleeping with on and off for the last three years at work. Instead, she sat docilely by as the baby was dressed in an outfit her mother-in-law had chosen and nodded her head when she was informed that she would be attending church every Sunday so that Miranda could be properly baptized. Later, when she told the story of the baby's birth, she always made sure to say that she would never have been able to make it without Jimmy by her side.

By the time I got home, Sol was asleep on the couch with the television on. I bent down so that my head was level to his, and as if on cue his eyes opened and he smiled. He wrapped an arm around my neck and brought me closer to him so that he could kiss me. His lips felt dry and cool, which suddenly made me realize that I was burning up inside. I unbuttoned my coat and let it fall to the ground and then I pulled off my skirt and underwear. I lifted my shirt over my head and then I slipped off my bra. Sol stayed where he was on the couch watching me.

I pulled him down with me, and he laughed like I was playing, and when I didn't laugh back he got quiet. We pushed the coffee table out of the way and then he took off his shirt, and when our skin touched again, I was reminded of how hot I felt and how cool he was. He rolled on top of me so that my backside was rubbing against the coat I had just taken off. My mother had chosen it for me because it was practical and warm and made from wool. As he got on top of me, it scratched my skin, but I didn't make him stop because something inside of me wanted it to hurt. His pants were pushed down halfway past his knees and the sex we were having was dark and uncomfortable and confused. I closed my eyes as he tried to rearrange the way we were positioned, tried to find a way to make it better, and when he couldn't I felt him give up.

It got darker and hotter, and I rolled and hit my head on the leg of an armchair but still we kept at each other in a frenzy that bordered on desperation. The blanket he had been using on the couch was now coiled between us, creating lumps and twists that made things even more unwieldy. Sweat stung my eyes, but I couldn't wipe it away because he was holding me so tight, he was crying, and I couldn't breathe and I couldn't let go and he whispered something into the curve of my neck.

"Don't talk," I said, which he must have heard because then he said nothing.

We held on to each other throughout most of the night, encased in our desperate sadness and our want and our need and our hurt. We laid on the floor of our little house on top of my scratchy wool coat, taking turns sleeping and then waking as if we were on watch for something important to happen, and in the morning when the sun came flooding in through the kitchen window and woke us, I realized that it finally had.

It was true what they said about the glow.

It was as if someone had taken a sparkly magic marker and used it to outline my face—and Sol's, too, for that matter. We didn't need to take a test because we knew that night that we had made our child. I took one anyway, simply because I wanted the pleasure of seeing that pink plus sign. The truth was that I took more than one and I collected them in my nightstand drawer, and every time I thought I was dreaming, I took them out and lined them up like little toy soldiers along the edge of my bed.

Sol made me quit my job, which was a relief because it wasn't the same without Anne Marie. Randy had already hired a new girl, blond and busty with a high-pitched squeaky laugh. He hung out more at the front desk again, with his sleeves rolled up to the elbow, showing off the thick gold chain around his wrist. The new girl laughed at whatever he said while I looked away because participating in their joke would have been disloyal to Anne Marie. Besides, it was quickly becoming clear that even though she was the new girl, I was the outsider. So, I was glad when Sol told me to quit so that I could stay home and rest.

In the mornings, I wandered around my house imagining what it would sound like to hear a baby's cry in the rooms, to watch a baby crawl across the unleveled floors that so long ago seemed like such a big deal. I went to the library and took out books on babies, and the old librarian smiled at me when I went to check them out.

Sol insisted I change my eating habits. Every morning, he handed me a plate of bright red strawberries and thick creamy yogurt that he flavored with real vanilla beans. He poured me glasses of ice-cold water with slices of pale green cucumbers floating inside. He bought organic milk from the farm an hour from where we lived and made fresh ice cream at his shop. He baked muffins using zucchini and carrots from a friend's greenhouse and topped them with sweet pats of melting butter. We were cliché and corny and probably did what every young excited expectant couple does.

At night, Sol laid his head across my belly and talked to our baby, calling it Sweet Pea since we didn't yet know if it was a boy a girl. Sometimes he would hum songs and the sound of his voice would vibrate across my skin and make me giggle. We decided to keep our secret to ourselves for as long as we could. When my doubts would creep in, I would push them aside, telling myself I was being childish, and instead focus on the fact that I was holding the most magnificent creation inside of me and that everything was as it should be. I was smiling most of the time now, and I'm sure that my behavior seemed odd to people I randomly ran into on the street but I didn't care.

We heard Sweet Pea's heartbeat at our first appointment in Dr. Goldman's office. She covered my belly in sticky, slimy goop, warning us that it was early and that there was a possibility that she would not be able to find it, but then there it was, loud and powerful and real, and we both cried and she handed us tissues that she had on a table next to the exam table. I pushed out of my head the idea that sometimes she had to hand them out for a different reason than why she was giving them to us. We celebrated that night with Sweet Pea Cream Pie that had a graham crust and a cream topping that Sol colored with kale juice. I scooped it into my mouth not even caring that it tasted faintly of grass.

Afterward, Sol went into the hallway closet and brought out a box. "This was mine." He turned it around in his hands a few times. "From when I was little."

He removed the lid and handed it to me. Inside was a worn teddy bear, its brown fur matted and rubbed off in spots. It made a crinkly noise when I squeezed it, and when I turned it around, I could tell that the seam in the back had been opened, probably more than once to be restuffed and then refastened in perfectly spaced brown colored stiches.

"Even after I got too old, my mother still hung on to it. She was always repairing it."

He grew quiet.

"I found it sitting on the dining room table the day that she disappeared."

His face sunk as he spoke and his sadness hung on him like a piece of clothing. There had been fewer stories about Sarah Jacobs, as if somehow the world had forgotten her. I wished that the police would hurry up and identify that bone. I was sure that once he knew for certain that it was Sarah we had found in the lake, he would feel relief, and by then the baby would be born and he would have a happy distraction.

I started to speak, to reassure him, but he walked out of the room and so I followed. During the months when we were trying to get pregnant, Sol decided to paint the second bedroom yellow because he thought it would cheer us both up. It was still empty since we hadn't yet bought any furniture, so I placed the bear on a windowsill, pushing it up against the windowpane. Sol put his hands on my belly and I leaned back into him, putting my hand over his, sealing our promise as the afternoon light turned the walls a perfect shade of gold.

I stopped at the deli to pick up his favorite lunch.

It had been so long that I didn't know if I should knock or just let myself in, so in the end I did a little of both. There was music playing, sad and dark and slow, and even though it was bright outside, it felt as though there was a shadow turning everything inside gray. Canvases of different sizes hung from hooks suspended from the ceiling. They were painted in solid blocks of color, and as they moved, they reminded me of laundry shifting in the breeze. He came out of the bathroom rubbing his hands on a dishtowel and his features softened when he spotted me.

"Fishhhh." He kissed my forehead.

I handed him the bag of food.

"Lunch time already?"

Like we hadn't missed a beat.

He put his hand on my face. "You look beautiful."

He turned off the music and we sat together at the table. "Nothing for you?"

"I'm not very hungry."

The truth was I had promised Sol I would stop eating fried foods so I took an apple that I had brought from home out of my bag.

He dipped three fries into some ketchup and popped them into his mouth at the same time. "Are you enjoying being an old married lady?"

I nodded. "I quit my job." I took a bite of the apple and some of the juice ran down my chin.

He used his napkin to wipe my face and then he looked down at his plate and got quiet.

"You already knew."

He cracked his knuckles. "You know how your mom is."

I stole a few of his french fries.

"Are you cold? I can turn up the heat."

I realized that I was still wearing my coat, keeping my secret. "I'm fine."

He stood and cleared the table.

"What's that you're working on?" I pointed to the paintings.

"Let me show you."

He went inside the kitchen and put the dishes in the sink, and as he did, I slipped off my coat. I was still wearing the wool one my mother had bought me, but it was getting harder to button. Brian walked closer to the canvasses and began hitting them with a metal stick. He had attached the rods of a wind chime to the bottoms, and as I closed my eyes it felt as though I was in the middle of a rainstorm.

"Beautiful."

When I opened them again, he was looking at me.

"Even the colors of paint you chose remind me of rain."

He nodded but he wasn't looking at the paintings anymore. "Looks like you are enjoying your husband's cooking."

I doubted the changes in my body were noticeable to anyone who didn't know me well enough because I didn't necessarily look bigger, just softer, as though the sharp edges had been rubbed smooth. The moment we realized I was pregnant, Sol insisted on documenting every second of my progress. He made signs on green construction paper announcing how many weeks along I was, which he had me hold while he took my picture. There were funny ones where I stuck out my tongue and more serious ones where I cupped my hand over my belly and looked straight into the lens of the camera. Afterward, Sol downloaded the images onto his computer and we picked our favorites to hang on the refrigerator in the kitchen. We did it once a week, sometimes even twice because Sol said he didn't want to miss a thing. But I could see from the photos that I wasn't far enough along in my pregnancy for anyone who didn't really know me to know for sure.

Except for Brian, who thought my name was beautiful because it reminded him of mermaids. Brian always knew things about me without my having to tell him.

"Salmon." He was holding my hands in his and he was crying. "Oh, Sam."

And then I was crying too but the joy was tinged with bits of sorrow.

"She should know."

I shook my head. "I'm not ready."

"Please. Don't keep this a secret from her. You will break her heart."

Air moved in from the window I hadn't even realized was open, which made the chimes hanging from the paintings sing.

"I'm not ready. Not yet."

He brought my hands to his lips and blew on them. "Okay."

"Thanks, Dad."

I couldn't remember the last time I called him that. He put his arms around me and kissed my forehead a second time.

Chapter 24

I met Susan for lunch on a Saturday. Sol was working weekends, trying to earn extra money for when the baby came, so I was left to entertain myself.

After the second time Susan caught me throwing up, it didn't take much to get me to tell her the truth. I hated that she started referring to me as *Mama* because it made me feel like I should have been wearing a hair net with an apron tied around my waist, but she insisted so I just ignored her. Besides, I was used to being called by a name I didn't think suited me and this was no different.

"Mama!" she shouted from her seat at the table. She had arrived first and had already ordered herself a cocktail.

I smiled uncomfortably at the host who led me to where she was sitting.

"How are you feeling?" She was sipping her drink at the same time she was speaking so the words came out muddled.

"Good."

When the waiter walked over, I ordered an orange juice and a salad and Susan asked for another margarita.

"How's your mother?" I asked.

She lifted her half-finished glass into the air. "To my mother."

A group of women sitting a few tables away looked over at us. "Are you okay?"

"I'm great. My mom's great. John's great. We are all great."

She dipped her lime into the drink and then put it into her mouth, making loud sucking noises. "He dumped me."

"I'm sorry."

She shrugged and then downed the rest of her drink. "He said it wasn't working out, but I'm pretty sure he met someone else."

"You'll meet someone better."

"Of course, I will."

"Besides, he was bald."

Her face softened. "But I like bald."

"You like sexy bald. John was not sexy bald."

At first, she looked as though she was going to get mad, but then she smiled.

After we ate, I talked her into getting dessert. We decided to split a slice of chocolate mousse cake which I mostly ate since she said she wasn't hungry.

"Let's walk," she announced after we paid the bill.

The weather was starting to warm and people were outside pushing baby strollers and walking with small dogs whose leashes got tangled every time they stopped to talk with someone they knew. Susan pulled me along, and finally we stopped in front of a children's clothing boutique called Baby Birds.

"Let's go in," she urged.

I shook my head.

"C'mon, Mama. Have some fun."

I let her take me inside. A saleswoman came over to help, but Susan shooed her away.

"Isn't this adorable?" She held up a onesie covered with painted Japanese koi fish.

I nodded.

"Do you speak? Or does Sol not let you do that either?"

The orange juice from lunch was now dangerously close to the back of my throat. "What's that supposed to mean?"

"Never mind. Let's get this." She held up the onesie in her hand.

"No."

"Why not?" Even though she was smiling, there was an edge to her voice.

"I don't even know what I'm having."

"It works for a boy or a girl plus look at the design." She puckered her lips so that she looked like one of the fish. "You know you want it and it will be my treat."

"I'm not ready to buy anything yet. It's bad luck."

"You're being ridiculous." She marched up to the cashier and took out her wallet. "Why can't you ever appreciate what you have?"

As we left the store, she tried to push the bag into my hand, but I refused so she stuffed it into her purse instead. "Sometimes you are such an ungrateful bitch."

She turned around and walked away without saying goodbye.

When I got home, my phone buzzed a few times and the texts slowly rolled in.

"Sam."

A pause.

"I really am happy for you."

A siren wailed past the house as the next text came in.

"And I'm sorry."

Sol took off early from work so that we could go to our first ultrasound together. I couldn't wait to see our baby and had been asking Dr. Goldman for months, but she insisted on scheduling it closer to the halfway point to limit exposure to radiation. We sat in a waiting room where most of the men were scrolling through their phones while the women flipped through magazines. I was too nervous to do either, and so was Sol, who didn't let go of my hand, making the sweat forming between us feel like glue.

He followed me into the room and sat in a chair at the foot of the exam table. The technician came in and smiled. I think she tried talking about the weather or maybe it was the traffic, but I was too nervous to listen.

Even though it was warm in the room, my fingertips felt frozen.

"First baby?"

We both nodded.

"Just relax."

I laid back and closed my eyes and talked to Sweet Pea like I had been doing since the beginning. Sometimes I told stories, but today I whispered a lullaby and imagined the song moving from my lips past my heart and then down through the umbilical cord.

"There's your baby," the technician announced as she moved the probe over my belly.

I hadn't realized it, but my eyes had been shut. When I opened them, I saw a baby more perfect than I ever could have imagined, and when I looked over at Sol, I knew he felt the same. He stood and held my hand.

"Do you guys want to know the gender?"

"Yessno," we said at the same time.

"How about if I write it down on a piece of paper and put it in an envelope and you can decide later?"

I nodded because I was so busy staring at the images of our baby I couldn't speak.

The technician kept moving the probe, clicking away at her computer.

"Everything is fine, right?" There was panic in Sol's voice.

The technician smiled. "The doctor will be right in."

She helped me sit back up before leaving the room.

When Sol touched me, I realized his hand was even colder than mine.

Finally, the doctor came into the room, smiling, and waved for us to go. "Everything looks great. Congratulations."

We went out to dinner that night to celebrate.

"I don't remember ever feeling this happy."

That I was responsible for his elation made me feel high. Sol dug out the envelope holding the sex of our child from his pocket. "Interested?"

One of the games we played when we went out to eat was to order banana cream pie from every restaurant that served it to find the one closest to his mother's. Just from looking at what the waiter placed on the table, I immediately knew this was not it. I picked my spoon up anyway.

I shook my head, "I want it to be a surprise."

"Why?"

"Because so few things are."

The piecrust was dry and crumbly. Sol picked at a piece of banana.

"You can find out if you want."

"Really?"

"Only if you can keep a secret."

He scooped a dollop of whipped cream into his mouth and then tucked the envelope back into his pocket. "Of course I can."

I woke up at 3 a.m.

Maybe it was the excitement or just all the sugar I had eaten, but suddenly my eyes opened. I felt a movement within me like I had never experienced before, a glide, a twirl, a twist.

A swim.

Quickly, I reached for Sol's hand and laid it across my belly so that he could feel it, too, but it was too late. When he woke, he was confused and caught too far in the depths of sleep to understand what it was that I wanted.

"Next time please try harder to wake me," Sol demanded in the morning after I told him what had happened.

I assured him that based on the baby books I had read it was simply the first of many movements and that there would be more opportunities. He kissed my belly before he left.

Once he was gone, I went upstairs to take a shower. I took off my clothes and stood in front of the bathroom mirror. My breasts were rounder, and even though Sol told me they were beautiful, I was still not used to their size. I stared at my profile, turning left and right, and rubbed my belly, amazed that there was a life inside of me, capable of moving, capable of swimming.

Like a fish.

Sol must have forgotten something, because I heard his key in the door and then he came upstairs. He was standing outside of the bathroom looking at me.

"Sam," he whispered, and I watched as he moved quickly to get his camera—slowly like I was a tiger from the wild he was afraid to frighten off.

I crossed my arms across my chest, covering my nipples that, because of the pregnancy, had grown darker than I had ever seen them.

"You are beautiful."

He was snapping pictures and I couldn't stop him . . . and then suddenly I didn't want to. I let my hands drop and I turned so that I was looking straight at him, which must have surprised him because for a minute everything froze. We stared at each other, him fully dressed with the camera dangling around his neck and me completely nude with his child inside of me. I walked toward him and then I put my arms around his neck, and we moved across the cold bathroom tile as though we were dancing. I brought his lips to mine and kissed him, and then I watched as he closed his eyes like he was floating, and I took his hands and put them on my belly and this time when the baby swam, we felt it together.

Nothing was the same after that because I now understood that there were things I knew that he didn't.

And so did he.

Whenever the baby kicked or moved, he looked at me in awe, as if I was responsible for the miracle. I started sleeping naked because I liked the way my skin felt when Sol brushed up against me with nothing to separate us.

There were physical changes, as well. My skin took on a pink glow and my nails, which I had a terrible habit of biting down to the quick, were long and graceful. For the first time, I didn't turn away from myself when I looked in the mirror. Even my orange hair, which had taken on a copper hue, curved more softly around my face and sometimes in the right light, sparkled.

Now when we went shopping, Sol let me take charge. We chose baby furniture based on what I liked and what I thought would work best in the room. He simply shrugged when I insisted that everything be white even though he wanted pine. He said nothing when I arranged to have the pieces delivered immediately even though he wanted to wait until after the baby was born. He even gave in on names, only asking that if it was a girl we could choose something to honor his mother.

At my doctor's appointments, I stared at other pregnant women and wondered if they felt as important and special as I did. I noticed that many of them placed their hands on top of their bellies and I started doing the same. I liked how the nurses called me *mommy*, not at all in the same way that Susan did, and I liked that I was being told what a good job I was doing. My days finally began to have meaning, purpose, and I started to feel accomplished.

In the mornings, Sol squeezed fresh orange juice, which I drank while he showered. Afterward he would lie on my abdomen, his wet hair leaving spots on my chest, and trace circles around my belly button. Every time the baby kicked, he would look up at me and smile and I would smile back. I had never felt so desired and so necessary and so powerful.

After he left for work, I sat in the rocking chair Sol brought from his father's house. He told me his mother loved it and that sometimes when he came home from school, he would find her there asleep. It had a soft, soothing creak, and I wrapped my arms around myself, matching the words in my lullabies to the rhythm of its squeaks. I rocked back and forth, loving and growing the baby that had already given me so much joy and wondering what it was the Sol's mother had thought of when she sat in this very same spot.

Chapter 25

Sol must have forgotten to turn off the television before he left for work, and the sound of the reporter's voice seeped through the kitchen walls like a bright red wine stain. The first thing I saw when I walked into the living room was his sweet smiling face on the screen, and I wondered how many photo albums his mother had to search through before finding the right one, knowing it would be plastered all over the media for the world to judge.

The reporter was talking loudly, but I wasn't listening to what she was saying, because in the background there were tents and police in uniform, some of them with FBI scrawled across their backs. Maybe the pressure had finally gotten to him or maybe he felt some form of remorse, which is the only way I could explain what Stephen Markworth had finally decided to do.

Confess.

They cut to a video of him standing in a courtroom, his hands cuffed behind his back, staring down at the floor, and I felt relief because even though I had known he was most likely the one responsible for her death, I didn't want to see it in his eyes. I didn't want to confront the possibility that you could love someone with such dangerous desperation that it would lead you to destroy them.

To break them.

I muted the sound just so I could give myself a few minutes longer to pretend it wasn't real. When I turned the volume back on, the reporter was describing the scene, and as the small hairs started to rise on the back of my neck, I realized something was amiss. I stared at the screen harder, focusing all my energy on the spot where she was standing and looked in the direction she was pointing. I blinked a few times, but when I opened my eyes, I was still faced with the same perplexing and awful conclusion.

Something was terribly wrong.

The reporter turned her head and pointed toward the trees where most of the action was taking place, and it was then that my breakfast began to rise in my throat. I managed to make it to the bathroom, and after cleaning myself up, came back into the living room still hoping I had misunderstood. I turned up the volume, but even as the reporter's amplified voice boomed through my house, I knew there was no mistaking what she was saying. Stephen Markworth had led the police to where he had buried Sarah's body, near his home beneath a sprawling oak tree in the forest on the edge of town.

Which was at least fifteen miles away from Daphne Lake.

Everything around me slowed as I contemplated the consequences of the news that was being broadcast on the television. If Sarah was buried under that tree then it was impossible that the bone Sol and I found could have belonged to her. Even though I had adamantly assured him that it was.

Even though I had promised.

I thought about the despair in his eyes and how with just a few words, I had been able to make it magically disappear. But now there it was on the television screen, pushed into the light of day, exposed for all to see. It was up to me to protect Sol, to help him believe whatever it was he needed. I had to figure out a way to fix this, but at that moment, I was so lost I couldn't imagine what it was I would tell him or what he would want me to say or whether I would even be capable of saying it. So, I did what I always did when I needed to disappear, when I needed to make the world around me stop.

My art was no longer in the house, so I made my way outside and then into the garage. The door was rusted and difficult to open, and when I finally got inside, I was so overcome by the gray mustiness that filled my nose that I found it difficult to breathe. My desk was shoved into a corner and covered with boxes. They might as well have been cinder blocks for how heavy they felt to move, and I gave up after a few minutes, but not before finding a piece I had been working on from before, poking out from one of the stacks on top. It was a water scene with weeping willow trees dotting the banks of a lake.

I started to feel dizzy so I tried to steady myself, but all I could see was Sarah's smile and then how she must have looked once the life was squeezed out of her. As more of the dank, stale air in the garage filled my lungs, Sarah's face was replaced by the image of my hamster, Fluffy, dangling from the jaws of the cat while I sat idly by, paralyzed and incompetent. I was suddenly over-whelmed by how hopeless it all seemed, and it was then that everything began to close in around me and go dark.

When I opened my eyes again, Brian was standing over me in his unas-suming way and not in the least bit aware that he couldn't have been more of a hero if he had come in wearing a cape. I had forgotten he we had planned to meet that morning.

"You're okay, Fish." It sounded more like a question than a statement as he pushed away the hair that was now plastered to my face.

I tried to stand but lost my footing before he caught me. "Stay here." He left and came back with a glass of water, which I sipped slowly. He held me tight, buoying me up until I found my balance and made it back inside the house.

"What were you doing in there?" he asked.

But I didn't want to talk or think about it.

About any of it.

"Are you okay?" he asked.

I nodded.

"I should take you to the doctor."

I shook my head. "Just dehydrated, I'm sure." I didn't want to go to a doc-tor. I didn't want to be reminded of what had happened or what had caused it or what was being televised on the news. I wanted the things that were threatening the perfect trajectory of my life to just blow away like a coating of dust on an old piece of furniture and be replaced with better things—like the beautiful house my husband had fixed up for us. I wanted Brian to be proud of what we had accomplished. I wanted him to see how good my life had become.

He was still trying to decide if he should listen to me or call an ambulance so I just started talking. At first the words were slow to come, like they were stuck in honey, but soon it got easier, and I watched his face as I pointed out the kitchen cabinets that Sol had refinished and showed him the bathrooms he had repainted. I opened the pantry, displaying the foods Sol picked out for me, and saw him looking at the ultrasounds attached to the fridge door with magnets in the shape of ice cream cones. The faster I talked, the further away I got from thoughts of Sarah and everything that the location of her remains implied.

When we walked into the baby's room, Brian carefully unwrapped the brown paper from the canvases he had brought to reveal a series of giraffes and elephants done in soft pastels that fit in the room as if they were made for it, and in that moment, everything really did feel perfect, and I understood, maybe more than I ever had before, that he had always been the one to save me from the world, from my pain, from myself.

I was lost in thought and hadn't noticed that he had managed to retrieve my half-finished water scene collage from the garage floor and propped it on the windowsill next to the stuffed bear.

"This is beautiful, Fish. When are you going to get back to work on it?"

But I didn't want to talk about the art or what had led me out into the garage, and as it started to rush back, I could feel the panic beginning to rise.

It was as though he could read my mind. "Let's get out of here."

He took me to a diner, and I let him treat me to an order of onion rings. Afterward, we shared a plate of donuts still hot from the fryer. "Sam," he said as he kissed me goodbye, "I really hope you have everything you want and that you are happy. Really happy."

I was sitting in the rocking chair when Sol came home. He walked into the room, and the moment I saw his face, I knew he had heard the news about Sarah Jacobs. I couldn't look at him, knowing there was nothing I could do to take it away.

I took his hand and he followed me without asking where we were going, and I handed him the car keys. We hadn't been out together for a drive in a long time. As he drove, he stared straight ahead like he always did. I tilted back into the headrest. Maybe everything that had happened was finally catching up to me; I suddenly felt achingly tired.

"Are you okay?" Sol turned to look at me.

"Fine." I put my hand on his knee. "Let's go shopping. For the baby."

It was what I had been searching for all day, and it was Brian who made me see. Brian who showed me what I needed to do just by being my father. It was how I would be able to turn things around so that instead of staring into the sad abyss of the past, Sol and I could look ahead toward the brightness of our future. It was what would hold Sol and I together and remind him that now he had a family of his own and he was safe. It was the answer that had been right under my nose all along.

Our baby.

We ended up at a hardware store. Sol grabbed a cart and seemed to know where he was going so I just followed. We walked from one aisle to the next, and I watched as he pulled things off hooks and then checked them off his list.

It started as a cramp.

"Sam?"

I realized I was holding my side.

"I'm okay."

He looked me up and down. He trusted me.

"Indigestion. It's normal."

He rubbed the lower part of my back. "Maybe you should sit."

"I'm fine."

He stared at me for a minute longer and then continued down the aisle. I waited until he finished paying and we were settled back in the car before I said anything more. If I kept it to myself, then it wasn't real. Besides, I really was sure everything was fine, but when he turned to me, I could tell he knew something was wrong.

He dug into his pocket and pulled out his cell phone. "Call the doctor."

"I'm sure it's nothing."

He pushed the phone toward me.

I spoke to the doctor covering for Dr. Goldman, and when I hung up, I told Sol that he could see me if I insisted but that he agreed things were probably fine.

Sol turned the car in the direction of the hospital.

The television in the waiting area of the Emergency Room was on a news channel but no one was paying attention. Sitting across from us was an old man with a walker and a woman beside him who kept looking up anxiously any time a nurse called out a patient's name. There was a teenage girl with her hair pulled back into a ponytail and her wrist wrapped in an ice pack and a three-year-old who kept running from one end of the room to the other. His mother was rocking a baby in her arms and he finally calmed down after she handed him a toy. I put my hand on my belly.

"Sam Green?"

Sol and I stood and he put his arm around me as the nurse led us through the swinging doors and into an examination room. "You can change into this," she said pointing to a gown.

"Is that necessary? I don't think this is a big deal."

She handed the gown to me anyway.

I took off my clothes and watched Sol fold them into perfectly formed squares, and then I jumped up on the bed.

But he saw me grab my side.

"It's just the donuts I had for lunch."

He turned away, and I wanted to tell him to trust me, but I said nothing and then he found the remote and turned on the television, flipping around until he landed on an old episode of *Law & Order*.

I felt another one, but this time I could cover it up by sliding under the thin blanket the nurse had given me. "I read about this thing called Braxton Hicks. They're these contractions that start early as a way for your body to prepare for delivery."

He was focused on the television screen, watching the detectives handcuffing someone.

"Do you think we will still have time to put the crib together tonight? I would love to see what it looks like."

He didn't answer.

Dr. Lapin had a head of yellow-white hair and a voice that was so soft you had to strain to hear it. He pulled the curtain back and walked into the exam room with a chart in his hand. "Now, young lady, what is this trouble you have gotten yourself into?"

I felt like a five-year-old.

"She's been having pain," Sol said.

I hated that in a span of minutes, I had gone back to being the person about whom things were said. "It's really not that bad."

"I'm sure it's not," Dr. Lapin said. "How far along are you?"

Sol answered before I could. "Twenty-four weeks and three days."

"When did the discomfort start?"

"Earlier in the evening," Sol answered.

I glared at him but he ignored me.

"Let's have a look."

He laid me back in the bed and lifted the gown. He smiled and apologized for the fact that his fingertips were cold and then he felt around my belly. "Everything looks good here. Why don't we send you in for an ultrasound just to be sure."

Sol let out the breath he must have been holding the entire time.

"All just a ploy so you could get a glimpse of your baby." He winked at me as he left the room.

The woman in the room next to ours began to yell, and as she got louder, Sol turned up the volume on the television. The lawyers on the show were giving closing arguments, which made me think of the law school I had refused to attend, which made me think of my mother, whom I wanted more than anything, so I was relieved when the orderly finally came to bring me to radiology.

The technician spread the now familiar goo over my abdomen and pressed the probe hard into my belly.

I winced.

"Sorry."

She pressed even harder, but I didn't care because just at that moment the baby kicked. "Did you see that?"

Sol was smiling as he grabbed my hand. We stopped paying attention to anything else except for our baby, who as far as we were concerned was making every effort to wave to us.

The technician didn't say anything, but I didn't care, because we were both staring at the baby, whom as I had promised, was fine. She continued taking measurements, tapping away at her computer, and when she was finished, she handed me a box of tissues and told me to clean myself up.

We were back in our room a few minutes later, and Sol handed me the bag of pretzels he had bought from the vending machine. There must have been a *Law & Order* marathon on because now there was a different episode blaring from the television. I stuffed the pretzels into my mouth, and just as Sol was about to go find me something else to eat, Dr. Lapin walked in.

"I have the results of your test." He was looking down at the floor, which made his voice sound even more muffled. "Your cervix is measuring short. I won't really know anything until I do a manual exam."

Sol turned to me as if he didn't understand what the doctor was saying and I could translate. Unfortunately, the pretzels had turned to paste in my mouth, and it was all I could do not to choke.

The nurse dropped the bottom half of the bed down and lifted the stirrups. Sol came and stood beside me, holding my hand so tight that his fingernails dug into my skin. The doctor apologized as he slid the cold metal speculum inside of me. I closed my eyes and started to pray, and soon the whispers in my head became words that turned into cries that flew around the room, bouncing off the faces of the detectives from *Law & Order*. They shot out through a crack in the window and then up into the night sky where they dissipated soundlessly into the murky black air.

Chapter 26

There is a physical thing that happens to me when I panic. It happened when my mother threw my father out of the house, and again when I was in high school and the girl who sat two seats behind me in chemistry class hung herself in her walk-in closet. It's an uncontrollable tremor that begins in my core, making my shoulders bounce and my teeth chatter like I am standing naked in the middle of the North Pole.

One of the nurses laid a warm blanket across my legs but I was still shaking. The doctor was holding my hand, but because I was trembling so intensely, my vision blurred and I could barely see him. Sol was on my other side, and he had this weird smile on his face, the kind that looks strange because it's so wrong—like when it rains on a perfectly sunny day.

I was shaking so much I wasn't even sure who it was that spoke.

"You are five centimeters dilated and your bag is bulging."

I shook my head. "My baby isn't due yet."

This couldn't be happening. I had done everything right. Through my chattering, I looked over at Sol. How would he ever forgive me?

The shaking was unstoppable regardless of how many blankets the nurses laid on top of me. They took my temperature and the doctor shook his head, and he and Sol talked in the corner of the room as if I wasn't even there.

"It's going to be okay, Sam." Sol was beside me, smiling that pretend smile, and then I threw up all over myself, pieces of the half-chewed pretzel I had eaten before I lost my innocence. The nurses came to help change me out the soiled gown and put me in a new one, and as they removed it, I got a look at my round naked belly and I shook my head no, back and forth, violently, like a crazy person. The despair was like a brick sitting on my chest, making it impossible to breathe, and the only way I could think to relieve myself was to wail so that's what I did: high-pitched and ear-piercing like what I imagined an animal must sound like as it is being slaughtered. I covered my face and I screamed and I shook and I sobbed until it was quiet and everything got dark. I must have slipped away for a few minutes; when I opened my eyes again, I was in a different room and Dr. Goldman was at the foot of the bed.

There was an IV in my arm, and for a minute I forgot what had happened. I felt like a spectator, watching things from above like when I was a little girl and got tired of walking and Brian lifted me up onto his shoulders and I got to see the world from high up.

"Feeling better?" Dr. Goldman asked. She was wearing a black cocktail dress. I wondered where she had been when she got the call.

Now that she was here, things would be fine. She would tell that stupid doctor that he had made a horrible mistake and everything would go back to being how it was when all I needed to worry about was matching the crib bedding to the color of the walls.

I nodded.

"Salmon, I need to explain what is going on."

"Everything will be okay now, right?"

There was that smile again. "Your cervix is opening and you have an infection."

"But it will be okay."

She was looking through some papers and then she leaned up against the railing of the bed. She didn't usually wear makeup in the office and I wasn't used to seeing her lips colored so brightly. "I won't lie to you."

The shaking started again, and Dr. Goldman buzzed for a nurse who handed me a cup with some pills inside of it, but I pushed them away. "I don't want to take anything that will hurt my baby."

The nurse tried again, but I shook my head.

"Take them, Sam," Dr. Goldman said.

"Where is Sol?"

"He needed to make some phone calls."

I could feel my insides shrink and the breath inside of me with it.

"Please make it easier for yourself."

I hated myself for giving in . . . and for the tremendous relief I felt that Sol wasn't there to watch me.

Be weak.

Pathetic.

Helpless.

I swallowed the pills.

Things moved quickly after that. Nurses bustled in and out, and after a while I stopped trying to cover up the cramping I was having. Sol came back into the room and stood by my side, but he couldn't look at me and I couldn't look at him, and whatever they had given me made me feel like I was wrapped in cotton. I tried to fight my body, fight the urge to push out the baby that was still too small to live outside of me, but it was too hard. No matter how hard I tried, I couldn't make it stop, so finally I gave up and the baby whom I loved more than anything else in the world came swimming out of me. When I opened my eyes, Sol was on one side and my mother was on the other.

"It's okay, Sam." She wiped my face with the cloth she was holding in her hand.

Dr. Goldman was so close I could see black mascara tinted tears running down her face. "This is your son." She handed me a tiny bundle wrapped in a blanket. I held him in my arms and I sang to him and I told him that I loved him and I held on to him for as long as I could because I knew that once I gave him back, I would never see him again.

"I want to name him David," Sol said. "It means beloved."

I nodded because at that moment I would have agreed to anything to make it up to him.

"That's a beautiful name," my mother said.

There was an unrecognizable softness in her voice that made me even more aware of the fact that something catastrophic had happened. She leaned in and kissed my son's forehead.

The movement in the room got less frantic because there was nothing to try and prevent since the worst had already happened. The nurse assured me I could hold him for as long as I wanted, for as long as I needed. He was so small and fragile, and all I could think about was that he was beautiful and that his tiny finger fit perfectly in my hand. It was my mother who finally took him from my arms and handed him back to the nurse. Sol was sobbing in the chair beside me, but I was silent, light-headed, like a balloon precariously tied to the handle of a stroller about to free itself and float away. I rolled over in the bed. This time when I closed my eyes, I prayed that I would never open them again.

My mother took over.

She told Sol to go home, and at first, he fought but then it was just easier giving in, easier than sitting in the room where we had lost everything. He finally left, and she spent the night in the reclining chair beside my bed.

When I woke, it took me a few minutes to remember what had happened, and when I did I was overcome with such tremendous sadness that I choked on my own spit. Just then her eyes opened like she could sense I was in distress. Just like she knew when Fluffy was in that cat's jaws, because she had the instinct.

The one that I didn't.

She pushed a button so that the mattress lifted and I was sitting in an upright position. A resident knocked on the door and tried to come inside but she shooed him away. After that, she stood guard, deciding who could come in and when. The only time she went away was to get some cookies from the hospital cafeteria, but they just sat on a plate next to the untouched breakfast tray that came and went. Even though she made sure the door remained closed, I was still on a maternity ward and I could hear other patient's visitors walking past.

Sometimes I could also hear laughter.

Sol came sometime around eleven. I was rolled over pretending to be asleep because I couldn't bear to see his face. He and my mother whispered to each other so as not to wake me, and the part of me that was going crazy inside wanted to pull back the blanket and show them that I was awake and that it had all been a silly practical joke—all of it.

My mother shook my shoulder when the lunch tray arrived.

"Try to eat something," she urged.

Sol had turned on the television but the sound was muted. He was so pale, he looked as though he had been rubbed in chalk dust. "Hey," he said when he saw me looking at him.

The tips of my fingers were frozen and I felt completely numb inside.

"You should eat."

I wanted to tell him that it didn't matter anymore and that I didn't care if I ever ate again. I wanted to tell him other things, too, but I said nothing, and instead I took a bite of the sandwich he offered. It was tuna salad, which he had always teased me about never wanting to try. I ate half not really tasting it anyway, and he smiled. There was a knock at the door, and Dr. Goldman walked in and both Sol and my mother stood.

"There is something I want to talk to you about." She sat at the foot of my bed, and this time she was dressed in her white lab coat. "We can do an autopsy if you want to see if there was something genetically wrong. And you should decide what you would like for us to do with him, afterward."

"I want an autopsy," Sol said.

I said nothing.

"And my son will have a burial. In a cemetery."

I listened to the cracks in my husband's voice as he made our child's funeral arrangements, and after Dr. Goldman left, I slipped down under the covers. I could hear their voices, mostly my mother's trying to talk Sol out of a formal ceremony so that it would be easier on me.

When it was time for me to go home, instead of a baby, they handed me a blue satin box tied with a ribbon. Inside were some Polaroid shots of David and a card with images of his hand and footprints. I held it on my lap as Sol drove back to the house. He helped me out of the car because I was still too sore to walk on my own. He put his arms around me and I waddled beside him, cursing the sanitary napkin wedged between my legs. Dr. Goldman assured me that the bleeding was normal, but all it did was remind me of brutality.

Brian was waiting for us when we arrived. He had called while I was in the hospital, but my mother told him not to come since I would be home soon anyway. When I saw him, I started to cry short, smudgy tears that had some-how managed to survive the frost that had taken over my insides. He held me in his arms and, even though he tried not to, I could tell that he was crying too. "It will be okay, Fish. You will see." I wanted to believe him. I wanted to feel like he could make it all go away like he always did, but I knew that nothing could relieve the kind of pain I was feeling.

He led me into the house and helped me get comfortable on the couch. If I thought the sadness would stay outside of our little white house and not follow me in, I was wrong. It sat in the back seat of Sol's green car and marched up our walkway, slipping itself like a noose around my neck.

Brian brought out a tray that had belonged to Sol's mother. He placed several teacups on it and filled them with my favorite candies. He lifted some red licorice strands up to his nose, and even though I wanted to, I could not even force myself to smile.

Sol was in the kitchen unloading grocery bags. He and my mother got busy cleaning, buzzing from one room to the next, and then I heard clanking noises coming from the kitchen. I closed my eyes and leaned into Brian's shoulder, but every time I fell asleep, I would wake gasping for air like I was drowning. They made small talk over lunch, but I just kept moving the food around on my plate, hoping that if I did it long enough, no one would notice. My mother brought out a chocolate cake with glossy brown frosting, but I didn't ask for a slice. I wanted to disappear, but I also couldn't bear the idea of being alone, so instead I sat on the couch where I listened as they cleaned up and tried not to hate them for being able to shift so effortlessly back into life.

Finally, my mother helped me upstairs. She handed me a pink nightgown, but instead I chose a bra and a T-shirt and a pair of baggy sweat pants and she didn't fight me. I laid down and closed my eyes. When I woke, my shirt was wet with round, sour milk stains. Sol was asleep beside me, and I managed not to wake him as I slipped out of bed and went downstairs.

My mother was still rummaging in the kitchen.

"I don't want anything," I said.

She came back with leaves of green cabbage in her hand. "It's an old wives' tale but hopefully it will work." She slipped them inside my bra, the coolness soothing my full, aching breasts.

I sat on the couch and she sat beside me.

"It will be okay, Salmon."

The cabbage leaves lost their coolness and began to feel clammy against my skin. "It will never be okay."

She held my hand. "I promise that it will."

"How do you know?"

"Because," she said as she kissed the top of my head, "I made you and I know what you are made of."

She put a pillow in her lap and helped me lay across and that is how I finally slept that night.

With her watching guard.

Chapter 27

The day of the funeral was cold and gray.

Drifts of black, dirty snow lined the path to the part of the graveyard where babies were buried. I was propped like a cripple between my mother and Sol. I am not sure how many people were there or even if I spoke to them. Mostly, I focused on the geese that flew overhead, their long mournful wails more of a tribute to my child than anything the man in the black overcoat reading aloud about God.

People came to the house afterward. Henry Green sat in an armchair tapping his cane against the hardwood floor just as he had the day of my wedding celebration. If he looked at me, I didn't know because I could not look at him. I just focused on the sound of the tap that matched the beating rhythm of my heart.

"Drink some tea," Susan said.

My fingertips still felt frozen and the warmth from the cup hurt.

She sat beside me on the couch, her weight on the cushion causing me to topple slightly, which she didn't seem to notice.

"Let me know if there's anything I can do. If you or Sol need anything."

I took a sip and burned my tongue.

She sighed. "It will be fine, Sam. Don't worry. You will have another."

When she stood, the couch sunk back down deeper as though we had been sitting on a seesaw. Some of the tea spilled onto my lap, and I could feel it seeping through the skirt my mother had given me to wear. It was thin and black and long, and I knew that once this day was over, I would throw it into the trash because I never wanted to see it again.

My mother came and sat beside me, and again I felt myself tilting over as if I was on a ship. The couch was new, bought in a material we thought would withstand a child's touch, but I had not noticed before how unsteady it felt. I began to feel queasy and the room started to spin, faces and sandwiches and pieces of furniture flying around me in wild abandon. I didn't even bother to excuse myself, just went straight upstairs, where I stripped off the black skirt and put my sweatpants back on.

The old wives' tale was true, and the green cabbage leaves had drained the milk out of me, leaving my breasts deflated and empty. I got into bed and my mother came up and tucked a blanket snugly around my shoulders like she did when I was a little girl. She went to turn off the light, but I told her not to. There was too much darkness inside of me already and I couldn't stand any more. I tried to sleep, tried to silence the sound of the people below me who were pretending to be kind when I knew what they were really thinking: I had let his hand slip from mine, I hadn't been vigilant, I hadn't protected him, and now he was gone and there was no one to blame but myself.

Sleep came again without me realizing and when I woke, I felt unsteady and confused and then I remembered David's face and the pain was so fresh it made me cry out loud. Sol was in bed and it was night. He rolled over but didn't wake. I stared up at the ceiling, running my hands over my belly, reminding myself that David wasn't with me anymore.

In the morning, after I convinced them I was fine, Sol and my mother went to work. My mother laid out some clothes for me but I chose my sweatpants instead. I went downstairs and stood in the middle of the house like I was trying to decide what to do even though I knew where I would end up.

Someone had emptied David's room of the boxes and furniture. All that was left was Sol's mother's rocking chair and the bear that was still wedged into the corner of the windowsill. I tried to sit and rock, but I didn't fit the way that I used to, and I knew that I didn't deserve to sit in her rocking chair anymore because I was not like her.

I was not perfect.

I sat with my back propped against the wall with the bear in my arms. That's how I spent the first day and every day after, only moving to the couch in the living room when I heard Sol or my mother's car pull into the driveway. It was all I had in me to greet them with a smile and tell them that, yes, things were getting better. But all I wanted, all I dreamed about, was for everyone to leave me alone so I could sit on the floor in that room holding the little crinkly bear in my arms.

It was harder to fool Dr. Goldman and even harder not to cry when she told us that the autopsy results had come back from the lab and that David was genetically normal. Sol seemed relieved, but all the information did for me was confirm that what happened was entirely my fault. Dr. Goldman explained that sometimes the cervix can open and there is really no way of knowing if a patient is at risk until it happens. She reassured us that there were ways to prevent it from happening in the future and then recommended waiting a few months before trying again. On our way out, she pulled me aside and asked if I was all right. I assured her that I was even as she scribbled the name of a support group on a piece of paper. I waited until I got to the lobby before I crumpled it and threw it into the trash.

In the car, Sol seemed relieved. He asked if I wanted to go get a piece of pie. I didn't. All I wanted was to go back to the house and sit in David's room, but I knew he wouldn't understand, so I agreed.

He ordered apple and I ordered cherry, but I had no appetite so I just pushed it around on my plate until it looked like a big red gloppy mess, but he didn't say anything and just motioned for the waitress to bring the check.

He reached across the table and patted my hand. "We'll be able to try again soon, Sam. You'll see."

After a while, you get used to smiling when you want to cry because you've learned that is what you are supposed to do.

Sol smiled back.

He tried to touch me a few times.

Slipping his hands around my waist and pulling me in close to him. If he noticed that I tried to pull away, he didn't say anything. I didn't know how to explain that I did not want the body that had betrayed me to feel any kind of pleasure.

As the days passed, I grew more restless, but I didn't want him to know so I waited until he was asleep before I slipped away to sit in David's room. One night as I sat up to leave, he pulled me back down. We were facing each other and he put his hand on my cheek. I had long ago stopped sleeping naked. He slid his hand underneath my sweatshirt and tried to lift it over my head but I stopped him. I could not bear to have him look at me. He left his hands there anyway, cupping my breasts and squeezing them hard. As he kissed me, he pushed his tongue into my mouth. He coaxed the waistband of my sweatpants down so that they sat at my knees and then he pulled my underwear down, too. As I turned away from him, the scruff on his face burned my skin. I put my arms underneath my bottom and grabbed a handful of the sheet between my fingers and then I closed my eyes, counting the seconds until he would finish. He rolled on top of me and moved in and out of me quickly and precisely, like he was pumping gas. When he was done, I waited until he was asleep before I let out the cry that had hidden itself inside the folds of my vocal chords, but he must have heard because his breathing pattern changed and I knew he was awake.

"I lost a baby, too, you know. You aren't the only one it happened to." He was sitting up now, covering his face with his hands.

I went into the bathroom and stripped off my clothing and turned the water in the shower on as hot as I could stand. I scrubbed myself until my skin was raw, and as I cried and my tears disappeared down the drain, I wondered if I he would ever find it in his heart to forgive me.

When I came back out, he was gone.

He left a note on the nightstand scribbled with a pen that had slowly run out of ink.

Going to sleep in the sto.

I sat at the edge of the bed, holding the paper in my hand, and even though I hated myself for it, I breathed an irrefutable and unmistakable sigh of relief.

That's how it went for the next few weeks. He would come home for a few hours after work and then leave again, as if I was toxic and spending too much time near me would poison him, too. He stopped touching me, stopped kissing me. On the rare occasion he slept at home, I stayed downstairs on the couch since it seemed kinder to us both.

One morning my mother showed up. I wasn't quick enough to greet her at the door, and she found me sitting on the floor of David's room. She was so fast, in fact, that I wondered if she had her own key. I started to feel angry, but it had been so long since I had felt that way toward anyone else but myself, that I had almost forgotten how. She handed me a sweater and led me outside.

The sun was shining.

I hated that the world was moving on without acknowledging that the most terrible thing had happened.

She pushed me into the passenger seat.

"Let's take a drive."

My arms were crossed at my chest like I was a sulking teenager.

As soon as we turned the corner, she began to sing. I had forgotten how pleasing her voice was. I had forgotten how easy it could be to slip into serenity. But I didn't deserve relief or comfort, so I covered my ears and soon she stopped singing and just continued to drive. I closed my eyes so I could no longer see the perfectly cloudless blue sky.

After about half an hour, she drove me back to the house. She used her key to open the door, and I felt a flicker of rage that again quickly subsided. She led me back to David's room, and I was relieved that she finally seemed to understand that is where I belonged because that is what I deserved.

But the rocking chair was gone, and in its place sat my art desk surrounded by piles of magazines stacked precariously high. Brian was carrying in more, and his sleeves were pushed up above his elbows. I knew I was supposed to smile, and because I had become so good at it, that is what I did. They both smiled back.

Pleased with themselves.

After that, it didn't take long to get them both to leave. I even waved out the window as they drove away. The desk was just as I remembered, but I couldn't even picture the girl who had once loved working at it. All I could think about was that day, about Sarah Jacobs and how I ended up back in the garage in search of my collages even though I should have known better. Maybe I was crazed and irrational, but at that moment I was more certain than ever—it was the art that always brought me pain.

Someone walking outside distracted me and I stared out the window. Spring was slowly easing in, and the grass was just beginning to turn green. The previous owner must have planted tulips in the corner of the yard because they were starting to come up. I felt hot and sweaty and enraged. I hunted through a drawer until I found a pair of scissors. I stood over Susan's art desk, stabbing at it unmercifully like it was a person I was murdering. I scraped at it, grunting with each plunge, gauging out holes and hacking out chips of wood hoping for relief.

But there was none.

I ran into the yard. I was in my usual sweat-pant attire, which these days I wore both day and night. My hair was pulled back into a ponytail that had gotten so tangled inside the elastic I had given up on brushing it. I fell to my knees in the tulip bed and began to snip them at their base. But it was taking too long and was too civilized and controlled and didn't match the savagery I felt inside. I threw the scissors onto the grass and began to rip each flower out with my bare hands. Soil caked beneath my fingernails as I pounded my palms into the ground, which was still hard from winter. Green leaves and dirt and death surrounded me.

I wanted the world to stop turning and for people to stop living, but I also knew that nothing would take away the pain. I went back inside the house and sat on the floor of David's room and that's when I saw the collage still propped against the windowsill. My hands shook as I ripped it in half, then into fours, and then into so many pieces that they fluttered around me like confetti at a parade. Fragments of something that had once made sense but now made none surrounded me and none of it mattered because any bit of hope, any bit of self-confidence I had managed to nurture, had disappeared with the death of my child. I wrapped my arms around my knees, moving softly back and forth. Minutes and then hours passed, and when I heard a car drive up, I didn't have the strength to stand.

Sol called out: "Sam?" As though he was home for the evening and ready to talk about the events of his day like we were a perfectly normal couple.

I didn't answer.

"Sam?" This time there was tightness in his voice.

He turned on the light in the hallway and opened the door to the room I was sitting in. I hadn't realized how dark it was until the brightness streamed in.

"Are you okay?"

He was looking inside the room. He was looking at the desk and the pieces of collage that surrounded me like the dirt mourners sprinkle onto a coffin. He hesitated, and for a minute I was sure that he was about to turn around and leave, but then he didn't.

He lifted me up from the spot where I had been sitting, and because I was too tired to fight, I let him. I wrapped my arms around his neck and buried my face into his chest. He carried me upstairs and stripped off my clothes and then filled the bathtub with cool water and helped me get in. He got a washcloth from the linen closet and cleaned the dirt and the smell and the grime from my skin. He untangled the elastic from my hair and helped me tilt back, and when I wanted to sink all the way down, he forced me back up. He filled his palm with shampoo, softly rubbing it into my scalp, and then rinsed it clean with a pitcher he brought from the kitchen. He helped me stand and then he wrapped me in a towel and rubbed my back until I was warm and helped me change into the white nightgown he had picked out.

He led me downstairs, and I sat at the kitchen table while he made me a grilled cheese sandwich. He sat across from me while I ate, and when my hair fell into my face, he reached across the table and tucked it behind my ear.

"I will always take care of you, Sam."

I finished the sandwich and he took the plate to the sink. When I stood up, he put his arms around me. "I shouldn't have listened to your mother and moved out all the furniture. It makes it like he didn't even exist."

My cheeks felt like someone had rubbed them with fire.

His hands were still around my waist and he pulled me into him, and I could feel myself giving in to the warmth and the comfort of being held. "Soon we can get to work on having another." He smiled. "Then all of this will just disappear and we can start fresh."

I didn't mean to tell him the way that I did.

"What did you say?" he asked.

I thought the words were still safely inside my head. I hadn't even realized they had slipped out into the air, but there they were, ugly and mean and honest. The words confirming what I had known for so long but kept hidden. "I can never be someone's mother."

"Of course you can, and you will." He looked at me funny, like he didn't recognize me, like he was no longer familiar with the monster I had become.

I had already lost everything, which meant that I had nothing left to lose.

"I can't, Sol." I took in a breath that sounded like a cry, "And I won't." He was staring at me in a way he never had before. "Ever."

Perhaps it was the look in my eyes or the darkness in my voice, but I could tell that not only had he heard but also that he believed me. He still had his hands around my waist and pushed himself away as though he had been electrocuted. He pushed back so far that he knocked over a kitchen chair. He kept backing up slowly until he reached the car keys on the counter, and the next thing I knew he was out the door with the sound of the engine rumbling in my ear.

He came home less often after that, and when he did, there was an uncomfortable air between us. I tried hard to make things better once I realized I could not give him the one thing he wanted most. I started showering and wearing makeup again and waited in the living room around the time he usually came home. I sorted through his mother's recipes and tried to prepare the easiest ones I could find. He would eat what I made and then wash the dishes, but afterward he would leave me to go back to the store.

One night I waited in our bedroom, and when I heard the front door unlock, I called to him. It had taken perfect timing, but I managed to fill each flat surface in the room with a candle and lit it before he came up the stairs. I turned out the light and listened as he climbed up the stairs. The room was bathed in a golden warmth, and when he opened the door, he squinted for a minute as his eyes adjusted.

"What are you doing?"

I turned around slowly, and I stood before him completely naked and exposed. I reached my hand out to him.

He stood at the threshold of the doorway but he did not come any further. "I'm sorry, Sam."

"Please." My face turned red both from the heat in the room and from my shame.

He stepped backward. "I can't."

He ran down the stairs, and when I heard the door slam, I blew out the candles, each wisp of rising smoke a memento of my despair.

My mother came by a few times to make sure I was eating. She quickly figured out that things between Sol and I were strained.

"You know you can still think about law school."

We were eating lunch in her kitchen, my little girl daisies innocently hanging above our heads.

"I'm not sure how Sol would feel about leaving his business and moving to New York."

She took a bite of her salad, crunching hard on a green pepper and making it look as though she was deep in thought.

"Maybe some time apart would do you both some good." She finished her meal and stood to clear the table. "Come work with me. You know I would love to have you."

I smashed the crumb topping from the piece of coffee cake I was eating. Lately, she let me eat all the dessert I wanted. "I'll think about it."

She smiled. "Would it really be so bad?"

When I got home, I realized Sol must have come in while I was gone because there was a big pile of laundry sitting on the floor in front of the washing machine. He had gotten himself a canvas bag with a drawstring and carried his things back and forth like a soldier on leave.

I wonder how many people can pinpoint the exact moment their heart breaks.

It was innocent at first, loading his things into the washing machine and holding up a pair of his jeans. Gliding my hand across a bump that felt unnatural like some kind of cancerous growth. My fingers tingled slightly as I unfolded what looked like an innocuous note.

Can't wait until tonight. I miss you so much. See you at 7.

It was hard enough to read, but what was worse was that in the place of a signature was an imprint of a pair of lips the shape of which I recognized immediately. The shaking began so quickly that the note slipped from my fingers and fluttered to the floor. I could feel my knees hitting each other, and the next thing I knew, they had given out from under me and I was sitting on the ground with the rest of his dirty things. I rubbed my arms up and down, waiting for my teeth to stop chattering. Shock has a way of slowing time and then speeding it up, and as I relived every moment of my discovery, the sun went down and the house became dark.

Jiggling keys in the door and then his footsteps on the stairs startled me. Was he coming back to retrieve what he had left behind? I waited on the floor with the note unfolded at my feet.

Chapter 28

When I opened my eyes, my fingers were covered in glue and scraps of magazine were littered around me like shrapnel. The collage of Birdie I had started was now finished and sitting in my lap. It was morning and I was here, back in my life, and even though I knew I was safe, I couldn't stop seeing it all in my head, over and over again. What I had uncovered about myself, about Sol, even if it was only in a dream, was so disturbing it left my insides raw.

I wanted to pull the covers over my head. I wanted a drink. I felt trapped with nowhere to run. I wanted to disappear into thin air so I wouldn't have to live this life or dream about the other. The only reason I finally got out of bed was because Alice had a doctor's appointment that morning and I had promised to open the store, and if nothing else, I couldn't let her down. I took a shower then stared at myself in the foggy mirror, running my fingers along the lines of my face in the reflection. In this life, I was sad and broken and lost. In my dream life, I had been someone's wife and mother.

I had failed at both.

I got to the store and pulled out my keys, which slid effortlessly into the lock. Attached to the knob was a peace sign with two silver butterflies that chimed whenever the door moved. I turned on the lights and only had time for a few sips of coffee before the chime sounded again. When I looked up, I saw Birdie pulling off her hat. Propelled by static electricity, her thin hair flew straight up like a halo above her head. Her mother was crouched in front of her, helping to undo her coat.

Time is supposed to be constant. No matter what you are doing, the duration of the first sixty seconds is supposed to be the same as the next. But when Birdie's mother turned to face me, everything came to a sudden and screeching halt.

She hesitated for a moment and then cocked her head. "Sam? Is that you?"

Birdie went to the table to gather her supplies, not remotely interested in the possibility that her mother and I might know each other.

I pushed a piece of hair behind my ear. "Hello, Susan."

"What a funny place to run into you."

Even though I knew that this was a different Susan from that other Susan, something inside me clenched.

"The last time I saw you, your dad was packing you up for law school. I can't believe that we lost touch. It's been too long. How are you?"

"In between jobs. Helping Alice out." I tried to keep the conversation light to distract Susan from the sound of my heart beating out of my chest, but I didn't need to because just then her phone buzzed in her bag and she got distracted. She didn't look at me again until she turned it off. "She's doing me such a favor by letting the kid stay here two mornings a week."

I was grateful for the change in subject and motioned toward Birdie, who was already hard at work on a drawing. "She's great."

Susan had a strange look on her face, as though she wanted to say something, but then she didn't. "Anyway, I have to get to class. Maybe we can get together some time? Get a drink? I'd love to catch up."

I nodded, knowing that would never happen because that's just what people said when they ran into the people who had fallen out of their lives, forgetting that they usually had fallen out for a reason. Susan kissed Birdie on the top of her head but the little girl didn't react.

"Have a good day."

Susan waved, and perhaps it was petty of me, but I was secretly delighted that her daughter didn't wave back.

Birdie got busy with her drawing while I worked on washing down the tables and then covering them with tan-colored craft paper. There had been a birthday party the afternoon before, so there was a little more cleaning up than usual, but I was grateful for the distraction. I tried to concentrate on washing the brushes, focusing on the steaming water running over my hands, but even that didn't stop the thoughts from pushing their way in.

After I was finished, I sat down beside Birdie to paint a figurine. I picked out a dolphin because I knew Birdie liked them. I was so lost in painting that I didn't notice when Alice came in.

I walked over and watched as she put her things away. "I met Birdie's mother today."

"Oh yeah?" She was looking through the mail on her desk.

"We used to be roommates."

Alice stopped what she was doing. "Small world."

I wasn't sure what I wanted her to say, I just knew that I wanted her to make the uneven feeling inside of me go away. I didn't know how to make Alice understand because I didn't understand myself. She must have known something was wrong, though, because she put her hand on my cheek. "Don't look back, Sam. Only look ahead."

Now that I knew when Susan would be coming, I was able to time things to avoid her. I reminded myself that as long as I worked at The Creative Outlet and got to spend time with Birdie, nothing else really mattered. It probably was not healthy to allow myself to get so involved with her, but I couldn't help myself, especially when I realized that Birdie was beginning to smile when she saw me, and that if I walked away from the table to get something, she would get up with me, slipping her tiny hand inside mine.

At noon, I would give her a hug goodbye and then go and pick up lunch, which was always a salad for Alice and a grilled cheese sandwich for me. Birdie would be gone when I returned and Alice and I would eat together. Alice told me more of her myths, her voice and the rhythm of her words so soothing that when she spoke, I closed my eyes like I was listening to the most beautiful music. Being with Alice, in this place in those moments, I could feel the parts of me that had unraveled slowly starting to mend.

One day, Birdie and I were working on a figurine that she had chosen—a mother elephant and her baby. I had struggled to fall asleep the night before and ended up watching a special on animals from sub-Saharan Africa, so as we painted, I told her what I had learned. Every few minutes, she would stop and look at me, waiting for the next word to leave my lips. I had never met anyone so interested in what I had to say.

"Girl elephants live together for most of their lives."

Birdie nodded, mixing black and white and a tiny bit of blue as I had shown her. She dabbed at the elephant's hind leg, swirling in a circle, seemingly pleased with the effect.

"But boy elephants live by themselves."

She watched as I added black to the underside of the elephant's ear to give shadow and dimension. She was a talented artist with a good eye and so easy to teach. I poured a little more paint onto the palette, but then I felt her stand and run, the air whipping past me like a deep breath. We had gotten so involved in what we were doing that I had forgotten the time, and now there was a man, who I assumed was her father, bending down to meet her at eye level. She wrapped her arms around him and the intimacy of the moment reminded me that she belonged to someone else.

It looked like she was whispering something in his ear and my heart broke again. Could it be that she could talk but that she just chose not to talk to me? I didn't want to watch anymore, so I turned back to the elephant we had been working on. It took a few minutes for me to realize that he was standing at the edge of the table extending his hand.

"I'm Rachel's dad."

I looked up into his face and into his eyes, which were so familiar that something inside of me broke.

Sol.

He said it at the same time that I did, so I didn't have to explain how it was I already knew his name.

"Nice to meet you," I mumbled realizing that as far as he was concerned, it was the first time we had ever met.

"Rachel really likes you. It's nice to finally put a face to the name."

He knew about me. Even though I didn't think she could talk, she could, and when she did, the words she chose to say were about me.

Birdie came back wearing her jacket and hid behind Sol's leg.

"I'll see you around?"

He said it casually, like you would to any stranger you'd just met, but to me it felt meaningful and like it required a response.

"Sure."

I tried to stay focused after he left, but I couldn't. Everything inside of me was shaking. Alice must have realized something was wrong because she offered to get lunch, but I insisted on going myself. I needed to get outside, to breathe fresh air so that I could remember that I was real and that what had just happened was real, too.

Snow was falling gently, the individual flakes landing on my coat disappearing before I could appreciate their beauty. People rushed about, their faces wrapped in scarves through which the occasional puff of white breath emerged. I took my time allowing the coldness to seep through and revive me like I was just waking from a dream. I tried to walk with purpose, even though everything inside felt loose and wobbly. Somehow, I managed to get to the deli and make it back to the store even though I couldn't remember anything except for the way the cold air felt against my skin. I walked in, half expecting that he would still be there, like he had suddenly remembered who I was and was waiting for me to return, which of course he wasn't.

Alice talked while we ate. I nodded at the right times, but the whole time I was somewhere else. I was making promises to myself that I would not fall again, that I would not slip.

That I would not let him break me.

Maybe it was the result of curiosity or a tiny flicker of courage, or maybe it was simply out of fear, but that night when I went to bed, I knew what I wanted.

I needed to understand. I needed to know more.

I took out my sketchbook and a stack of magazines. I thought about flight and being free and then it began as I started to draw.

Chapter 29

Sol stood in the doorway but neither of us spoke.

Seconds collapsed into minutes, but I didn't cry because I felt so broken inside, I wasn't even sure I'd know how.

Finally, he spoke.

"I'm sorry." He picked up the note and shoved it into the front pocket of his pants.

"For how long?"

He shrugged. "Doesn't matter."

I stood, leaning against the side of the washing machine, not trusting my legs, which quivered like jelly. He extended his arm but I pushed it away. Somehow, I managed to make my way downstairs to the kitchen and pour myself a glass of water. My head was spinning and my hand was shaking so much that the water splashed outside of the glass.

"Let me help you," he said as he pulled out a chair.

"I don't want your help."

He was quietly staring down at the uneven linoleum floor he never believed was uneven in the first place. "I didn't mean to hurt you."

Something inside me got ugly, and then all I wanted was to hear all of it in excruciating detail. "How many times?"

He turned away from me. "It doesn't matter, Sam."

"It does to me."

He ran his hand through his hair. "What difference does it make?"

"Because I want to know how many times you fucked her, and then I want to know how you live with yourself."

His face turned red. "I can't tell you how many times because I've lost track. Do you want me to tell you how good she is? Because I can do that too. Do you want me to tell you that she makes me happy? Do you really want to know all the details, Sam?"

Each sentence was like a blow that hit me squarely in the gut and I had to fight not to double over from the pain. Susan had once told me that she and I were the same, and I finally understood that she was right. I hated that of all people he had chosen her. I spit my words out like watermelon seeds. "How could you betray me?"

He was almost to the door when he spun around. "You," he came close and pointed his finger at my chest, "betrayed me." He was so angry, his chest heaved up and down like he was blowing up a balloon. "You left me a long time ago."

He stomped out, slamming the door so hard the entire room shook.

I was frantic, and the rest of the night passed in a blur. The movie playing in my head was of Sol and Susan making love in my bedroom, in the store, in my old apartment. I imagined the two of them laughing together and of him sharing with her the parts of himself that he had only ever shared with me. No matter how I tried, I could not make the images stop, and each was more difficult to bear than the next.

I stayed awake that night, pacing the hallway from the kitchen to the living room, hoping that he would come to his senses and come home and beg my forgiveness and tell me the whole thing had been a terrible mistake.

But he didn't.

He didn't come home that night or the night after that. On the third night, I was just about to call him when I heard his car in the driveway. I had stopped at the bakery and bought his favorite cookies, which I ended up eating over the course of the last two days since he hadn't shown up. Today's batch was sitting on a plate on the kitchen table. I motioned for him to sit and pushed the plate toward him, but he shook his head.

"I don't want this to be awkward." He slid into the chair.

I had thought all of this through. What we needed was a neutral party to help us sort things out. "I think we should talk to someone."

He nodded again. "I already have. But you should have your own representation."

Saliva pooled in the rounds of my cheeks and then slipped down my throat and I choked.

He stood up and the chair made a screeching sound as it scraped against the floor.

"Let's not make this harder than it has to be." His eyes were red, as if he had been crying.

"Don't do this, Sol." I felt like I had just been kicked and I couldn't catch my breath.

Someone was knocking at the front door.

"Sam?" my mother called out as she let herself in.

Sol started to back away but I blocked his path.

My mother made her way into the kitchen, holding my sweater up into the air. "You forgot this."

He tried to push past me.

"Don't leave me, Sol." I was crying and panting because breathing was still too hard.

"Let him go, Sam," my mother said.

But I couldn't. Even though I knew how pathetic I looked, I didn't care. I couldn't lose him, because I couldn't imagine who I would be without him. I tried to grab onto him, but he slipped out of my grip. Tears and snot covered my face and I tried to think of what I could say that would bring him back to me. He was getting closer to the door, and in a matter of seconds it would be too late. I had to do something to make him stop, to make him love me again. "I need you." Weakness and shame pulsed through me, and I felt myself beginning to collapse.

He stopped and turned and looked at me and my mother, who I hadn't even realized was standing beside me, holding me up.

"No, Sam. You don't."

Then he walked out without ever looking back.

She made me tea and I drank it because I thought the heat would thaw my insides. I held the cup in my hands, hoping to stop feeling numb, but then the pain came rushing back and all I wanted was to feel frozen again.

My mother didn't say much besides asking whether I wanted sugar or honey, and when I didn't answer, she made the choice for me. When it came time for bed, she led me upstairs and then helped me change and got into bed with me. The last time she slept in a bed with me was when I was ten and got sick with the flu. I remembered how she had wiped my forehead and given me sips of flat ginger ale to drink.

I tossed and turned for most of the night, and each time she repositioned the blanket so that I was covered. I didn't fall into a deep sleep until early morning and only woke because of the smell of sweet, buttery pancakes. My stomach grumbled and I hated it for betraying me, but then I had no choice but to get up.

I sat at the table holding my head up with my hand, and she slipped the plate of food under my nose. Each cake was puffed in the center and covered in white bursts of powdered sugar. She sat across from me, blowing small rippled waves across the surface of her coffee. "What do you feel like doing today?"

I shook my head. I had lost track of time and reality and did not have the faintest idea of what day it even was. The only thing I knew was that there was pretty much nothing I wanted to do that day or the day after that or any day for that matter.

"Get dressed," she ordered.

The way she said it made me understand that doing what she wanted far outweighed the aggravation of disobeying her. Anyway, I didn't have the strength to fight. I found a pair of clean sweatpants and put them on.

Brian was waiting in the living room when I came downstairs. He kissed the top of my head and hugged me for what was probably a few seconds too long since I suddenly felt like I couldn't breathe.

I sat in the back seat of the car like I did when I was little. My mother drove and Brian turned on the radio.

"Remember when we went to Disney World?" Brian asked.

"You were eight," my mother said, looking at me through the rearview mirror.

I nodded.

"All the other girls loved the princesses but you loved Dumbo the Flying Elephant."

I was quiet.

"You wanted to ride it over and over."

Even then I wanted to fly.

No one spoke and Brian turned up the music. A song my mother knew came on, and as she sang, I closed my eyes, but all I could picture was Sol.

Leaving me.

We got to the beach, and my mother parked in the lot that was nearly empty. She popped open the trunk and brought out a basket and some chairs, which Brian and I helped carry. It was still not warm enough to be considered beach weather, and there weren't many people on the sand. A few little girls were running around with their pants pushed up above their knees. They raced to the edge of the water, getting closer each time as their mothers shouted at them not to get too wet.

We walked away from them until it felt like we were the only ones there, and my mother laid out the blanket and set out the chairs. I tried not to remember the last time I had been to the beach. Brian reached over and touched my cheek.

"It will be okay, Fish."

My mother looked up and then went back to arranging the blanket. She positioned the chairs on each corner so the wind wouldn't blow it away. "Let's walk."

We started off together like we always did, but after a few minutes, my mother went on ahead. For as long as I could remember, it had always been like that. No matter how much she tried, she couldn't be held back; it was as though her legs were too long, her stride too fast, and they always took her a few steps too far. I watched as her hair whipped in the wind. When she turned toward us, it covered her face and her lips and made her laugh, and I was suddenly struck by how young she looked. She turned back around, bending a few times to pick up shells that she collected in her pockets.

Brian put his arm through mine and pulled me close. Smooth salt air rushed up through my nose and settled inside my throat. I tried to lose myself inside the movement of the wind, but the pain I was feeling kept me weighted down. My mother was now far enough ahead that the only thing that made her recognizable was her gait, steady and strong and determined.

Despair rose from within me like carbonated bubbles. "What am I going to do?" The sound of my weakness made me tremble, and Brian must have thought I was cold because he hugged me tighter.

"To thine own self be true," he said softly.

After my mother threw him out, I would go to his apartment after school to do my homework. We never talked about what had happened or how much I felt to blame; instead, we sat at his kitchen table eating potato chips and slices of American cheese, and together we would read Shakespeare. I loved *Romeo and Juliet* but Brian preferred *Hamlet, Prince of Denmark*, a story about a man destroyed by his failure to act. When we were feeling especially silly, we would read parts of the play aloud. I wanted to ask why he was quoting from it now, but two dogs chasing each other distracted me, their movements wild and unrestrained. A young boy threw a stick into the ocean and they ran after it as if their lives depended upon its retrieval. Brian was staring up ahead, looking at my mother, who was already making her way back. While she was still out of earshot, he repeated, "To thine own self be true."

I waited for him to say more, but then my mother was there and he grew quiet.

"You two and your secrets." She looked from me to him and then she laughed like she thought she was making a joke.

Once we were home, I could barely keep my eyes open. My mind went blank, and when I woke, I was dazed and unsure of where I was. It was only after a few seconds that the memory of the last few weeks came crashing back making it hard to sit up.

My parents were in the kitchen, and I could hear them talking but I could not make out their words. When I was little, I remember thinking that they spoke in harmony, their voices complimenting each other as though they were singers in a choir. That's what it sounded like now, a sort of music floating through the air.

My mother made dinner, and afterward we washed dishes like we had when my father was still living with us. It was easy to fall back into routine. It felt effortless to stand between the people who love you in the spot you have stood in so many times before. They were there with me for the next several days, and we made food from my childhood and watched our favorite movies. Although no one said it out loud, I knew they were doing everything they could to hold me up.

To help me forget.

On the morning of the sixth day, I woke and showered and got dressed. I packed the few things my father had brought from his apartment and then put water to boil for tea. When my mother came downstairs, she smiled because I had opened a fresh box of Earl Grey and placed a tea bag in her mug. I set the timer for exactly four minutes, the perfect amount of time for it to steep, just as she had taught me. After breakfast, I assured them that I really was feeling better and then I walked them to the door. As we hugged, I couldn't help but think that we were acting as though a plague had been lifted and we were no longer under quarantine.

After they left, I sat on the couch, trying hard to remember the person I used to be.

Before.

I didn't realize how late it was when I got up to make myself something to eat. My mother had stocked the freezer with enough food to keep me going for a while, and I was sitting at the table eating a bowl of soup when it happened.

The lights went out, and suddenly I was alone in the dark.

Helpless.

I tried not to panic, even when I stumbled into a wall and the bowl went crashing onto the ground. I looked for some paper towels, but I didn't have a flashlight so I just gave up, sliding along the wet floor that was already tilted to begin with.

I took a few breaths and thought about what to do.

I knew that I shouldn't have, but I did it anyway. I made my way across the room and found my cell phone and typed in just one word.

"Help."

Then I sat in the dark and waited.

He was there within twenty minutes.

"Sam?" he said my name differently than he had in the past. Like we didn't belong to each other anymore. It made me catch my breath.

"Are you okay?"

I motioned toward the lights even though it was pitch black and he couldn't see me. "Lost power."

He disappeared and when everything came back on a few minutes later, I felt assaulted by the rush of sound and light.

"Just the fuse box." His eyebrows furrowed as he explained, and I thought it was odd that I had never noticed him doing that before.

"Maybe you could show me where it is so I know what to do if it happens again."

He smiled. "You can just call me."

My eyes finally adjusted to the light, and I couldn't tell if there was pity in his voice.

"I don't mind." He smiled again.

I walked him to the door.

"Take care." He waved like he was a repairman leaving a service call.

That night, I turned off all the lights and sat in the dark until morning.

I watched a lot of television.

I commiserated with the women whose husbands failed lie detector tests on daytime talk shows. I learned to get everything in writing from the cantankerous judge on court TV. I even taught myself how to make my voice perky like the reporters on the entertainment interview program so that I sounded happy whenever my mother called to check on me.

No one really knew that I had given up.

Sol sent a few emails asking if I had hired a lawyer, which I hadn't. He then sent me a list of the items that he wanted from the house, which I didn't really care about. I left his things in boxes in the foyer and made sure not to be home on the days he said he would be by to pick them up. The date we had arranged to sign divorce papers was nearing, and my mother asked if I wanted her to come, but I didn't because I just wanted to be alone.

I wanted it to end.

One night I got a text from him. I think there was an infomercial on television, because all I remembered hearing was someone's loud booming voice in the background shouting about cleaning fluid that could take the grease stains out of anything. I had spent the last several nights mesmerized by the notion that just a phone call away laid the perfect vegetable chopper, the perfect diet pill, the perfect windshield wiper.

My cell phone was sitting on the coffee table, and I picked it up when I heard it buzzing. It was Sol making one last request. He wanted the bear that his mother had given him. He probably had every right to it because, in truth, it was deservedly his. But the thought of giving it to him made my heart race so fast that the room began to spin. My hurt solidified into rage that then melted and seeped through me. Second to his betrayal with Susan, asking me to return the bear was the unkindest thing he had ever done.

I tiptoed into David's room, as though there might have been someone there to wake. It was dark and empty except for my art desk, which was pushed up against the wall. I hadn't gone near it since the day I had attacked it with a pair of scissors, which now felt like another lifetime ago. I picked up the bear from the windowsill and squeezed it to my chest, but when I turned it over I saw that the stitching in the back had started to come undone. I don't know why, but I pulled at the thread, unraveling it even further. I'm not sure if I was surprised or if, somehow, I had always known what it was I would find inside.

Her poems were written on scraps of paper just as Sol had described. I carefully pulled them out, flattened out each one with the palm of my hand. They were exquisitely worded and hauntingly beautiful and hidden from the world so that they wouldn't distract her from being the perfect mother she was supposed to be.

After I laid them on my art desk, I found a heavy book to help iron out the wrinkles. Some had yellowed with age while others had so many crossed out words it made the paper they were written on ripple. The top of each page was fringed with the uneven tear marks that come from being ripped out of a spiral notebook. I couldn't help but notice how different they seemed from the precisely cut recipes displayed in her albums.

And then, just when I thought she could not surprise me anymore, she did.

It was on the back of a poem about an oak tree, about acorns falling to the ground, that was so simple and beautiful it made my heart stop. I flipped it over, thinking there might be more on the other side, and that's where I found it, scribbled in her same determined handwriting. What I held in my hand was not precisely a poem but still as original and meaningful and poignant. What I held in my hand was her recipe for banana cream pie.

She was sharing her technique, giving away the magic that made her pie different than any other. It was the vanilla beans stored in extract that gave the custard its rich flavor and the whipped cream stiffened with cream cheese that made it sit up like a sculpted cloud. I read it over a few times, but it took a few more minutes before I noticed the note that was scrawled like an afterthought at the bottom and partially obstructed by the curl of the page.

"Sol—I love you. I'm sorry."

I held it in my hand, running my fingers over her words, her atonement. There was a wide space between his name and her apology, like there was more that she wanted to say but she could not find a way, which is maybe why she decided to write it on the page that held her most beloved recipe. Had she intended for him to find it? Why had she kept all these poems hidden inside the bear where all they did was serve as a daily reminder of who she'd always hoped she would become?

Before she became perfect.

I held her poems in a bundle, tight to my chest, and as I closed my eyes, I tried to hear her voice so that I could understand if what happened to her the day she disappeared was an accident.

Or if it was a choice.

I sat on the ground with the deflated bear in my hands and I cried for all that she had wanted and all that she believed she could not have. I cried because she thought there was no other way but to disappear and because I understood so well how she must have felt. I also knew that I loved her more than Sol ever could and that now her secrets were mine to protect.

I found a bag of cotton balls in the medicine cabinet and re-stuffed the bear. It took me late into the night to recreate the stitches, but I worked slowly and methodically until they were perfect.

Just the way that she would have done.

Chapter 30

And then I was back.

But this time, I woke swallowing and gulping for air like I was drowning.

Suffocating in sadness.

In my hand was the collage I had created—a swan whose neck was curved in the shape of an *S*. The water on which it floated sparkled with blues and greens, transformed from the car ads I had ripped from the pages of a magazine. A swan floating peacefully above the water was the perfect tribute to Rachel.

And to her stolen dreams.

That morning, as I showered and ate my breakfast, I thought about who I had become in that other life, and as I got ready to leave for work, I did so with new resolve. I told myself that I would not let him back into my life.

I would not let him break me.

I repeated that promise to myself for days, lingering over the words like they were an enchanted witch's spell. I whispered them as I was falling asleep, believing that they would protect me and make me stronger, more resilient. Even if this Sol was not the same as the one in my dreams, it was not something I could risk.

I had to remain vigilant.

It started with a hardly notable strike of lightning that developed into an engulfing, thunderous roar, which then launched into an all-out hurricane. It was as though I had no other choice, as if it had always been a foregone conclusion and my only option was to hold on tight as my world swirled around me. I really did try to slow it down, contain it, make it stop.

At least, that's what I told myself.

I made sure to come to work later, avoiding Susan, and leave earlier to bypass Sol. I tried to pull back from Birdie, which was the hardest part of my plan since she was the one constant, the one reason things made sense.

He started coming earlier and slipping into the seat beside Birdie while she and I were together. As hard as I tried to ignore his pull, sometimes it was so strong that even getting up and moving to the other side of the store was not enough. I tried to brush away the electrical currents that danced around my chest whenever I saw him. One day I caught him staring at me in a way that felt so familiar and intimate that, as I turned away, I felt my memories of THEN collide into my memories of NOW, and I lost my breath and my footing. He was there in an instant.

To catch me.

After that, he started coming before lunch and bringing food. I recognized his mother's recipes instantly, watching as he cut up sandwiches into triangles for his daughter to eat. I heard him whisper things into her ear that made her giggle, and even though I tried not to, I couldn't help but imagine what he might have been like with our son.

After a while, he began bringing in things for me too. At first, I declined, but Birdie seemed to take my refusal personally so finally I just gave in. He brought the fried chicken he had made the first time he cooked for me and bags of fruit like he had made when I was pregnant. I had to remind myself that in this life, he had never made those things for me and that this Sol was not the same as that one, but soon drawing the distinction between the two became more difficult. I tried to pull back, but it was so hard, like denying yourself the pleasure of sinking into a warm, comfortable bed after a long, cold, winter storm. Sol provided familiarity and relief even though he had no idea why.

Once the weather started to improve, Sol and Birdie and I would take walks after lunch. At first, Alice would raise her eyes but then she stopped, maybe because she respected me enough to know that I was a decent person and that I wouldn't do anything to cross the line. That was probably the hardest part for me, knowing that she didn't really know who I was. I tried not to think about the person I was becoming, or worse, the person I had always been. I would try and walk ahead of Sol and Birdie like I could somehow forget them, move away from what they meant to me, but they would always catch up and then Birdie would run ahead like it was a game. When she returned, she walked between us, holding each of our hands.

Connecting us.

Sol told me he had chosen to name her Rachel after his mother, but that Susan had nicknamed her Birdie because of the squawking sound she made as an infant when she nursed, like a hungry bird. He told me about her selective mutism and about how she could talk in some places but not in others, and I wondered if the fact that her parents could not even agree on what to call her might have been a reason she had chosen to go silent.

It was odd to be at the start of something with someone with whom you'd already lived a lifetime. One time I made the mistake of asking Sol how things were going at the ice cream shop, and he looked genuinely confused. "My father closed that place years ago. How'd you even know about it?" Somehow, I managed to distract him by pointing out something sweet that Birdie was doing. From then on, I was more careful, trying to let things unfold naturally, trying to keep hidden the fact that I already knew so much about him.

Sol had opened a photography studio. He took Birdie and I there once, and she practiced making shadow puppets against the white backdrop while he showed me around. The jobs he was getting were mostly wedding and family portraits, which he confided that he hated. I knew him well enough to understand that this wasn't the type of photography he dreamed of doing. He pulled a box out from a closet, picking out photos to show me, handling each one like it was a delicate piece of glass.

"This," I announced, "is what you should be doing." I picked out one of a bridge with the lights blurred out in the background. He smiled, clearly touched that I held his work in such high regard.

"Too bad my wife doesn't agree," he said as he gathered them back into the box.

I pushed back my hair, which I had started to wear down again. "Really?" I could hear the amazement in my voice and hoped it sounded genuine. "Maybe one day she will change her mind."

He smiled and looked at me for a second too long. "Maybe."

Sol started showing up even on the days Birdie wasn't there. He would suddenly appear as I was walking to the deli. At first, he acted like it was a coincidence, but when it didn't seem like I expected an explanation, he stopped pretending. As we walked along the streets, sometimes we would talk about Birdie and his photography and his dreams.

As the weeks passed, he stopped showing up at lunch, and instead waited for me after work in his car. It was not the green Civic we had owned in my dreams but instead a small hatchback with a car seat set up in the back row. Sol would take me driving, and I would sit quietly beside him, staring at his profile, admiring the elegant slope of his nose. Sometimes my breath would catch in my throat and I would open the window so that I could feel the wind whip past my face, hoping I could remember all the things I had promised not to forget. But he was like a drug I couldn't stop inhaling, and as soon as I rolled up the window and leaned back, I could feel myself wanting him even more intensely than I did before.

Thursday morning, Susan cornered me in the back of Alice's office.

"Seeing anyone?" she asked without even trying to make it sound nonchalant.

I shook my head, trying to ignore the red that crept up my neck and across my cheeks like a slap. I felt guilt and shame and anger at Susan for making me feel that way.

"I could set you up if you want. I'm sure I could come up with someone."

The skepticism in her voice felt cruel.

"Really, I don't mind. I like playing matchmaker," she continued.

I wondered if she knew about Sol and me. Because he came and went with such ease, it made me forget that he had a wife, and the fact that his wife was Susan made it even easier.

"What do you say? Interested?"

I sorted through some paintbrushes in the sink. "That's nice of you, Susan, but I'm really not."

"Sometimes you are such an ungrateful bitch." She smiled as she said it, like she was teasing, like it was a joke, but her words hit their mark with bullet-like precision.

The whole rest of the day, I couldn't stop remembering the last time she had said those same exact words—when I was pregnant with David and she insisted on buying baby clothes and then afterward my life began to unravel as if I was cursed.

And I lost everything.

I invited him to dinner on a Monday mostly because it gave me the weekend to prepare. He barely hesitated before he agreed, and for a second, I wondered how he went about explaining his absences to Susan. But then I just stopped caring.

I wasn't a terrific cook, but I had learned to make a few things. During my time in New York, Mickey's grandmother taught me to make a delicious fried pork dish with a tangy dipping sauce. I made it with a side of sticky rice and steamed asparagus for Sol. As I breaded the meat, I tried not to think of Mickey and how I had stopped answering both her phone calls and her texts because I knew no matter how hard I tried, I wouldn't be able to explain. He arrived promptly at six-thirty with a bottle of wine, shifting from one foot to the other like a nervous prom date in the doorway. I invited him in with a wave of my hand, and he stood for a few minutes looking around. I wondered if it felt familiar.

"Nice place," he said as he put the bottle down on the coffee table.

We ate at the kitchen table my mother had bought. I knew him well enough to know that he was telling me the truth when he said the food was delicious. I didn't eat much, mostly because my stomach felt like it had risen into my throat. He poured the wine, first one glass and then a second. When we finished eating, we took the bottle into the living room and sat on the couch.

I hated myself for it.

But I wanted him with such urgency that my chest began to hurt, and I suddenly wondered if I was about to die. He sat beside me, chattering on about something irritating that Susan had said that morning. His hands were clasped in his lap, his wedding band glistening like it had magical powers, and as I stared at it, I knew that I had to do whatever it took to turn things around and put them back the way they should have been. Like adjusting a crooked painting, the responsibility was mine to make things right. I reached over and slipped my hand into his—the one without the wedding ring. He stopped talking, but he didn't move it away. It was quiet after that, probably too quiet, and just when I thought things were going to be okay and that he understood, he stood up.

"I should get going."

I had made a mistake, moved too quickly, and now it was all going to fall apart.

"Don't go," I said softly.

For a second, he hesitated and it looked as though he was playing out the options in his head. Maybe it suddenly occurred to him that what was happening between us was wrong and the guilt that he had managed to suppress up till now began to rise to the surface.

"At least stay for dessert. It's my special recipe."

I refused to take no for an answer and headed into the kitchen to get things ready. When I turned around with two small white plates in my hand, he was standing there, waiting.

"Just a few bites and then I really need to get going."

I cut thick creamy wedges from the pie I had practiced making all weekend, over and over until it was perfect.

"Banana cream," I announced, setting each of our plates onto the table.

He sat down but he didn't eat. "It's my favorite."

"Really?" I had gotten good at lying.

I tried not to watch as he took his first bite, but I couldn't help myself. Cream kissed the edge of his lip, and after he swallowed, he closed his eyes like he was in a dream. He didn't look up because all his attention was focused on the plate. His second and third bites were more frantic, like he was scared it might be taken away before he finished. He went to cut himself another piece, mischievously licking the cream off the edge of the knife like I was certain he had also done when he was a little boy. When he finished that piece, he went for another. I kept out of his way because I knew that each bite brought him closer to me. Once he finished, I covered what remained with plastic wrap and set it inside the refrigerator. Before I could turn around, he had his arms around my waist, pulling me toward him, kissing the side of my neck.

He smelled like bananas and vanilla, and we made love right there on the kitchen floor. I had never truly understood why people called it making love until that moment. My nerve endings were on fire and everywhere he touched me felt so good it hurt. I could sense the thing that had once bonded us rebuilding, tying and reknitting itself hundreds of times over so that, once again, we were attached. When he came inside of me, he wrapped his hands around my head, keeping his eyes on mine, making sure that I wouldn't look away so that I would understand, so that there could never be any question.

That I was his.

He didn't come around the store after that, and at first I was worried. But late on the fourth night, when I was already in my pajamas, he knocked on the door.

He smiled when I opened it and I could tell he was drunk.

"Got any more of that pie?"

Before I could answer, he pushed his way inside. His lips were on mine and his fingers were unbuttoning my top. I liked feeling how much he wanted me, so I gave into him, allowing his bourbon-heavy breath to wash over me. This time we made it to the couch, the roughness of the cushion rubbing against my bottom. He plunged his tongue deep into my mouth like he was trying to inhale me and then afterward rubbed the ends of my hair across his lips.

We never spent the entire night together, but it became our habit to lie entangled for as long as we could, and once we were up, Sol would make breakfast even though it was pitch-black outside. We sat naked at the kitchen table, scooping soft mounds of scrambled eggs onto buttered white toast. Our lovemaking left us both ravenous, and sometimes Sol would make a second round of breakfast before getting dressed to leave. We never spoke about the fact that he couldn't stay because he had a wife and child waiting for him at home. We ate our breakfast and carried on with our routine like it was the most normal thing in the world.

Because I knew him so well, I knew exactly what to do the moment I sensed his interest starting to wane. I knew exactly what to do to pull him back to me. One evening I left the door unlocked, and when he knocked, I told him to let himself in. He came upstairs where I had filled the room with burning candles, their light casting golden warmth around my naked body. I stood holding a camera lens in my hands, frozen in my position like a statue. He smiled as he came closer, taking the lens from me.

He turned it around a few times in his hands. "How is it that you know me so well?"

I hesitated for a moment, feeling guilt over my deception, but then I reminded myself that the only thing that mattered was turning things back around to where they should have been in the first place. He spent the next few hours posing me in the light and snapping pictures, and because I knew he was happy, so was I.

I could pretend that I was not falling in love with him again and that I was in complete control of what was happening between us, but that would have been a lie. Even though it should have been a happy time, my mind flipped recklessly between then and now while my body got tangled within my sheets, trapped inside a prison of uncertainty, distrust, and confusion. The things I lived through in those dreams frightened me, but there were moments when my real life scared me even more. The dreams had become my rearview mirror through which I could find my bearings and predict what was coming up ahead. To know how to proceed in this life, I needed to find out what transpired in the other one. There was no other choice; I had to know what happened.

To us.

To me.

I sat at the desk my mother had given me when I graduated from law school, pushed away the blotter, and pulled a sheet of paper from the drawer.

I began to work on a collage.

Chapter 31

I was staring into a mirror brushing my hair on the last day I would ever be Sol Green's wife. I even used new eyeliner from the drug store because it was so dark it made my eyes recede into my face and I thought maybe it would be harder for him to see inside of me.

I chose a dress that he was especially fond of, but then I changed out of it. Instead, I wore a skirt and top I had bought with my mother after she convinced me it made me look stylish. It was a little more tailored than most of the things in my closet, but by the time I decided it was constraining, it was too late to change.

I sat on the bus with the bear in my lap. I had wrapped it in toilet paper and put it inside a used gift bag I found in the back of a kitchen drawer. The woman sitting across from me was staring, and I wondered if I looked like I was heading to a party instead of the dissolution of my marriage.

When I got off at my stop, I began to walk, and even though it was warm, I started to feel the shaking. It began in the back of my throat, subtle and faint, and I clenched my teeth to stop it from spreading. It was only a few blocks to Sol's lawyer's offices. I passed his family's ice cream parlor and wondered if his father was working inside, covering Sol's shift so he could take time off to undo the mistake he had made.

A few blocks later, I walked by the coffee shop where Sol had taken me after we met that first time at Daphne Lake. I looked inside the window and then the shaking started up again so violently that I couldn't control it even though I tried to look away. There she was—sitting at the very same table where we had sat.

Waiting for him to be free of me.

More than anything I wanted to go in and slap the cup out of Susan's hand and then smash her head into the table. I could feel the anger surge and little balls of spit form in the corners of my mouth. The words I wanted to say got stuck in my chest, making it hard to catch my breath. I think I coughed, and maybe I even stopped for a minute and turned in her direction, but in the end, I did nothing.

Except shake.

A few panic-stricken minutes later, I was standing in front of the building. It was a long ride up in the elevator and a child pushed all the buttons before his mother pulled him away. As a result, we stopped at each floor, waiting in silence for the doors to open and close, time slipping away meaninglessly. I felt my heart race, like I wanted things to move faster, but then I remembered why I was there and I started to shake again until the elevator finally reached my floor.

Immediately, I wished that I wasn't alone.

My mother would have known exactly what to do. She would have announced herself to the receptionist and it would have been clear to anyone within earshot that not only was she important, but that she was someone to be reckoned with. I had to repeat my name a second time before the receptionist heard me, and even then, she acted as though I was bothering her. She pointed toward a beige rectangular couch where I sat until she remembered to call someone to come get me.

I held on more tightly to the bag with the bear.

I heard someone in the hallway, and when I looked up, I saw it was Sol. He was disheveled and pale, and when he turned toward me, I couldn't help but think that maybe it was because he had second thoughts and that he had finally come to his senses.

"Sam." He sounded like he used to sound when he used to love me.

Instinctively, I reached toward the man who was still my husband.

He sat down on the couch beside me, but he didn't take my hand. He looked like he was trying to find the right words to tell me something. A paralegal came out and motioned for us to follow, but Sol waved her off. He was staring at the cup in his hand as he spoke. "The police came to see me last night." He clasped his fingers around the cup. "They found my mother." He was staring down at the floor. "She was there all along."

A few more moments of silence punctuated by the ding of the elevator outside the glass doors.

"At the bottom of Daphne Lake."

I knew it before he said it. I had known all along even if my heart hadn't spoken it loudly enough for my head to hear. His face was ash gray, and the only time I had ever seen him look like that was at the loss of our child. I reached out to touch his hand and he let me.

"The car was a rental, which is why it took so long to trace." He took a sip of his coffee. "Remember that first time we met? You were holding that sketch-book of yours and you reminded me of her." He looked at me for a moment before turning away. "The bone we found was only dislodged because of the drought, because the water levels sunk so low." He shook his head. "Otherwise I would never even have known."

There were a few more minutes of silence and then I saw him trying to gather his strength, to tell me something—no, to ask me something.

"Sam?" His brown eyes were more gold than I remembered. Whatever anger or hurt I had inside drained out of me as he took my hand and held it between his.

"Sam?" he repeated and I squeezed him back.

"Someone did this to her. You know that, too, right?" Even though he had turned away, I could tell that he was begging.

Begging me to tell him that his mother would never made this choice of her own volition. It was my chance, my way back into his life, and all I needed was to say the words that he wanted to hear. And I started to . . . but then I looked down at my lap, at the bear that had belonged to Sol when he was little and had held his mother's secrets for so long.

For too long.

I had to explain things in a way that he would understand. I could tell him how she felt suffocated and hopeless and broken because she knew she was never going to be perfect because who she really wanted to be was never good enough, and that in the end she made the only choice she could—to simply disappear. I could make him see that it had never been about leaving him and that perhaps he was even the reason she had stayed for as long as she did. I could make him understand how much that must have cost her. But before I could get the words out, he turned to look at me, and I saw that he could read it in my face, see it in my eyes, and then he jumped up quickly, like he had just been electrocuted, and pushed me away.

Hard.

"Forget it." He was shaking with rage. "She loved me, Sam." He swallowed down his spit. "She would have never done this to herself. She would have never left me," he growled the last part under his breath, "the way that you did."

Then he turned and stomped down the hallway into an office.

I felt like I had let him slip from my fingers, like I did with everything that ever mattered to me. When I got to the room, Sol was sitting at the table, but he wasn't looking at me. The lawyer my mother insisted I hire was sitting at one end of the table, and Sol's lawyer sat at the other. She was pretty and blond and her name may have been one of the names in the entrance, but I couldn't remember. The shaking inside of me had now turned to a smooth drumming beat, pounding between my ears.

"Why don't we get started?" She motioned for me to sit.

I handed Sol the bag with the bear, and then I tried to speak again, carefully arranging the words in my head so that they would come out right. But as I opened my mouth, I watched him take the bear out of the bag and place it on the table where it toppled over the edge and landed on the floor. Instead of picking it back up, he pushed it aside with his shoe, leaving it there like worthless trash.

Which is when I understood there was nothing left for me to say.

We sat in silence until the paralegal asked if I wanted a drink, and I must have said no because she sat down again and then his lawyer spoke. It was a short marriage with not much property so there wasn't much to divide. I looked over at Sol, but he was looking away from me, and then all I could think about was David. In one of the art books Brian bought me when I was little, there was a painting of King Solomon. In it, the king decides that a child over whom two mothers are fighting will be split in half. Brian explained that he did it because he was searching for the truth, because he was searching for their humanity. I looked at Sol again, but he had his cell phone out and was scrolling through his messages.

More talk coupled with more paper shuffling signifying the end of my connection to the man who fathered my child and who promised to take care of me for the rest of our lives. There was a box of Kleenex on the table, which I didn't need because I wasn't crying, mostly because I was focusing so hard on controlling the shaking.

Everyone began to shift in their seats, and I could feel that things were coming to an end. The lawyer handed me the papers, and as I held the pen in my hand, I drew out each letter of my name slowly and methodically like I was sculpting a piece of art. Sol looked up, and I realized I had his attention, but then he turned away. I looked across the room at the floor-to-ceiling glass window, and I wondered what it would feel like to break free and crash through.

To fly.

Sol was tapping his fingers against the tabletop while his lawyer cleared her throat. I clicked the top of the pen a few times, and because it seemed to irritate him, I did it again. The lawyer left the room to get some water, and I continued writing out my name, knowing that each letter brought Sol one step closer to Susan.

One step closer to freedom.

I wished my name had more letters in it. I wished I could go on writing it forever, but I couldn't, and before I was ready, before I wanted it to end, it did, and we were finished.

Fractured.

As we stood to leave, he smiled, perhaps in gratitude or relief, but I wasn't sure which. Just then, I pushed myself away from the table. I needed to get out, run from the room, and get as far away as I could.

Part of me wished that he was following, but the rest of me knew that he wasn't and that he never would again. Streets and faces and honking cars blurred together until I stop running and realized that I was sitting on a park bench, the tears rolling down my cheeks like a toddler who had just dropped her lollipop on the ground. I cried harder, as if somehow that would make everything go back to the way it was, but at that moment, I was suddenly overcome by the realization that nothing would ever be the same again.

Because I had allowed him to destroy me.

To break me.

As the shaking intensified, I was overwhelmed by how damaged I had become. I tried to take deeper breaths to calm myself. I probably looked as though I was hyperventilating, but there was no one around to witness my breakdown. The panic started to recede but returned with a vengeance when I suddenly realized that the reason I could feel myself collapsing and literally crumbling away.

Was because I was.

I looked down at my hand and my fingertips, which were starting to disintegrate, to slowly but undeniably disappear. I told myself I had to be in shock and tried to ignore the sensation of watching myself slip away. It was as though, instead of cells, I was made up of hundreds of squares that began to topple in onto themselves, and when I looked down at my lap, I realized my hand had completely vanished. I was breaking up into the tiny bits of color almost the same as those from which my collages were made, disappearing inch by inch, piece by piece. I knew I should have felt terror, but all I felt was relief, and then because I couldn't make it stop . . . I didn't. I softly tilted my head backward so that I could more comfortably fall into the act of disappearing, and then I took a deep breath and closed my eyes because I knew:

There was no turning back.

Chapter 32

When I opened my eyes, it was morning and shards of sunlight flickered across the room, making everything around me feel warm and safe. I was here, back in this life, sitting at the desk my mother had bought to furnish my office after I graduated from law school. I held onto the armrest to steady myself and then I tried to relive the thing that I had just experienced that I knew beyond any reasonable doubt had been real. I focused hard and just as I was about to give up, it came, and I could see myself in those seconds and minutes right after the parts of me began to disappear.

When I slipped out of that life and back into this one.

There had been a blur, a swirl of light, and then movement so electrifying it felt like I was on fire. I was crumbling away, breaking apart, and I could remember the feel of the tremor in my head, the aftershocks dancing across the neurons of my brain tantalizing me with their insight. Even though I thought I was about to vanish into nothingness, that is not what happened.

Where I finally ended up . . . was back at the beginning.

It wasn't random. The reason I landed there was so that I could start again, so I could change my future. I was sent back to the point in time where Sol and I first met so that I could make sure that we stayed together, so that I could outrun my destiny. It had always been about Sol and me, about the two of us. Despite the hurdles and obstacles placed in our path, we had still managed to find our way back to one another. We were meant to be together, which not even a shift in time could disrupt.

I had been given a second chance, an opportunity to correct the mistakes of the past. I had never been a big believer in signs, but how could this be denied? Sol and I were never meant to be apart, and the fact that we had found each other even through irrefutable odds proved it. For the first time in a long time, I felt confident and hopeful and like I might explode with all my newly discovered insight. I needed to get out, to breathe real air and find the person I always went to when I needed to confide my secrets.

He smiled when he saw me at the door. It had been too long since we had seen each other and I let him squeeze me close.

"I'm so glad you're here."

I followed him into the living room.

"I've been holding on to this for you."

On my sixteenth birthday, four months after my mother had thrown him out, Brian took me to the post office and got me a passport, which he steadfastly renewed when needed. "For you, Fish." He handed it to me like it was my golden ticket—my promise of escape.

"Thanks." I tucked it into my bag. I wanted to tell him that I had fixed everything and that I didn't need Italy anymore, that I didn't need anything anymore, except for Sol.

"Maybe we can plan a trip together in the fall?" he asked.

I nodded but then neither of us said anything more.

"I've met someone."

His face brightened. "That's great, Fish."

I realized that I had been coiling the strap of my bag inside my fist as I tried to pick my words carefully, suddenly self-conscious of what they might sound like to someone on the outside.

"He's great and I really like him but there is one little thing."

For a fleeting moment, I hesitated, because there was something comforting about keeping it all to myself. But my father was looking at me in that open, sweet way of his that told me I could tell him anything.

"He's married. To my old roommate, Susan, and they have a little girl."

Brian was silent. I waited for him to speak, and when he said nothing, I suddenly felt as though I needed to explain. "He isn't happy with her. You of all people should understand."

It happened quickly, his face turning from pink to white, his lips gray. "Why do you think that is something I would understand?"

We had never spoken about why my mother had thrown him out but I knew it was because of what I had seen that day at school with my art teacher. My mother was a person of high morals, of principle, and infidelity was something she would not have tolerated. Even though it had never come up, I knew that was the reason their marriage ended and it was also why I was certain that my father would be more understanding about the circumstances in which I currently found myself. The silence between us went on for too long, and when he finally looked at me, there was something in his face that I didn't recognize. Even his voice sounded different, distorted.

"I have never been disloyal to your mother. The only person I have not been honest with is you." He raked his fingers through his hair and closed his eyes. "You deserve to know the truth."

I suddenly wanted him to stop talking.

"The reason that I left was because Jayne wouldn't tell you the truth."

I tried to remain calm, but my face felt wet, and I realized I was crying flat, wide tears that spread out like pools of ocean across my cheeks.

"We grew up in a dirty little town in Alabama. In a trailer park called Crystal Manor."

My nose began to run, and I wiped it with the back of my sleeve. "You're a liar. My mother grew up in a cottage with flowers in the window boxes and a white picket fence around the garden. Just like the little white house I live in."

"No, Sam, she didn't. She grew up in a tiny broken-down trailer with a mother who kept a collection of empty whiskey bottles next to her collection of mean boyfriends. The most Jayne saw of her mother was the back of her head as she led them into her bedroom each night."

My mind began to spin, searching for a way to prove that what he was saying was untrue. It was not possible that my mother could have lived the life he was describing and I hated him for lying to me. I steadied myself on the arm of the couch. "Why are you telling me these things? How do you even know?"

He was composed now, like he was suddenly released from his cage. "I know because I was there. I know because Jayne is my sister."

Sweat beaded above my upper lip and plastered my hair to my face. The light faded and closed in around me, first a sickly shade of brown that got deeper and emptier until it turned black. The pinhole through which I was seeing the world became smaller until it finally closed, and then everything simply disappeared, and I let it because I was just too tired to fight.

Brian was leaning over me with a damp towel.

"Fish," he cooed, and for a minute I forgot everything that had happened. It came back in slow motion, each piece of the puzzle fitting in perfectly until the image was complete and undeniable.

"I'm sorry," he said.

I tried to push myself up, but the room began to shift again, so I let myself sink back down. The towel felt cool against my head.

"Tell me. Everything." I didn't know why, but I suddenly needed to know all of it.

He looked down at his feet as if he had second thoughts.

"Please."

He took in a breath and blew it out like he was clearing the dust off the words that had been sitting inside of him for too long. "Jayne took care of me. Even when the fridge was empty, she made sure I was fed. Some nights it was just Rice-a-Roni and ketchup, but I never went hungry. She played games with me while our mother was busy entertaining. That's what we called it—'entertaining.' Jayne was always good at making things sound prettier than they really were." He took a sip of water. "But then it got too much for her."

He twisted the glass between his hands, the water swirling inside of it like a tornado.

"One night she went to a party and got really drunk. I don't know what happened because she never told me, but a few weeks later she found out she was pregnant." He wasn't looking at me, just staring straight down at his feet. "She decided to leave and I begged her to take me with her. We drove for days until we ended up here."

I could feel my insides breaking apart, brick by brick. "Why did you pretend to be a couple?"

He looked away. "People just assumed we were married, and it was easier to let them think that. At first, I did it for Jayne, and then I did it for you."

I took the glass of water from him, hoping it would cool the fire that was leaping at my throat.

"Didn't it seem strange to you that we didn't wear wedding rings? Sleep in the same bedroom? That you called me by my first name?"

Before I could answer his face turned red.

"I'm sorry, Fish. None of this is your fault. None of it."

The truth was it had never occurred to me to question them, not for a moment, because I believed all of it. I believed all their lies.

"I knew that it wasn't right and I've wanted to tell you. For so long."

The fire inside of me began to transform into something misshapen and unrecognizable.

"I've always worried that if you didn't know who you really were that you would never be able to be true to yourself." His words were hushed like he was making confession.

Lights flickered inside my brain, illuminating everything that had been beneath the darkness. I came into the world under false pretenses. It was their fault that I could never commit to anything, never feel like what I was doing was right, never really understand who I was or what it was that I wanted.

I never stood a chance.

The thing I was feeling inside was no longer blurry or unformed. In fact, it was now patently clear what the red flame had turned itself into.

Rage.

It took half an hour to convince him I was okay to leave. He didn't want to let me go. Even though there were no visible scars, he could tell that I was broken and he was right. I'm sure I looked drunk as I staggered out of his apartment. I weaved across the sidewalk as though I couldn't find my footing because I couldn't.

Anger and grief fueled me, propelling me forward. It felt like minutes, but it must have been longer, because the next thing I knew, I was standing outside my mother's house, my hand on the knob, breathing in the sweet smell of something baking inside. I used her spare key to let myself in. She was leaning over the open oven door, a pretty ruffled apron tied around her waist. If she was surprised to see me, she didn't let on.

"Hey there, stranger." Out came a sheet pan of cookies that she set down onto a waiting trivet.

Bringing baked goods to a closing was what she did to make both the buyers and the sellers feel good. It was how she kept up appearances and made people believe she was something she was not. Now I knew why. I had avoided her since losing my job with Stu because I was scared to admit my failures, scared of what she might think of me.

But I wasn't scared anymore. Fury bubbled up inside of me, and even though I had never been violent in my life, I had a sudden urge to strike her.

"It's. All. Your. Fault." Breaths that sounded too much like sobs separated my words.

She turned away but not before I saw her upper lip twitch. She focused with the intensity of a surgeon, carefully transferring each individual cookie onto the cooling rack.

"I thought you would be a good match for Stu's firm. I had no idea things would fall apart. I'm sure we can find you something else. I'm sorry but you can't blame me for this."

She thought I was talking about losing my job. I walked over to the counter, and with the swipe of my hand knocked everything within my reach onto the ground, but the fact that the rack made an unsatisfying thud as it hit the linoleum floor left me even angrier.

"What is wrong with you, Sam?" She went to the pantry and came back with a dustbin.

I watched as she crouched down to sweep up my mess and I suddenly hated her even more.

"I went to see Brian today. You know. My uncle?"

She looked up once and then went back to what she was doing.

"Did you hear me, Mom?" My voice sounded as fragmented as the cookie crumbles she was collecting.

"He shouldn't have told you. It wasn't his to tell." She walked to the trash beneath the sink while I waited. I wasn't sure what it was I was waiting for, what it was I expected. I had pulled back the curtain and exposed her and I wanted her to hurt.

I wanted her to pay.

She went to the refrigerator and took out another tube of cookie dough. She got out a second cookie sheet and went about her task as if nothing had happened. I stood in front of her, blocking her access to the counter.

"You're acting like a child, Sam."

I shook my head. "How do I even know that's my real name? How can I ever believe anything you ever tell me again?"

"What is it you want?" Her voice went up an octave, and although it wasn't much, I felt a small sense of victory.

"I want you to stop thinking that things can be fixed with your stupid doctored-up desserts. I want you to tell me the truth."

"Really, Sam? Is that what you want?"

She sat down at the kitchen table beneath the daisies I had drawn for her when I was a little girl.

"Do you want to know about the trailer park? Her boyfriends? The ones that fucked her or the ones that tried to fuck me?"

The drawl that I remembered from our dinner with Lucas. Except now I understood why.

"Maybe you want to hear about how all she cared about was getting money for her next fix? I can tell you all the gory details because I'm sure that's what you really want to fucking hear."

In all my life, the worst word I had ever heard my mother use was *damn*, and even then, it was used sparingly. Her face was contorted, and for a moment she looked much older than she was.

"I swore that things would be different for you and I kept my word. I have done everything to make sure you are independent and will never need a man for anything. I have given you everything and more." She held her head in her hands, her fingers moving slowly across the smooth surface of her forehead.

"Except for the truth," I whispered so quietly I wasn't sure that she heard. I waited for some semblance of remorse, and when it didn't come, I hurled my last question at her, this time loud and clear and encased in an unquestionable roar. "Who is my father?"

Her head was still in her hands, and when she finally looked up there was a tear. I saw it slowly make its way down the curve of her cheek. One lonely solitary tear was all that I was worth. "I was very drunk that night. There are several possibilities. None worth mentioning." Then she sighed as she stood. "Why does it matter? The minute you came into this world, you were mine. You belonged to me and I promised that I would always take care of you."

She came closer to me. "And I have."

I had expected her to beg my forgiveness for lying and cheating me out of any chance of living a normal life. Everything she had given me, taught me, told me, was a lie. But instead she acted like she had given me a gift. I backed away from her, and then because I couldn't think of what else to do, I pulled the daisies off the wall and smashed them onto the floor, cracking the glass in the frame. Even though it was what I had wanted all along, when I heard my mother gasp, it left me feeling even more unbalanced than when I first arrived. She didn't look at me as I walked out, just crouched down onto the floor holding the broken flowers in her hands.

There was only one person I wanted.

One person who could remind me of whom it was I was meant to be. I called him on the cell phone I was supposed to only use for emergencies, deciding that what had just happened qualified. He could tell almost immediately that something was wrong and half an hour later was at my front door.

I didn't want to talk, didn't want to admit that everything I once believed was a lie and that I was a fraud. I wanted him to hold me, make the room stop spinning so that I could go back to being who I was yesterday—the girl Sol loved. I pulled off his clothes because I wanted to be beneath him so that the weight of him would ground me and stop me from floating away. He read my frenzied movements as passion and bit my breasts and left red finger marks where he clenched my thighs, but I didn't care because it made me feel like I was real, legitimate.

We lay side by side for a few minutes, and then he rolled over so that he was on top of me again. He lifted my arms above my head, pinning me so I couldn't move. He laid his head inside the soft part where my neck met my shoulder and then he was inside of me again. "Marry me," he said as he pushed himself deeper, putting his tongue in my mouth so that I couldn't breathe. I stopped struggling against his force and gave in, letting him take me, letting him have me. Because at least when I was with Sol, I knew who I was.

I never officially answered his proposal, but we went about our lives as though I had. He spent time researching divorce attorneys on my computer and making plans for our life together, and I let him because it was easier than the thought of being alone.

"Do you think we can clean up this room?" he announced one evening as he stood in what had gone from being my home office back to my art studio. He flicked on the light. "I thought Rachel could stay here when she visits."

I couldn't imagine spending one more moment than I needed to living in the house my mother bought, pretending that it resembled the one in which she was raised, the house where in another life I had lost everything that mattered to me. "I was hoping we could get a place of our own."

"Of course we can." He came up behind me, slipping his hands under my shirt and squeezing my breasts. Something uncomfortably familiar clenched inside of me. "I can try to do more weddings, and once you get back to work, we should be fine."

I spun around but he didn't loosen his grip, just pulled me in closer. "I love working at Alice's. I don't want to go back to the law."

"We don't have to talk about it now. I'm sure it will all be fine." He smiled. "Don't worry, Sam. It will all be perfect. I promise." He kissed the tip of my nose. "We'll paint it pink. Rachel likes pink."

That night after he was gone, I cleaned up the room, putting everything away into the garage, including one of the pieces that had fallen to the floor and had then somehow ripped clean up through the middle. I folded it in half, gathering everything else up in a box, and as I walked through the kitchen, my phone buzzed. A voice mail from Mickey; I hadn't even noticed my phone ring. Her voice sailed through me, calling out like my long-lost conscience.

I hit delete.

Chapter 33

Sol moved into his father's house because he didn't want to give Susan any ammunition against him. He came over more often and we spent the nights just lying in bed together, sleeping. I curved myself into his body like a pearl inside an oyster and lost myself in the rhythm of his breaths. I needed him even more than I had before because when I was with him, I had clarity, definition. When I was with him, I knew who I was supposed to be.

The problem was that once things became more serious between us, Birdie began to distance herself. She stopped sitting beside me or smiling when she saw me in the store. She rarely even lifted her head, keeping it bent over whatever she happened to be working on until it was time for her to leave. I missed her desperately, and I blamed it all on Susan, whom I was sure had convinced her I was the reason her father had moved out of their house. During the times when the truth crept in and I knew that I was to blame as well, the only thing that comforted me was the feel of Sol's breaths on the back of my neck.

One night I woke with a start, and I saw that he was awake, as well. He was lying on his back, his fingertips pressed together in the shape of a church steeple.

"Make me that pie. Again. Please," he whispered.

I kissed the round of his shoulder. "Of course."

"It tastes just like my mother's." His voice sounded small.

"I'll get the ingredients tomorrow."

He rolled over so that he was facing me. "Did you know it's why I fell in love with you?"

I did. Because that is how I had planned it. "No," I lied.

The tapping of his fingers sounded like a muted drumroll. "She disappeared." He stared into my eyes. "Did I ever tell you that?"

I shook my head.

So many lies.

Too many lies.

I put my hand on his bare chest, feeling it lower and lift faster now because he had suddenly started to sob. "Sometimes," a soft cry came up from inside of him, "I wonder if someone took her away from us or if . . ." He didn't finish his sentence. Even though he didn't realize it, this was not the first time he had asked for reassurance from me that the woman that brought him to the earth would never have left him.

This time I didn't hesitate, because I wasn't going to squander away another opportunity. Maybe there was something compelling about us each having mothers who had betrayed us, another link in our chain, an everlasting connection. When I turned to him, his face was wet with grief and I knew what I had to do. "Of course she loved you. I'm sure she will come back to you one day."

I pretended I didn't hate myself as the words slipped past my lips. How it works with lies is that they must be placed carefully, one on top of the next to avoid collapse.

"She had this stuffed bear she carried around with her that used to belong to me when I was little."

I was staring at a crack on the ceiling that looked like a bolt of lightning. "Maybe it reminded her of you. Maybe that's why she carried it around."

He was quiet for a few more minutes, like he was deciding if what I had said could be true. I knew he needed to believe that he had been important to her, and what I said must have convinced him because he held me tighter, kissing the side of my face and tracing a circle around my nipple. I could feel his erection growing against my leg. His worries had been laid to rest but mine were suddenly heightened. "Where is the bear now?"

His fingers danced over my belly as he spoke. "I think my dad must have sold it at a garage sale or donated it somewhere after she was gone. I don't really remember." He kissed my lower lip, sucking it between his, and then he rolled on top of me and I let him because he needed me, and anyway, I couldn't move even if I wanted because I felt frozen inside.

When he finished, I made my way to the shower and turned on the water as hot as I could stand. I cried for Rachel, for her lost scraps of poetry, for irretrievable hope, and for the bear that was now in the hands of a complete and utter stranger.

Then I cried for myself.

In the morning, I left him in my kitchen finishing up the last of his breakfast. I told him I wasn't hungry, but the truth was that I just needed to get away. I walked to the grocery store to get the things I needed to make the pie. I found bananas that were so sunshiny yellow they almost didn't look real. I swung the grocery bag as I walked home, the movement careless and cheerful, reminding me of when I was little. Walking helped extinguish the worries that had begun to spark inside of me, and as I approached my front door I was even humming.

She was standing in the middle of the living room with a tall cup of coffee in her hand.

"Good morning, Sam." My mother smiled as if nothing had changed between us.

Sol came out of the kitchen with the plate of donuts she brought because she still thought I could be easily bought.

"I've just been talking to your friend." She lifted her coffee in his direction, and I caught a glimpse of her self-satisfied smirk.

Sol was oblivious. "You mother brought you this." He handed me an envelope that I recognized immediately as coming from her stash of fancy stationery. The back was embossed with a swirled gold letter J.

"Open it," she encouraged.

I put it down on the coffee table because there was nothing inside of it that would make any bit of difference.

"Sol's been telling me that you work at that painting place."

"You should go."

She smiled as she gathered her things to leave. She realized that she didn't need to stay because not only did she know how to get to me, she knew she already had.

"You two talk things over and let me know. Pleasure meeting you." She beamed her perfectly polished real estate smile at him, and he smiled back completely unaware that she despised him.

Even a few minutes after she left, the room still vibrated with her presence and her perfume. I crumpled the letter into a ball before tossing it into the trash can.

"You aren't even going to open it?"

I shrugged. "Why should I?"

"She said it would make you happy."

I could feel the anger lifting inside of me. At her for putting me in this position and at him for making it so that I had to explain. "She doesn't have the first idea of what will make me happy." But he kept staring at me until I finally retrieved it from the garbage and ripped it open. I pulled out a note that smelled faintly like lilacs and handed it to him. "You read it."

He glanced over it quickly and then smiled. "It's the name and a phone number for some law firm in town with whom to contact at the bottom. It says here that there is a job waiting for you if you want it."

We looked at each other for a few more minutes before I took it from him, crumpled it back up again, and threw it away. "Not interested."

"I think we should talk about it." His words came out slowly like he thought I didn't understand what I had just read.

"I told you. I am not going back to the law."

His eyes darted back and forth from one corner of my face to the other, and he looked like he was about to say something but then changed his mind. "Let's not make any decisions now. We can talk about it later." He pulled me into him and kissed the hollow valley at the base of my throat.

He went upstairs to shower, and I listened to the water as it rushed downward from the upstairs pipes. If her intention was to cause me discomfort, it worked. I felt trapped, cold, uneasy and I started to pace around the room like the tigers I had once loved so much at the circus. I walked a circle between the kitchen and the living room finally ending up in what had been my studio. I was staring out of the window when he came and found me. He smelled like clean cut grass, and as I leaned up against him, I was reminded of how well we fit into each other.

"It will be okay, Sam."

Of course, it would. The only thing that mattered was that we were together.

It was our destiny.

"I've got to go now, but when I come back, I'll bring you home a surprise." He kissed my earlobe, squeezing me even more snugly into him.

I stayed by the window, listening to his sounds as he got ready to leave, the jingle of the house keys I had given him and the smooth swoosh of the door as it closed. I reprimanded myself for giving in to my doubts. Things were different this time. Everything was going to be different, and anyway, this was meant to be . . . and not even my mother could ruin it.

I went into the kitchen and that's when I saw it. Sol had dug her note out of the trash, smoothed it out, and stuck it onto the fridge with a neon-colored pink cupcake magnet. I wanted to cry, to scream, but I was alone so no one would hear me anyway and it wouldn't have made a difference if they had. It was as if nothing I said mattered, like I was gagged, voiceless.

Grounded.

I did what I always did when I felt powerless.

I made my way into the garage where I had haphazardly tossed my supplies and brought them back inside. I unfolded the last piece I had been working on and taped up the ragged tear, trying to ignore the fact that it made it look bandaged.

When I was living in New York, Mickey and I took her mother to a performance of *Madame Butterfly*. It was an opera about a young Japanese woman who gave up everything for the love of an American sailor who ultimately betrayed her. Heartbroken, she ended up killing herself so that her son could be free to go and live with his father and his new American wife. Her passion and her pain haunted me, and I could feel the beginning tingles of despair starting at my fingertips. I spread my things out onto the kitchen table and began to cut squares out of magazine pages.

Chapter 34

I waited.

Cutting and pasting and then cutting some more until I could feel the breath fill and empty from my lungs. I focused harder, arranging and rearranging and shifting and breathing.

But there was nothing.

To hear.

To feel.

To see.

I worked harder, doing what I had done many times before. I tried losing myself in the swirl of movement, in the brilliance of color, but nothing came. It was just me sitting alone at the kitchen table with a collage of *Madame Butterfly* in my hands. There was no magic, no visions, no answers. I felt more lost and alone than ever, and I realized how much I had relied on those dreams and what it was they offered.

Escape.

Yet no matter how much I tried, there was nothing. It was as if I had read the very last page in the book and the story was over. Or maybe there was nothing left for me to see because my life in the dreams had actually come to an end. On that day when it happened, when I lost Sol, it really did break me in half—broke me into then and now. Threw me back to the beginning and I had made my way to the end. I could feel the fear building up inside of me like a hurricane, whirling and tossing about my insides. I was completely on my own now, left to make whatever decisions I was going to make without the foresight of what had happened to me.

Before.

I was desperate, and as the tears clouded my eyes, I tried again one last time but it eluded me, as if it had all just been a figment of my imagination. Even though I knew it wasn't. What I had lived was real, and it had delivered me to who I was now, into this moment. But I was uneasy, the frenzy pumping its way through my veins. I looked around the room in desperation, searching for relief. And then I saw it.

I pulled the sheet of my mother's stationery off the refrigerator door and smoothed out the wrinkles. I used my scissors to slice into her words and her letters, carving into the elegantly curved *J* until it turned into flakes of lilac-scented confetti. I arranged the pieces so that they looked like butterflies, moving them back and forth until they covered the gash in the middle of the page, which only hours earlier had reminded me of a wound. My fingertips were caked in glue, and I closed my eyes one last time because I was still hoping, wishing.

And then there was something.

Maybe it wasn't a dream but it was something. I stopped what I was doing and sat in silence. I could feel the chaos inside of me quiet, and what was left behind was not entirely defined, but as I nudged it further I recognized the feeling because it was what I had felt in the coffee shop so long ago when I had broken up with Lucas, when I had started to take care of myself, when I started to believe.

Accomplishment.

As frightening as it was to lose my past life and all that it held, there was also an exhilarating sense of potential. Of taking off into the unknown—of flight.

Of freedom.

I held the collage like a trophy in my hands. It symbolized everything that had led me here, to this exact moment in time and the realization and I had never felt truer or more alive. I took in a deep, cleansing breath, and it was in that instant that I heard someone at the door.

"Sam?"

Fate had brought Sol home at the absolute perfect time so that he could share it all with me. I finally had something tangible that I could use to explain, and I knew that he would understand.

About whom it was I wanted to be.

I was still staring at the work so I didn't notice that there were two sets of footsteps. When I looked up, Sol was standing in the doorway with his hands on Birdie's shoulders. When she saw me, she slipped behind his leg.

"Don't you want to say hello?"

She shrunk down into a size even smaller than she already was. She looked at me again, but this time I was the one to look away. I could not bear to see what it was that I recognized in her eyes.

Betrayal.

"Come see what I made." My olive branch.

She continued to stare as though she didn't understand what I was saying. Or maybe she understood all too well.

"What do you think, Rachel?" He was trying to untangle her from his leg, but she refused to budge. Her little body shook with anger, tremors that made their way up to her lips so that they chattered like she was cold. She turned her head and buried herself into his side and he put his hand on her shoulder. "Salmon missed you, Sweetheart. Why don't you just say hello? C'mon, you know Salmon."

But she didn't move. Just kept shaking like a frightened little mouse.

"Maybe you should take her home."

He nodded then mouthed, "Sorry."

"Guess she's just tired. We'll try again another day." As he turned to leave, Birdie gave me one last look, and if I ever doubted it before, it was clear now. There was no question that she saw right through me and that nothing else mattered.

Because she knew exactly who I was.

After he came back, the only subject he wanted to discuss was Birdie. My collage lay abandoned on the kitchen table, hanging off the outer edge like a piece of debris.

"She'll come around," he said.

But I knew better. I knew she would never forgive me.

"Why don't we give her a new brother or sister? That will make her happy." He wrapped his arms around me, lacing his fingers around my belly as we made our way to bed.

I pushed him away but he held on tighter. "I don't want to have children, Sol."

He nuzzled my neck. "Of course you do. Everyone does."

"Well I don't." Every bone in my body tensed at the horrible familiarity of the situation in which I suddenly found myself.

He pulled away for a minute, his face cocked to one side like a confused puppy. "You'll change your mind," he said confidently, falling asleep a few minutes later, breathing into my hair and making what had once been comforting feel suffocating.

I had convinced myself that because he had Birdie, he wouldn't want more children. How could I have been so wrong? Once his sleep was sound and his snores grew further apart, I slipped out of his grip, trying not to feel like I was stealing away like a thief in the night.

I went into the kitchen and pulled out the green tea Mickey had given me that I hadn't made in months. I was shaking, like Birdie had, like I did when I was scared. Why was it that anytime I felt like I had moved forward there was something that pulled me back down again? My revelation from earlier in the day felt like it happened a lifetime ago. Words and images shot around my mind like ricocheting pinballs, and I couldn't help that every time I closed my eyes, I remembered the Sol from my dreams. The one who told me what had finally stopped his mother from leaving the only time she ever tried to escape. It was his father's words that rang in my head. In that perfect kitchen with that perfect pie, he had chosen the perfect words to compel her to stay. Because he knew they would forever bind her to him.

"Rachel, don't leave the boy."

Sol's father had taught him well.

On the Sunday night before Sol was to sign his divorce decree, he wouldn't leave my side. He begged me to make him the pie for good luck, and he sat at the kitchen table while I worked.

"I love how it smells while you're making it almost as much as I love eating it." He closed his eyes, taking in long exaggerated breaths.

I cut my finger while I was slicing up the bananas, and it took a few minutes for me to realize that the bright red ooze was coming from me.

Sol ran to get something to clean it up with while I stood paralyzed, watching my insides drip out. He was back in minutes, squeezing my finger and running it under water. He cleaned and bandaged it and then kissed the tip like I was a child. "Think you are good now." He smiled.

I felt removed from my head, from my body, as though what was happening was happening to someone else. He wrapped himself around me that night, whispering in my ear: "Tomorrow we start our lives." I pushed myself against him, trying to find warmth. Even though it was spring, I had never felt such coldness from the tips of my fingers to the bottoms of my feet. Cold feet. Except they were beyond cold—they were numb.

He fell asleep quickly and again I slipped out of his arms. I sat in the kitchen with a cup of green tea and uncovered the Madame Butterfly, which had been shoved beneath a stack of mail. I stared at the words inscribed on her dagger: "who cannot live with honor must die with honor." Maybe I should have pitied her but I didn't because I was envious of the fact that in the end, she had figured it out.

How to make things right.

He found me in the kitchen where I had stayed up all night writing the word *honor* in black magic marker across the center of Madame Butterfly's kimono. The letters were stylized and pointed and difficult to read. They reminded me of the tags scrawled across the subway cars I missed so much. I was trying to understand how to give honor to Birdie, to Rachel.

To myself.

He invited me into the shower with him, and we took turns rinsing off the soapy water like some intimate baptism, cleansing ourselves of sin.

"You look perfect," he said as he tucked my hair behind my ear, and his words sent shivers up my spine.

"You too," I said, and he smiled, not noticing the tremor in my hand.

We drove to his lawyer's office in the hatchback with the car seat in the back. When we got out of the car, I hesitated.

"What's wrong?" he asked.

"I don't think I should be there."

He began to speak but I cut him off. "It will only make things worse."

He didn't respond.

I pointed to the coffee shop on the corner. "I will wait for you in there. Come find me once it's done."

He looked down at the sidewalk. "Order me a slice of cherry pie, and when I get out, we'll celebrate." Like he was about to be released from prison. He kissed me hard almost as if he was angry. I pushed him away because I couldn't breathe. He began to walk toward the building but not before turning one last time and waving.

He shouted something I couldn't make out. *See ya,* or *I'll be back soon.*

Or maybe *goodbye.*

I wasn't sure.

The coffee shop was busy with the sound of chattering old ladies and clinking silverware. I took a seat by the window, which was covered with droplets of rain that looked surprisingly like tears. I ordered Sol his pie and got a coffee for myself. When it came, I didn't add sugar or cream, cringing as its bitterness filled my mouth but feeling that was what I deserved.

It was her oversized umbrella that caught my eye first because it looked like something you might bring to the beach. It made her seem small and inconsequential, and as she tried to hold it steady, I turned away but not before she saw me. She walked inside, the umbrella flapping like a bird, and once she managed to twist it closed, she used it like a walking cane, each thump matching the beating of my heart. A few minutes later, she was sitting in the chair opposite mine, scooping up cherry pie with the side of her finger. "You don't mind."

It wasn't phrased as a question so I didn't respond. That enormous umbrella had not been enough to protect her from the mist and drizzle, and there was a thin line of mascara running down her face. A smear of pie filling clung to the lower part of her lip and looked like blood. "It's only fair since you are fucking my husband." She took another swipe at the plate, this time sticking her finger into her mouth and pulling it out with a *pop.*

"I'm sorry, Susan." And part of me was.

Something inside of her gave way, like the air escaping from a balloon.

Her eyes got bigger and her cheeks became hollow. "You wouldn't understand. How much I love him. I would give up anything for him. Anything he
wanted."

It was an explanation, maybe more for her than for me, and I hated how
well I actually did understand.

I hated it.

The waitress walked over but then changed her mind and walked away. I
wished she would have interrupted this thing that was happening between us,
happening to both of us.

"Sometimes I ask myself." She coughed like she was choking on her spit,
and I saw that her face had suddenly changed with the realization of how
much what she was about to say would cost her. "If I had to do it all again, if I
could go back in time and do it all the same, would I?"

I promised myself it was just coincidence because there was no way
she could have known, but it would have been a lie to say I wasn't curious
about what she would have done. Would she have handled things differently
or would she also have ended up back in the same exact place as I had? She
looked down at the plate, tracing the rim with the tine of her fork. She was
quiet for so long that I wasn't sure if she was still considering her answer or if
she had simply forgotten the question.

Finally, she stood, the umbrella thumping loudly against the floor like
a punctuation mark. "Maybe I love him more than I love myself or maybe I
just need him. Whatever the reason, I would do the same exact thing all over
again."

If she thought revealing her truth would have given her some form of
relief, she was wrong. She looked even more broken than before. I hated that
I recognized the despair that had plastered itself across her face, and I hated
that it looked familiar because it was exactly how I had looked.

When Sol had left me.

A little girl sitting in a highchair a few tables away screamed one of those
ear-piercing shrieks that made everyone in the room turn to look. It was an
everyday moment, and one that only lasted for a few seconds, but when Susan
turned back around something about her had changed. Her breathing had
quickened and she seemed to be filled with a newly discovered awareness.
This time when she spoke, it was with powerful authority, maybe even a religious clarity. I could not take my eyes off her, and then it was as though we

were two halves of a whole, because as the realization came to her it also came to me. She smiled an ugly smile as she spoke: "Sol will never leave us."

She didn't need to say anything more because I already knew that she was right, even before the hateful words slipped past her teeth. "He will never leave us because he will never leave Birdie."

She looked through me like she didn't really see me anymore, maybe because I no longer mattered. She turned to leave, and I watched her walk away in the rain, walk in the opposite direction of the lawyer's office. She no longer needed to travel up inside the elevator, holding her breath between floors. She no longer needed to sit across the table, watching him sign her away because now she knew he never would. She had exactly what she needed to keep him bound to her side. Just as his father had done to his mother, Susan would do to him.

I closed my eyes, watching the colors in my lids explode like fireworks. Faces and places and words blurred together, rewinding like a television program, and I watched it carefully as it became sharper and clearer. Susan and I had traded places, traded lives. The last time I was near this coffee shop, she was the one waiting for Sol and I was the one heading into the lawyer's office, waiting for my life to be destroyed. Always waiting for something to happen to me, someone to fix me, someone to take care of me.

Someone to make me whole.

The waitress walked over and refilled my coffee, and this time I poured in some creamer. I had never really noticed how free it looked as it spiraled and swirled against the darkness with unrestrained abandon. I thought about the future and Sol and irony and about how Susan had finally figured out how to get what she wanted.

And then I thought about outrunning my destiny.

Chapter 35

It's funny how when things are right, they just fall into place. How all it took was a flick of my thumb for a taxicab to appear seemingly from nowhere. How easy it was to purchase a plane ticket at the airport since I still had the passport Brian had given me tucked away inside my purse.

As much as I wanted to disappear, I knew that I owed the people in my life some form of explanation. I planned to email all of them once I settled in. An apology to Alice for leaving her empty-handed and even more for not fighting harder against whom I had permitted myself to become. Mickey's note would be the easiest because I knew she would be smiling the whole time she was reading it. I felt compelled to write to my parents because even though I was still angry with them, I knew that in their own way they had contributed to the fact that I was finally ready to stand on my own. If there was anything I had learned from them, it was that love was complex.

Sol's would be the hardest.

I understood now that he would always need to be with someone who would be willing to give up everything for him, and even though it had taken almost two lifetimes to learn, I finally knew that person was not going to be me.

I managed to get the last window seat and decided the heavens had sent me a sign of approval when a group of Italian nuns dressed like penguins sat around me. I closed my eyes, falling slowly and gently into their words, unfamiliar yet soothing, like spoken music.

I opened them just as we were taking off, as I was overcome with the sensation of lifting high above the Earth. It was, as we emerged over the clouds, soft and billowy and impossibly perfect that I finally understood that where I had gone wrong was believing that my second chance was about being with Sol. It all seemed remarkably clear now as I floated high above the clouds with the voices of the Italian nuns singing in my ear. It suddenly made sense why I had found myself back with Sol in the same house with the same conflicts as before. It was because the question had never been about *doing* things differently.

It was about *choosing* things differently.

I finally understood that no matter how many lives I lived, I would still always come back to the same question over and over until I figured out the answer, and there was only one way to make it so that it was worthy of all I had sacrificed.

The only way to alter my destiny would be to finally choose myself.

The first thing I planned to do when I landed in Rome was visit the mosaics. I rifled through my purse to recount the money I had taken out of the ATM at the airport. Which is when I found it, folded over a few times and tucked at the bottom of my bag, waiting for the perfect time to reveal itself. It was one of the notes that Birdie, when she had loved me, scribbled and gave to me as a gift. She must have tucked this one in my bag when I wasn't looking. It was frayed in the corners, reminding me of Rachel's poems because it also looked like it had been there a long time just waiting for me to find. I unwrapped it carefully, like a present, and then there it was. Her word, the letters long and gangly like the tentative legs of a baby giraffe, but spelled out clear and crisp and undeniable in their profound honesty.

Birdie's final message to me.

F-L-Y.

Acknowledgments

Thank you to Caroline Leavitt, Anne Bohner, and Nicole Frail for shredding and untangling. Thank you to Liliana Ossowski for believing that I could still make a beautiful dress out of the tattered remains. Thank you to Maya London, Rita Zoey Chin, and Connie Hertzberg Mayo, who remind me that how you organize words on a page can be magical. Thank you to Catherine Kim, Lisa Gersten Shapiro, Carolyn Gutilla, Julie Comenzo, Jennifer Cotell, Roni Ross, Lisa Duke, Stephanie Moore, Adriana Kopinja, and Lindsay Gravin for having faith and offering distraction just when I needed it most. Thank you to Ruth Kashi, Amie White, and Jeremiah Healy, whose voices I hear. Thank you to Richard Ossowski for being the first man in my life, literally and figuratively. Thank you to my children Noah, Ben, and Chloe for letting me run away when I need, and most of all, to Rich Crable, for helping make the escape possible and to whom I am forever grateful. Finally, thanks to my sister Talia, who listens to all my gripes and always reminds me that I'm good enough.

Thank you to all the ones who fill the fractures
With love
With hope
With comfort.

But especially to the ones who teach you that, without those fractures, you cannot become the person you are meant to be.